# THE SCULPTOR

# THE SCULPTOR

A Novel

Michael Aronovitz

NIGHT SHADE BOOKS
NEW YORK

Night Shade books may be purchased in bulk at special discounts for sales promotion, corporate gifts, fund-raising, or educational purposes. Special editions can also be created to specifications. For details, contact the Special Sales Department, Night Shade Books, 307 West 36th Street, 11th Floor, New York, NY 10018 or info@skyhorsepublishing.com.

Night Shade Books™ is a trademark of Skyhorse Publishing, Inc.®, a Delaware corporation.

Visit our website at www.nightshadebooks.com.

10 9 8 7 6 5 4 3 2 1

Library of Congress Cataloging-in-Publication Data is available on file.

ISBN: 978-1-949102-54-3

Cover illustration from Shutterstock
Cover design by Claudia Noble

Printed in the United States of America

# FOREWORD BY JASON HENDERSON

I'm honored to have a chance to write an introduction to *The Sculptor* by Michael Aronovitz. I first met Michael about a year and a half ago, when he submitted a story to the *Castle of Horror Anthology*, a series of short horror story collections now on its fifth volume. The one thing I noticed about Michael's work is how he has remarkably broad focus in his writing. He presents texture that is instantly evocative and recognizable, so that you can feel your way through his worlds. The corners and edges of Michael's world seem dangerous. But he also has a keen understanding of the way people tick. So I was thrilled to get to look at his new novel.

On its face *The Sculptor* is a highly commercial piece of work (as a publisher this is something that matters to me; it might not matter to anyone else, but there it is). The "Sculptor" of the title is a serial killer known, like Ted Bundy, for stalking universities and choosing what in the Bundy days were called "pretty young coeds." And after murdering them in various torturous ways, he leaves them mounted upon a rod and displayed to be found later. It's this display that has led the police to call them Scarecrows. In one of several unreliable narratives, we learn (at least we probably do) that the Sculptor has very particular ideas about the value of leaving the bodies on display, that the most amazing moments are those when cars are zipping past in the early morning, as the sunlight only begins to shine on the bodies. It is this moment, without the context of flashing police lights there later, that the casual passersby would most experience complete cognitive dissonance as they saw these bodies. It's the pure, strange moment of discovery the Sculptor most enjoys.

The story in *The Sculptor* is very fast moving, but we meet a number of characters who will be familiar to us in the world of the commercial thriller. Most reliable to us is Captain Bill Canfield, the policeman who has no intention of getting involved in investigating a serial killer—until he happens to be dragged into it. Erika, the "unsworn hired help" (that is, an office worker) with the police has caught the eye of the serial killer, and now her presence has a tendency to put Canfield in danger. We meet a whole array of cops, sad victims, and loved ones. With each of these, Michael Aronovitz takes the time to show us how they're thinking and how sometimes, they don't tick *right*, whether that means they deserve to die or not.

What really sets the book apart is that in the end, *The Sculptor* is not really so much a serial killer book. It's a book about stories and narrative and the way we understand ourselves. Over the course of *The Sculptor*, we hear many different variations on the history of the killer. In a narrative move that I don't think I've ever seen before, we receive almost an entire chapter of reflections on the killer's early life that may or may not be true at all—and that's not the shocking part. Many times in the book, even when we know that the story we're hearing is false, we sense there is more truth there than the characters know. For instance, when one of the characters writes what is clearly a piece of fiction, we as the reader are lulled into a sense that what we are reading is truer than any of the narratives we have seen so far. *The Sculptor* is a book where we are constantly needing to be convinced about who is to be believed, and which story is to be countenanced.

I really admire Michael Aronovitz's writing, especially in the way that he conveys the almost mystical power that men can ascribe to distracting beauty. There is a meditation on beautiful college students that is angry, perverse, and instantly recognizable to the reader. These are ugly thoughts we have heard and avoided and sometimes stumble into ourselves. We recognize the writer as somebody very akin to those "incels"—self-labeled "involuntary celibates"—whom we've heard about and who sometimes commit awful crimes. And yet this too is exactly the sort of assumption that Aronovitz has his character or characters constantly taunt us with. Because that might just be *what the killer wants us to think.*

The character of the Sculptor himself is very much like a writer—he knows that words matter in a way people don't always think of. Little details he shares will not just convey ideas but trigger responses. "Incidentally," of course, but that's just the narrator's sleight of hand—witness how one character on the road convinces another of a third character's depravity through an unrelated story full of carefully chosen details. I don't want to give it away, so I'll have to leave it vague. But the Sculptor—and therefore Aronovitz, of course—can predict where we as the reader are going to go next. But not vice-versa. If you are the kind of reader who likes serial killer stories, you will definitely enjoy *The Sculptor*. There are twists upon twists and you will *not* see them coming.

But I think you'll enjoy *The Sculptor* even more if you're the kind of reader who enjoys knowing how readers think. Pay attention, as you read the book, to how many times you're being narrated to in such a way that you're being asked to make associations, and then see if it turns out, not that you were wrong, but that something in the story was relying on you making those assumptions.

I was honored to have a chance to give this book an early read. You have a lot to look forward to.

Jason Henderson<br>Publisher, Castle Bridge Media<br>Denver, Colorado<br>May 2021

# CHAPTER 1
## PETALS
## (1986)

"Daddy."

"Hmm?"

"There's a dead girl in the flower bed."

He was standing there in the archway, soaking wet because he'd been in the backyard again, pretending to be a scary clown running through the sprinklers.

"What?" I said.

"A dead girl," he repeated. "Out back. She's staring up into the sun, and I saw it make her eyes change colors."

"What do you mean, change colors?" I was buried in weekend work, writing up price policies and clearances for bakery, seafood, and deli at the Shoprite where I'd been recently moved up to day manager.

"Michael . . ."

"You know," he said, nodding, smiling, exposing the vacancies where his baby teeth hadn't yet been replaced. "First her eyes were dark blue like the flag, but then they faded to a color like robins' eggs."

He ran off, feet pounding down the stairs, the hard rhythm broken only at the bottom where he jumped the last three to the living room floor. I squeezed my eyes shut and pushed up my glasses with my thumb and forefinger.

"Michael!" I called. "Mi—"

I stopped myself when I heard the back door slam. He'd be waiting now and wouldn't budge until he had satisfaction. Back at the flower bed.

To show me the dead girl.

I pushed up out of my chair, feeling it in my Achilles tendons. Time for less take-out and a few workouts at the gym. But we'd stopped going last year when Michael had crept away from his group at day camp during first lunch and found a dead squirrel under the walking bridge. The story went that he grabbed it by the tail and ran back with it, whipping it around his head lasso-style and finally dancing around it like a wild Injun in view of the kiddie pool.

I walked down the stairs. Passing through the kitchen, I thought about the way Michael was always asking me weird shit at the dinner table, like whether your eyes dried and cracked when you were dead before your kidneys shriveled or how they kept fitting bodies in the boneyard when the property borders never changed. That one had sent me to the library, and when I told him they honeycombed the caskets, he found it hysterically funny.

I pulled hard on the back door because it always stuck in the summer, and the construction paper partly scotch-taped to the glass of the storm door wafted up from the suction and settled. It was Michael's drawing of the creature he'd named "Shadow Man," untethered at the top now, hanging upside down and backward. Had to fix that. I mean, a kid's creativity was important. I'd seen it on the shows, and like most kids, Michael was always sketching phantoms and creatures. He also said monsters lived in "the pockets" we could see when we blinked, and that wasn't like most kids. None I'd ever heard of. Maybe he was going to be a poet or something.

Outside, the sun made me put my hand above my eyes for a second as if I was saluting, and I moved down the walkway, avoiding the bird-shit splattered on the old decorator stones. Michael was waiting for me there at the bottom of the backyard hillside that was a bitch to mow, down where it flattened out and Madeline had her flower garden in front of the lattice fencing.

I went sidestepping, since it was steep enough to make you pull a hammy, and when I reached the bottom and continued on, looking up, Michael had his hands over his mouth, laughing.

"I know," I said, "I look like a dork, but it isn't nice to . . ."

I stopped about ten feet away from the garden presentation. There was no dead girl there, of course, but there were impressions in the mulch, like a chalk-line sketch where you could see the vague shape of a small person that had been lying there: head, shoulder, hip, and knee. The outline was pressed into the woodchips between a grouping of Madeline's tulips and a larger throng of daffodils that were bordered at the back edge by two of those elf garden gnomes.

I moved closer, arms folded across my chest, and leaned over it. Some of the loose flower petals were pressed into the black mulch, flattened as if something of weight had reshaped them as part of the imprint.

I called the police. Not that I thought a dead girl had been lying back here, not really, but a family that lived over on Trent Street had reported their little girl missing last night—everyone knew this, it had been on the news. Michael had seen the show with my wife and I. We never hid things from him, and just in case, I had a responsibility to be over-cautious. Silly, I know. Nine times out of ten the missing kid showed up, there was a mundane explanation, and I would consider myself to have been ridiculous in thinking the mulch had been shaped in some suspicious way to begin with.

The cop didn't think it ridiculous.

He squatted down at the edge of the garden, picked up a flower petal or two, then looked up at me quite mechanically through his mirrored sunglasses. I thought he was going to take something for evidence, maybe for that new-fangled "DNA testing" I'd heard about, but he didn't. He explained a couple of things, gave a few theories, then glanced over at Michael and called him a genius. He also suggested that I get the kid some therapy, and I thanked him for his time.

Evidently, this was Michael's first art project in the great outdoors. The cop—his name was Officer Bill Canfield—showed me one of the flower petals up close. There was a faint tracing on it, and when you looked hard you could see that the mark was made up of extremely small flecks of paint, the metallic type. It was a ghosted capital "E" and part of the "V" that followed. Michael had flattened the petals one by one with the double-A Eveready batteries we kept in a Ziploc bag on a shelf in the pantry. He'd been affected by the girl on the news, sweet little thing that she was, and had made a bed in the mulch looking as if she had been lying there.

The cop asked him why.

Michael smiled, rocking side to side.

"She looked like a dolly on TV," he said. "And I thought she'd like flowers."

He ran off, up the incline that was a bitch to mow, far faster than I think even Officer Canfield could have run if he wanted to show off his skills of pursuit, and I shook his hand stiffly, wondering to myself what to make of all this. I trudged back to the house, got Michael in the shower, and helped with the groceries when Madeline came back from the store.

At the table for an early lunch, she was reaching across for the pitcher of iced tea, and Michael was staring at her chest. She was wearing her loose, off-white slouch T-shirt with the wide neck off the shoulder, and for a second you could see the top of her breast, almost down to the nipple. Eyes turned to slits, Michael started groaning through one of his rictus grins, and I noticed he was doing something under the table. I cocked my head and glanced down, and he had his spoon, the one that he'd been using to eat his oatmeal, inside his shorts.

"Michael," I said.

"Ahh," he said back. Wide-eyed, I looked over at Madeline, and she said simply:

"It's normal. Michael, get your spoon out of your pants. It's a breast. Women have them." She adjusted her shirt. "Honey, I need a new Walkman. It's eating my Jane Fonda tapes. Michael, stop scratching." She took a bite of her Caesar salad, all teeth on the fork, making it "ping" on the exit. Swallowing, she pointed it at me a couple of times. "Forgot to tell you, I took out a hundred for the Phils game next weekend, but the teller said we were overdrawn. I had to fill out a form. Michael, stop turning your eyelids inside out, it's disgusting." She shifted so she could cross her legs along the other corner of the chair. "We need to get the car inspected and the washing machine is making a noise. Michael, use a napkin, not your forearm." She kept her eyes on him, then put down her fork daintily, scrunched her shoulders, and smiled as if she was about to tell him a secret. "Michael, sweetie, you need deodorant or something. You smell like boy." She turned to me, beaming. "A red-letter moment! You can welcome him to manhood with your Old Spice. It's like a Disney story or one of those telephone commercials that make you tear up!"

I nodded along, but I was still stuck five issues back, wondering what a first-grader was thinking in the first place, looking at a grown woman's chest, especially a strange camper like Michael. Breasts weren't Maddy's thing in my eyes, I was a leg-dog for life, but she was, in fact, built firm up and down, being an ex-college cheerleader who was sweet, petite, and elite and all that. But what the fuck . . . I mean, when did you start getting "feelings" as a kid? This wasn't puberty, couldn't be, but stuff came before that, didn't it? Shit. Now I had to hit the library. Again. This kid was making me a regular book-nerd, I swear it.

But I forgot about the library. I had all that work to do in the upstairs office, and it took me through until dinner. Then I ate too much pasta with clam sauce, drank too many Miller Genuine Drafts, and got loopy in front of the living room television that had those fucking green blurry shadow-traces no matter where we positioned Maddy in the room with the rabbit-ear antennas. I went upstairs, turned in early, and in the middle of the night my eyes flew open.

I'd been dreaming, and it was a bad one, the type with flying in it and monsters advancing through strobe lights.

I sat up. I'd been sweating in the air conditioning. The television was on with the volume off, and I looked down watching the images wash over Maddy lying on her tummy, covers down to her waist showing the curve of her back. She had big ole hair like a country singer, I teased her about it all the time, and it flowed long on the shoulder except for a renegade strand stuck to her lip. Her profile there on the pillow looked perfect, like one of those artsy outlines that they could have used to animate a logo for perfume or a clothing line. She was a living Barbie doll, so tiny and pristine. Shit. Michael had gotten a big dose of my thick clumsy genes and was almost as tall as she was at this point, the top of his head about an inch from her chin-line.

I thought of something . . . connected to the flying dream that had those maniac images as flash-points . . . smiling jesters juggling dead puppies . . . carnival creatures squatting around a campfire eating spotted human remains . . . Michael's fascination with a missing girl who looked to him like a "dolly."

Like his mother?

Oh.

Fuck me royal.

But no, he couldn't be that smart, that twisted and "advanced" for lack of a better word.

I was careful coming out from under the covers, and after putting on shorts and a tee I moved into the hall, closing the door ever so carefully, turning the knob so the latch would catch slowly, slowly, and then I walked off down the dark hallway as quickly as I was able.

To make my way downstairs to the pantry. To get a flashlight and slip outside.

To the tool shed.

To get a spade shovel.

Soon I was standing over the mulch in the flower bed out back, training down the harsh cone-shaped light of the Rayovac, making the image at my feet stark and over-bright. Michael's artwork. Impressions in the mulch, head, shoulder, hip, and knee, with flower petals flattened by Eveready batteries to match with the contours of the imprint. It had prompted me to call the police, and Michael had earned a measured and critical evaluation from Officer Canfield. He also might have set up one of the greatest pieces of misdirection and hiding something in plain sight by a first-grader in all history. Shit, I'd have to look that one up too, though I didn't look forward to it.

Was it possible?

Was it at all plausible that Michael made it seem as if the issue was on the *top* of the mulch, making the presentation the thing to "figure out," therefore causing the figurer to think he was himself a real Sherlock Holmes to connect the batteries and flecked paint? Had my seven-year-old son actually come to what would have otherwise been a seasoned adult's conclusion that when a pro like Canfield investigated and evaluated something with such "clever insight," he would check off that box, move on to other scenarios, other mulch beds as it were?

I set the flashlight on the ground about a foot away from the imprint of the head and placed the tip of the spade between it and the indentation made by the "shoulder." Adjusted my position. Put my foot on it and pressed down.

The tip of the blade went through the mulch and the dirt fair enough, yet three-quarters of the way down to being buried to the hilt, I felt something change. It went from the gritty feel of steel working through soil to the smoother and more distinct sensation of running a good knife through meat product.

Startled, I looked up.

Michael was at his bedroom window looking down at me. The moon reflected off the glass, giving him ghost-glare and a slight red tint to his eyes the same as when you used a flash taking pictures of dogs.

He was smiling.

Wide as the world.

Because he had in, fact, properly predicted the deductions, assumptions, and actions of Officer Canfield, and that being said, my son knew exactly what I was going to do with that shovel.

# CHAPTER 2
# UNSWORN HIRED HELP (TODAY)

She had a great ass. She was a tall, Scandinavian blonde, daringly thin, "statuesque" even. She'd always worn slacks at the station, even in July and August, but you still couldn't help but happen a glance after her now and again. Women's dress pants were sterile by design, but they never could hide a good ass. Not Erika's anyway.

She was bending over the coffee machine just outside the office, reaching for the cup of red swivel sticks. Captain Bill Canfield wasn't looking. It looked as if he wasn't looking, but his open-door policy worked both ways, keeping him visible, subject to scrutiny. Fair trade. There was no door at all; in fact, he'd had it removed. His desk was centered next to the Westinghouse fan facing up so it wouldn't blow around all the papers, and he wanted the sightline regardless of the things he chose not to stare at.

From his position in here, he could survey the front entrance, public information and complaints, and the space for his desk sergeant, watch commander, and patrol supervisor. If he leaned left, he could see who was going in and out of equipment storage and the report writing room, and if he rolled his old wooden banker's chair a foot to the right, he had a clear view of department communications and dispatch. The view was *panoramic.* He liked that word . . .

liked to be "panoramic," it kept him connected. And this had nothing to do with Erika Shoemaker's ass, even though he'd never quite gotten around to moving the coffee pot to a more peripheral location.

Officer Blake poked his head in.

"Evidence repository is almost fully reorganized," he said. "I'll have a report on your desk by ten o'clock."

"Nine-thirty's better." Canfield looked back down to review the annual grant proposal in front of him. Needs, Approach, and Outcomes looked good, but the subsection covering Future Funding needed more finite explanation and detail. Someone walked by and Canfield didn't even look up.

"Tully," he said.

"Yes, Captain?"

"Those shoes have clicky heels. Get rubber soles. Then you can run faster and you won't advertise around here like a broad in stilettos."

"Yes, sir."

The officer clacked off and another figure was soon in the doorway.

"Chief . . . sir."

Canfield looked up.

It was the jumpy new kid, redhead, chin-zits showing through his peach-fuzz goatee. Probably safe to assume he had a beanbag chair at home, a long-board, a pet snake, and the latest version of *Call of Duty.* Canfield leaned back and webbed his fingers behind his head.

"As far as titles go around here," he said, "Captain is good enough for me. That's my rank. 'Chief of Police' just means I get stuck with more paperwork, which I do, so let's keep it plain."

"Well, Captain, my service revolver is faulty."

"What you mean, faulty?"

"Feels sticky."

"It's a Glock Nineteen," Canfield assured him, "an oldie but goodie like a greatest hits record. If it feels sticky, go beg Sullivan for some table space, get some Radcolube, and take a dry cloth to the trigger assembly. You replace something, fill out a req."

"I want a Smith and Wesson M and P Nine. Sir."

"Why?"

"The Picatinny rail."

"What about it?"

"Takes accessories. Want to install a laser sight. Bought it myself."

Canfield sat forward and rested his beef-bull forearms on the edge of the desk. He had to have some Tums around here somewhere, or an old bottle of Pepto-Bismol.

"If the schedule hasn't been changed," he said, "you're on parking lots and meters this month, speed traps by the high school the rest of the spring. Stick to the purview, no lasers."

Officer Mullin's eyes went half-lidded, and he gave a strange gentle smile.

"Of course, Captain," he said softly. "Your feelings are paramount." Canfield was about to say that his feelings had nothing to do with it, but the kid moved out of the doorway too fast. Detective Bronson filled it. He'd been waiting there behind the jamb. He was always doing that . . . lurking behind the jamb. He was a big man, black moustache, thick neck bulging over the collar. He pressed his palms above the archway and leaned in, ducking his head.

"You hear about it, Bill?"

"What?"

"The thing."

"What thing? I got shit to do."

Bronson grunted, took a step in, and fished out his Newports. He didn't smoke them. He'd quit two months ago, but he liked playing with a new pack every few days, squeezing it like a stress doll.

"They found another scarecrow," he said. Canfield stared at him for a second.

"Don't call them that."

"Why not?"

"Gives the press an easy headline, that's why. Helps nobody. And it's not our case."

Bronson smiled unevenly.

"This one was discovered at the edge of a construction site on the Northeast Extension up by the Lehigh Tunnel. The bastard's getting closer."

Canfield sighed. Heartburn. He hated heartburn.

"It's not our jurisdiction just the same," he said. "He's for the Feds and the Staties. If he puts one of those poor girls up on a pole here in Lower Merion, I'll give you first dibs."

Bronson's eyes were shimmering. He was still smiling, but the flavor had changed.

"Have you seen one of them?" he said. "One of the victims?"

Captain Canfield didn't like lying. He did anyway.

"No."

"I've got a file. I can show you."

"No, thanks. You have other fish to fry, and I don't need you running off, trying to validate the size of your prick and giving some maniac's handiwork shape and contour. He kills coeds. He disfigures them. He puts them up on display thinking he's haunting the highway or some such lame horseshit. Don't help round his edges."

Bronson opened his mouth to say something, then closed it, putting the wrinkled pack of cigarettes back in his pocket.

"All my life I played by the rules," he said softly. "I got food issues, I got bad skin, I got allergies."

"You have plenty of solid convictions."

"Small fish."

"Lots of small fish change the color of the water."

"And some criminals get to swim in it anyway, keeping us tied to the dock by our own rules and protocol. That's a paradox."

"That's the job," Canfield said. "Why don't you get going doing it, here in your own jurisdiction where we need you?"

"All for one and one for all, huh?"

"That's the idea."

"Minor vice and domestic disputes."

"We're a small town on the Main Line, Detective, white picket fences and all that, so don't be so eager to rewrite the script. We got it good. We keep it simple. You want to be a hero, go join the Peace Corps. Or try teaching kids in public school, special ed., maybe. That's heroic. I'll write you a rec."

Bronson gazed at the floor for a second and then ducked out of the doorway.

"And put that file in the shredder," Canfield called after him. "If it's on your hard drive, delete it, or else I'll go through your desktop and give it an enema." He pulled open the drawer in front of him, noted the two empty antacid bottles he hadn't yet tossed, and hauled out his hardcover thesaurus. The wide spine was worn and the cloth binding was ripped at the top, the Scotch tape coming loose. He'd have to use Gorilla tape. This was a real synonym finder, the thick kind, old school, tons of words, far superior to Webster's or the shit that came up on a Google search. It was better than a dictionary too. Instead of explaining the word with harder words, it gave you alternatives, made you figure it out, made you learn it.

He turned to the P's and looked for the word "paradox." Hmm. "Puzzle, Maze, Quandary, Dilemma." He had initially thought it was an unsolvable riddle, like the chicken and the egg business. Pretty close; in fact, his version was better. He loved it when that happened.

"Captain."

"Come."

It was Erika, files in her arms, stacked up to her chin. She'd removed the blue slim-fit blazer she usually had on like a uniform, showing that her white dressy blouse was sleeveless. Nice forearms and biceps. Tan and lean. Maybe she played weekend beach volleyball or did Namaste in the park.

"Morning," she said. "You mind?"

He nodded and brushed aside the pile of parking citations that had to have the appeals weeded.

"What's all that?" he said.

She clapped the pile down and faint dust rose into the light bars coming through the slats of the blinds.

"Correspondence from the mayor," she said, "five complaints from the school board, twenty-five complaints from concerned parents *about* the school board, two messages from that family on Sycamore claiming the renters across the back alley are using their trash cans again, the electric bill, a statement from Aqua, a few DWI's, a few more underage drinking citations, and a ton of formal appeals to get rid of the township siren at the firehouse, the usual."

She curled the backs of her knuckles on her hips and did that subtle head-juke that made her hair gather down the back. She had nice hair, long, fine, and tailored at the edges. She taught a grooming and cosmetology elective at Upper Darby High School and the local JCC up on Haverford Avenue on her off days. Beauty and brains. She'd graduated from Penn, the Wharton Business School, and she'd said she was saving up for her own salon. Captain Canfield had no doubt that she'd be successful. Though "unsworn hired help," she pretty much ran things around here.

"Ruben is out today," she continued, "so we'll have to dump the trash ourselves. We're good with arrest forms, but I'm running short on offense and complaints. I need extra paper towels signed out of supply for the ladies', and the holding tank needs a wipe-down. Something with industrial sanitizers. Smells like a barn." She turned to go. "Oh, wait." She stepped out toward the coffee table, grabbing her aluminum storage folder, and she came back in, thumbing through stuff bunched under the clip. "Sorry, Captain. This was at the bottom of my in-bin. Addressed to you. Wasn't sure if you'd want it left buried in the pile."

She slid off a small envelope. Looked like something that would hold a bar mitzvah invitation. Canfield bent forward and took it between the tips of his index and middle fingers.

"For me, huh?"

"By name."

He leaned back in his chair, making it creak on its worn tilt-lock, flipping the envelope to the front side. It was his name all right. CAPTAIN WILLIAM TIMOTHY CANFIELD: CHIEF OF POLICE, spelled out with small magazine letters, all uniform so they came from the same article apparently, and so finely cut in outline that it almost looked like professional labeling.

"Gloves," he said softly. "And the letter opener." He'd only touched it at the edge, and Erika's prints were on file. Maybe there was something pristine. She was swift with it and handed him the implements like a nurse assisting a surgeon.

He opened it carefully, but he didn't need to work hard at it. The top flap was only stuck at its corner-point, and he was willing to bet it hadn't been licked. Sponged. Probably with a cheap, generic product taken right out of the package from Walmart with a pair of powdered rubber gloves. Gingerly, he unfolded the page.

The magazine letters on it were a contrast with the modest presentation on the outside—big and slashing, alternating in size, purposefully cut for uneven dissonance. To establish a brand. For newspaper headlines and people like Bronson.

I MAKE PRETTY DOLLS, NOT SCARECROWS, CAPTAIN.

CALL THE FEDS, AND I KILL ANOTHER COED.

DO NOT CALL THE FEDS, AND I KILL ERIKA SHOEMAKER. TONIGHT.

GET IN THE GAME

LOVE

THE SCULPTOR

# CHAPTER 3
# GUESS WHAT'S IN MY HEAD

Erika's apartment was more a workspace than a portrait of comfort, the living room filled with makeup tables, cosmetic cases on wheels, a vanity with a double-sided round looking glass, and two oblong mirrors on tilt frames. There were also a number of mannequin heads on tripods or straight-rods affixed to the desktops by table clamps. The heads were adorned with wigs she could practice on, cutting, coloring, straightening, and curling, and Canfield felt bad for her.

Protection and protocol outweighed social semantics, and Erika had been the one treated like a criminal, standing by rather helplessly as the CSI unit had advanced methodically through the living room and the galley kitchen with the open-wall bar space. They checked the hallway linen closet, the cloak closet, the bedroom and bath, and finally the closet catty-cornered by the back-door terrace exit. They engineered two meticulous walk-throughs, making a final determination that there were no hidden explosives on the premises, no traces of poison laced in her drinking glasses, no potential hazards in the wiring, nothing nefarious in the airducts. And when the last of them had finally exited, the apartment looked ravaged, as if dogs had gotten into the laundry basket. Erika seemed exhausted. Canfield politely adjusted the brim of his cap in an indication that it was time for him to be on his way, and she made to follow him to the door.

"Well, you sure know how to treat a girl," she said.

"Only the best."

"I'm not good at small talk."

"Nor I." He turned. "Erika, there are two black and whites in front of the complex and one out back in the parking area by the Goodwill storage bin. No one is getting in here, repeat, no one."

"And who are the officers in the squad cars?"

"Dutton and Ramos, Trigoso and Clark, and White and Scarduzio."

"They're clean?"

"To the best of my knowledge, yes."

"To the best . . ."

"Yes, Erika. I made sure the timesheets ruled them out as potential persons of interest. I concede that we are being observed, but I haven't yet determined the vantage point. Admittedly, I haven't ruled out the idea that someone at the station could be suspect, but I'm convinced there is some other explanation."

"That letter wasn't mailed, Captain. It was planted in my in-bin by someone with access behind the glass."

Canfield nodded.

"Noted, and today I interviewed almost everyone at the station on day shift with a W-2."

"Almost."

"Yes. As you had said, Ruben is out sick, and Bronson had a series of field interviews in the Morrison case that took top priority. Henderson, Dietrich, Getz, and Albano are still open, and I have details to confirm concerning Brooks, Willis, Sanchez, and Youngblood. I passed down the order to Deputy Chief McMaster to alert Internal Affairs, and I called the FBI three times as well as giving a report to the commissioner. This hasn't been taken lightly, Erika. We've covered every angle except getting you to a safe house."

She moved across to one of her long tables where there was a litter of accessories from different makeup cases mixed and strewn across the surface. Among the disorder were a few mannequin heads lying sideways, and she took up one and twisted it gingerly back onto its clamp-rod.

"No safehouse," she said reflectively. "Stuck on a cot somewhere with bars on the windows."

"You don't know it would be like that."

"Thanks anyway, no." She peered back at him. "So where were the Feds today, anyway?" she said. "I would have thought they'd be all over the station like storm troopers."

Canfield pushed his tongue into his cheek. He'd been thinking the same thing.

"Don't know," he said finally.

"Who did you talk to?"

"Special Agent Rutledge."

"No, you did not," a voice said. Erika banged back against an end table, knocking over a lamp, and Canfield reached for his sidearm. The voice was robotic and insectile, the product of one of those voice-changer apps, and it came from the flat-screen positioned over the mantel, no picture, just audio.

"You spoke to me, Captain Canfield," it continued. "There is no 'Special Agent Rutledge.' I have control over all the station telephones, car radios, and two-way Motorolas. I'm listening, and your methodology today was weak and predictable. First, your search of the apartment was a waste of time and resources. There are no explosives except those I wired to the undercarriages of the squad cars outside. Attempt to signal them or anyone else on the force in the next ten minutes, and I detonate all three, killing six field officers. The responsibility will be all yours, Captain Canfield, just like the coed you sentenced to death by calling the FBI in the first place. Is she not real to you? What do you think her parents would say if they knew the killer made a specific demand, specifically to you, Captain Canfield, that would have saved their dear daughter's life if simply obeyed? Would you have responded differently if you knew her? What if we made this up close and personal?"

An image on the flat-screen clicked on, and Erika gasped. It was a live feed, seemingly, from a fixed camera showing a dingy warehouse space with moisture-stains on the walls beneath exposed overhead piping. There was a steel chair bolted to the floor center-screen, and a young woman was sitting on it, naked, feet duct-taped together at the ankles, hands bound similarly at the wrists on her knees.

She was fixed at the waist with a belly-chain snaked through the bars of the backrest. She had sassy brown shoulder-length hair, arched bangs, pouting lips. Wetness that shined on her cheeks jigsawed down like broken glass, indicating she'd been sitting there long enough for new tears to cut through those that had dried. There was a noose around her neck made of thick manila rope, going straight up behind her out of the shot with only the barest hinting of slack.

Expressionlessly, Canfield tried to see her as the kidnapper might . . . college girl, unassumingly pretty, wholesome, confident, probably a tomboy until she discovered Revlon, upturned breasts, small mole inner-right just below the tan line. Long waist, flat stomach, belly ring, dull silver ball stud, narrow hips, long legs, she was an athlete maybe, lacrosse or field hockey, possibly soccer. She was weeping. Begging. Saying the word "please" over and over.

"Captain," the mechanized voice interrupted from off screen, "here is your second chance. Please follow these simple directions and consider the basic stipulations. I have been torturing my plaything. You must guess what exactly I have been doing to her. She is not allowed to move. If she were to shift or jerk more than half an inch it would trigger the cable and pulley system I have hooked up to her noose, applying a foot-pound of torque per five seconds, separating her spine vertebra by vertebra. Slowly and lovingly. Once tripped, there'd be no going back, and to this point she has been a good girl. So what torture have I been inflicting upon her, Captain Canfield? Look at her closely. Use your deductive methodology. I have not groped nor raped her. There is nothing planted in any orifice, and the duct tape does not conceal anything. The chain holds her in place around her middle firmly, yet comfortably, and has not been tightened. I have not fed her anything harmful. She has not been given electro-shocks of any kind and she has not been tazed. I have not touched her teeth, nor anything in her mouth or nostrils. There has been no use of gasses or pepper spray, no needles or pinpricks, toxins, eye drops, or pharmaceuticals. There is no corrosive, acid, or chemical on the chair, and I repeat, she has not been penetrated in any way, shape, or form."

"Wait," Canfield said.

"No waiting," the voice replied. "I am torturing this poor girl. You must guess how. I'm going to continue doing it every three seconds. She's not crying the way I want her to. Not yet; that's a hint. Guess what I am doing to her and her life will be spared. Fail, and she becomes Doll Fourteen. Clock's ticking."

The screen went blank.

Canfield was silent for a long moment, considering the idea that there was no way to elicit help without putting six of his officers at risk, let alone the girl, considering the time limitation. In a way, the killer had already won.

He'd gotten Canfield involved, gotten him to play, and besides that, Erika had become his new sidekick. But why? She was no cop.

He sucked on his front teeth and looked down at the floor. That one was obvious. Erika was pretty. They were both single. He liked her. This altered the social conventions between polite co-workers, and it was probable that the killer wanted them to fuck. It would make her better collateral. For later. But Canfield thought there was more to it.

She had taken a seat on the sofa. She looked as if she was trying not to shake.

"Any ideas?" she managed.

"No. He's listening, Erika. He could be watching somehow as well."

She shuddered and folded her arms so that she was cupping her elbows. Canfield stayed silent. The killer evidently wanted him to listen to his receptionist's input, and there was no choice but to play this through as it seemed to be scripted. Erika rested her hands on her knees.

"He's playing with words," she offered. "And I don't trust him. He claimed he was going to kill the coed if you called in the Feds, then he didn't, and he never claimed he wouldn't kill her in the first place if you hadn't."

"I thought of that."

"He wanted me here with you, that was the point," she said hollowly. "But why?"

"Thought of that too. I don't know," he lied. Second time today, a red-letter moment.

She looked at him.

"Do you have any idea what he's doing to her?"

"No."

"Should I?" she said. It was a whisper.

"I don't know that either." He moved to the couch, sitting next to her a full cushion over. He put his elbows on his knees and folded his hands. "He thinks he's an artist. You're an artist with makeup and hairstyles. Maybe he feels you'll understand him in some fundamental way that's relevant."

Her eyes widened and she straightened archly, flipping the hair on one side of her face back over the shoulder.

"I don't see that I could possibly have anything in common with him," she said. "He's a monster."

"Making sculptures."

"Statues are beautiful. Those disfigured girls, impaled on poles on the highway, are hideous."

"You've seen them?"

"Bronson showed me. I think he thought I'd be impressed or awed. Speaking of which . . . "

"It's not him, let's eliminate that as a possibility."

"You sure?"

"Yes, Erika. I've known him for twenty years."

"Well, the images are disgusting."

"Not to the killer," Canfield said. "There's a reason, some kind of bizarre explanation. This is the kind of guy who wants to change our perspective. Play guessing games so we're questioning the way we see things." His hands slowly made fists. "So what does our 'number fourteen' have to do with the paradigm? She's not disfigured. He's torturing her, but there is absolutely no visible evidence of this. Sculptures are physical entities, so I doubt he'd be going for some sort of smoke-and-mirror psychology."

Erika stiffened. "Wait," she said.

"What?"

She closed her eyes, leaned forward, elbows on the knees, and made her hands into the praying shape.

"I style hair."

"And?"

She opened her eyes and looked at him square.

"We didn't see the back of her."

"What's that mean?"

She blinked. "Captain, have you ever tweezed your eyebrows?"

"No, of course not."

"Well, it stings. We get used to it. But what if he has been tweezing out strands of her hair from the back? A single application wouldn't mean much, but it's cumulative, like the Chinese water torture. My God, he's been scalping her one follicle at a time!"

"Too slow," the mechanized voice barked through the television speaker bar, making them jump. "And you only decoded the initial, more obvious clues, passing over the more important latter. This will not do. If you are going to operate with such sluggish dysfunctionality, Captain, I'll find someone else to share secrets with."

The picture blinked on, and the camera had been taken out of the tripod, handheld now, slightly unsteady, showing the victim from behind. She was motionless, head drooping, noose raised, and rope taut. The back of her bared skull was a scattershot of blood-points, the few remaining strands making her witchlike and haggard. The hair had been plucked out all along the brain casing up to the forehead region, where it cropped back in to give the frontal illusion they'd been first subjected to. And the bastard had worked all the way down past the cranial base to lay bald the whole of her neck, where the rope had yanked it to a curved apex. There you could see the shapes of the separated vertebrae jutting up into the skin as clear as dinosaur bones in a museum case.

The killer slowly walked the camera around her.

"While the two of you fumbled around, wasting precious seconds figuring out the more global theme of my removing her hair, her false periphery, you missed the most obvious crucial detail. Did I not tell you quite bluntly that she wasn't crying the way that I wanted? Well, don't fret. All's well that ends well, as your ignorance helped transform her into a purer, more classic type of beauty. Just look at her now, Captain . . . so pure and so haunting . . . the glorious mask of Greek tragedy both you and Erika helped me create."

The camera shot came to full front, and for an awful moment Captain Bill Canfield didn't see a dead coed.

He saw a lovely broken statue weeping blood.

The killer had ripped out her eyelashes.

# CHAPTER 4
# MOVING PICTURES

Detective Bronson lived on the far side of Montgomery Avenue in a nook of dense woodland, and he no more believed that the Captain's letter had been planted by someone employed at the station than he trusted the Feds, who hadn't yet made their grand aristocratic appearance. Truth be told, he was glad to have been given the green light to get the hell out of there, though it had meant a long day of tedious field interviews he'd inherited from the Juvenile Division because of his expertise in narcotics—a marijuana ring orchestrated by a couple of high school juniors who'd gotten in over their heads. Depressing. Bronson didn't like interrogating teenagers. He preferred to be immersed in lab analysis, biology, photography, and criminalistics, getting his geek on, and he'd been chomping at the bit to get home.

Now, like every night, he was in his living room wearing the flannel-lined rugby bathrobe with the hood up. The curtains behind him were closed on either side of the hearth, which was also flanked by two steel contractor's storage containers housing all his investigative paraphernalia. The desk lamp was cocked left. Up the staircase the hall light was off, but the bathroom had the vanity lights turned to the dimmest setting. The middle room, which he called the "hoarding den," had a path snaking through all the accumulated bric-a-brac, brightened only faintly by the stove light he always kept on in the kitchen back there, no overheads.

He settled into his chair. Before him, the desktop computer was on, the cursor blinking in the Google surf bar. The unit was sitting on the double-pedestal rolltop desk with the plinth base. The old dinosaur belonged in the office upstairs, but Bronson had hired Gentle Giant Movers to bring it down here. That was one year, three months, and five days ago, when the first scarecrow was discovered next to a pyramid of concrete piping and two Bobcat mini-dozers a hundred yards west of the Blue Mountain Service Plaza on the Pennsylvania Turnpike.

Bronson took a deep breath that made his nostrils flare; today's events changed nothing. Few on the force knew exactly what had been in the Captain's threat-letter, but Bronson had seen it. To him it was no more than a massive inconvenience, a hoax, most probably kids. This killer wasn't about involving cops, let alone manipulating them. This killer was about stealth and voyeurism, fetish and obsession.

This killer was all about the girls.

The first scarecrow's name had been Brittany Barnes. Her file and spare folders took up a good amount of the drawer bottom-left, and it stuck for a second when Bronson made to pull it open. He thumbed past the divider and pulled up a fat manila pouch stuffed with pictures he'd downloaded and printed from her Facebook and Instagram accounts, along with all the exchanges she'd shared publicly on both platforms before her parents had deleted them. There were also all the newspaper clippings discussing her disappearance, online blogs talking about her, and three or four tablets of yellow lined paper filled with Bronson's notations about comments he'd found from friends, family, and acquaintances. He'd drawn possible connections, made inferences and multitudes of spare notations when it seemed he'd found something between the lines.

At the end of the Barnes girl's fourth tablet, there were a few blank pages. This is where he'd pick up where he'd left off to do the compare and contrast after he'd officially "mapped" the new corpse. Then he'd get out the file on Victim #2, then the next, and the next. It was becoming an all-nighter. And he was running out of drawers. He jotted down on his "to-do" pad that along with new tablets, he had to get a few plastic hanging file units at Staples or Ikea. Soon he'd have to rent out warehouse space . . .

The latest victim was named Melissa Baumgardner, freshman at Widener University, Chester, Pennsylvania, nursing major, found yesterday morning three hundred yards from the south side of the Lehigh Tunnel up the Northeast Extension. She'd been positioned on the high shoulder past the breakdown lane where PennDOT was setting the foundation for sound barrier walls. She had been decapitated, the head reattached and disfigured, the whole of her body impaled on a pole set in some sort of flag-base seated by a pile of crushed stone and a border-ring of dented steel drums.

Victim #1, Brittany Barnes, had attended Shippensburg University, which sat at the bottom of the state, halfway to Pittsburgh from here. Her dump-spot had been a mere six miles away from her dorm residence. Melissa Baumgardner went to school up 476 South, twenty-five minutes from where Bronson was currently sitting, and her dump-spot was an hour and twenty-nine minutes north, 75 miles. The longest the killer had driven to deposit a body was Victim #10, Trisha Sugarhill, sophomore at the Penn State Brandywine Campus who'd been left impaled on the roof of the construction trailer on I-68, Eastbound Mile Marker 6, down in Maryland.

Bronson grunted, put down the tablet, pushed up, and reached for the shoebox with the two jars of pushpins—one with yellow, the other dark blue. There were also a few balls of red yarn and a small pair of sewing scissors, and he approached the wall in front of the desk with a sort of ritualistic reverence. He'd glued cork to the paneling going from the inlaid shelving to the corner by the stairs with the stereo system and old-school CD tower he rarely used anymore, and upon this makeshift board presentation he'd tacked up a detailed map, now littered with Post-It Notes marking times and dates and arrows drawn with a Sharpie tagging rest stops along what would have been the most convenient routes, as well as the weigh stations, gas stations, welcome centers, and motels, anywhere the killer might have been seen. The yarn connected the points of contact (yellow pushpins) and dump sites (blue), for perspective and overview, and it created what was now a complex patterning that looked more like a Native American dreamcatcher than an instrument that tracked spatial tendencies.

One thing, however, was blatantly clear. Though the killer was steadily putting more distance between point of first contact and that of disposal, his general choice of hunting ground had gotten closer. To Philly and its suburbs. Bronson had a gut feeling, in fact, that the son of a bitch lived somewhere nearby, and that's why that prank letter to the Captain was so goddamned frustrating. False alarms were alarms, after all. They were loud and obnoxious, getting everyone's radar up, just when this guy had been getting more comfortable.

Bronson put in his pushpins and tied off the yarn, then shimmied out from the short space between the desk and the wall. He backed up and gave it a look.

Dreamcatcher, hell! It was like a movie cliché, or worse, the efforts of the sap on the Car Gurus commercial who mapped out where to buy a used clunker like some obsessed stalker. Looked like a shrine. It was only missing the candles.

He moved back behind his desk and sat, rubbed his thick moustache, one side, then the other. Charts and graphs were a necessary part of the process, but logistics weren't the final point. Bronson had known all along that he wasn't going to catch the killer by interpreting (and acting on) the travel patterns; he didn't have the resources. He had to do it the other way, victim-first through the eyes of the killer, and he'd spent months trying to figure out what made someone a mark. What was the trigger specifically? What was the reason? All the victims were females between the ages of eighteen and twenty-one, all of them students living at college, all of them fit and attractive. That part was a no-brainer, but what was that special something, that sexual specificity that had made these particular coeds unique? He had notes, cross-notes, details, and inferences, but much of his work looked like random annotations from a modeling agency, each girl described in detail, with cross-references that sometimes matched, sometimes didn't. Collectively, it read like a blur of "t & a" that evaded a pattern. Frustrating, but Bronson knew he had to be patient.

Tonight's compare and contrast would be Brittany Barnes and Melissa Baumgardner, numbers 1 and 13. He picked up the old packet for Brittany Barnes and fingered through it for the photos he'd printed, pulling out the two that showed the most skin. The first was from her old Facebook account, shot down the shore from her beach chair, showing her bare legs in the close foreground, then the sand and the water. She had her toenails painted powder blue, skin smooth and tan, cluster of freckles (three) high on her left thigh.

The other pic came from her Instagram, showing her sitting with a girlfriend on a padded bench in the waiting area of what looked like a South Philly restaurant, potted plant on the floor to the right and a large reprint in glass behind them of the 1932 construction workers having lunch on a skyscraper girder. Both the young women were giving their "signature smiles," both in short black dinner-dresses, both with their legs crossed. Neither had on pantyhose. Brittany's hair was up, wisps coming down along the sides of her face. Her friend had close-set blue eyes, a long nose, straight hair, big teeth, and an ankle tattoo that looked like a butterfly. Monster calves. Her hand was on Brittany's knee.

Bronson put down the photocopies and reached for the mouse. He'd seen Melissa Baumgardner on the news as had everyone else . . . the high school yearbook picture her parents had released to the press . . . and she was a looker too, no doubt about it. Still, Brittany Barnes was the type you pictured lifeguarding, riding horses, and trying out for the pep squad, while Melissa Baumgardner was more the youth beauty pageant girly-girl, all spangles and curls, stardust and unicorns, at least that's the way it looked from her headshot.

He wanted to see her body.

He put her name in the surf bar, and three options down was "Melissa Baumgardner (@lissygirl) Instagram photos and videos." He clicked it, and the computer went dark. Bronson stared at it. There was no power loss in the room otherwise, and he hadn't had his feet anywhere near the power strip on the floor.

The screen brightened suddenly, and there was a photograph there. It was a cell phone close-up, the device apparently held sideways, revealing a naked girl lying on her back on some sort of steel table. She was long and supple, and her eyes were gone. Below the shot, words in italics floated in like a title. They said:

*lissygirl*

The image on the screen changed. Another girl, same table, same pose, then another and another, all thirteen scarecrow victims shown in rapid-fire, and then more familiar images came up on the monitor. It was the mini-episode Bronson had watched three nights ago on the porn site *Bang Bus,* where they convinced a Bostonian blonde twenty-something protester to hop inside the van and get paid for oral sex and intercourse. He'd . . . *used* the frontal shot where she rode it like a horse, and cried out "aww fuck" over and over in her pixie voice. He'd gone and found the site because his nephew Ralphie had wanted to show Bronson and his brother the YouTube show he'd liked so much called *Hot Ones,* where a celebrity guest was interviewed about deep personal issues while eating chicken wings laced with hot sauces. It was funny. The guest they'd had on was a guy named Bobby Lee, who had apparently shat himself on a prior episode. He'd mentioned talking to someone about an appearance he'd made on *Bang Bus,* and they had posted a pic with him posing with one of the porn stars. Bronson hadn't known she was a porn star. He'd only known she looked nice in those shorts, and when he got home he'd visited the site.

To be honest, however, he had known what it was the second he'd Googled it, since it was offered on *Porn Hub.* He'd gone on anyway. He'd been on other sites like it, but he had weaned himself off all that shit. Not that it had been easy. It wasn't as if he was about to go "contacting mature singles in his area," or sharpening his skills on the club scene. He was forty-nine years old and overweight, with a number of issues including toxic social shyness and halitosis anxiety.

But he'd kept it legal and above-board, always eighteen and over, never "candid" with that peeping Tom hidden camera bullshit.

Didn't matter.

His browsing activity was being flashed before him on hyper-speed, and he recognized every single thing that he'd ever clicked. Everything. Eight years' worth since he'd bought the system at Best Buy, and even though he'd been altogether more prudent than lecherous, exercising temperance and avoidance for up to three months at a time, the number of accumulated visitations was staggering. Images he'd long deleted out of his browsing history were still flashing onto his computer screen faster than camera cuts in a music video, and he'd been watching in shock for a number of precious seconds already.

He bent down for that power strip.

The phone rang. He froze. He had a retro-style rotary phone that he'd bought on Amazon to go with the desk, and the ringer was startling, especially in this context. It was three inches from his nose, and he slowly straightened back up. Picked up the receiver and brought it to his ear.

"My friend," the voice said. It was enhanced, mechanized, robotic, inhuman. Bronson was sweating, forehead, base of the spine.

"Yes."

"You've been naughty."

Bronson paused.

"Yes," he said finally. "What's the game here?"

Now the pause came from the other side.

"My friend," it repeated, "do you know what a doppelgänger is?"

"Why don't you tell me?"

"Of course. In your case it's your hard drive. Your ghostly counterpart. Your double. Or better yet, maybe it's the truer 'you,' the one we wouldn't want anyone to see. Wouldn't you agree?"

Bronson looked at the screen. It had come back to Melissa Baumgardner's death shot, lying on a steel table under the bright overheads, shapely legs, neatly shaven pussy-stripe, short poking breasts, eyes bloody craters.

"Here's the thing," the mechanized voice continued. "You have made a clear distinction in your mind between these victims and your addiction, though your brothers and sisters in the SVU wouldn't see it that way, would they? They'd look at the material on this hard drive and consider them linked to the files in your desk and the patterns on your wall. They would conclude things about you. Deviant things. They might even think you're the Scarecrow Killer himself, and it might be difficult to explain away, wouldn't you say?"

"Yes," Bronson said. It was from behind clenched teeth.

"Good, we're on the same page. Listen carefully. Every pornographic website you have ever clicked into is locked in a file now, mixed with all the visitations to the Instagram and Facebook pages of the girls you call 'Scarecrows.' I have added in one hundred and seventeen more 'visitations,' including 'Hot College Girls,' 'Blonde Dorm Duos,' and 'Naked Babes in the NCAA,' for spice and good measure. And I'll be watching. If you try to alert anyone about this or sign out equipment that could wipe clean that hard drive, I will hit 'Send' from my superior system and deliver your entire enhanced portfolio to Captain Canfield, everyone else at the station, Karen Rogers from the Channel Six News, the FBI, your mother, your best friend from high school, your worst enemy from college, Matt Garter, the *Daily News*, the *Philadelphia Inquirer*, and ten cable news sources."

"And to avoid this . . . inconvenience?" Bronson said.

"Easy. You have your doppelgänger and now I have mine."

"And who's that?"

"You, Detective. Time to self-actualize. Surprise is waiting for you down in the basement."

# CHAPTER 5
# NIGHT GAMES

Officer Randall Flint had been a Navy Explosive Ordnance Disposal technician, and his report concerning the three squad cars outside Erika's apartment was no less than dire. In fact, he'd never seen anything like it. What had been affixed to each tailpipe was a sophisticated, military-grade device, incredibly compact, each one housing an exotic porous silicone in a vacuum unit that could cool it to the temperature of liquid nitrogen. The detonators were electro-pneumatic, simply adding compressed air, and if triggered, each unit would have reacted seven times more impressively than TNT.

If the officers were shaken, they weren't showing, yet Erika sat deep in the corner of the sofa, feet up on the cushion. She was hugging her knees.

Canfield stepped outside and called Bob Silver again, this time on his Samsung, and the commissioner agreed that for tonight at least they'd go cell to cell, as station communications had been compromised. Canfield made his current report. Commissioner Silver assured him that his procedural execution had exposed the department to the least possible liability regardless of what the killer had suggested, and the captain thanked him for his support.

"It's long after business hours," Canfield added. "If the Bureau is going to be properly briefed, I'm going to have to—"

"Already done, Bill. I gave the rundown to Special Agent Lester Shanahan an hour and a half ago, FBI Philadelphia office, 600 Arch Street. He's bringing a team to the station tomorrow, 10 A.M. sharp. Give him what he needs. Otherwise, he'll try to stay out of your hair."

"What about Erika Shoemaker?"

"They want to move her."

"Where?"

"Undetermined. There are minor issues with location and the deployment of her escort."

"How long?" Canfield said.

"Two hours. Three on the outside, nothing past midnight."

"She's scared to death, Commissioner."

"Then look after her. Get her out of that apartment. Take her to a diner. Run her over to your place and let her get cleaned up, maybe convince her to take a long nap. Just don't take any black and whites along for the ride. Until we figure out who planted that letter and wired those squad cars, we keep this close to the vest."

Canfield looked out the window.

"My people are embedded here," he said. "How do I keep this covert?"

The commissioner laughed shortly.

"Bill, you're the best cop in Southeastern Pennsylvania. Figure a way to sneak her out the back, for Christ's sake."

By the time things were wrapped up at the scene it was well after 9:00 P.M., and just after 10:00 there had been another call from Bob Silver. They'd just pulled into Canfield's driveway. There were more delays at the FBI field office, and it was agreed that it was best that he and Erika stay put at this point.

*"Handle it, Bill. I can't think of a 'safer house' or a more qualified guard-dog. We still want to keep the visibility low on this, but if you need any sort of assistance, give me a shout. Put me on speed-dial."*

Captain Canfield had complied, and he was sitting on the edge of the mattress upstairs in his bedroom. He'd put on his oversized Villanova tee, loose black sweat pants, and tube socks that sagged; he didn't have stylish casual stuff. He didn't have party clothes, or date clothes, or Metro-clothes, or attire for houseguests. He had his uniforms in the bedroom closet, pressed and sheathed in plastic next to the hooks for his caps—one for the station, one for all-weather field duty, and the third with the braid and gold clusters for ceremonies. He also had a dozen suits, all double-breasted, two from Boyd's and ten from Men's Wearhouse. There were a couple of windbreakers next to his duck-quilted flannel-lined Active Jac, and separated by a hanging divider was an array of industrial button-downs, insulated coveralls, polyethylene bib overalls, and heavy-duty work trousers hung with clips, never folded, all for when he was playing carpenter in the garage, or prepping the ride mower, or wire-brushing slag and mill scale off the iron fencing, or tinkering with his Harley Dyna Wide Glide that sat like a trophy in the carport. Clothes had a purpose. They made the man, and he was sitting on the edge of the bed in his casuals, sending a message to Erika Shoemaker. That she was safe here with him, that there were no strings attached.

She was in the shower.

The shower was connected to the bedroom, and for Canfield this felt incredibly "close" and intrusive and awkward. It had actually been the compromise. She'd initially wanted him in there with her, sitting on the toilet. He'd convinced her otherwise, claiming the bathroom porthole window was not big enough for human infiltration and she was just as safe with him playing sentry out here. What he hadn't said aloud was that back at her place on the sofa he'd caught the scent of her perfume, or skin cream, or body spray, and it was excruciating for him even to entertain the idea of having her a foot and a half away from him, naked as a jaybird and visually shielded by nothing but a thin coat of mist on the shower door.

The water shut off and he tried not to picture her drying off, moment for moment. There were sounds, however, frank sounds of movement, the door sliding in its groove, a wet foot on the tile. Skin. Supple. Smooth and warmed. He imagined her patting herself dry under the chin. Behind her knees. Between her thighs.

"Hi," she said. He looked up, and she was standing in the doorway. She was wearing his oversized cabana towel like a cocktail dress, and with the matching hand towel she was smoothing the damp lock of hair gathered over her left shoulder. She had deep collarbone lines. She'd removed all her makeup, eyes raw and fragile, but the shadows cut along her Nordic cheekbones and jawline as if she'd used an artist's highlighting brush. She was a diamond. Shelved here in this dingy bolt hole.

"Sorry about the amenities," he said clumsily.

"They're fine."

"I'll sleep on the floor," he said, pushing up.

"I'd rather you didn't."

Canfield settled back to the bed. It made a creaking noise.

"It's . . . that's exactly what the killer wants," he said.

"I want to feel safe, Bill."

"I think we should keep this official."

She came toward him.

"I want to feel safe, *Captain*. What we saw on that television scared the shit out of me. And I don't care about posturing and political correctness right now."

He stared down at his hands.

"So you want me to . . ."

"I want you to pour me a glass of wine from the bottle I brought from the apartment," she said. "It's in my bag on the chair. You can use that drinking cup on the night stand. Then I want you to take that .44 Magnum Desert Eagle that you have holstered on the bottom side of the bedframe, and I want you to pull it out of there cocked and loaded. I want you to let me under the covers and then get in with me, holding me from behind with your right arm crooked under my neck and across the chest to the shoulder in front. Hold the piece in your free hand, I know you can shoot right or left, I've filed the range-records. I don't trust the window. It gives me the creeps with the shadows of the trees playing across it, and if a perpetrator came through there, you'd have a clear plane and good positioning. Through the door, you'd just have to look back over your shoulder. Less comfortable that way, but your body would be a shield from that angle. That's the set-up I want."

She was standing close. He moved his head an inch in acknowledgment, keeping his glance aimed down at her feet. Dark-tint lotus flower anklet tattoo. Faint light shimmering along her shins highlighting a small nick just below the right knee. He cleared his throat.

"It's not a Desert Eagle," he said. "It's a .480 Ruger Super Redhawk with a two-and-a-half-inch snub-nosed Alaskan barrel, and I don't have it strapped to the bottom of the bedframe. I keep it in the bureau, top drawer. The underwear drawer. Anticlimactic, I know."

"It'll do," she said. "I'll take your service revolver. Where is it?"

"Clothes closet. Under the caps in the belt scabbard."

She crossed past him to get it. She also let the towel drop off. He had raised his gaze, following her as a natural sort of reaction, and he looked down again quick, jaw making shapes in his cheek. Her ass was better than he had envisioned. Heart-shaped and smooth, and she had long, toned legs like those he'd seen on commercials for *Dancing with the Stars.* His sweat pants were suddenly revealing; he got up brusquely and made for the underwear drawer.

"You forgot to pour me my wine," she said.

"First things first," he said. He took his time getting out the weapon, looking it over, checking the trigger, the hammer, the barrel.

"This place could be bugged," he murmured.

"Yes, I'm aware."

He heard the sheets move.

She was expecting to be held now, in his bed—all caution be damned.

He took a deep breath, all right then, ten-four. He'd just keep his trunk and lower parts backed off, like that prissy hug you gave acquaintances at those uptight social gatherings he tried his best to avoid. And if she backed her backside into him? Well, you know what they said about bridges . . .

He turned. She had poured her own wine, and she was sitting with the pillows propped behind her, comforter folded down, legs stretched out over it, feet together at the ankles. The tiny patch of blond hair disappearing between her thighs was smartly trimmed in "Bermuda Triangle" style, yet thinned more like a sleek arrowhead. Her breasts were wide-set and upturned, sun-freckles in the cleavage, her hair slick and darkened. She took a drink. Slowly. Carefully she drew in her feet, legs mirrored in parallel before they slipped under the folded-over bottom-sheet beneath her. She reached over to put the drinking glass on the end table next to the service revolver, then moved down and in, shifting and giving a half-turn, weight on her right hip, ass making a shape under the covers. Canfield didn't move, and she looked back over her shoulder, eyes naked and brittle.

"I'm a gem when it comes to hair, makeup, and personal grooming, Captain, but I'm poor at seduction. Get in with me, don't make me beg."

He took a step forward, feeling as if this was one of those "out-of-body" experiences.

"Captain."

"Yes?"

"Take off your clothes."

"Pardon?"

"Please," she said. "Take off your clothes. I want to feel you."

He reached for the bottom of his shirt.

Downstairs, something tapped on the front door.

"Oh, my lordy-*fuck*!" Erika cried, jerking back up to a sitting position, covers in fists up in front of her chin. Canfield turned to snatch his cell phone off the top of the bureau. He hit the touchscreen home button and got nothing. He hit the on-button: dead. Erika scrambled out of bed and rushed over to her bag. She got out her phone, thumbed at it, and shook her head "no." Canfield reached for the Cisco wall unit by the light switch, grabbed at the receiver, and pulled it to his ear. No dial-tone. The tapping downstairs continued, methodical and deliberate, and Erika's eyes were wide moons.

"It sounds like fingernails," she whispered, "doing that slow ticky-tack thing, like the maniacal villain, grinning and scheming."

"I don't know what it is exactly," Canfield replied. "The acoustics in this place amplify things, but still, you wouldn't hear fingernails." He ripped open a drawer. "Put these on, hurry."

He chucked over a pair of blue gym shorts with a drawstring and a sleeveless white T-shirt.

"Stay here," he said.

"Are you kidding me?"

"Back into that far corner, sit Indian style, and get comfortable. If anyone comes through the door or the window, be patient, get a good look, and aim at his middle, the biggest part of the trunk, right above the belly button. Knock that safety off, that's it."

"But we shouldn't split up, should we?" she said.

"I can't have an anchor, Erika. This room has only two points of entry, but downstairs there are multiples in a three-sixty: windows, mudroom, kitchen door, basement. I don't have eyes in the back of my head and I have to be ready to turn on a dime, shooting at movement the second I see it. Put the gun down on the bed, it'll be easier to get your arms through and put your pants on. Hurry now."

She hesitated only a moment, then hurried.

"Get in the corner."

She got there quickly and sat down hard, knees pointing at ten and two o'clock.

"Good girl."

She brought the gun upward by the side of her face.

"Talk to me like a doggie again, and I'll MeToo you so fast you'll get whiplash." She smiled crookedly. "Now get going. Maybe it's Avon or Girl Scout cookies. And I like peanut butter, not those cardboard-thin fucking mints."

The tapping had stopped, but now it continued. Slower. A bit harder.

"Go!" she hissed.

He went.

The hallway was dark, the bottom half of the staircase dimly illuminated by the faint secondary glow from the night sky filtered through the living room bay windows. Had he kept on any of the downstairs lights he would have been at more the disadvantage with the glare on the glass from in here, but he didn't feel all that reassured. Windows could be weapons, and like Bruce Willis in *Die Hard,* Canfield was caught in the moment without footwear, just sagging white tube socks. He came off the landing careful not to slip on the hardwood, gun in extended low ready position, forty-five degrees downward.

The front foyer area was recessed, opaque, yielding the vague dark forms of the half-round console table where he always tossed his wallet and keys, the wall-mounted coat bar, and the antler plaque up high to the right with the deer horns he'd brought back from the hunting trip last year out in Altglen. The front door loomed before him like a massive black tombstone. He'd been torn between installing a hanging lantern in here or an arched window over the frame made of stained glass, the modern type, nothing "churchy," and he wished he had made up his mind. He moved forward, firearm now in CQD Power Point, in front of his face so he could look over the muzzle-tip in line with the alleged threat.

From the other side someone kicked the door, rocked it in its jamb, and Canfield almost shot his damned nose off. Another kick, then a third conjoined with a splintering sound, and Canfield reached and twisted the deadbolt, grabbed the handle, and ripped the door open wide. Night wind, night sounds, and a huge, hulking figure stood in the dark on the stoop. Canfield leveled his weapon.

"Hands up," he said, "then get on your knees. I'll shoot you like a mad dog, I'm not fucking bluffing."

The figure raised his hands, crooked at the elbows. Something glinted in both palms.

"I can't go to my knees," the man said, voice rough and thick. "I almost passed out stomping the door just now, it's my arthritis. Same with my hands. Why do you think I had to tape silver dollars to my palms? I can't curl my knuckles, let alone rap them on wood."

Canfield reached for the switch just inside the doorway, fumbled for a moment, and flipped it on, flooding the stoop with a sharp blaze from the exterior bulb that tossed shadows, hard slanted left. The figure moved his hands slightly to shield his eyes, and indeed, he had silver dollars taped to his palms. He was a big man, red baseball cap, snow-white hair. He had blue rheumy eyes with dark saddlebags under them, and deep-set age lines on both sides of his mouth. He had on a windbreaker, a loose work shirt with the "Giant" supermarket logo, old jeans, and cheap sneakers. Canfield took a step closer.

"Why didn't you ring the doorbell?"

"Doorbell's out. Take a look, you can see the exposed wiring."

"Convenient. But I'm not taking my eyes off you."

"I wouldn't either," the man said. "But remember, I came to you, not the other way around."

"Why?"

The man blinked a few times and drew his hands closer to his face defensively.

"Captain, I have photophobia. I'm sensitive to light. Bring me inside. Please."

"What for?"

"My confession."

"Are you this 'Sculptor' character?"

The man smiled sadly, eyes closed as if some mental anguish had risen in him equaling the pain of the harsh exterior lighting.

"Is that what he calls himself now?" he said. "Well hell, I'm not him, never could be. But I was his accomplice back when he was a boy." He made himself open one eye to a squint. "You and I, we've met before, Captain. By a backyard flower bed when you were a junior officer investigating a missing persons case, a three-year-old girl. No. I'm not the Sculptor killer. I'm his father. And now that he has resurfaced, he's going to try to put a warp on the world. Captain, you've got to trust me. The killing has just started, the mind-fuck is in its infancy, and you're a goddamned fool if you think that *I'm* bluffing."

# CHAPTER 6
# DOLL #15

Detective Bronson flipped on the basement stair-light and it popped hard and darkened, making him jerk so dramatically he nearly pulled a muscle. There was a streak of afterimage and a burning smell from the filament. He swallowed dryly.

Upstairs, he had quickly changed into a dull yellow T-shirt with rippled "bacon-neck," and old faded jeans, loose in the leg, high on the ankle. Work boots, thick socks, and he was trying not to squeeze his Sig Saur P238 by the grip too damned hard.

Not that he thought he'd have a chance to use it. Wrong game; more likely, there was a victim down there in the darkness, Bronson's victim now, brutally slaughtered, strategically positioned, and any second he expected to hear sirens. If he got raided right now, he'd be mistaken for the Scarecrow Killer, and if he could manage to hide the body he was an accomplice, or better yet, a copycat, the infamous "doppelgänger."

He had turned on all the living-room lights behind him, but the glow lost its warmth at the top end of the stairway, filtering only three or four steps down on a dull gradated angle that looked like the blade of a guillotine under water. Past that was a spread of darkness so thick you could very well anticipate the last stair too soon, miss the lip, pitch forward, and break your damned neck.

Of course, the replacement bulbs were down there in the basement, in the off-white veneer storage cabinets at the back end of the house by the fuse box. So was the flashlight. And he'd misplaced his cell phone, couldn't find it this morning, and it seemed pretty clear that this was no accident. He'd have to make it way back to the bulb with the pull cord hanging above the washer and dryer.

Bronson stepped to the short landing and the floor creaked. He stopped. The sound had never seemed malignant before, but everything was magnified, sensory hyperbole. He moved forward and put his weight down on the first step, then down to the next as if being careful and delicate would lessen his exposure. At the fourth stair he felt the darkness start to slide over his face, and by the seventh he was disoriented, as if everything was unhitched and weightless.

He got to the bottom, or at least what felt like the last stair. He dipped carefully with his toe, touched down gingerly, and felt the surface change from woodgrain to the rough industrial carpeting.

Suddenly the lights blared on—not the bald sixty-watter he'd been going for, but a pair of footlights with red and blue color gels, both facing straight upward in each of the north corners in front of the white masking fabric that ran floor to ceiling to cover the piping.

The lights were not the only new props. Centered between them was a decorator side table—a rickety thing painted black with small claw feet. It had a mirrored top that reflected the new luminescence like thunderheads, and there were two items sitting on the glass.

On the left there was a large capsule, what Bronson's mother would have called a "horse pill." On the right was a drinking glass, two-thirds filled with blood. Or at least it looked like it . . . wasn't burgundy or merlot, wrong consistency. Wasn't V8 or cranberry juice either. It had swashed up to the lip on the inner side and streaked down in a cone shape like a sample in a test tube.

"I know that you know what it is in the glass," the mechanical voice blared, amplified by hidden speakers and loud enough to make Bronson's teeth buzz. "You just don't know where the blood came from. I am going to tell you, and then you are going to have to make a choice. A moral one, since that particular muscle of yours has so tragically atrophied."

"What choice?"

"Don't interrupt. I didn't want to involve her, but you have now enticed me to put another card in the mix. I currently have my fist clenched deep into the gray hair of an unconscious librarian from Wilmington, Delaware. I have a

Tactical Custom Triple Edge bowie knife. You speak again out of turn, I'll cut her throat like turkey gizzard and send you the head. Are we clear?"

Bronson nodded.

"Good boy," the voice said. "Let's see if you're clever. Tonight for dinner you had planned to eat the salad you made this morning, waiting for you in the small Tupperware bowl on the second rack in the fridge, but you caved and had the leftover spaghetti with lobster and cream sauce from the other night when you sat alone in the back corner by the kitchen at Fellini's. When I broke into your house today to arrange things, I laced the dish with strychnine. I added a homemade compound for a delay in order to account for your typical fourteen-minute rest in the Laz-Y-Boy after dinner, the three minutes to change out of your work clothes, and the nineteen minutes you would expend pinning the wall map, looking at the file on Brittany Barnes, and clicking the *Lissygirl* Instagram that offered my lovely presentation of dead girls for ambiance. Right about now you should be feeling the first symptoms of the poison: restlessness, increased audio and visual sensitivities, escalated heart rate, mouth filled with copper."

It was true. The dryness in Bronson's mouth had gone metallic and his pulse was starting to pound in his temples.

"Here's the deal," the voice said. "In about two minutes the condition advances to convulsions and asphyxia, leading you to be added to the tally of those like Alex the Great and Jane Stanford, though they will be remembered more fondly, I assure you. The antidote is on the black table in pill form. It is laced with a powdered explosive, sensitive to force, triggered by saliva, and only dismantled by stomach acid, so considering the arid condition of your mouth and your throat, I would not advise trying to swallow it dry. Similarly, if you bite down, snort it, or try to let it melt on your tongue, your head will explode like an M80 in a watermelon. You cannot insert it anally and you can't stick it in your ear. You cannot open the capsule and sprinkle the contents on your eye, and you can't run upstairs to the refrigerator for a Coke or a Deer Park. I also doped your spaghetti with Acetazolamide, same delay mechanism as the poison, so by this time it's live. It is a remedy for Acute Mountain Sickness, usually meant to cure those who feel ill at eight thousand feet. This special blend has been engineered to climax impressively at the height of eight stairs, exactly three from your basement door, where your breathing would immediately accelerate, a side effect typical for this drug yet thirty times as extreme, and therefore, in concert with the poison, your lungs would explode. Tick-tock, Detective. The implements for survival sit right in front of you, but I sense hesitation. Speak now, it's appropriate."

"Why this? What's your motive?"

"Very brave, Detective. Taking some of your precious time to find meaning and substance. Still, propriety forces me to offer information more practical. The blood in the glass belongs to a teenager named Meagan Mullin, redhead, wide face, yellow lashes, lots of freckles. She's insecure about being so frightfully 'ginger,' and she listens to 'stoner-sludge' and 'black metal.' She often thinks of suicide and rips her stockings on purpose. We met online. She sends me her blood. It's a thing nowadays—crazy kids."

"Why her?" Bronson said. The name was familiar, but it was out of context somehow.

"So that you can be wed. You see, I'm going to kill her tonight . . . make another doll, and her DNA will be part of your fiber. It endures seven days in its host, so I own you for a week. Understand that I don't think the threat of exposing your hard drive is enough. It frightens you, but it won't make you kill for me. This will. Drink the blood, Detective Bronson, and save yourself. Meagan will be Doll 15, yet number 16 will be all yours, that's a promise."

Bronson paused for a long moment thinking of the librarian he couldn't see, of risk, reward, and collateral. Was she a bluff? Undeterminable. His instinct said no, but his best play was risk. He squared his shoulders and stalked over to the table to pick up the glass, careful not to spill, head pounding, eyes bulging, pulse burning. He turned and moved as quickly as possible to the splash basin, steeling himself, expecting at any moment to be stopped somehow, but there was no resistance, nothing, just silence. Bronson leaned in over the front of the basin. He lowered the drinking glass. Poured the blood down the drain and set the glass down next to it. Then he looked right. On top of the Maytag there was an array of detergents, a spray bottle of Shout, a box of Borax, and the fabric softener with the white fucking teddy bear on it. There was also a half-gallon of bleach. Bronson put his gun down, picked up the container, and again leaned across the edge of the basin.

"Here's a nice chaser for your fucking DNA," he said under his breath, pouring half the jug down the pipe. Then he covered the entire bottom surface of the sink and filled the glass so it spilled over the rim. He would have preferred an ethylene oxide treatment, but beggars couldn't be choosy.

Now for something to drink from. Behind him on top of a folding card table half under the staircase was the red dented toolbox without its tray, a tube of caulk, and a claw hammer. There was also the Maxwell House can with the fuses, wall anchors, staples, finish nails, and other miscellaneous junk. His heart was thudding hard in his chest—not much more time. He grabbed the coffee can, dumped out the contents, and stomped back over to the utility basin. He didn't expect the water to work, too easy, but it was worth a shot pushing up the faucet handle. He got what he'd expected, a long groan followed by a throaty knocking from deep in the pipe. The spigot bucked in its mount. The main valve at the curb was cut off, probably hours ago. If Bronson had tried to take a piss or do the dishes after dinner he would have known, but the killer clearly knew he usually did both before he went to bed.

There was one last hope that maybe the bastard hadn't accounted for. Behind the dehumidifier in the right corner was the French drain built into the floor, the circular trench that had never worked very well, often overflowing years back. Bronson hadn't had a significant flooding down here since he'd had his plumber put in a sump pump, but he knew water swirled in there regularly. Sometimes, however, it was bone dry. He didn't know why, he wasn't an expert with water tables, soil erosion, and the sedimentation and runoff of nearby rivers and streams. No choice here but to gamble.

He moved to the killer's decorator table and picked up the capsule, next advancing deep right, kicking aside an old suitcase and elbowing past an empty steel rack unit. The wide heavy-duty plastic drain cap on the floor was about three good feet in front of the masking cloth, and it was mildew-spotted and covered with a light coat of masonry dust, the ribbed hose of the sump pump coming out through the small side-recess. Bronson used his toe to push aside the filthy drain cap. Inside there was water, thank God, about eight inches deep and rust brown. The pump was stagnant in it. Back in the farthest reach of his mind, Bronson noted that he'd have to call his plumber again about that.

He bent to a knee, dipped in the coffee can, and pulled it out, dripping. He put the pill in his mouth. He squeezed his eyes shut, forced himself to raise the can to his lips, and took a big swallow. Tasted of rust and iron and silt like a sewer, and he almost threw it back up. He forced it down. The pill, however, stayed stuck on the back of his tongue. He dipped the can again and brought it up, almost biting at it, this time taking in so much his cheeks bubbled out. He jerked back his head, face wet and shirt soaked.

He'd done it. He put his forearm against his mouth, willing himself not to retch, and then turned and coughed hard into his shoulder.

There was a popping sound through the speakers, and for a moment it was difficult to determine what it was. Then not so. It was clapping, slow and sarcastic.

"Well done," the killer said finally. "But I am afraid you missed the entire point of the exercise. I told you this was to be a test of morals, while you seemed to deduce that it was solely about your resourcefulness. I think the key here is that you took some of my conditions and interpreted them as staples of fact, like mathematical postulates assumed true as a basis for constructing your reasoning. But what if I lied from the beginning? What if I told you now that your spaghetti wasn't laced with poison, but rather a hard dose of time-released and harmless adrenaline . . . that the blood in the glass came from a farm pig, and that it was the capsule that contained Meagan Mullin's DNA? No, don't bother putting your finger in the back of your throat. I don't just talk a good game, I am an expert with chemical manufacture, and I assure you that I am even more adept at quick-releases than I am with delays. The capsule in your stomach has been fully absorbed, you and Meagan are already wed, and now I'll give you a bridesmaid."

New spotlights blared on from behind the gauzy white fabric that masked the horizontal piping against the front wall. Now it was see-through like mesh, and Bronson screamed. Crab-walked backward.

It simply gave him a better view.

There was a naked woman there, tied fast to the pipes like Jesus with duct tape over her mouth, the product cut in the shape of a coy smile like a cupid's bow. She was tall and bone-thin, black hair plastered to her neck from exertion, flesh ghostly and translucent with exotic blue vein-work marbled beneath like irregular flagstone paving.

And there were needles.

A swarm of them, yet only inserted on her left, Bronson's right, each pin slightly puffing the flesh at the given point of entry like wire in a sheath, inlayed in multiple penetrations beneath the eye, in the cheek, above the lip, through the front of the chin, the soft tissue beneath the jaw, and likewise down the rest of her body like some strange work of one-sided acupuncture. Each needle was connected at its outer end to a length of micro-thin vinyl tubing, the entire lot bundled a few feet from her with a zip-tie and apparently funneled into a single conduit the size of an eighteen-gauge extension cord.

The footlights changed, rear off, front on, cloaking her again. Bronson had seen her for about a second and a quarter. For him it was enough for a lifetime.

"Hope you took note of the details," the voice said. "Did you have time to follow the length of master-tubing? It snakes out from under the masking cloth and connects to the sump pump in the French drain. When you approached with your coffee can, I am sure you noticed the dirty well-cover, but I would bet you didn't see how shiny and new was the anti-kink hose coming out of it, nor the aforementioned tubing inserted into the filter trap. Yes, it is my pump, not yours, jerry-rigged not to work by a float rod, but by remote control, the instrument I am holding right now in my hand. Behind the curtain you just got a glimpse of the one and only Bridget Ballentine, starting center for the Drexel University Dragons basketball team, Division One. A champion, but she has an eating disorder, never seeing herself as quite thin enough. As remedy, the needles I have inserted in her fatty tissue have been sucking out different portions of that particular layer bit by bit. I could explain the process to you scientifically, Detective Bronson, but I am afraid time is of the essence. A few more applications will kill her, but look at the effect of a quick engagement with the device."

The footlights switched back.

The sump pump flipped on and jumped in the rust-colored water. Bronson cringed, ground his teeth. The young woman breathed in hard against the duct tape as the skin sucked to her bones, making her eyes bulge and her face look like a skull covered in Saran Wrap. The pump disengaged and the rear floodlights went dark again.

"Final deal," the voice said. "You can save Bridget by removing the needles as carefully as you can. I have given you a measure of .0125 of a millimeter's play surrounding each insertion, and like that old game *Operation,* one slip in any direction except for straight back kicks on the sump pump. Except this time there is no shut-off after one and a half seconds. You'll drain her. Your other choice is to save Meagan Mullin, who thinks she is meeting me in exactly twenty-three minutes at Saint Mary's Cemetery on Sproul Road in Broomall. She is walking into a trap. I will kill her if you do not get there before me. She will be in the vicinity of the towering woman who cannot see: that's the clue you must dissect on the fly. And no phones, so don't waste precious time. The moment we hung up after our brief introduction, I disabled the landline. Since it will take you thirty seconds to exit the house, you have exactly one minute to make a decision, as I have calculated the following driving time to get two towns over, plus your walk from your vehicle parked at the chapel, across the field of flat ledger stones to the grave site. Chop-chop, Detective. You can't save both. Which will it be? You'll have to alter your foundations for logic. One girl is in front of you, and the other could very well not exist at all. Moreover, I am a liar, an unreliable narrator. I tell you something, tell you it's a lie, and then I say that I lied about lying. Fact: you don't know Bridget personally, and I will tell you now if you choose to believe me, that Meagan Mullin is Connor Mullin's sister. You work with Connor Mullin. He despises you, wants to unseat you, thinks you depend on rank more than courage."

Bronson stood up. Connor Mullin, yes, redhead and chin-zits, the newbie who was asking Captain Canfield for a different gun this morning so he could put on a laser sight. Bronson hadn't known the kid had it in for him. Didn't know now. Liars lying about lying, right?

"Question," he said.

"Clock's ticking."

"Why not just lace my spaghetti with Meagan Mullin's powdered DNA? Why the dog and pony show?"

A pause, but a slight one.

"Where would be the sport in that, Detective Bronson? Besides, I wanted to see you drink gutter water."

Bronson didn't bother with a comeback. He turned abruptly and charged hard for the basement stairs, to take them two at a time, get to his car, and race to the cemetery. This was no moral choice; it was a practical one. First, in a cold sort of pragmatism, there was a distinct possibility that he had, in fact, swallowed Megan Mullin's DNA. Then again, maybe not. Maybe Connor didn't even have a sister. Regardless, the play wasn't here in the basement, and it had nothing to do with ripping down the masking cloth and playing *Operation*. Bronson wasn't meant to have the chance. Even though he was overweight and insecure, he was a quick study, and this son of a bitch was, if nothing else, becoming predictable in the ways that he cheated. Plainly, the killer had control of the lights, which were most likely about to go off, leaving Bronson to fumble around for the pull cord by the washer and dryer. And it was probably burned out like the one in the stairwell. That was meant to take up his precious time, not the careful removal of needles.

Concurrently, the brief glimpses he'd been afforded of the girl tied to his pipes had told volumes. Her eyes like eggshells with pinpoints for pupils were not filled with fear, and instead of screaming into the duct tape swelling it, she'd inhaled, making it dimple. In terms of Bronson's skill with psychological profiling, he'd additionally noted that everything about Bridget Ballentine said *wallflower*, a "Plain Jane," the one who volunteered to serve punch at the prom and sew the dress for the homecoming queen. Athletic prowess aside, it seemed the Scarecrow Killer had tried to transform her, make her into a terrifying hood ornament fastened to the front of a hearse steered by Satan.

In the killer's eyes, she'd been in her glory.

And she'd been dead as a doornail for hours.

# CHAPTER 7
# KILLER BACKGROUND

"Who is he?" Captain Canfield said.

"Can I lower my hands?"

"No." That came from Erika. She was on the stairs, one bare foot two steps down from the other. She was a silhouette, pointing the service revolver straight ahead at eye level, and from this angle Canfield was as much in the line of fire as was their prisoner.

"I've got this, Erika," he said. "Go back up to the bedroom. Closet. Four pairs of handcuffs in the hanger mate with the black pockets, right side. Bring down a set and check the cell phones again, hurry."

She shot up the stairs, clumped around overhead, and returned, similar positioning.

"No cuffs, Captain."

"You sure?"

"Yes. And both our cells are still dead, same with the house phone." She was aiming the revolver again.

"Erika," he said, "lower your arm carefully, aim the barrel in front of your toes, and come down here. My eyes have adjusted to the darkness, but yours haven't as much. Turn on the overhead. There's a switch at the bottom of the stairs."

"No, please," the man said. "Lamplight only, deeper room preferable."

Canfield pushed the muzzle up harder into the nape of the man's neck and used his other hand gripped in a horse-collar to guide him around to the leather bench at the open end of the three-sided living room sectional.

"Sit," Canfield said.

The big man sat.

"He's photosensitive," Canfield said, not taking his eyes off his gun and its pressure point against the back of the skull. "In the den, Erika. On the desk. Table lamp. Has a push-button in the base."

She came off the stairs and obliged. It took a second or two as she tooled around in there, but soon the living room was feathered with secondary light and soft shadow.

"Lower your hands slowly," Canfield said. "Good. Now slide them palm-down under your legs, that's right, sit on them. I'm going to go through your jacket pockets on either side of you. If I find so much as a toothpick, I'm going to hog-tie you to that newel post at the bottom of the stairs."

"Understood."

Canfield ran his palm between the man's shoulders and felt nothing but backbone. He went through the pockets. In his peripheral vision he saw that Erika was in the archway between rooms, watching, and he reached back up and pulled down rough on the back of the collar, sliding the jacket down the man's arms to the crooks of his elbows.

"Up," Canfield said.

"My arthritis."

"Up and sit on this windbreaker that I'm going to jump-rope under you. I saw a girl tortured today and I'm not feeling charitable."

The man pushed up into a squat and grunted. His knees made soft cracking sounds. Canfield shoved the coat under him, reached to his shoulder, and shoved him back down so he was sitting on his hands again. Another grunt, louder, but for all intents and purposes he was wearing a straitjacket now, poor man's version that would slow him down if he tried something.

"Erika," Canfield said, "come in here and take a seat on the sectional directly across from this man. It'll be soft leather under you, so sit at the front part of the frame. Put your elbows in the middle of your thighs making a solid tripod. Keep your hands relaxed. Eye behind the notch and line it up with the post the way you did before, but keep your head straight, no tilting. Aim the weapon at the middle of this man's chest as soon as I move to his side. I need to reach around front to see if he's wearing a tactical vest, the kind like a bib, since I didn't feel anything around the back."

"He's not," she said. "When he went up on his haunches for you to slide the windbreaker under him, his shirt hung for a sec at the neckline. I saw curly gray chest hair and ribs, big ones like webbing around a barrel, no vest."

"Good. Take the position then and point at the middle of his breastbone. If he moves in a way you don't like, squeeze the trigger, nice and easy, don't pull it, you'll kick right."

She moved around and passed quickly on the left, and Canfield pressed the snubnose hard for a second. It was a subtle reminder to the subject not to move during the transition, and he noticed that the back of this guy's thick neck had those creases you usually saw on jobsite foremen and farm workers.

"I'm going to take my gun from the back of your head," Canfield said. "I'm going to move to a seat to your right and down a few feet. Reminder: I know the furniture, I won't falter or stumble, and if you move while I'm moving, I'll aim for your teeth, then your right eye, one-two, just like that, no questions, no hesitations."

"Got it, Captain."

Canfield moved. He sat. The marble coffee-table top was too close to his knees for his taste, but he adjusted. He took a position, aiming his .480 Ruger.

"Now tell me, who is he? I'm not going to ask you again."

The man blinked, close-set blue eyes, soft jowls, big chin with a cleft.

"I ain't a bad guy."

"Didn't say you were, but you'd better get ready for a long, uncomfortable evening. I'm not going to transport you to the station in the black of night with only one piece of iron on you while the other drives. I'm also no more keen on walking you to a neighbor's house and creating more pedestrian liability than I am on sending this young lady out into the dark by herself for assistance. So. I'm going to hear your confession with said witness present, and next get a legal pad so you can write word for word in your own hand what you did, what your son did, where he is now, everything. Tomorrow at around 8 A.M. when the mail comes through the slot, I'll ask my postman to drive us to the station. Two guns, daylight, federal employee, and a jeep. Sounds like a winner. Then I'm going to call the FBI field office on Arch Street and tell them to prepare for your transfer when they show up at ten o'clock."

"Fair enough, but you're not going to catch him by passing the buck."

"It's the way we do things. There are procedures in place for a reason."

"Right, and he's well aware of them, Captain. Bureaucracies are his kingdom, and he floats like a ghost through the blank spots and loopholes. The Feds were phase one because they were *meant* to be phase one, picking through the rubble and sucking his exhaust while he put those poor girls up on poles on the highway. He won that round, and since then he's moved on, going up-close and personal, intimate and psychological. You're the game now. And so am I."

"Did he contact you?"

"Didn't have to. Your department's movements today weren't subtle."

Canfield shook his head slightly.

"Well, I don't play games."

"You don't get it, Captain, you're already playing. Everything you're doing . . . that we're doing right here and now . . . all of it, he's already thought of and written into the plan. Tomorrow? Feds? Transport? All a pipe-dream. There might not be a tomorrow, not for the three of us, anyway, not if he doesn't want there to be."

"Give me his name," Canfield said flatly. "Date of birth. Color of eyes. Estimated height, approximate—"

"Captain, excuse me," the man said. "Please, his name is Michael Leonard Robinson. He was born in 1979, he went to Lower Merion High School, and he played snare drum in the marching band, but all that fluff isn't going to help you. Forgive me, let's get off the script they handed out in 'Interrogation 101' and cut to the chase, if you don't mind my bluntness. More important and more relevant is that he dropped off the grid in 1997, the day he turned eighteen and left home, and you gotta understand, Captain, that by then he was doing things with technology that no one could understand, nor would they today."

He glanced over at Erika.

"Pardon me for telling you this, ma'am, but even back as far as '89 Michael had a set-up in his room with coaxial cables that could take over the television downstairs and show porn. He could record himself, project it on the boob tube like Skype, predict your answers, and make you feel you were having a conversation with him in real time. He figured ways to obtain unauthorized access and find bank numbers and hospital records, police reports and government bids for the navy yard, and all when he was just ten."

He peered back at Canfield.

"He grew up with computers, they shared a coming of age. The best birthday that boy ever had was his twelfth. 1991. That's when the first digital library was developed at an American university, the Mercury Electronic Library at Carnegie Mellon."

He paused as if looking for some kind of response.

"He predicted the Dot Com Boom!" he said, eyes wide like saucers. "He claimed commercializing the World Wide Web would be the death of the world. He was thirteen. He didn't know the 'Internet' would become a household word three years later when everyone and their mother started going online, but he knew exactly what it would become. He nicknamed it 'Space Vomit.' He predicted Facebook too. Said it would be public graffiti that would make us naked without knowing it. He was sixteen. He was reading constantly, breaking into college research databases mostly, reading anything he could get his hands on: physics, philosophy, anatomy, all the subjects. Mostly, though, he liked history, killers both military and criminal, like Genghis Khan, Shaka Zulu, Jeffery Dahmer, Joan of Arc, John Wayne Gacy, General Patton, Hannibal, Jack the Ripper. Pardon me, Captain, I couldn't name them all if I tried, but the point is that he studied their strategies and created computer animation scenarios to act them out, making them modern, making up horror games before horror video games even existed. Put that on the television too. Rough stuff, most often through the eyes of the killer. Torture. Mutilation. Burning. Delimbing. Skinning. Decapitation. Sometimes he even played MC, talking through a robotic voice scrambler and representing himself as a hooded skull with red eyes and steel teeth. Years later, in 2009, I saw the debut of *Deadliest Warrior* on TV, and I remember laughing out loud, thinking that by comparison it came off like *Sesame Street*."

"I'm no psychiatrist," Canfield said. "I'm also no lawyer. I need data I can use, and all you've really told me so far is that he was ahead of his time making video games."

The man's face reddened right up into the scalp, making his hair look whiter.

"I'm telling you that he was practicing, Captain! Creating simulations. Getting ready. For this." He glanced back at Erika. "You saw a girl tortured, ma'am?"

"Yes."

"Was it live?"

"Seemed so," she said.

"Did he speak to you?"

"Yes," Canfield said.

"I'm willing to bet it was recorded. Enhanced. Might not have even been real, but don't think for a minute he wouldn't carry out what he showed you. I'm just saying that by now he would have advanced the craft of projection and computer animation thirty years ahead of what NASA or Disney, Pixar or Hollywood or anyone in Silicon Valley could even begin to conceive."

He turned to stare at Canfield for a moment, eyes burning, but then he lowered his glance to the floor, heaving a sigh.

"I'm sorry," he said. "I'm doing my best here, but I'm not good at telling stuff, never have been." He glanced up toward Erika. "I'm a nuts-and-bolts kind of guy, miss . . . I'm a union man, worked as the daytime manager for a supermarket my whole life, no frills. I was a champ at putting my head down and earning a paycheck, putting food on the table, you know the deal. But I was always clumsy at parties, slow on the uptake, the last to get a joke, or worse, being the guy *telling* a joke and then having to start all over to fill in the backstory."

He glanced back, nodding slightly.

"If you would, Captain, humor me. Let me go in reverse here just for a heartbeat and paint you a fuller picture . . . make it so we don't have to jug handle and do a one-eighty later, repeating stuff we don't have to. Michael was breaking into college databases and he was also a product of his generation, a gamer but five steps ahead. I, on the other hand, am also a product of *my* generation, good and tech-stupid, but some of the details, at least the early ones, I do remember. The folks who made *Pong* put out the Laser 128 Apple II clone in 1990. It was Michael's first computer, age eleven, and he had it in pieces up in his room the minute it came out of the box, reassembled one night and then hooked up again in a different way the very next, and the next and the next, all connected together with stuff he'd been collecting from yard sales for years, all sorts of mechanical trash neighbors left at the curb, churches, synagogues, small businesses, school dumpsters filled annually with antiquated equipment they regularly weeded all through the Central League trying to have visible evidence they were keeping up with rising standards politicians kept promising.

You wouldn't believe what they'd throw away, especially the high schools: old ham radios, CB's, VCR's, televisions, eight-track recorders, cassette recorders, video cameras of all shapes and sizes, stuff from the Sixties sometimes, others more current. It was like Michael was some kind of mad scientist. I was his gopher, his dumpster-diver so to speak, his 'grave-robber,' and I bought magazines to keep up with the new stuff. Thought it was my duty to encourage him for his interests and all.

"My only screw-up was in 1992, when I presented him with an IBM ThinkPad he didn't care for and left in the corner of his room like an abandoned stepchild. But it was 1993, when he celebrated his fourteenth birthday, that I hit the motherlode for him, all because I got a hold of what those Sega AMZ people developed, the *Virtua Fighter* that had 3D graphics using polygons. Soon he had his Atari Jaguar console hooked up to a bunch of the other paraphernalia in his room, and his Sega Saturn connected in some strange way to his Apple Power Macintosh along with some of the other stuff, the other tech that had been popping up all over the place, like the Talkboy, the Discman D121, a minidisc player, PDA's, zip drives, digital cameras, webcams, QuickCams. The Be Box with its peripheral ports never got popular, but Michael had it wired into the mix when the Nintendo 64 hit the streets, and after that—well, forgive me, I couldn't follow what he was doing if my life had depended on it."

"He was a busy boy."

"Yes, Captain, making false realities. Can you imagine what he's capable of presently? When I tell you he's off the grid, I'm not just telling you that he's erased his digital footprint. I'm telling you he could be anyone. I'm telling you that he knows how to be everywhere and nowhere, haunting the matrix, decades ahead of the big current industry programmers, top-rate engineers, white and black hat security hackers, elite information tech specialists, secret service, military, special ops, you name it. He could take out a power grid just as easily as he could put a ghost in everyone's cell phone at a Phillies game, rigging them all to explode when the choir hits the high note in the national anthem. And it's not just wires and circuits, Captain Canfield. He's good with weapons and tools, fear and pathology. All that reading, remember? He liked biographies as much as philosophies written by dictators, and he enjoyed studying parts breakdowns of pneumatic jackhammers as much as plumbing blueprints and building schematics. He could very well put out all the lights in all three grids in the lower forty-eight: east of the Mississippi, west of the Mississippi, and Texas, all ahead of any countermeasures US Cybercommand could begin to institute. Then he could live in the sewers for ten years. He could come up with fifty ways to kill you with a backscratcher, and a hundred reasons that would sound good to you to go slice your sister's face up with razor blades."

"Where is he?" Canfield said softly.

"Nowhere, I told you. Everywhere."

"I get your point, but riddles don't help me. Seems you enjoy telling them too."

"I came to confess. And '*where*' isn't your biggest problem."

"What is?" Erika said.

He looked at her.

"Plainly, ma'am, it's the '*why.*' I know him. At least I knew him as a boy, and I'm telling you, he's not doing this for gain. He's not doing it to feed an addiction or make some sort of gory artistic statement, even though he'd probably try to sell you that line."

"Then what's he doing it for?" Canfield said.

Robinson looked at him square.

"Glee," he said. "For the fun of it."

Canfield was grinding his teeth.

"It doesn't add up," he said.

"What?"

"Small town. Someone would have outed him. Kids talk. Kids tattle. Somehow, some way, I would have heard about him."

The man shook his head.

"He blended, Captain. Like a seasoned assassin. Never got associated with any particular friendship group, and he spent most of his time in the house, the quiet genius no one ever really knew. I'll bet you most of his graduating class wouldn't remember him, even with a yearbook picture."

"Speaking of which . . ."

"Yes," the man said. "You're right. Even though he fell off the face of the earth in 1997, we still have the old public photos. Yearbook. Driver's license possibly, you'd have to check the records at the DMV. Heck, I have his graduation shot in my wallet. It's a bit dog-eared at the edges, but you're welcome to it, maybe when you let me have use of my hands to get it out for you."

"Patience," Canfield said.

"Of course, Captain. I doubt it would do us much good anyway. He's in his early forties now and I would assume he's had plastic surgery. Might even be a woman for all we know. You're not going to catch him by regular means, and neither will the Feds. He wants to lead you all into a maze of alternate ID's, disguises, fabricated digital representations, false trails of breadcrumbs."

"Then how are we going to catch him, Mr. Robinson?"

"By getting involved, Captain. By learning everything you can about him, right here and right now. I'm here to give you everything that I've got. I'm going to tell you about the three-year-old girl I dug up from under the mulch and reburied for him. I'm also going to tell you about how everything changed after that, his gestation period where he inverted and ate himself alive while he was hiding up in his room hacking into college databases and building renegade computer-projection systems."

"You've already briefed me on the latter."

"Layers, Captain. Bad storyteller, remember? There's more to it."

"So now you're going to try to tell me he had a guilt complex."

Robinson laughed bitterly.

"Heck no. At the age of seven he killed a three-year-old and thought of it the same as a good game of Stratego. I'm not talking about guilt. I'm talking about his weakness."

"He's got a weakness?"

"Everyone has their Kryptonite."

"And his?"

"Women," Erika said rather sharply. "Girls on the highway—isn't it obvious?"

The man nodded.

"Hmm, yes, I suppose you're right, ma'am, at least generally. It's the typical story, isn't it . . . the common denominator, as they say, launching a thousand ships and all that. Beauty untouchable. Innocence and standoffishness, softness and at the same time all the sexy stuff cutting you like a razor, all the contradictions, but I'm no romance novelist. Neither is Michael. And his weakness goes further than being awed by a pretty face and a good bum, pardon the French-reference."

He paused.

"Umm," he said, voice falling soft. "I'm . . . uh . . . I'm talking here about the very first doll . . . before little Cindy Chen, or Brittany Barnes—when he unveiled his first roadkill and started counting them like playing cards. I'm talking about the one who had him starstruck straight out of the box."

He looked up, eyes moistening, big cowboy jaw quivering.

"Don't you see, Captain? I'm talking about the only one who ever got to him, and she did it in ways you'd never expect, never in a million years. I'm talking about Madeline. I'm talking about his mother."

# CHAPTER 8
# LOVE NERDS IN THE FRIEND ZONE

Meagan Mullin's Apple iPhone XR did magic tricks, and it had nothing to do with the backlight design that stretched the screen into the corners or the A12 Bionic chip they advertised with the *"Next-Generation Neural Engine."*

Meagan's phone had a man in it.

A psychedelic ghost-man.

When he came to her it was always at night, and he made his entrance in an explosion of pixels. They literally jumped out of the phone.

And you could . . . taste them.

Three weeks ago to the day, Meagan had been here in her room, sitting on the bed with her knees drawn up and her toes under the covers, watching the candle in the skull on the bureau toss shadows. They made the walls seem longer, dark chocolate. She had a ton of homework, but she was pretty much stuck in "D" territory across the board, except for the A-minus in college-prep English and the B she had going in her nursing elective. Over on the desk by the window, her textbooks looked like a random scatter of upended gravestones. That was symbolic somehow, and she almost smiled, moving her head to the slow, seductive rhythm of the tune she'd pulled up on her iPad. She didn't have earbuds. It was one of the mutual decisions she and Mother had agreed on, but the reasons were different.

Meagan didn't like the idea of being disconnected, shut out and deafened to the rest of the world. She was convinced it was the older generation's ploy to be able to sneak up on kids. Mother, on the other hand, wanted to be able to hear everything she was listening to, like they were bonding. As if. You couldn't feel the groove of good stoner-doom-sludge or hard-ass deathcore metal from down the hall. That was like saying that Black Sabbath could be appreciated on the tinny public address system at school during swim class . . . in that awful torture chamber made up of long tile floors and polished block walls where the glassy echoes made you sad for no reason. I mean, maybe it would be good on some television ad about the opioid crisis, but Meagan didn't listen to music for background or commercialized theming. She hated sellouts, like Asking Alexandria's Danny Warsnop, and his solo "Shades of Blue" Hollywood comeback bullshit, or the idea that a lot of her classmates listened to whatever was the most popular thing in the mainstream. Music was supposed to be her soundtrack, her *soul*-track, something she felt in her—in her what?—in her *balls*, yes, straight to her *balls!*

She folded her arms hard. That type of thought usually made her giggle like an insane person, but the context here bummed her out. Her Sonos speakers were only six inches tall. Back in the day, they had cabinets you could sit on, with tweeters that shrieked and woofers that actually moved and vibrated in their mounts as if they were on springs, she'd Googled it. She was born in the wrong era. She should have been a teen in the '70s, her mother the '60s; in fact, they would have been better as sisters that way so they could have hated each other more openly.

The light changed, hallway light, door open, immediate downer. Meagan hit the button to cut off the tune, making the room seem awkward and dumb, like a hangover.

"What?"

"That was interesting music," Mother said. "Who are they?"

"Acid Bath, Mother. From the Nineties. And you only like it because it's slow. It's called 'Scream of the Butterfly,' Dax Riggs's interpretation of love."

"Well, I did like it. Seemed sad and luxurious, like a broken antique."

"You interrupted the second verse, Mother, when the drums come in. It's my favorite part. What do you want?"

The woman just stood there in the doorway, thread tassel earrings dangling, bony hip pressed to the jamb on one side. She was wearing one of her sleeveless "wearover" dresses that looked like a sock on a branch, leather boots, and that amazingly annoying scarf she thought fashionable in all kinds of weather.

"Meagan," she said. "My darling sunflower."

"Don't call me that."

"Why not? Sunflowers are lovely and yellow and bright like the sky."

"I'm not a blonde, Mother! I'm red-headed, pie-faced, and plain, and I'm sick of you rationalizing me!"

"Not true."

"Is so! You butter me up as if it comes out of some parenting manual! Nothing is real in this house! Ever since my asshole-brother became a cop, he's been impossible, keeping logs of how long I'm in the bathroom and what I eat and how many times I just so happen to leave a room with the lights on, and ever since you started your doctor dissertation, you've been off in the clouds like a bad cliché. I live with a Nazi and a hippie. *God,* it's so frustrating!"

Mother clasped her hands in front of her.

"It's not a 'doctor' dissertation, Sunflower. It's 'doctoral.' And Connor is no Nazi."

"He supported Trump!"

"It was a phase. And I'm not a hippie."

"You've got to be joking!" Meagan grabbed her own hair on both sides. "Mother! You wear oversized buckles, gaudy chokers, and furry hats that have ear-flaps in class when you teach! You sing sappy old folk songs like they're opera, and write chapters about Jonathan Swift and the language of birds! You can't cook, you drive like a drunk, and you dance with yourself, hugging your own shoulders. I see you doing it in the bathroom when you leave the door cracked open!"

The professor's answer was just to gaze back, a slow smile working into her face.

"Mother, stop staring, please."

"Why should I?"

"It's yucky and weird."

"No, scrumptious and weird, just like you, Sunflower." She padded into the room and stopped halfway, going pigeon-toed, biting a fingernail, the oddball scholar at the exhibit now. Tentatively, she came over and sat on the edge of the bed.

"Uncomfortable," Meagan said.

"Yes, but I wanted to know when you were going to start practicing again."

"I quit marching band."

The professor kept smiling, but there was a dent in it.

"And why?"

"I want to learn bass, electric, with an amp and everything."

"I thought you loved the clarinet."

"I don't," Meagan said stiffly. "I only practice what I have to practice, and I never want to go jamming with it, go sailing, flying outside the lines and into the margins. I mean, if there was anyone who could understand that, it would be you, Mother!"

Becky Mullin folded her hands in her lap.

"I think," she said, "that since you got that lip piercing—"

"It's called a 'Spider Bite,' Mother."

"Yes, of course it is. I'm saying that the jewelry makes you more sensitive to working the mouthpiece, and if there was anyone who was wired not to give up on something because of a trend, it would be you. Sunflower."

Mother pushed up and made her way over to the doorway. Once there she looked back "meaningfully," but Meagan had absolutely no response, and she hated her mother bitterly for it.

The moment the door closed, Meagan's phone rang. Odd, she hadn't yet changed the stock ringtone that sounded like neurotic xylophones, but instead, her cell was blasting a stereophonic version of "See You in Hell" by Electric Wizard, the power chords right after the short intro.

Meagan just stared at it as it vibrated and moved like a live thing, playing her old favorite song by her longtime favorite band, clearer and crisper and harder than her Sonos speakers. She reached for the device.

"No need," a voice blared from it, music fading behind like black velvet. "We are already connected. *Sunflower*."

It was a mechanical tone, genderless yet somehow quite "male," like a kidnapper talking through a mixer or something, and Meagan braced to push off the bed and run as fast as she could. Down the hallway. To Connor's room.

"He can't help you," the voice said. "I'm far too advanced, he couldn't shoot his way out of a paper bag, and . . . well, forgive me . . . he smells."

Meagan felt as if her eyes were going to pop out of her head. Her heart was thudding.

"Who . . . ?" she said.

"Someone who understands you," he said. "Don't speak, let me show you. First, we will see a mother's distorted interpretation of a daughter's inner self."

Something started coming out of the cell phone, like a movie animation with rich golden pixels bursting up in a small lovely plume—a mermaid's tail that quickly grew a pinwheel of multiple fins that elongated and curved downward, waterfalling in miniature fountain cascades and bouncing gently around her phone in granules that finally made a sparkling half-sphere. Then in the center there grew a stem, creepy like a snake coming out of a basket, and from the stem came two leaves soon turning to four, all lightly bobbing in a way that seemed insectile, then two more small leaflets with larger ones protruding from underneath, and from the center grew the round head, still green but sporting a host of tiny disk-buds that bristled like an alien seedpod infested with threadworms, and from around the perimeter came the bursting of yellow ray sunflower petals, quivering, wriggling.

Then the petals started to shrivel, to die, curling in on themselves. Meagan was transfixed, hands clenched up in front of her chin, fingers webbed white.

*"I'm melting,"* she whispered in a cracked, hoarse falsetto. "*. . . melting . . .*"

There was a burst, and Meagan gave a short screech. The flower had exploded into spores, the haunted Tinkerbell pixie dust floating all around her. The specks quickly vanished like the flashes coming off a 4th of July sparkler, but Meagan had already breathed in some of them; she felt them go up her nose and to the back of her tongue. The taste was strange and at the same time familiar, both foreign and personal . . . somehow earthy, like dead vegetation combined with the squat flavor of her own thumb, which she still tended to suck when highly upset even though she was in the tenth grade. Gross! It reminded Meagan of those awful Harry Potter jelly beans that had come out years ago, some sweet and delicious and others amazingly real and disgusting like "booger" and the one like bad fish.

"That is not you," the voice said. "It's not even close, though your mother would picture you thus, the traitorous sunflower, not directly facing the sky, but eventually tilting toward the dishonesty of the east. Clearly, the substance and soul of Meagan Mullin is more the dandelion, so often ignored, considered almost weed-like and common, part of the collective background, but in actuality she is the star of the daylight, making the long grass fields look like portraits, a dreamscape soft under foot that turns vivid and wondrous in death, leaving sweetness and beauty that floats on the air."

From the phone came another small sculpture of pixels, same waterfalls, same golden granular mound, same growth of a stem, but this one was straight and fibrous, its tip sprouting small green leaves like a royal neck-choker, yellow petals spreading open above it in a glorious roundlet. Green leaves that were layered just above the choker came up to embrace their golden head-feathers, engulfing them and making a warm cocoon from which a bud came up through the center like birth. The leaves of green then peeled off, unveiling the statuette finally actualized, the lovely core of soft fur, spreading upward and outward, forming the seed head, the feathery half-moon becoming the full sphere of cotton that made you feel safe and peaceful and happy and grounded.

The weed-flower bowed toward Meagan is if caught in a low breeze, and the fluffy seed parachutes came off, back end first, and they collectively swirled upward in a cyclone, next fluttering down, and for a moment the room was a glittering snow globe. Most of the tufts disappeared, the sparkler effect, yet the remaining ones floated gently around Meagan, and like she had as a small child, she put out her tongue. These weren't cold and teasingly brief, but potently warm and lastingly divine, somehow merging the flavors of caramel and Skittles, Meagan's favorites, yet changed in some odd subtle way that made the combination make sense.

"As I said," the voice continued, "I don't read minds, but I understand you. I can create images that define you, and I can share your imagination as if we were lying on our stomachs right next to each other, ankles crossed, listening to doom-sludge and deathcore, and looking at some raucous dark graphic novel come alive in our fingers."

Meagan stiffened. Right next to each other? What was she doing? She shook her head as if she'd been hypnotized. This had gone too far, and she spoke again, this time with a bit more authority.

"You don't prove you know me with a dandelion," she said, "so I'm going to ask you a question, mister whoever, and if you get it at least partially right, I might consider not throwing you out the window and getting my smelly brother to trace you and find you and shoot you for being the perv that I think you might be. Get a question *really* wrong, like dead-wrong, and I'll call his boss too. Captain Canfield. He's no joke, and at the station, he's got—"

"Got what, Meagan?"

"Equipment!"

"Mine's better. And I like ultimatums. Ask your question. Let's do this, but let's up the stakes. I get it wrong, you never hear from me again. No pixel shows, no dandelions. But if I get it right, you give me a gift such as I've given you with said pixel show, such as I am giving you by not telling your mother that you have experimented with cutting yourself, high on the inner right thigh, to let out the pain, only a mere three times, but that would be enough for her to sink her hooks into you, get you into therapy, force you to talk to her."

Meagan felt like screaming. Instead, she amazed herself by answering calmly, "What's your gift if I lose?"

"A lock of your hair and a thimble of blood. Put them together in an empty pill bottle and leave it in the Saint Mary's Cemetery, Section 2, Plot 16, Row 1 at the foot of the gravestone marked "Cindy Chen (1983–1986)."

"She was three?" Meagan said. "That's sad as fuck. So why do you want my hair and my blood?"

"I like dandelions, cemeteries, red stuff, and danger, and you well know nothing is real without sadness."

"Who is my favorite guitar player?"

"Trick question, there are two."

"Name them," Meagan said. "And tell me why I love them."

"Ah," the voice said, "you have made this too easy, not making me choose, but no worries, I'll celebrate with you the headlines. Liz Buckingham from Electric Wizard is your longtime dread-sister, gorgeous and pale, sticking to the chords, avoiding the platform solos played by her husband Jus, and therefore matching with you . . . *Dandelion,* like some exotic mirror, showing more the sweet background mural of the landscape itself as opposed to its steeples and monuments."

Meagan's lips thinned.

"And the other?" she said.

"Well . . . Herbert, of course, the artist with no public last name from the Brazilian metalcore band April 21st When their new album, *Courage is Born From Fear,* was released through Eclipse Records, you bought it for the title alone, your life story in one simple phrase. Then, you listened, laser-focused on the melodies, the speed, the monstrous heaviness. And let's not forget that when you first saw their band pics you died a little inside, as Herbert, Lucas, Helbert, and August, each in his own way, seemed a cornerstone of some bizarre sexual dreamscape. In the end, however, it was Herbert, forever Herbert and his electrifying guitar work, like lightning from heaven that split the earth in two with savage rhythm designs and intricate lead-work. In a way, you are Herbert's pioneer, his first fan, his best fan, the primary witness to his potent aesthetic."

"You win," Meagan said quietly.

"Then give me what I want, Dandelion. A lock from your crown and a drop of your soul. Tomorrow night, at full dark, 9:20 P.M. at the appointed place at Saint Mary's."

"Will you be there?"

"No, Dandelion. That would be creepy."

"Ha, ha," she said. "And what do I get out of this?"

"Adventure," he answered. "And an exotic mirror that visits you faithfully."

Her phone went dead.

And the next night she did it. She took one of Mother's bottles of Esomeprazole and mixed it with another half-used canister the woman always opened early, losing track, because the ninety-day prescription left so many of them on the shelf in the kitchen cabinet next to the spices and extracts. Then she went through Mother's sewing basket she kept at the top of the linen closet and pilfered a thimble, an old one that looked tarnished, one that Mother wouldn't miss, and a pincushion needle. In her room she cut off a tiny lock of her hair, left side, between her ear and her neck where you wouldn't notice unless you really were looking. No worries. She was landscape, collective background, lovely to her new friend, blur to the world.

She cut herself. She did it with the needle, sitting on the toilet with the lid down, one bare foot propped up on the edge of the sink, bending in on herself for the close, meticulous work. She filled up the thimble.

Scary part over.

I mean, she'd been to Saint Mary's hundreds of times in the daylight. She and Laura Fitzsimmons used to ride bikes there, all the way down the winding asphalt pathways to the mausoleums and back, and if there wasn't a burial that day there was no one there to say you were trespassing.

She liked Saint Mary's. Out of her window you could see the edge of the west lawn between the border trees. Twenty-six headstones, she'd counted them numerous times, marveling at how peaceful they looked in the moonlight. During the day, passing by on the way to school at Cardinal O'Hara, the place in general looked groomed and tailored to the point it seemed almost royal, totally demented in a way, as the best-kept places were graveyards and golf courses. And since you couldn't gaze out your window to look back at your own house, you had more connection actually to your neighbor's property, almost as if that was more your house than your house, and so, in a way, Meagan lived in the cemetery. She felt more at home out there than she ever had down the hall from scummy Connor newbie-cop, and weirdo Mother teacher-hippie, that was for sure!

Three weeks ago Meagan Mullin had put her hair and her blood, thimble and all, in a pill bottle that she placed at the foot of the gravestone marked "Cindy Chen." Above her, the sky was a scatter of stars, and the night was warm and windless.

Before running home, Meagan had stepped back for a look-see. She had ripped off the label, of course, and the little blue pharmaceutical container perched on the granite base seemed odd, like a tiny idol on the wrong altar, so she took a basket of dead flowers from the grave next to it and wedged the plastic bottle behind it.

Since then, the ghost-man had visited five times on the phone in her room, making pictures dance and pixels turn to sweet candy.

Tonight, in a matter of minutes, she was finally going to meet him.

Section 2, Plot 16, Row 1 at 9:20 P.M. on the dot.

He'd promised he would not touch her—it wasn't like that. He'd said that he wanted to return the favor of the blood and the hair, and that he would remove one of his teeth, drill through it with a micro-bit they used for delicate glassworks, and put it on a thin braided band-necklace so she could wear it in secret under her blouse, feel his presence when he wasn't making her phone do magic tricks.

"What do you look like?" she'd asked. "I don't want to run into some stranger who might be there gravestone-rubbing or smoking tree or crying like a mental patient with the dead in the dark or whatever."

A plume of pixels swirled up, jet black, settling into the shape of a reaper's hood. Inside formed a skull with red eyes and steel teeth.

"You look like an album cover," she'd said, hiding her awe and her fear.

"I'm being extreme," he said, as the virtual figure eroded to micro-drops falling to the tabletop, bouncing like marbles on stone, then disintegrating with the faint smell of licorice. "But Dandelion," he continued, "I will, in fact, be wearing a hood. For my own protection and anonymity. And for your own peace of mind, bring your Vigilant Personal 130dB rape alarm. Also Connor's service pistol. Make sure it's loaded, and practice putting the safety on and off. He won't miss it, I assure you. He's off duty, out drinking with Officers Justin Finch and Tony Cabrera. They're Ubering to a dive bar in Springfield. Your mother will also be a non-issue. She just received a message on the desktop in her bedroom that has her mesmerized. You know how she gets when she uncovers something academically eccentric and creatively challenging . . . she says it's like being trapped in a 'dream-chasm.' Trust me, she will be deep in the abyss. She's even going to lock her door, which you know she never does unless writing literary criticism for publication, and she's going to pull an all-nighter tonight, leaving her so spacy and trippy and happy and weary that she wouldn't know if you brought acrobats from Cirque du Soleil into your room and practiced double backflips off the bed and the dresser. Climb out your window, Dandelion, fifteen minutes before our meeting time."

She looked at the clock.

9:01 P.M.

She went down the hall to get Connor's pistol.

# CHAPTER 9
# I'LL MAKE YOU FAMOUS

Professor Becky Mullin would never let on something like this to the kids, but she was utterly overwhelmed, and she sat at her desk with her face in her hands. There were papers piled log-cabin style to her right . . . six classes' worth, which was two above the contracted course load, totally unfair, but she teetered on ABD status (all but dissertation), making her the English department's pack mule. On the bright side, there were just three more chapters for her to complete . . . three more to draft, pore over, redraft, and copyedit for the committee, and following the dissertation defense, everyone could finally call her "Dr. Mullin."

She preferred "Becky" actually. Some of her students referred to her as "Wacky Becky," and that was okay if she knew them a little, but once in a while someone would call her "Bucky" in class. That hurt her feelings, made her eyes smart, but she always took the high road and joked back that her two front teeth weren't "bucked," just a tad long like an elegant bunny's. That usually got a laugh, maintaining at least the appearance of the warm and welcoming collegiate aura she worked so hard modeling. Sometimes, though, she wished she had a rough-and-tumble high school gym teacher's starch so she could unleash clever comebacks and quick stinging reprimands.

In truth, most of her students adored her, but unfortunately, this semester she'd gotten a heavy concentration of the clunkers, like her first-year kids in

Comp 101, a group that was peppered with immature proletarians who missed due dates, whispered constantly, and purposefully made their empty plastic water bottles crackle and pop during lecture. And all her sections, the whole lot of them including her Monday–Wednesday graduate students, seemed unable to get past the darned basics, the run-ons, rambles, comma splices, fragments, and passive constructions they were supposed to have mastered in middle school. What a waste, what a shame! Becky wanted to celebrate their ideas, but spent most of her time writing grammar lessons on their papers and editing line by line their untidy prose as if she were making their beds. They usually ignored it all and just flipped to the back page to see the grade.

Becky sighed wistfully and put her palm-heels together, resting her chin there making the shape of a wine glass. She smiled softly, letting her mind wander to more comforting pastures. Even though she'd separated from Bruce, she hadn't missed a step when it came to her Meagan. Her sunflower was blossoming right before her eyes, artsy and eccentric, like mother like daughter, and Becky found the depth of love between them to be complex and enchanting. It was all a clear result of Becky's remarkable perceptions and the way she shaped their communications with sweet and gentle control. She only wished she could make similar strategies work in the classroom, or among her colleagues, or in front of her superiors. Sadly, it seemed that when confronted outside of the house, Becky regressed, suddenly unable to use her oddities effectively to her advantage, especially with men. Maybe that was why she'd worked so hard to raise her son to be so patient and sensitive.

Poor sweet Connor. Such a manly young man, so strong and so tangled in his own emotional tapestry. Inside, under the steely exterior he'd built to fit the police uniform, his sentiments were amazingly eclectic. Years ago Becky had thought him bipolar, but after a number of diagnoses coming up negative, she had come to the conclusion that he was actually wired inside like a woman. Not gay, God no, and she would never say any of this out loud, but he was intuitive like a lioness, emotionally connected to the world with its beauty and fire. How else could you explain the way he handled his occasional bouts of frustration and anger with such grandmotherly empathy, letting his eyes go to half-mast, pursing his lips into a knowing smile, and saying something like, *"I'm on a different wavelength right now, but your feelings are more important to me than my own."* And speaking of which, her Connor *loved* to sit at the kitchen table and talk about feelings! Of course, she'd encouraged this practice (nightly) since he was in middle school, and at this point she didn't quite recall if it had originally been his idea or actually hers.

Her cell phone rang, the Woody Woodpecker sound. The thing was buried in here somewhere, and Becky started moving around the cluttered symphony of folders, notebooks, and freak and geek circus memorabilia: the pamphlets and the figurines, buttons, magnets, stuffed toys and puppets she used as paperweights to pay homage to Jonathan Swift's lifelong obsession with human oddities, like Lobster Boy, Tom Thumb, and Carl Unthang, the armless fiddler. Suddenly she made an unpleasant association between this mess and the grammar in the student papers, and she promised herself that she would halt the excruciating process of writing her dissertation to actually straighten and clean off her desk in the morning. The paper grading could wait till the weekend.

Found it.

"Hello?"

"Look at your email."

The caller hung up.

She took the phone away from her face and looked at it like a sample in a beaker. Her circle of acquaintances was rather small, mostly comprised of Connor when he needed to let off some steam, Meagan when she grudgingly admitted she needed something, and Bruce when he wanted to complain about his little aches and pains, the way his jaw was clicking and driving him nuts, a nosebleed, a knee brace issue.

This hadn't been Bruce.

Nor one of the kids or the dreaded fourth possibility, Dr. Laure, the third outside reader on the committee evaluating her doctoral work . . . the monster who seemed to hate her with an exceptional passion, claiming she tended to lose focus and exercise intimate and awkward personal illustrations littered with wild, unsupported generalizations.

She hit Google Chrome and pulled up her Gmail. There was a message there from "Editor HarperCollins," and she clicked it.

Ms. Mullin,

My name is Helen Juniper. I am an editor for a relatively obscure division of HarperCollins that focuses on state-of-the-art academic writing with unconventional social or political context. My team is familiar with your work, as your graduate thesis on Swift was an unusually profound argument for his architecture of endothermic symbolism mirroring human behavior in the archetype illustrating Edenic, Pentecostal, Rosicrucian, shamanic, alchemical, and Newtonian reverberations.

In short, Ms. Mullin, we are in the process of expanding our focus and mission to include fictive work written by scholars who demonstrate exceptional metacognitive strategies and aesthetic sovereignty. Plainly, we have found strong evidence of this hybrid in your master's work and are positioned to make you an immediate offer. If you check your PayPal account, there is an advance we have designated to you of $1,000 in good faith. In return, we would like at least part of a first chapter, 2500 words minimum, to be delivered back to us in the form of an emailed attachment by 6:00 A.M. tomorrow morning.

We are aware of your ongoing doctoral work as well as your responsibilities in the classroom, and we apologize for the late notice. This new platform is experimental, similar in many ways to a pilot for television, and to gain office and desk space, phone lines, and designation on the website even available through the "Search" icon, we need the program to show immediate success with tangible content. Unfortunately, our proposal had been put on the back burner and is only now being considered at the end of this fiscal quarter, hence the rather close deadline.

Our model is this. The books coming out of this division will focus on the subterranean labyrinth positioned deep in the human psyche, lying unseen beneath the socially accepted worldview constructed by the mass media. We will take the public evidence of living criminals and miscreants not yet identified and incarcerated, and invent their "life stories" in real time. It is like a scholarly (and dark) version of fan fiction. Should you choose to accept our offer, your first assignment will be the serial killer who has been kidnapping coeds and impaling them on poles on the highway. Some have called him "The Scarecrow Killer" or, more recently, "The Sculptor."

We have a tape we have obtained from the local police in your area. It is attached below, next to the contract you must sign, and we suggest you listen to it. Remember, you must turn in the first 2,500 words of the first chapter by 6:00 A.M. tomorrow morning, or we would trust that you would be so kind as to simply not accept the $1,000 advance.

In terms of the writing itself, be aware that genre fiction, even literary genre fiction, is a different mechanism from academic work. Please don't make the mistake that Barbara Lazear Ascher made with her short narrative "On Compassion," through which the first half written in "story voice" was riddled with logic errors and physical improbabilities. She gained control in the second half of the document where she moved to more familiar block paragraphing and straight exposition, but you will not be afforded such opportunity.

We have heard that you have been criticized by the doctoral committee, concerning your current dissertation in progress, for "slipping into fictive structures"—and these very structures are the ones we want you to explore! With the completion of each chapter you will receive a fresh assignment with information pertaining to the grisly work of a new and unidentified sociopath. You will create his or her personality, motivation, and methodology through the lens of what we call "psycho-connective narrative." Our goal for you is a twelve-chapter collection, and your advance for the manuscript in full upon completion will be $100,000. You will then receive 15 percent royalties following print and distribution as is indicated clearly in the contract.

Listen to the tape.

Invent who this person might be.

The results will be extraordinary!

Helen

Becky Mullin checked her PayPal account. As promised, the money was there for her to accept, $1,000, offered in faith. My goodness, who did that? What a wonderful organization, what freedom, what encouragement! Helen wanted 2500 words? Absolute child's play. Becky Mullin was a worker-bee and was no stranger to marathon all-nighters; in fact, she'd probably finish the whole chapter. Her creative juices were really flowing now, and she was as excited about writing as she had been as an undergraduate.

The real issue was the commitment to twelve stories altogether. What about the dissertation, the committee, her students, their papers?

Yes, and what in reality was there for Becky even after attaining the coveted degree? Truth? Seven more years of servitude as an associate professor before getting tenure, discouragement on one hand and grammar lessons on the other. But if she could complete this little collection on the side, this pleasant little romp around the barnyard, the payment of $100,000 would be an absolute godsend. It meant paying the mortgage on time, keeping up on future student loan payments she'd long been deferring, better supporting Connor as he saved up for his own apartment, maybe putting on an extension that would make the kitchen big enough to have an island in the middle of it. And most importantly, it translated to leaning less on Bruce every few weeks like she was a teenager asking for gas money.

Becky's mother used to say that you were never really free until you handled all your own finances. Well, this smelled like freedom and then some. With bonuses.

Becky read the email again and her eyes dampened. She was built for this. Dark fan fiction of the real, born of Professor Becky Mullin's intensive psychoanalytic ability and eccentric intellectual daring. She almost giggled. She knew nothing about gambling, but she knew what a "ringer" was. She was the ace here, and this was a lock. It was almost like cheating.

She took her cell phone, turned it off, and walked it over to the bureau, where she put it in the jewelry box under the removable tray. No interruptions, not tonight, not now.

She floated back to her desk, sat, and clicked on the police interview.

And listened with awe.

*

It was the most beautiful and terrifying thing Professor Becky Mullin had ever heard.

There were parts cut out, audible "redactions," similar to those mentioned on CNN when they discussed FBI communications and court filings. Still, the edits did not cloak or alter the content. Nor the syntax; in fact, it made the presentation more frightening, as the imperfections gave it an uncomfortable closeness, a realness, like a snuff film made on home video. It was a father's partial confession concerning his disturbed, brilliant son who dropped out of sight in 1997.

There was a woman in the room. She was referenced a couple of times by the speaker, yet never heard. The cop was cut out of the recording as well, but it was easy to fill in that side of the interrogation by the contextual nature of the given responses.

Of course, the killer's name had been spliced out as well, and the reason was obvious. The editors at HarperCollins didn't want Becky to have a name, a label. As far as the actual investigation was concerned, the killer's real name would be inevitably kept hidden by police until incarceration, and this was a wonderful circumstance built into the deal by default, at least in this case. It protected the mystique of Becky's artistic version of this beautiful fiend over time. And she had a strong feeling that this one would never get caught. Ever.

She clicked the tape again and sat back in her chair, eyes closed, moving her fingers softly to the rhythms of the confession as if appreciating an orchestral performance. She reveled in the tones, the phonetics, the allure of the tragic spookiness of this heartbroken father describing his son's toxic and deadly weakness for women, fueled by an Oedipal complex.

The ending to the interview was the perfect coda, abrupt and disturbing. Clearly there was more to it, Madeline's story in particular, but Becky didn't need it. She had her building blocks, her cobblestones if you will, and now she had to just fill in the fog.

She sat forward, pulled up a blank document page on Word, and set the font to Calibri 12, double-spaced with no space between paragraphs. No header. No worries. She didn't have to trade her creative instincts for the cavalier parameters of literary discourse. And talk about building blocks, the connections between her own experience and the raw data was staggering. Maybe God was involved. How else could the stars align thus?

The father on the tape was a supermarket union man, and Becky had been a cashier for the Pathmark at the corner of Lawrence Road and West Chester Pike all through high school and her first year of college. She knew the sounds of a grocery store, the smells, the hubbub of the crowded aisles, the end caps that always needed refilling, the bone-chilling cold of the walk-in box behind the milk case, and the back room with the baler and the stacks of product on thick wooden pallets next to the carts by the rear alcove where the maintenance men shoved scraps and leftovers down the trash chute with a snow shovel.

Like father like son, no? The killer, at least in *this* piece of spooky fan fiction, was going to be in the supermarket business.

And he killed coeds, so he also knew his way around a campus, just like Professor Becky Mullin, soon to be "Doctor." He liked power tools and weaponry as did her Connor; *God,* that was no stretch! Through the years, she'd heard enough about mechanical gadgets and engines, pistols and big rigs, buck knives and generators, battle hatchets and circuit boards, that she probably could have built her own space ship by now!

And the connections she could draw from her daughter? Ah, Sunflower was the perfect resource offering the perfect tidbit, the dark sludgy doom music. It was with a similar frame of mind that the killer realized his craft, making murder his dark art, creating his sculptures in the spirit of beautiful terror and doom through reanimation.

And a "thesis" if you will? A bottom line?

Ah. She was going to construct him as a tech genius who paradoxically despised tech! But more, he was disgusted by the incompetence of the neophytes of the world trying to use it, thumping the buttons and squinting at the screens like cavemen, the way Becky felt about grammar and her freshmen.

The one thing that wasn't on the tape was this business of removing the eyes of the victims, something everyone knew from the news, so it deserved mention. She'd figure that one out in the course of creating the draft. She curled her fingers over the keys, eyes gently closed. Atmosphere first, leading to introspection and action both working as a bridge to epiphany. Okay. She bent to it, wrote the first line, re-read it, and smiled.

*"There's mist on the football field."*

It was good, it was solid, old-fashioned yet fresh, filled with mystery and Americana, starting at the very beginning . . . a very fine place to start. The lyrics from the Rodgers and Hammerstein musical danced in her head, creepy in this circumstance, and Becky Mullin got a beautiful chill up the spine.

The next thing she knew, her fingers were flying.

# CHAPTER 10
# STRANGE LAND

There was mist in the graveyard. Meagan had tried to slip through the gap in the wrought iron fencing at the edge of the west lawn as she always did, but someone had welded-in three replacement posts. She'd had to go all the way around to the front entrance, and she was late and out of breath at this point. She was wearing her knee-high combat boots, skinny-cut jeans, and the devil-laced midriff tee that had looked boss in the house yet slutty out here. She had on her favorite black leather jacket, vintage punk with shoulder studs and waist buckles, but the pockets were angled and the gun had almost fallen out twice.

She passed beneath the huge gateway arch with ivy growing through the black letters, and everything seemed weird from this perspective. Ahead, dead center, was the darkened chapel at the end of the mild rise of the access road, and to the left were the first grave markers, many with small American flags wedged into the grass next to them. There were short pine trees between the rows, and the gauzy haze crept through the branches and needle clusters in what seemed like slow motion.

Meagan made her way past the first lot, listening to the scrapes of her bootheels on the asphalt, close and hurried and echoless. Ahead at the crossing in front of the church was a street sign, and when she got to it, she put her hand out and leaned on it. "Section 2 / St. Luke's Drive." Meagan looked off to the broad expanse to the right, and the sky was starless with a low crescent moon thin as a shaved apple slice just above the tree line. The long rows of headstones on both sides of the roadway advanced through the threads of mist like an army of the dead, the ground at their feet littered with sentimental keepsakes: wreaths, small stones, teddy bears, candle baskets, flowers, all loving tributes, but to Meagan they made the place seem like a ghost town with one of those rotating weather vanes tacking against the stop in mindless repetition.

Was she insane?

She almost turned around to head right back the way she had come, but thinking like such a chickenshit made her temper flare up. Where was her courage, her courage born from fear like the April 21st album title? Hell, back in middle school she and Fitz used to smoke cigs near here on the bench in front of the monument of the unnamed lady, and if memory served, the edifice was to the left of these very grave markers at the far edge of a flat grassy lot. Shit, once she got to the statue Meagan could use it for cover, looking around it to the other side, down across the lower field to check out who was waiting for her at Cindy Chen's gravesite. An unexpected angle from which to observe.

She did a "ready-set-go" in her head and darted in before she could talk herself out of it, bursting a diagonal to the left through the headstones, zigzagging a bit in the shadows, new energy, trying to make her way toward the middle before the hard left leading to the upper field. She started really moving too, using her hips, one hand in her pocket holding the firearm in place, but gaining a rhythm nonetheless, dancing L-shapes in and around the headstones, like the thing knights did in chess, forward two, over one, again, once again . . . and now I'm a rook, going straight, going strong, my mother's a bitch and my life is a song, and a hut and a two and a three and a four, and my dickhead brother is some dirty whore.

That made Meagan think of the dumb game he invented when they were younger, trying to scare her in the car by saying you had to hold your breath while passing a cemetery, and then suddenly it hit her, *really hit her,* that she had surrounded herself with buried corpses, an ocean of dead people, all around her, right now.

She slowed, slowed more, and then more so . . . looking over a shoulder, then the other, eyes wide and heart thudding. Her hands had crept up to her throat now, all girly and everything, but she couldn't help it. *Fuck!* This kind of thing had never bothered her before, sitting on the knoll with the twenty-six plots within view of her bedroom window. She'd always focused on the art of the stones, the comfort of the night-sky draped above the foliage like velvet, but the whole thing was a trick, a clever diversion making it seem to people that it was okay to visit and leave flowers and keepsakes.

Damn.

There was body after body here, lined up in graves like stalls in some massive slaughterhouse, a bizarre museum where the exhibits were right beneath your feet facing upward, each with a grass curtain, each six feet down, just a measly six feet, and they weren't friendly. They were all in various stages of nasty deterioration, all of them skull-grinning with bugs crawling in and out of their eye-holes.

Her chest hurt. Her mouth tasted sour, and she suddenly feared tripping over her own feet for no reason like a horror movie bimbo, and there was a Y in the pathway she didn't remember from the old days, and she was disoriented, right or left, and she chose left and happened to notice a few names on the gravestones.

Saunders, Schneider, Slessinger, Sullivan.

She came to a dead halt. What?

Alphabetical order? Could they actually do that with different families? Mind whirling, she did the Boy Scout compass-thing, turning east then west, north then south, and the stones were a maze and she was hopelessly lost.

It started raining, cold, the type it took a few minutes to get used to before you just said, *"Fuck it, I'm soaked."* Meagan hunched her shoulders, shivered, and grabbed the dangling belt-straps of her coat, squeezing hard. Now she was going to look like shit, like a drowned rat, and Goddamnit, they were *graves* all around her, that's all! They didn't go on forever. And they weren't an army either. They were aunts and uncles and daddies, and grandmas, and she had to conquer these childish fears.

Meagan focused on the stones to the right. A breeze blew across and she shook her wet hair off her face, noticing that the markers there said Engel, Abbot, Zwick, and Christiana, the last of which had a carving of Jesus holding a lamb with a sprig in its mouth.

See?

Nice and peaceful.

Jaw firm, Meagan cut across a plot to get to a wider row, and even though there was a mild curve up ahead, she felt she was still moving in the right direction generally. She wanted to run, but she controlled it. She wanted to get out the gun, but there was nothing to shoot at.

After a minute or so the row straightened, and up ahead there was something she recognized, yes, thank God, of course, the gray stone crypt with the mild pitch in the lid and the vine-and-ivy motif on the sides. She still remembered the name etched on the front of it. "Lipschutz." LOL, "LIP-Shits!" Hell, she and Fitz had sat right on top of it and smoked weed their first time. Pure blast, rude rush. They'd laughed like hyenas, and this was like coming home.

She touched the wet stone for good luck in passing, and now that the mist had blown off she saw the familiar stand of big tall bushes shaped like those fancy hats that archbishops wore. The gap in the middle to the right was still there, and Meagan passed through and stopped short.

The broad dark field that spread out before her looked wrong for some reason. The robed, unnamed lady was a few hundred feet ahead, a dark form in the rain, but she wasn't the issue. It was the field itself, made up of flat markers, the ones that lay even with the ground instead of coming out in perpendicular, and there was something out of place here. Something subtle, but she couldn't quite nail it.

She moved forward anyway. She was late. It was possible that her mystery man had thought she'd choked by now, but there was also a chance he was waiting. For her. To give her a necklace that was so fucking bad-ass even Liz Buckingham would have been jealous.

She started to jog. The rain wasn't making puddles yet, but she could feel the grass getting heavier under her boots and she wanted to step on the stones. Naturally, she knew Connor would say that this was bad luck, so for spite she started moving in this crazy game of hopscotch, and the aunts and uncles and daddies and grandmas were nice, regular folk, right? No complaints—shit, they were probably rooting for her!

She was making good time, only slipping once yet recovering, jumping even faster now, and when she stole up a glance halfway to the statue, the image jerked up and down like something from that *Blair Witch* movie, but besides the lame remake, that film was old school, and Meagan was new school, and she was going to get that damned necklace if it killed her.

Meagan slowed; she was here. Her breath was high and she had a delicious cramp in her side. There were long, wide cement steps leading to a border walkway going around the statue on all sides with those spiky plants that had red waxy berries looking plastic and poisonous. Inside the square, the statue had its own border presentation, surrounded by ferns. On the short wall at ground level was the inscription BLESSED IS SHE WHO HAS BELIEVED, and mounted on a grand marble sphere and rising into the dark was the woman in the robe, made of that copper product turned dull weathered green, oxidized black on the ridges especially down toward the bottom of the garment.

Meagan stepped to the walkway and promptly climbed up on the top edge of the border stone surrounding the granite sphere. Squatting, she reached up and grabbed the cold statue at the hem, going hand over hand, feeling for the nips and tucks, pressing forward like one of those weird Russian dancers, or the pros they brought in at the bar mitzvah she'd seen recently on the *Mrs. Maisel* Netflix show. It almost made her laugh outright, but she held it in, biting the inside of her cheek. She didn't want her hooded psychedelic ghost-man to see her spying on him, let alone laughing like an idiot, so she worked her way around, turned the corner, and sat on her haunches, a shadow under the robe.

She gasped.

Before her the ground sloped down a hundred feet or so, gradually leveling off, and she realized what had been so peculiar about the field she'd just hopscotched through. There had been no keepsakes. The field had been totally bare, because the remembrances had been stolen, gathered somehow and spread out here before her, down through the lower field from here leading to Cindy Chen's grave. It was like one of those red carpets they rolled out for kings, but wider, massive, thirty feet across at the least and a football field long, chock full of flowers and prayer tokens and other glitzy shit; and there, across the access road at the far edge of the field where Meagan had been a few weeks ago leaving a pill bottle with her hair and her blood on the short granite slab, there was a shrine now, the gravestone absolutely smothered and covered with bouquets on top of wicker baskets on top of baby toys and half-puckered balloons, and crosses and grave blankets, and Christmas tree ornaments and pottery, scarves and hats and cards and limp ribbons, all of it making the buried stone look like a strange obelisk, a humongous shark's fin cresting and pulling up night surf in the hard rain.

All for Meagan Mullin.

She carefully hopped down from her perch and put her hands in her coat pockets. She jerked her head to shake the hair out of her face, but it was plastered to her neck and her forehead.

A massive metaphorical red carpet.

She started to make her way down the hill.

# CHAPTER 11
# CONFESSIONS, CONTINUED

"First things first," Canfield said. "Tell me where you hid the body."

Robinson shifted as if he wanted to move his hands, and Erika stood. "Don't you dare."

From the corner of his eye Canfield saw she had her arms extended, feet squared.

"Sorry," Robinson said. "Itch. Spine, lower back. It'll pass."

"Mister," Canfield said. "I'm not going to tell her to sit down, and I'm not going to tell her not to shoot either. 'Fess up. It's getting stale in here."

The man nodded.

"Of course, Captain. It makes the story go out of order, but like I said, I never made a living spinning yarns that went in straight lines to begin with."

He paused as if expecting a friendly laugh to flutter about the auditorium, and then he closed his eyes, bowed his head.

"Sorry, trust me, Captain. I'm not trying to make a case for my innocence anyway." He was silent for what felt like a long time, too long, and when he finally raised his glance it seemed he was caught between giving it straight or looking for pity. Canfield had a feeling it was about sixty-forty.

"When I made the plans to rebury Cindy Chen," he continued, "I was desperate, saddened, scared beyond belief, and all I kept thinking about for some reason was one of the few things from my high school years that stuck with me. It was this Robert Frost poem. I can't claim I remembered all the words or even the title, but I did recall that the character was out in the woods. There was something about roads less traveled, and I connected that with my favorite book my ma used to read me when I was a toddler, *The Little Red Caboose.* Not that I claim to have remembered the blow-by-blow of that one either, but I knew it was about trains. I thought about Frost's foliage and untrodden paths, and I connected them with the regional rail lines running through town. Merion Station was close enough, there on Idris and Hazelhurst Roads, marked by one of those small station buildings backdropped by a short grove of woodland. I knew that people drove past these types of outposts and ignored them the same way they did construction sites, power stations, and drainage basins, and if you were a commuter standing there waiting for a train there was a solid concrete wall and an overhang blocking the view back over the shoulder. It all made sense to me. Sneak in from the back edge of the trees at night and dig a shallow grave no one would ever find."

He swallowed, making his big Adams apple move up and down. Then he studied his feet again.

"Yes, Little Cindy Chen, here goes," he said thickly. "I dug her up from my backyard garden that midnight. I had gone through her throat most of the way with the shovel earlier, so when I lifted her out her head swung like a trapdoor on a hinge. I was moaning, weeping, trying to cradle her, trying to transfer her body to the duffel bag and position her in there so she looked more human. But the rigor mortis had her elbows stuck to her ribs and her forearms tree-branching outward, little fingers hooked in like claws. And she was bone-white with dirt in her eyes . . . God forbid, I couldn't look at her anymore, so I arranged her the best I could and covered her with mulch before zipping her closed."

Erika sat, her voice choked with disgust.

"You bastard."

He didn't raise his head.

"Yes, ma'am," he said, "you're right. I don't deserve to live, let alone enjoy another moment of freedom, but I didn't come here to be free. I didn't come here for you to understand either, but I hoped that you might anyway." He looked up at her cautiously. "Do you have kids, miss? Did you ever love someone so much that it ached? Michael was my boy, my only son. We played ball together. I taught him how to hit a slider on the outside corner, how to hold his glove-hand when he pitched, how to eat a Rita's water ice without getting brain freeze. I took him fishing at the reservoir in Broomall, joked with him, told him stories, took him on hayrides at Linvilla Orchards during pumpkin season. He was my boy. He was quirky and weird, with a goofy smile that warmed you right to the gut, and before the murder I was in denial about all the psycho nonsense. I wrote it off as creativity and kid stuff."

"Until he killed Cindy Chen," Erika said flatly. "The real creativity exposed."

"Correct."

"And after? How did you go to him and approach this?"

"We didn't discuss it. I couldn't, to tell you the truth. I couldn't get my mind around it. And he kept acting so natural, the way he always had. That was the part that got me the most. His game-face."

"So you started being wary of him," Canfield said. "Scared."

Robinson turned to him, eyebrows up.

"Wouldn't you be?" he said. "I blocked out the reburial mostly, only recalling bits and pieces like a film with most of it spliced out and trashed." He sucked on his teeth for a second. "Oh, don't worry, Captain. I remember exactly where I put her. Back of the station building dead center, twenty-five paces in from the other side of the thicket of ash, oak, and sycamore, five paces west. She's in there, trust me."

"You bastard."

"Yes, you said that already, ma'am, pardon my mentioning it."

"Easy," Canfield said. "Make your point. Tell us the whole thing; we won't judge."

"Why the hell not?" Erika said.

"That's for the court and a jury," he said to her patiently. "We're here to listen. And so, Mr. Robinson, you're saying you blocked most everything out and carried on as if nothing happened?"

"No, sir. I'm saying that I blocked out the reburial. Are you kidding me? Sir, I couldn't ever get the image of that precious little girl out of my head. We knew her . . . sort of . . . I mean, after the fact, when I was driving the duffel bag in my trunk to the train station, I remembered the day Michael first saw her, the day he probably marked her and started planning his first real 'art project.' It was a few months before the—incident—in the winter, a bleak day, hard gray, one of those stale hangers-on in late February with the stiff winds that steal your breath right from your chest at first. There was ice on the backroads, old ice with tread marks in it, and there were snowdrifts the plows had pushed to the sides with those black exhaust marks, you see what I'm saying? We all had cabin fever, it was the weekend, and Michael wanted to go sliding on the ice in his Converse sneakers, so instead I took him on one of our hikes through the neighborhood. It ended up being an adventure, fun getting 'lost.' We were talking about the kind of jazz-first graders always talked about, but it was Michael-style, like bugs and the way he liked the word 'exoskeleton,' and how he wanted to eat frog legs like rich folk but right off the frog the way you ate chicken, and the way he dreamed about having a spider for a pet on a leash. We were a ways away from the house, about a mile or so, and we'd ended up in a neighborhood of those twin houses, where the streets back-to-back shared the same alleyways."

He stopped as if he couldn't continue, breath shaky.

"She was there," he managed. "She was . . ."

"Say it. I want to know," Erika said.

"She was this tiny precious angel," he blurted, "playing in the back driveway with her father watching her over his shoulder every few seconds, using his car's scraper to chip ice off the bottom of the garage door. I remember I thought he looked comical, squatting down so low his butt almost hit the ground between his ankles. Little Cindy was in this puffy pink coat with the hood up, and she had on these matching snow pants that were stuffed with so much down it made the whole thing look like a miniature space suit or something. She had taken sidewalk chalk and drawn what looked like a snowman on a mound of ice at the corner of the driveway where the trash cans were, and she was jumping and laughing and clapping her hands. Then from the opposite direction that me and Michael are coming, this haughty lady is walking down the alley with these uptight, hissy-bitty steps, wearing big fur ear muffs and a fancy winter coat with brown fluffy wrist cuffs, most probably mink, and she's walking this cocker spaniel puppy, soft black with a gray circle around the left eye. And by God, that little Cindy Chen starts going bananas, running to the edge of the driveway and stretching out her arms, shouting, 'Cute! Cute!' Naturally, her father hurries over all quick-mannered and strict, and he scoops her up, scolding her in Chinese. And the dog-walker, yeah, she sure could have let the kid pet the spaniel. She could have picked the pooch right up and walked over, but no, she struts on past, purposely looking away as if the style of fencing of the house opposite is suddenly fascinating and the vinyl siding is some kind of marvel."

He stopped, mouth moving wordlessly for a second.

"But Michael wasn't looking away," he said softly. "He was staring at Cindy Chen in her father's arms, reaching after the dog and crying, and my boy was staring at her hard, yes sir, laser focus, mouth open, cheeks flushed. He was almost drooling. He'd made his first mark, the first target."

"Where did he kill her?" said Canfield. "Where and when? Be specific."

"Don't know, Captain. Never asked. And as for the 'how,' I don't know that either. When I dug her up from the garden it was pitch-dark outside. I had the flashlight on the ground, and I moved the body quick as I could in and out of the beam, never studied it." He smiled as if he'd just hit his thumb with a hammer. "I remembered her, though . . . like a shock hitting me straight in the chest when I'd first, you know, gone down on my knees to start the digging process, to know where to get my shovel under exactly, rubbing away the top layer of mulch and soil with my fingers to find that bloodless oval face in the dirt. I was nose to nose with her, don't you see? And the next day I saw that face everywhere, then the next day and the next, in the frozen puddles on the street, in the sun reflecting off cars, in store windows, in the bathroom mirror, always out the corner of my eye when I was in the process of turning my glance elsewhere. She recurred in the flickers, Captain, haunting the edges. The visions wouldn't go away, so I made myself numb to them. I had to, and after a while I owned it, normalized it, glossed it over so much so that I made myself go to the ceremonial burial of the empty casket at Saint Mary's Cemetery. I did it to punish myself, to remember that it was real. By then Michael was nine. I'd thought about taking him with me, but there was enough going on in our lives, other issues, lots of them, and I didn't see the point of forcing him to watch the Chen family standing around the grave."

"Wait," Canfield said. "Michael was nine? No, your math's bad. A declared death in absentia isn't valid for seven years—look it up."

"Not to contradict you, Captain, but Chinese law is different. They can make the call in two years, and her parents clearly wanted to have quick closure or whatnot. I don't know which judge they had to make an appeal to or what court they had to show up at, but I was there when they lowered that empty casket into the ground. It was 1988, June fourth to be exact, two years after her disappearance to the day."

"You attended the burial."

"Yes, ma'am, as I said."

"You stood with the family."

"I watched from a distance like the coward I was and still am. I pretended that I was mourning at another gravesite. There was a monument there to my left, a green copper lady in a robe, and I had a clear view down a short hill and across a field. Most of them wore white, strangely. It was windy, and I remember it ruffling their clothes while they stood there like statues. After the lowering, they put strange things by the headstone. Looked like food and sticks, maybe incense, and slips of paper they put pebbles on to keep them from blowing away."

"Must have been tough on you," Canfield said.

"It was. Cleansing too, but more of the first."

Canfield's fingers were falling asleep, so he switched the gun to his left.

"You mentioned there were issues in the house," he said. "Spill. Keep it relevant."

"Yes, sir. I honestly don't know if Michael would have ever killed again if what happened in those next two years hadn't happened. I make no excuses for him, he is what he is and he was what he was, but I'm just saying it's entirely possible that after Cindy Chen he might very well have moved on from murder. After all, he was only seven, and maybe he'd have wanted to go from kickball to Crazy Eights. I mean figuratively, if I'm using the word right."

"I'll look it up for you later," Canfield said. "What happened when he was seven after Cindy Chen's murder, Mr. Robinson? Enough drama. For a guy who can't tell a joke, you can sure tell a story, out of order or not. Let's get to it."

"Right."

"Yes, let's talk about *Madeline,*" Erika said, "Michael's weakness. His mother. His kryptonite. I have a feeling I know where this is going, but since you opened that door before you can have the honors. Spill, Robinson. All the gory details."

"All the . . ." Robinson's blue eyes were burning, and the smile he worked up was cracked thin like ice.

"This is a confession, ma'am," he said quietly. "All due respect, I'll give it to you, but there are some things that stay holy here, or I clam up, take my punishment, and let my son ravage this town like the Black Plague of London."

Canfield wanted to intervene, but he kept his mouth shut.

"Go on," Erika said. *"Please."*

Robinson's eyes softened at the edges.

"Sarcastic, but I'll take it. Ma'am, please trust me, I'm telling you that Madeline was innocent. Always. Of course, she was no saint, no one is truly, but she was as close as you could get to it." He nodded his head as if he were tipping a cap. "She was like you in a way, ma'am, if you don't mind my saying so, and at the same time different as the sun and the moon."

His face colored slightly, but he put his chin up.

"What I mean is that . . . well, pardon my noticing, ma'am, but you have straight blondish hair and Maddy was a brunette wearing it teased up, long and curly the way they did in the Eighties. You're tall and she was tiny, four foot eight inches to be exact. You have faded freckles dusted across the bridge of your nose and she had a beauty mark on the side of her chin. My point is that even though you pitched your tents in different yards, as it were, you would have still shared the same fence I was referring to. Natural prettiness and all, and I don't mean any disrespect, ma'am, but you're asking me personal things about the only woman I ever loved, and I'm going to discuss it the best I know how."

"I get your point," she said coldly.

"Yes, ma'am, so then you understand that Maddy was too good for me, out of my league and all that. She went to West Chester University, cheerleader, biology major, and I met her at a mixer. She was standing across the room at the punch bowl and I was on the other side of a steamtable wearing a white apron. Part of the food service crew. I'd barely managed to get my high school diploma, but I didn't need to have a dorm and a major to realize how lovely this girl was, and I mean classically or whatever fancy word you might want to use, sort of the way we all agree to appreciate art on cathedral ceilings or fancy pictures of hummingbirds painted on porcelain."

He closed his eyes.

"She had on one of those tight red front wraps straight across the chest showing her shoulders," he said. "Short leather skirt and Gladiator sandals, cherry-blossom pink with gold Egyptian bow straps." He looked at Erika. "I'll never forget the first time I saw her. I was in awe, and like Frankenstein's monster, I stumbled from around the corner of my station and caught the edge with my hip, almost knocking over three hot table trays and the sterno canisters underneath them. She was talking to two of her girlfriends, and when they saw me coming, their eyes started laughing. I understand why. I'd been six foot seven since my second year of high school, and standing there at the punch bowl, Madeline and I looked like something out of a bad fairytale, the clumsy giant and the tiny princess, and what she saw in me I'll never know. Maybe she realized early on that I'd do anything for her. Maybe she could tell how thankful I was that she took the time to talk to me while her girlfriends looked on, crossed their arms, rolled their eyes, and finally gave us some space. You see, miss, I was smitten, hook, line, and sinker. And I suppose you're inferring that Michael was too, that he had some kind of obsession with his mother."

He made shapes with his jaw.

"Yes," he said finally. "He grew fast just as I had, a big ole boy early on, and when he was in first grade he was almost as tall as she was. I guess the issue here is that Michael was an odd soldier, sometimes looking at things bare and literal instead of the way you were supposed to. To him, there was a woman in the house, a woman with breasts and privates, high cheekbones and pretty legs who paid attention to him, coddled him, fussed over him. He noticed all of it in the wrong way is what I'm telling you. See, some women give birth, and forgive the bluntness, but they get a worn look to them, wider hips, can't keep the weight off. I'm sorry but it's a damned fact of life." He sighed. "Not for Maddy, though. She kept her figure, still looking fine in a cocktail dress, or jean shorts showing the pockets, or her white tennis outfit with the terrycloth ankle socks that had the pink pompoms on the back. Mostly, though, it was that smile, sparkling like the flash and 'ding' effect on toothpaste commercials. She was a living doll, sharing that smile for me and for Michael alike, and I think it had my son transfixed, as they say."

The room seemed to be ringing.

"Did he see you have sex?" Erika said. "Is that what you're getting at?"

"Yes," he said evenly. "Twice. In a house you make imaginary borders, but sometimes they're breached. Once he came into the bedroom at two o'clock in the morning. We didn't expect him in the dead of night, and we didn't think to lock the bedroom door . . . See, Maddy was a light sleeper, and if I had a restless night, it was typical for her to go get us iced tea and a bowl of tortilla chips and salsa, or even Stone-Ground Wheat Thins and Gouda on a cutting board to stick between us on the bed. Then we could talk and gossip as if we were teenagers having a sleepover, she loved that kind of thing. That night like every night she looked good to me. That night I did something about it, picking her up and walking her to the corner of the room where I was holding her under the thighs and she was straddled on my hips. Michael burst in and saw."

He gnawed at his upper lip.

"A week later he used a screwdriver to unlock the door. Me and Maddy were under the covers, so it wasn't bad as the first time, but *boy*, was she mad, up on her knees with her side of the sheet wrapped around her! Yessiree, I think it might have been the first time she wasn't going to look past Michael's weirdness, the moment where push came to shove and she was finally going to punish him, maybe smack him in the face good and hard, but she bent over with cramps right there in the bed."

He stopped. With a strange sort of dissociated pity, Canfield realized the big man before him was trying not to cry.

"Cramps," he said. "They were just cramps, and the next day, indigestion. Constipation. Pain in her abdomen that flared up the next couple of weeks here and there for no reason, off and then on again while she was lying on the couch watching television, or vacuuming the rugs upstairs, or talking to me in the kitchen eating her celery snacks while I was washing the dishes. It made her leave her scrapbooking club early twice, and we were still just thinking it was a thing that would pass, a bug, something going around. Until the Phillies game."

He smiled sadly.

"You have to understand," he said, "that Maddy was a freak for the Phils, a 'personality' in the stands. She knew the other season-ticket holders in our section by name and brought tote bags filled with rally towels and hats, kazoos and noisemakers for the boys, face paint and sparkle makeup for the girls, rattles and binkies for the babies. I kid you not. She had everyone's phone number too, and she arranged color-coordination days just to get us on television."

He took a breath that made his shoulders move.

"When it happened," he said, "it was mid-July, hot as hell, and Maddy was chewing bubble gum that was cut like tobacco, pounding my old middle school glove between her knees, and booing the Pirates like a true Philadelphian. She had on her overalls that turned into shorts with the white frays on the edges, and a Phillies cap she pulled her hair through—out the back in a humongous tail like something you'd see in the bush. There was a foul ball that came our way, and Maddy jumped for it, clapping her hands at it clumsily. She missed and got a hearty round of applause, to which she took a couple of bows and one ladylike curtsy."

His eyes were red with emotion.

"Did either of you ever go to one of those old Phillies games at the Vet?" he said. "Not trying to guess anyone's age here, but you can look it up on Wikipedia if you like. Philly fans back then were stone-crazy. Our seats weren't in the 700 level where they were using the aisles for urinals and throwing toasters over the railing, but no one, and I mean *no one* ever got applauded for missing a foul ball. Except Maddy. Then she keeled over and fell forward two rows, where they caught her, just barely, and I'll never forget seeing her Laverne and Shirley sneakers sticking up and out of the fray."

Dead quiet. Canfield thought Erika was going to prod him on, but she didn't. Robinson cleared his throat.

"Uh, yeah," he said, "she . . . we . . . got her to the hospital and they did tests. I'm no doctor, and to this day I still wish I'd been as sharp as those conscientious folks in the movies, always a step ahead of the specialists, knowing what the beeps from all the machines mean, figuring what all the conditions are called, which nurses are on shift when, and what doctors have the files when they do one test or another, but all I knew was that the head honcho in the big office with all the diplomas on the wall said it was a combination of pancreatic cancer and the type in your bones, and both were mid- to late-stage, and there was bad stuff wrapped around the good arteries and operating was out of the question."

His gaze shifted from Canfield to Erika.

"I'm not asking for your sympathy, and I'm not making excuses for Michael, but we both lost the love of our lives. It took a year, two weeks, and three days, which seems like a lot or a little depending on how you look at it. Funny how time is like a rubber band, isn't it? If I gave you two minutes to live it would be the shortest amount of time you could imagine, but if you were in pain, it could be an eternity. Maddy's illness was an eternity, for her of course, but it was especially brutal for Michael. Again, no excuses. People with sick parents don't necessarily grow up to be serial killers, but I think you should know that these circumstances were odd and extreme in an odd sort of way. What's the word for the opposite happening of what you'd expect?"

"Irony," Erika said.

He nodded.

"Yes, irony, of course. In this case . . . *ironically,* it was Maddy's spirit and beauty that made it so horrible, especially for Michael, I'm afraid. Not that it wasn't awful for us all like I said, but I keep seeing her the way a seven-year-old, especially *this* seven-year-old would have seen her as she deteriorated. See, she was one type of doll to him that turned into another, and it made her more horrifying because she kept fighting to keep the mannerisms of the first."

His breath hitched, but he swallowed it.

"I'm not being clear," he said. "Maddy had gestures and body language she'd developed from the time she first realized she was the best-looking girl in the room, not selfishly, but more naturally, and she knew that the way she presented herself had an effect on people. She had a big smile, all teeth, and when she flashed it at you, scrunched up her shoulders, and crinkled her nose, she knew you thought it was cute as all hell. When you told her something you were proud of and she put her fingers in front of her open mouth and her eyes widened with joy for you, it made you swell inside, no lie. She had that gift of being pretty and making you feel as if you could be pretty too in a way, whether she was painting her toenails, putting on eyeliner in front of the makeup mirror, or looking at you over her shoulder while she was making you a sandwich. Don't you see? She was like a calendar model in your private home movie and she acted like it. Most couldn't pull it off, but she could, and even when things had gone really bad she tried to keep up the act that wasn't an act, and that made it worse. Think about it. The radiation made her lose her hair, and her scalp was eventually liver-spotted. Her eyes were still huge, but the sockets had shrunk like air going out of the tires. Her lips thinned and drew back, making her big teeth buck out, and her whole face went gaunt and skull-like. And she got thin. I mean, she was petite already, but after nine months or so her arms were twigs, her legs brittle sticks. She wore a loose flowered housedress and walked with a cane. Her voice had been sexy and low, yet now was dusty and dry, understand? She went from being a Barbie to that old chipped and mud-spattered doll that had puppet mouth and haunted your basement."

He shuddered. Went on carefully.

"She was afraid that Michael would think she abandoned him because of the pain, and so, *ironically* . . . she went out of her way to show him constant love and attention, as if nothing was wrong, as if she was still so outwardly beautiful that she could brighten his day with a look of approval. She'd bang her cane on the bedroom floor, begging and pleading for her son to come to her. She'd sit there tucked back in her favorite comfy chair and ask him about stuff, flashing that same signature smile, shucking up her shoulders and scrunching her nose, but God forgive me, the gestures were hideous now, coming from a broken doll with a bald spotted crown, bulging eyes, drawn-in cheeks, and a skeleton's grin. I know. You might expect that a character like Michael would have actually liked something like this, considering things such as exoskeletons, frog legs, and spiders on leashes, but it didn't work that way. She was his pretty doll gone bad, he tried to avoid her, she knew it, and it broke her damned heart. Each night she wanted to have just one more Kodak moment with him in case she passed by morning, and she'd make her way down the hall with the cane clacking on the hardwood, shuffle, shuffle, tap, shuffle, shuffle, tap, and she'd creak open his door and make her way to his bed in the thin glow of the nightlight, sitting down close to him and smoothing his hair off his forehead with her spindly fingers. I followed once, looking over her shoulder. Michael had his eyes squeezed shut, pretending to be asleep. That broke her heart too, but I never mentioned it. She knew I knew, and still, she never stopped making that trek down the hall, shuffling and tapping that cane like something out of a horror movie. Maybe that was her sin, but the punishment, especially in the final month when she was totally bedridden, was absolute overkill, pardon the pun, and didn't at all fit the crime."

He'd hung his head, but he raised it, eyes burning.

"Michael retreated," he said, "into his room, into himself, as did I. He is human. Or he was. I suppose your question way back in this long sad story might have been how and why we let him hack college libraries and make computer games of such viciousness, but you have to remember that Maddy was gone. I was heartbroken and still sick in my soul over Cindy Chen, no pity asked for here, none given I'm sure. I'm just telling you that Michael was all I had left in this world, and if you think people, even 'good' people, always tell the truth, admit to their sins, and welcome their punishment like the big man they pray to on Sundays, well, you're closing your eyes to reality. Again, I'm not asking for a pardon or clemency or the hope that I'd be added to your Christmas card list, but I'm telling you that at that point in my life I was going to do anything to stay out of jail. Anything. It was pure survival, self-preservation for me and my boy, who was a murderer, a recluse, a genius, a ghost. While he lived under my roof, I protected him. He got even smarter, then smarter still, and he also got stranger. Uncommonly strange, so much so that by the time he left home and disappeared I was relieved, to tell the truth, and when Brittany Barnes was left impaled on a pole on the Interstate, I knew. Not like that old movie *Halloween,* where Michael Meyers had come home. No. In this case, Michael Leonard Robinson woke up. The seven-year-old was fully grown now, fully realized, the dark soul who never moved on from Cindy Chen, from kickball to Crazy Eights."

"And you?" Canfield said.

"Me what?"

"Why come here now? What changed you, Robinson? What woke you up?"

Robinson's eyes filled.

"It wasn't about waking up . . . more like I couldn't stand being awake at all hours, day after day with no relief from the pressure. It got too crowded, the faces, Captain. The faces of all his victims flickering in the puddles and reflections and the windows and mirrors."

A tear fell down his cheek.

Erika shot at him immediately.

She pulled too hard and the gun kicked right. She was shouting something. At the periphery Canfield saw movement in the window to the left and he turned toward it, aiming with two hands. There was a flurry behind him and another gunshot. She'd missed again; he heard the bullet smash the oversized coffee mug on the console table. In the window there were two hands cupped like parentheses, someone looking in, cutting the glare. One of the hands moved, there was a flash of dull silver, a weapon possibly, and Captain Canfield discharged his pistol. The report was harsh, and the window shattered. He heard the front door open, footsteps thudding off, and Erika shot toward them again, cursing, the sound of her voice dwarfed by the ringing aftershock of gunfire. The place smelled like sulfur.

Canfield approached the window and stopped a few feet from it, current threat imperative, possible accomplice on the property, jagged glass in the frame. It was dark outside with a burst of new rain. Nothing else in the window. Canfield kept his eye there and stepped to the side to the hearth, reaching down for the poker. His fingers closed on the tongs, good enough, and he moved back to the opening to clear the rest of the glass. Most of it had been blown outside, but he slid his feet just in case, since he was still in his socks. He banged the tongs, breaking off the big pieces, and rubbed it along the inner edging. With his gun in front of him, he leaned out.

The rain was cold on his head and neck, but otherwise there was nothing. The basement egress window-well was in place. Lock unmolested on the tool shed across the lawn. Wind in the trees. Nothing.

He ducked his head, coming back in, and turned. Erika's hair was limp, her face ashen.

"It was him," she said quietly. She came over and handed him a throw blanket in case he wanted to towel off. Their fingers touched, she twitched, she was shaking.

"Easy," Canfield said. "Who do you mean?"

"Him," she said. "It was him in the flesh, sitting right here the whole time. The Sculptor Killer."

"How do you know?"

"It was the teardrop. He wasn't at the tail end of middle age, not even close. He was wearing makeup, a lot of it. That was why he wanted the lights low. I'm telling you, the jowls and creases, they were all fake, nicely applied, but he made the mistake of using silicone primer with a water-based foundation, so instead of having a nice layer like spackle, he got a tear track. I saw it."

Canfield nodded. He wanted to comfort her, maybe hold her, but his primary responsibility was to secure the premises the best he could. He moved to the foyer to shut the front door. Window later. When he returned, Erika had taken a seat on the sectional, and she was staring at the padded bench the man had been sitting on throughout the interrogation. There were two round pieces of metal there, the silver dollars that had been taped to his palms so he could knock on the door and not aggravate his arthritic knuckles. But the disks hadn't been taped. They'd been affixed to a pair of flesh-colored straps with small catch-releases, and they weren't silver dollars.

"Arthritis, sure," she said dully.

"Of course, it wasn't arthritis," a robotic voice blared, the one they'd heard on the torture video, but with higher tonality, coming through one of the disks. The object wasn't flat like a coin exactly, but had an indentation down center and a chamfer cut on the edging with bantam fiber optics, or something like it, now glowing red.

"It also wasn't Commissioner Silver that you spoke to earlier today," it continued, "any more than the father-character I just portrayed told you pure truths. You can parse through and decide for yourselves at a later juncture what is or is not useful to you, but mark my words, the notion that I am thirty years ahead of you in terms of technology is a modest estimate. I am speaking to you out of a mechanism that has many possible modes of operation. It is an amplifier, a recording device, a transmitter, and a projector, but the last function does not require a screen; in fact, it works better utilizing the darkness for backdrop. That is why it was best to persuade you, Captain Canfield, to blow out the window. Outside on the ledge you will find the mini-photonic optical device I planted and activated from under my leg just now before my exit. Note that the window made the recorded likeness of my cupped hands faint and lusterless, a convincing replication, while the beautiful darkness presently becomes the perfect canvas for my unholy likeness."

The disk on the padded bench glowed brighter, and in the window flashed the image of a hooded skull with red eyes and steel teeth, the rain passing through it diagonally. It disappeared as quickly as it had come into view, but it left a harsh glare on Canfield's eyes similar to looking into a laser. He squinted, rubbing hard with his thumb and forefinger.

A strange sound. It was the mechanical voice saying "Tsk, tsk, tsk."

"You can't look directly into the face of an angel without consequence, Captain Canfield. Don't worry, the impairment will pass. I held you here for this specific amount of time so you would be conveniently occupied with the bogus confession and therefore prevented from venturing out to borrow a cell phone when you'd realized I'd disarmed both of yours."

"Really," Canfield said acidly. "I'm no tech-nerd, but why not just cross all the neighborhood signals somehow and screw up the Wi-Fi? Seems a simplistic blockade for a magical angel, or whatever you are. Why all this dancing to get to the point when you could have just taken out a couple of cell towers?"

"Because there's no sport in that, Captain. Why don't I just kill you? Why don't I just slaughter every woman and child within fifty miles of this perfect little town and leave a bunch of broken men to sit in a bunch of shitty bars wondering why they shouldn't just jump off a bridge or straight into their nearest wood chipper? Understand, Captain, that while we were talking, I activated a number of pre-recorded false emergency calls to your station plus those in Haverford, Springfield, Drexel Hill, and Broomall, all realistic terroristic threats, all the insiders' buzz words. Get in the spirit of the game. Some of your fleet of black and whites are tragically unavailable to the residents of Lower Merion now, as the emergency deployment has you over-committed at the far borders of the precinct in twelve different locations. Your night-captain at the station has had to merge sectors, and the visible district-wide presence has thinned. You're weakened, Captain, and reinforcements even from precincts and agencies other than those I sent running will be slow to respond, too slow. Dispatch already tried calling you on your cell phone upstairs for guidance, three times, to no avail. They are alone, Captain Canfield, and so are you, no contacts."

"Why am I so damned special?"

"Mind your business. Erika was the original game for you, but that's changed. Three civilians are going to die tonight. Four are involved. They might all perish in addition to yourself and your . . . new girlfriend . . . but you can limit it to the initial inevitability of the mere three if you intervene with cunning or at least some measure of basic intelligence. You need to get in your car immediately after receiving these instructions. This is timed to the second, so were I you I would eliminate any diversions. Try to solve this by eliciting any sort of outside assistance from law enforcement or even neighbors or passersby, and I'll kill all four new protagonists immediately. I am not bluffing. Do not make the mistake you made with the coed by ignoring the conditions I put in Erika's in-bin. You divert to the station, I will, repeat, I *will* kill the four aforementioned players. Next, I'll give Erika my version of a skin peel and I'll sew your eyelids open to force you to watch. Finally, be assured that if you break my rules I will obliterate your entire police force, Captain . . . blood on the windshields and body parts in the storm drains. Again, I am not bluffing, have I been clear?"

Canfield said nothing.

"No worries, Captain, the question was rhetorical. Here's your briefing. The potential victims are two men and two females, one of them a teen. They are at three locations, soon to be two, located in Broomall, two towns over. None of you will arrive when you want to, and part of the fun will be working through these inconvenient delays. It's like a riddle, isn't it? You and Erika are going to determine who lives. You must decide on a course of action quickly, not only because the four players are headed toward their relative moments of confrontation like runaway trains, but because the other disk on the padded bench is a high-density explosive. It will take out the equivalent of two city blocks, meaning your house, the Mackenzies', the Goldschmidts', and half of Cedar Crest Park, right up to the push swings and walk-through botanical garden. If you do not leave the premises, I will detonate it in forty-five seconds. Go to 503 Elderberry Street in Broomall or Saint Mary's Cemetery next to it, in the vicinity of the towering woman who cannot see. Split up or choose one or the other to approach together, that's up to you. And Captain."

"Yes, what?"

"You should've fucked Erika before the shower while you still had the chance."

# CHAPTER 12
# A BOY'S BEST FRIEND IS . . .

Connor Mullin was caught out in the dark stinging rain, no Uber, no cell phone, and he had to admit to himself that he hadn't been ready for the police force, not yet, not by a long shot. Shit, man, after dropping out of LaSalle's philosophy program as a clueless junior, he should have taken a breath, saved up his money working at the Pet Valu or the IHOP, or maybe he could have even joined the Peace Corps or something. But he'd jumped right into the brotherhood, head first and all that, never thinking in his wildest nightmares that it was going to be like high school all over again.

Or childhood in general, if he was being totally honest with himself. As far back as he could remember public education had been a cold nightmare, and even though Mother had constantly praised him for wearing his heart on his sleeve and so openly sharing his emotional depth and sensitivity with the world, he'd stopped eagerly raising his hand in class all the way back in middle school. Freshman year he learned to speed-read online, but when he gave away the endings to *The Outsiders* and *The Hunger Games,* his classmates absolutely trashed him. He'd stopped trying to talk to girls altogether by tenth, and by eleventh he was afraid to put a like on a Facebook post, let alone have a profile or an Instagram. He liked power tools and machines, especially automotive and engine repair, but the Vo-Techers didn't go for him, wrong wavelength, where they didn't need some "psychology geek" telling them all about their feelings and shit. He liked guns, but the tough kids saw him as a target, not a "trigger," and in a literal way all the school shootings and soft-spoken liberals had made his interest seem low-class, suspicious, and, in the end, pointless. He became the shadow in the hallways, the weirdo with the red greasy hair that he kept parted way over on the side and combed across the forehead to hide all his acne.

College in a way had been worse. He'd never felt a part of anything because he was a commuter, and the whole experience had made him feel lost, more invisible.

Fuck 'em. Two days after he dropped out of LaSalle he'd done the buzz cut, deciding in a wild sort of a rush to become a cop and a hard-ass. He bought a Clearasil multi-step treatment kit, he registered Republican, he opened a savings, fuck 'em all, he started lifting weights, started running, kicked in a high-carb diet, and most of all, he worked his vocab, learning to talk tough and sell it like he meant it. When he passed all the tests and signed on at the academy, he'd felt he'd reinvented himself, and throughout the training process he made sure to talk as infrequently as possible. He made it a thing, wasn't hard. Everyone around him was careful and stoic and zoned playing soldier.

But earlier today he'd gotten too comfortable on the job, and the captain had dissed him about the laser sight. Connor initially thought his plea would show his enthusiasm, a student of the game with an interest in the tools of the trade, but he'd come off the stupid boy, misreading the play, raising his hand in class all over again. Christ, he hated this shit; he obsessed freakishly over his social miscues, replaying them in his head in "should-a, could-a, would-a" scenarios, and by the time it had become known that the captain had gotten that weird letter, Connor had decided he needed to cement things at the station, engineering some personal mojo so he wouldn't wake up in the middle of the night tonight grinding his teeth.

Of course, he could do nothing at first. The morning was a clusterfuck, with everyone having to file into the captain's office one at a time for questioning as if they were seeing the school principal. Fucking excruciating. Connor wanted to nip this in the bud, set a standard, break some balls for a change, yes sir, show-tough, strike first, make it clear that the new kid here was a player, and he spent hours stewing about it. Finally, that afternoon when the smoke had cleared, he had his chance in the break room, where he'd leaned forward, cupping both hands around his lukewarm cup of black coffee, and confiding with a sneer to Officers Finch and Cabrera that he thought Detective Bronson was an overrated, ineffective, pock-marked, fat faggot.

They'd stared back at him hard.

"Well . . . hey," Connor said, eyes darting between the two of them, "I mean, shit, I'm just backing you up, right? In the locker room yesterday, I was a row over and I heard you guys calling Bronson a has-been. I feel you, is all I'm saying. He stinks up the bathroom. He doesn't spray, trust me, I've followed him twice and it ain't no damned picnic."

More of the quiet. Connor suddenly noticed the overhead fluorescents buzzing and the second hand ticking on the wall clock. Christ, here we go again, fuck-up number two, and even though the bell was already rung and all that, Connor tried some haphazard clean-up for sure. He'd laughed and said he was playing, and that it was a humor thing for humor's sake, and that he wanted to try stand-up in some downtown comedy clubs doing a spin on how dumb redheads like him could be, and this was nothing more than a bit he'd been practicing to see how far he could put his foot in his mouth. No response, nothing.

Desperate, Connor had offered up drinks when the three were off duty, said he was buying, that he knew a good place.

Cabrera had looked him in the eye and said quietly:

"If you think I'm going to walk into a suck-ass rat's nest crawling with 'hip dudes' shaking hair out of their eyes and looking like they just came back from a Super Smash Brothers tourney, you're more of a fucktard than I figured."

"You pick, then!" Connor said. "Please, c'mon, guys, it's on me, name your watering hole. Let me make it up to you. We can even invite Bronson. I'll buy him a friendship ring and make him godfather when I have a wife and a brat, what do you say?"

They'd looked at each other and nodded, real subtle.

On the way to the bar, Finch had told their Uber driver to slow down and stop just before the exit to the Blue Route. Cabrera was in the front passenger seat. He opened the door and stepped out into the rain. That didn't make sense.

"Uh, hey," Connor said. Next to him, Finch ignored him. He was holding his right arm by the bicep across his chin, studying the Band-Aid on his elbow. Cabrera ripped open Connor's door, reached in, and grabbed him by the collar, both sides.

*Big hands,* Connor thought. His shirt was yanked up into his underarms, and from behind he felt something flat on his ass, something hard. Finch's foot.

He was extracted from the vehicle, pulled out face first into the rain, and hurled off like a cartoon character, arms windmilling, nose down like a plane approaching the runway. By the time he'd gained footing, the tail-lights were receding, cold rain bouncing off the asphalt like darts. In front of him was a rusted knee-high guardrail bordering a cattycorner of highway decorator foliage, maybe black gum or choke cherry, and he looked up and blinked hard. He was at the red light by the chute leading to the overpass where there were two big green signs anchored to the concrete announcing Route 1 and South Lima next to the blue icon shaped like a French lieutenant's chest medal saying 476. Beneath that were massive pitted support columns and darkness grinning from under the bridge.

Head hanging, shoulders hunched, he made for the on-ramp, walking up the winding incline, shirt soaked already, pants sticking to him. Three-quarters of the way to the ramp meter light at the merge, he noticed the high stink in the air. Up to the right there was a copse of Bradford pear trees with that trademark ripe stench, lining the edge of the road going southbound. He had to go north of course, and trees shouldn't have stunk so much in the rain, the way a fart in the shower always surprised you, and there was no surprise here, things stank, and Connor finally had to admit it. He was no psychological genius, just a pathetic savant, either reading people too well or not at all, as if he had military-grade focus in one eye and a blind spot in the other. And the worst part was that he had no mental filter to meter himself. He was an on-ramp with a busted self-signaling device, and he stepped onto 476 in the cold sweeping rain.

He turned up the collar of his shirt as if that made a difference and saw that the median was a high concrete barrier that sloped down to the grass a few hundred feet up. He started walking the breakdown lane. Where the fuck was the traffic? Was everyone afraid they'd melt in the rain? There was no high-mast lighting out here, no roadside emergency phone, and speaking of which, where the fuck had he left his cell? He was sure he'd had it at the house. But did he? He thought he remembered putting it in his pocket, but he hadn't been able to find his wallet at first, and that had taken all his attention. And he'd been in a hurry to meet Finch and Cabrera.

Someone was coming.

From behind, heavy engine. Sounded like a big rig. Connor turned and saw the headlights advancing along a high rockface that cropped up back where the road curved out of the sightline, and hell yes, Connor stepped out between the two lanes and put up both of his arms.

It came around the long bend, an eighteen-wheeler, a big semi with a jumbo trailer filled with timber, maybe cedar or spruce. The tractor had a pair of silver exhaust stacks and a big grille like a steam engine's cowcatcher, and like some eager kid Connor suddenly wanted to do the elbow bend and fist pump so he'd get one of those long hauling trucker honks.

The rig came on and then slowed, gearing down with hearty grinding sounds, and Connor lowered his hand to his eyes against the glare. There was a hint of mist threading up from the tractor's undercarriage, and Connor felt a soft wave of heat as it passed him and pulled over. The hazard lights reflected on the asphalt. The driver had his arm out, waving him around, so Connor jogged out across the front and made for the passenger side. He pulled himself up and opened the cab door. Inside was a big man, so tall he almost had to hunch over the wheel. He had snow-white hair and a red baseball cap.

"You look lost, mister," he said, and Connor almost let a smile betray him. The guy had that slow and childlike tugging at his tongue like the deaf. He was mentally challenged.

"You have a cell phone?" Connor said.

"Why sure, mister, but Lord have mercy, I could just give you a ride! Gosh, if I sit too long I got to throw down my road flares and triangles, and I sure don't want to leave you waiting for your lift in the dark. It's raining cats and hounds out there and it's warm up here in the cab. I got no one to talk to, so hop on in, why don't ya? I got seat covers on, so you don't have to worry about soaking the fine leather or nothin'."

Connor climbed up, pulled shut the door, and settled. The guy handed him a blue mechanic's rag, and Connor nodded thanks, twice actually, and oh yes, it was warm in here, yes indeedy. Nice even. And he'd liked the special ed kids at school. They made him feel safe and they'd occupied the only lunch tables at which he'd been welcome.

"This rig is sweet," he said.

"It's like home."

"You sleep in back there?"

"Yes, mister. Comfy as a cocoon."

Conner went up on a haunch to get a better look back over his shoulder between the seats, and there was a mattress on the floor with a comforter designed like a map of the states. A big American flag was draped across the back wall. There were some automotive supplies in a small tool chest in the far corner, folded clothes in a cardboard box, and on the near side-panel a coloring-book picture of a smiling horse filled in with crayon. The caption said, "Friends in the Meadow," and Connor was pretty sure the drawing hadn't been done so carefully between the lines by some kid brother or baby cousin.

"So where you headed, mister?"

"Other way, north, first exit will do," Connor said. He had turned back around and was looking at all the cool shit he'd YouTubed a million times in high school with longing: the oversized console, the needles and dials, the big toggle switches like the ones they had at the Franklin Institute. There were map holders and huge side pockets crammed with spray bottles, grease guns, and a few cans of WD-40, and below the iPad and the satellite radio, there was a nest of wires, curlycue cords, cables, power adaptors, and the kind of big gear knobs kids loved to go pulling on to "play bulldozers" at the park in the recreation area and the rides they had on coil springs outside the Walmart. A car was coming the other way, washing its pale light over them, and Connor looked over self-consciously. The man was watching him, smiling softly, leaning on the steering wheel with his big elbows and forearms. His hat said "Make America Great Again," and his green reflective vest had one of the tear-aways dangling because of the worn Velcro.

"You wanna drive it, mister?"

"Say what?" Connor said.

"You can drive it. I can show you."

"For real?"

"For sure! Then we could be friends like Bubba and Forest Gump, and it would be like this is our shrimp boat!"

Connor took a moment to study him closer, and he deduced that the guy was even lower IQ than he'd thought. And the two of them weren't like Forest and Bubba, yet more George Milton and Lenny Small from that book they'd had to read in tenth grade called *Of Mice and Men.* In that one, George was supposed to be the smart one, but it was clear that he was only smart when comparing himself to Lenny, the gentle man-mountain with severe special needs whom everyone, at least in Connor's class, had been fascinated with. When the big dude was shot at the end, some of his classmates had literally thrown their books across the room. Didn't seem fair to kill off such a friendly, loyal, simple, and hopeful man-child stuck in the body of a giant.

In the story he was also a killer, but everyone seemed to forget that part.

"Yes," Connor said. "I want to drive this hog. But don't you have to be somewhere?"

The man grabbed the bill of his cap.

"I'm ahead of schedule, mister, I swear. And this has been a long haul, from Jacksonville all the way to Delaware, and I can tell you the load ain't even a bit ugly back there. Ponderosa pine, and it even smells nice. Ya gotta believe me, I know this run, I done it three times before, and there ain't no low bridges or tight corners you'll have to worry about, you just keep your eye on the whole vehicle, not just the easy corner, and you'll be rolling just fine—you'll see."

Before there was a chance for protest, the man reached for the back of Connor's seat and yanked himself up to scramble into the sleeper cabin. Fuckin'-A, he was quick for his size, like a cheetah! Agile too; he didn't kick against any of the gadgetry and didn't stick his heel into Connor's jaw either, using his mattress as a landing pad and spinning around quick as you please. Now he was cross-legged Indian style, holding the back of both seats like a kid on a ride, face in between and eyes sparkling.

"Go on, mister," he said. "Get in the driver's seat, I kept it nice and warm for ya."

Connor paused, still not quite believing it, but then he climbed over the saddle-seat clutter-catcher. Connor didn't snag a toe, but he didn't go like the proverbial cheetah either. Palms pressed to the roof, careful with the hips, he straddled across and settled in carefully, taking extra time so he wouldn't hit any floor pedals. Finally he rested his back against the wood-beaded seat cover and thought, *Shit man, it's not just soothing, it feels like a damned back message.*

All right, Cap'n," the man said. "Now here's your lesson. I ain't no real teacher or nothing, but it's as easy as counting to nine. This here's an eighteen-speed Eaton Fuller trans, so think of it divided in half, there's your nine. You're gonna do an H-pattern, more like an M really, starting in the low range, just like your Ford or your Honda. Now for me, I might kick it off in the third or fifth gate, skipping those low-range granny gears, but you can go from the very beginning. First gear's down bottom left. Each time you change, you flick the thumb switch. When you get to five you flip the front high/low selector and go right up to six—top left 'cause fifth low and six high share the same ratio. So . . . one-two-three-four-five, flip up the front switch, six-seven-eight-nine, you got it?"

Connor nodded excitedly. The man kept on with his speech, but Connor didn't need it. The whole thing made sense. Besides, he'd seen so many video tutorials on the subject, he would have been able to feel his way blind.

He looked out his side mirror and then checked all around. The humongous man-child behind him was talking about taking the haul up 95 to Wilmington so he could show him the depot. It had other trucks and some rental cranes like a machine show, and even though there was a NO TRESPASSING sign since it was after hours and all, there was no one to prevent them from having a look-see outside the fencing, and there was a big rotary turn-around to head back to 95 North, so there were no back-ins or blind angles to worry about, no need for either of them to jump out in the rain to play spotter, and then they could run it back where they come from. I'm from Pineville, North Carolina, myself, so where do you live at exactly, mister?

Connor answered absently that it was Elderberry Street in Broomall, next to Saint Mary's Cemetery, and he absently heard the man laugh and say that it was good because cemeteries had big unmonitored parking areas you could sneak into for a nice nap, which was exactly what he was going to do, damned right he would.

Connor started forward, jerking it, some choke and spit, but goddamned right, he got this hunk of tin moving. Not quite a cheetah, not yet, but Connor was suddenly the kid again, playing bulldozer at the park in the recreation area while the other kids wasted their time playing baseball and Frisbee Tag.

Once he got going, he was going just fine, and when they passed Exit 3 Media/Swarthmore, Connor wasn't choking or grinding at all anymore. The road was near empty, and when opposing traffic ran headlights across the windshield, the industrial-grade wipers came across snug and clear, making the new raindrops glisten like prisms and jewels.

"They're pretty, huh . . ."

"What?" Connor said.

"The drops, mister. I know. I like it when the rain dots up like that and the wipers clear them away like a machine sweeping them into your private gem bag. And each time, just for a second, the window's so crystal clear you feel you could make it into a wine glass and drink out of it with your pinkie up like the British folk. Then it rains jewels again before you can blink. But don't get too dreamy with it, mister. Trucks will do that to ya. Too much, you know, too much . . ."

A minivan moved in from the left lane in front, and Connor down geared appropriately.

"Too much what?" he said. "Besides you guessing what was in my head, which was weird by the way, what do you mean, trucks will do that to you? Do what, too much of what?"

Connor couldn't see the man behind him, but he could have sworn he felt him bowing his head. In religious reverence? Shame? Did he drop a contact lens?

"Uh, mister," he said, "I never told no one before, but I guess I could say it to you because you're nice and we're friends, and maybe you wouldn't go laughing up a hurricane."

"What? Tell me what?"

"Trucks got a beauty is what I was going to say, too much of it, like they might hypnotize you, so you gotta mostly ignore that part of it and pay attention to the road." His voice went dreamy. "Trucks, though, they got sweet perfect angles and . . . you know, that word that begins with a P and sounds like . . . like . . . detective."

Connor laughed. "You mean perspective."

"Yes, sir! Perspective and portion!"

"Proportion."

"Right. Gosh, I wish I had you 'round all the time, mister. I used to remember all those words . . ."

The man didn't continue, and for a second Connor felt that maybe the poor guy lost his train of thought altogether. He was about to try to think of a technical question, and the man said:

"Ma."

"Huh?" Connor said. "What's that you say . . . Ma?"

"Yeah, mister. My ma. Don't you tell no one, but between you and me, she's the one who made me forget."

"Forget what?"

"Words like perspective. When I was a little fella, I liked to draw things. All the other kids in the neighborhood played Kick the Can and Groundsies and built forts in Scutter's Woods, and went down the creek chucking rocks and shooting bee-bee pump guns and lighting off TNT Poppers, Parachutes, and M80's, and smoking cigarettes, and later drinking beers and honey whiskey and going and getting girls and fighting for fun and sometimes for real, and playing Friday Night Lights and muscle cars and prom queens, but I just wanted to keep to myself, with my easel and oils. Ma worked at the quarry. Drove a dump truck. She let me drive it sometimes on Saturdays when she was making time and a half and the foreman, Jack the 'lecherous son of a bitch' Reynolds was off, and once I misread the flag girl and almost backed it off a cliff."

"That sucks."

"Yeah, but I loved trucks just the same, sort of became my backup plan that turned into my day to day. But, well, this is private, mister, but we're friends so I'll tell ya . . . when I almost run that rig off that cliff, Ma took me home at the end of her shift for the punishment."

"What punishment?"

"My day-to-day treatment, only worse, 'cause I almost ran the rig off a cliff."

"Where do I go up here?"

"Bear right but stay left inside it. Go slow in the curve and then we'll merge onto 95 South."

"Got it," Connor said. "Now tell me what you mean by the day-to-day treatment."

"Uh, well, now I kinda don't wanna."

"Why?"

"It's embarrassing, like stickers in your britches and all. Might make ya sick."

Connor paused. Now, he "kinda" didn't "wanna" know, but in a way he kind of did even more. He cleared his throat, and without being able to stop himself he fell into a Southern feel, almost the way racists thought they'd be better understood talking to Asians loud in the face with a mock Asian accent.

"She sex you up?" he said, almost wincing at the sound of it.

"Naw, mister, not so simple like that. She dressed me down, but in a way you could have written a book about. Ain't no law against it, but there should have been."

Connor gnawed on the fleshy part of the inside of his cheek.

"What do you mean?"

"She opened me up, looking inside me. Sat me at the kitchen table and made me admit things, over and over, like how dumb and irresponsible I was."

Connor smiled wanly. "That's every mom."

"No, mister, it got worse. See, everyone up here thinks folk south of Virginia live in trailer parks and tin-roof shanties and let their kids run around in diapers in the fenced-in front yard that's overrun with weeds and goose grass. But we didn't live on no dirt road and we didn't have no Copenhagen shacks down yonder, at least not in my neighborhood, thank you kindly. We had a nice porch, a weeping willow, and a garage with my daddy's carpenter shop where he made fox catchers and birdhouses on the weekends. What I'm saying is that everyone thinks Southern boys always get a redneck's version of a whoopin' growing up, but that's not the way it works. Some parents shove God into you. My mother stuffed me with sadness, made me see it in every corner of my heart and soul until there wasn't nothin' left to wake up for. See, my daddy hurt his back pulling out a stump in the back yard when I was in the third grade, and he went on painkillers he couldn't quit, and he run off by the time I was eleven. Ma had been a stay-at-home mom and she'd been happy, and I know that sounds kinda old-fashioned, but I'm sorry, she was. To keep hold of the house, though, she had to beg her uncle Reggie to get her the job at the quarry, and her new health care was super-cala-frajja, and it let her go talk to someone about her feelings and such."

"A therapist."

"Yeah, that's right. Problem was, she used the back 'n' forth back on me, like I was her patient."

"Come again?" Connor said.

"What I'm saying, mister, is that instead of whacking me with a leather belt she would've kept on a hook by the stove or a nail in the washroom, she sat me down every night and crossed her legs and arms and made me admit I was a big dumb failure, like a hunk of Jello that just wobbled. But she did it all professional-like, as if she was my doctor, my personal psych-eee-logist, shining a light on my cuts and sores and making me look and look and look until feeling sick about things seemed the way I was supposed to be all the time. Like her. Like she'd say to me stuff like, 'Son, I know you hate yourself and life has abandoned you. I know you're insecure and that sometimes, most times, you don't feel like a boy at all, like you're growing more womanlike, trying to connect with your misguided feelings. I know you like to paint, as the gutter-rats do in the mental institution out in Grayville, sitting on the lawn in hospital gowns and grinning like fools, and I know you don't have friends, and I know you touch your penis every night, and pick your nose, and sometimes don't wipe good enough, and chew the skin around your fingernails like a cannibal, and I know you think of yourself as someone who will always fail, and never find love, and never understand what life really means, and I want to help you. Talk to me. Tell me your fears, all of them, I know . . . it will take a long time, a lot of nightly discussions, a lot of digging, but in time, we'll get to the bottom of you.'"

Connor's bottom lip twitched, and on the wheel his knuckles were whitening.

"And what happened?" he said.

"Well," the man said, "I figured I wasn't good enough to live, so I took the thing I loved the most and tried to kill it, like inside myself, and I loved to draw and make portraits, so I went into the shed in the back yard and drank paint thinner. I don't remember how much I choked down, mister, but it almost put an end to me. When I woke up I wasn't so sad, but I couldn't think too well. It was kinda nice in a way, because Ma didn't go ripping into me no more. She just left me be, and I learned to drive that dump truck at the quarry without scaring the flag girls, yes sir, I did. Worked that muscle memory until I made my way up here to the big rigs, but I couldn't paint no more. When it came to thinking and drawing it had gone sort of blurry."

He paused.

"But I can do coloring books, mister! Like the horse on the panel here. I used different crayons this time, and didn't even run the colors together!"

Connor felt as if his head would explode. They had just passed the Port of Wilmington exit, and he was thinking about artists turned into happy-go-lucky village idiots all because they'd been taught to churn their feelings inside and out at the damned kitchen table. This wasn't a parent's discipline. It was a blueprint for getting your hooks in and examining your kid like a biology frog.

It was a profile of his own mother, Professor Becky fucking Mullin.

The story the man had just told was a shining light to Connor, showing the side of something that had always been right there in front of him yet cleverly shadowed, turned backward by his mother to make it seem normal. But this new . . . *perspective* made Connor reevaluate everything, sort of the same way you had to go back through that movie *The Sixth Sense* and figure out that Bruce Willis was really the unnoticed ghost in each scene.

Professor Becky Mullin, someone he depended on, confided in, sucked up to for constant approval. He'd always felt that their kitchen-table sessions had given him the advantage over his Gothic Emo fucked-up kid sister, because he was the one getting all the attention.

But what was it really?

What were those sessions she put him through every night under the unforgiving lights? Did they give him an advantage or just make him needy? And here was the real question: Were they even for Connor at all?

They gave his mother power.

Control.

Girl power making him a girl inside without his consent, without even knowing it.

In his ear the big guy was still talking, circling back, saying his ma had this weepy, disappointed look that made you feel useless. She could see inside you, she always said, and she claimed she could fix you, that you needed fixing, as if you were damaged goods she got at a yard sale and she was the only one with the Scotch tape and glue gun.

*Girl power making him a child,* Connor thought. *Girl power making me a girl.*

Professor Becky Mullin. Connor's personal "therapist." But move the letters of that God-awful word and you got:

The Rapist.

It was Professor Becky fucking Mullin who had made him what he was, a sensitive loser who had long been manipulated to wear his heart on his sleeve and smile at the world like an eager damned fool. He thought about all those times, raising his hand in middle school hungrily looking for that participation trophy . . . learning to speed-read and getting absolutely trashed by his new high school peers for it . . . being shunned by the Vo-Techers . . . getting thrown out of an Uber by his fellow officers straight into a rainstorm . . . knowing the decorator foliage was black gum and choke cherry and that the stink in the air came from Bradford pear trees, because he was never put into Little League or Pop Warner or martial arts classes or wrestling camp, oh GOD no, the competition was far too intense and inappropriate for Mother's delicate boy-girl, and it was better to sit and listen to the way birds conferenced and gathered in the choke cherry bushes and pear trees through the metaphorical way Jonathan Swift presented his blah-blah, and now they could share feelings and blah-fucking-blah.

His mother was his rapist.

The soft-sell type, the kind they didn't have laws for, as the simpleton said. She was a smooth-talking psychobabble sort of pedophile, playing your analyst, gently flickering her tongue in your brain, fondling your emotions, running the smooth tips of her fingers across them ever so softly in her rape den across from the oven and the spice rack. Every night was "time for sharing." Time to keep you there, vomiting stuff out of your soul while she scrutinized it with that pretentious feel-sorry smile . . . assuring you that you were hopelessly insecure and helpless and fragile and damaged while she slipped her moist, warm cock in your brain.

Yes, sir.

Yes, *mister*.

Connor was going to get this rig turned around, drive back, and let his new friend get some sleep in the graveyard.

It was only a short walk back home.

And Connor Mullin had a lot to say to his mother.

# CHAPTER 13
# DOING A DANCE DOWN DEEP IN THE BONEYARD

Meagan Mullin was tired of waiting.

At first she'd felt like dark royalty, anointed and cursed, sacred and terrified, walking down the hill among the keepsakes and treasures that had been tossed at her feet like rose petals from the netherworld. But up close now, the shrine just looked like a bunch of dirty, wet shit piled up on a rock.

And she wanted a more luscious nightmare, pretty please . . . with chocolate syrup and a cherry on top! Hey, maybe the lawn crypt to the left could start vibrating, right? There would be a rasping in the rain, a grating sound similar to when you caught the bottom of your car door on the curb, and in terror she'd realize that it was the mounting bolt in the granite cover scraping in its own pilot-hole. And oh-my-dear-*Goodness*, the stone was coming up, pushed from beneath by this skeletal flesh-rotted zombified miscreant!

But everything was just cold and wet and sad and forgotten. Plus, down a short bluff and about fifteen feet over, there was a bunch of cemetery paraphernalia that was a buzzkill up close, all rough and ready and dull and too real. There was a mud-spattered pickup truck on the grass down there with trash barrels in the back bed filled with digging tools. It was parked by this huge mound of fill with a tarp half blown off it, and lying at the foot in the runoff and runnels was a wooden apparatus that looked like a piece of elongated warehouse pallet racking. There were a few short stacks of folding chairs with see-through plastic covers on them held down by rocks, and earthy green mats rolled up next to a wreath on a tripod. In between it all you could see the big rectangular cavity they'd cut into the earth. There was a covering for it, but it was this low-budget warped sheet of plywood. The rain tapped off it sounding like a muted drum roll, a military tribute or something, and it just made Meagan feel hollow.

She looked back the way she had come, squinting into the rain. Damn. From up on the hill, this had all seemed like album cover material, the perfect backdrop for a famous new super-group starring Meagan Mullin on seven-string bass, Sophie Lloyd on guitar, Mia Morris on drums, and Carla Harvey on vocals, all traditional, no scream-o, and she'd wear a mask like Amerakin Overdose or Slipknot or better yet, Mushroomhead, and they'd open for The Butcher Babies all across the country, indoor arenas only if you please, and when everyone made the connection they'd go fucking wild!

Meagan sullenly walked across Cindy Chen's gravesite and gazed over yonder to the far right where she could almost see her house through the border trees. On the near side of the railing down there was the low end of the west lawn with the special nook that had her favorite twenty-six headstones, and suddenly Meagan stopped where she was. It was dark and grainy back in there with the overhanging branches blocking the spill of the moon, but sure as shit, that fence railing looked open at the bottom. You're kidding, fucking really? Now it appeared that the three familiar posts that had been rusted through, making the arch you could crawl through, were still rusted away the way they'd always been. But no, earlier she'd been damned sure they were rewelded, she'd seen the dried silver drippings, the solder marks or whatever they were. Had she walked all the way around here for nothing? Was she tripping? Had she lost all sense of place somehow and approached her little entry and escape hatch at the wrong point even though she'd been elbowing through there since she was a tween?

She walked through the headstones to the edge of the short bluff and sidestepped down carefully. Better question. Had her special someone temporarily made it *look* as if the iron railing had been repaired to make her go the long way and walk the royal carpet of keepsakes rather than look up at them from this angle once she got past the trees? Was he *that* obsessive, that conscientious, that . . . *romantic*?

She blushed hard. She didn't think it was about that, yet deep down she was hoping it was. But then why would he remove the repaired iron pieces he'd welded there in the first place? Was he afraid a maintenance worker would complain tomorrow that some phantom had secured the property better? Was he giving her a way out once he'd controlled her way in? Testing if she was still interested? Scornful? Turned chickenshit?

Well, she wasn't about to go checking it. What if he came down the hill while she was doing so? She'd have to come out from the shadows sheepishly. She'd have to explain herself and the fact that she'd been questioning his motives when the gifts on the hill made it obvious.

Well then, okay, c'mon already, where was he? She frowned. She'd been absolutely thrilled, and there was nothing that sucked worse than being stood up, confused, and wistful in the cold shitty rain.

She approached the ugly new gravesite before her and sighed. It was all so forlorn in the set-up phase before they packed the body in the ground with the headstone propped up behind it like a Hallmark card on the mantle. And so . . . who was to be buried here tomorrow anyway, boy or girl, man or woman? What was the cause of death? That was a good one. And where was the body now? Who picked out the clothes for the corpse? What time would they arrive tomorrow, what equipment had to be put in for the lowering, and how far in advance did they have to get it set up before the ceremony? Whose job was it, and what if he or she showed up late? What if the straps or the supports weren't set right and the casket tipped? What was the safeguard for that? What if the body fell out? What if—

Something moved. Meagan had been zoned, eyes fixed dully on the mound of fill, and she could have sworn something shifted a few feet off to the side.

She looked over at the truck. Yes, something was odd, something different, and it took a second, but she nailed it. Windshield wipers. They were pointing upward as opposed to the regular positioning. Had they been like that before? How would she know? She hadn't been looking that hard, why would she?

But she was sure looking now. It was a brown utility vehicle, an ugly old rust-bucket with cancer spots around the front wheel wells, a dent in the door, and a cracked headlight. The antenna was bent, and—

The windshield wipers moved, going back down slow as molasses, bumping on the glass the way you did when you went down a slide in shorts and your legs rubbed. Meagan pressed both of her hands to her mouth. The engine wasn't running. How on earth . . .

Wait.

Oh, fuck me, yes, there was something hanging from the rearview, you could see it through the glass, with the rain making the image jump as if reflected in shattered pieces of mirror. It was a braided leather necklace, and the pendant was a tooth, a big one, most probably a molar.

"Meagan Mullin!" someone shouted, rough but far off, gruff and older, like a school security guard threatening a blue slip, not a secret admirer making his grand entrance, and the suddenness of it made Meagan almost wet her damned pants.

"Meagan Mullin!" he hollered. "Come forward, right now! You are in danger, make yourself seen!"

Meagan knew that this place could play tricks on you with sounds, but it seemed he was on the other side of the monument up the hill, back deep in the field of flat ledger stones. Who the fuck? If he was her mystery-man he wouldn't be announcing himself this way—oh no he would not.

Decision time.

If he saw the keepsakes on the hill it was over. He would come down here just as she had, following it as if it was one of those huge highway arrow boards, and then he would notice the truck. He'd figure that she was hiding in it, in the cab, or if it was locked, the back bed. That nixed it as an option, and suddenly Meagan was furious. This "dude," this authoritative old fucking perv, was somehow in on this, tipped off, wrecking her magic meeting like a peeping Tom, and the thing that burned her the most was the idea that if the truck door was open, he'd go in and get her prize tooth.

Before letting herself really think about it, she made for the passenger door. The handle was the type you pressed with your thumb, and she pressed it. The door was unlocked and she pulled it open and climbed up on the diamond-tread running board. Inside was a dark hull with this old industrial-basement feel to it, and she ducked her head, pushed in, and pressed her knee to the seat, and it wheezed. Gritty gismos, levers, stark angles, and it smelled weird and dense, almost cloying, like sweet earth and flowers, and Meagan bit back a squeal, thinking of Harry Potter jelly beans, pixels, and snow globes.

*Dandelions. It smells like fucking dandelions.*

She snatched the tooth off the rearview.

She backed out, doggie paddling in reverse, wet hair hanging around her face, cold rain spattering up her back, her bare neck, and she hopped down backward to the grass.

To remain as noiseless as possible she pushed the door almost closed to a crack, and the guy up there shouted again, way closer than before, and she knew it was now or never, no time to guess whether the gap in the iron barrier was really there or soldered solid, and she turned on her heel and ran for the newly dug grave while trying to fumble her new prize tooth into her pocket. But the gun was in the way, handle up, and screw it, she stuck the molar in her mouth, and oh my fuck, she could taste the blood from the strands stuck to the root-stems that had been buried in his gums and it was like some bizarre French kiss with her mystery freak, and she dropped to the mud on her knees.

Hands shaking, she nudged over the plywood, making a short two-foot opening that looked like a black scalene triangle. To her right something squealed open and slammed shut, and simultaneous with the latter, the strange tooth in her mouth exploded, like pixels, and it tasted like caramel and Skittles, and she swallowed so hard she almost choked on the lanyard. She spit the leather band into the darkness of the grave and looked over to the right in stupid amazement. The truck door had re-opened all the way and closed its damned self, and the windows had tinted. Heavily. One part of her mind was spellbound by the taste of the tooth, another part grossed out, and yet another was thinking quite rationally that either her magic man had one amazing remote-control set-up or the truck was actually haunted, and she put her hands palm-down in the mud on either side of her knees, brought through her legs, and sat hard.

"Meagan Mullin!" the guy shouted from up past the hill, and God *damn,* if he didn't sound as if he was panting right over her shoulder! "Meagan, if you're out here, I am ordering you to give me a signal! It's a matter of life or death! You are in danger. I am a police officer!"

*Sure you are,* she thought, and with a slight groan she slid in her feet to dangle down into the darkness. Now, of course, there was something that was going to grab hold of her ankle. For sure, there was an escaped lunatic down there, a grinning demon squatting in the dirt, a blood-spattered clown lurking just past the shadow-line.

*It's just a hole in the ground.*

She leaned over and moved the board another couple of inches, took a deep breath, and carefully pushed herself into the void to the tipping point.

When she let go, she almost caught her chin on the slant of plywood, but she didn't, and she landed, her boots making a gritty sound on the dirt in the darkness. She cautiously put out her hands like a blind person, unable to see past her wrists. The air was thick as if it had soil in it, and she turned to the near wall.

As calmly as she could, she went up on her toes and reached up for the plywood's underside. It stuck on something and she moaned, nudging more urgently now, and it gave, it moved and it scraped across like a rusted prison gate that swept pitch-darkness into the grave.

From outside she thought she heard cursing, still far away but not that far away, and it was obvious he'd seen magic mountain. Eerie silence, more silence, then a muffled quick rhythm, as if a marching-band bass drum was being played far across a parking lot with heavy cotton covers pulled over the mallet-heads. Closer. Same bass drum played with wet socks filled with wood shavings, soaked oven gloves crammed with bread stuffing, footsteps.

Closer. Heavy breathing and wet treading right in front of the grave and then slightly past it.

"Meagan Mullin!" the guy rasped. "You are in danger. I am a—"

There was the sound of an engine roaring to life, and Meagan's heart leapt in her chest. The man out there shouted "Hold it!" and she could imagine him pulling a weapon and aiming it at the old pickup's windshield. She carefully slid the gun out of her pocket, not really believing she was doing it, but doing it just the same, as if she was in a theater watching someone in a theater watching a movie of a girl in a grave. The truck revved again, and it felt as if Mr. Man was approaching it.

"Exit the vehicle!" he commanded. "Now! This is real!"

Meagan clicked off the safety, Lord knew how many times her dickhead brother had shown her how. She still had the aftertaste of caramel and Skittles in her mouth, but the sweetness had soured. What happened when Mr. Man discovered the truck had no driver? What if he came over and ripped up the plywood? Would she shoot? Could she really—

There was a sound out there, sudden and coarse, truck tires spitting up grass and wet gravel, some spraying and ticking across the plywood above her, and from the truck's radio a song blasted out, so loud it seemed there must have been external speakers, and the theater in a theater was a world inside an album.

The song was that metal tune, "WWIII," by the German Industrial band KMFDM.

*Acoustic beginning with those hard-ass steel strings I love that beginning I—*

Meagan was grinning now in absolute terror and excitement, and she imagined she looked as if she had a coat hanger jammed in her mouth. The tires ripped and shredded the other way-away and then stopped short, then burst and halted again like a tease, and she heard Mr. Man pounding on the hood and calling her name, and then everything moved off down around back of her.

*Chasing the bait.*

The sounds receded, and it seemed the man and the truck were working their way over toward the mausoleums, and she couldn't be sure, but the fading sounds took on a different underscore, and it appeared that they'd possibly hit the paved roadway leading off to the columbarium.

*My magic man drew him away.*

Her smile softened, went dreamy.

*My magic man.*

Or wait a minute. Wait just one motherfucker.

Her smile withered. What if the old perv out there was doing all this himself somehow? What if he was playing her, playing both villain and savior, making it seem as if he was there to rescue her from this dark special someone he'd made up all along? Far off, the truck music had progressed to the recorded gunshots KMFDM had put right before the heavy riff, and—

Something in the dark moved behind her.

*What*

She whirled around.

*No*

She raised the revolver.

*Fuck!*

She fired her weapon.

# CHAPTER 14
# HONEY, I'M HOME

Connor brought the big rig to a halt on the shoulder just past the high school on Sproul Road.

"We're here," he said gruffly. "Thanks for the lift and letting me drive. All you have to do is take her across the street there right through that cemetery gateway arch. Chapel will be straight ahead of you and there's parking in front, on the sides, and around back, a ton of it."

"Thanks, mister."

Connor looked back over his shoulder.

"What you been doing back there, anyway?" he said. "You clammed up when I turned around early. No Wilmington, no depot and truck-show, I know, but I got shit to take care of."

"Yeah, mister, sure. We still friends, though?"

"Whatever. Answer the question. What the fuck are you doing? That a Playstation controller or something? Looks like a jacked-up Sony DualShock 4 wireless, but what's that screen in the middle for?"

"What screen?"

"Don't fucking lie, I saw it. You just turned it around almost upside down, mimicking your direction. It's better if you work your thumbs smoothly."

"You've changed, mister. You're mad. You're different."

"What's the screen for?"

"It's a video," the man muttered. "I got it hooked up at my house back home. My friend Larry made it for me. He goes to electronics school. It's like a seeing-eye camera with toys, and I'm playing with my pets out in the back yard between the little headstones."

"Headstones? In your back yard?"

"More fun if you picture it that way, mister."

"What's the game?"

The big man grinned foolishly, still looking down at his controller and moving his thumbs clumsily on the joy sticks.

"Cat and mouse. I'm working my remote-control jumbo toy ghost-truck, and I'm making it drive my pets looney tunes."

"You got a pet mouse?"

"Naw. A pit bull with a fat neck and a red-headed ginger cat." He started moving his right and left thumbs rapidly, tongue poked out the corner of his mouth.

"What's that you're doing now?" Connor said.

"Spin move. Cutting donuts with that haunted pickup truck, tearing up grass and making the fat-necked pit bull feel like he's chasing his tail, running down to the make believe mausoleums."

"What's his name?"

"Detective Fatso."

"That's what you call your dog?"

"Naw, mister. It's what you would call him. His real name is 'Hey You.'"

"Very funny. What's the cat's name?"

"Dandelion."

Connor's eyes narrowed.

"Yeah," he said thinly. "Better than 'Sunflower.' Fucking cunt."

The man was flicking the sticks and swinging his arms with it, moving the controller back and forth like a pendulum.

"That's a bad word," he said.

"Yes."

"But you said it anyway."

"Yes."

"You're even more mad, I think, madder than before."

Connor turned and stared out through the windshield.

"Fucking right I am," he said. "And if I say a bad word, I say a bad word. A cunt is a cunt and that's it."

"Who's the cunt then?"

Connor paused.

"I am," he said. "But tonight, that's going to change."

He pushed open the door and hopped down to the street. He didn't wave goodbye. He didn't make the sign for a trucker honk, didn't even look back. The rain had picked up and Sproul Road looked like a long black griddle popping bacon fat. Connor hustled across it, making a quick right on the far sidewalk. The rain was cold as hell, and once he was fifty feet down the road or so Connor moved into a shadow covering a portion of the cemetery gate fencing. He stopped to lean his forehead against an iron post and tried to regulate his breathing, gripping the neighboring posts like prison bars. He'd never been so angry, so cold, so immersed in black fire. It felt almost religious, like a dream state, and while on one level, standing there, he lost track of time for a spell, he knew with a certain surety it was only a few minutes or so.

Then suddenly he was back, awake and alive, striding through a long black puddle that soaked him up past both ankles. Felt good now. Wet leaves brushed his forehead from a branch overhanging the ornamental ironwork bordering the graveyard to his left, it felt good. A street lamp up ahead at the corner of Elderberry cast down its pale light with the rain passing through it. He reached out to bump his palm along the black iron posts as he passed them, and the dumb repetition of it felt good, it was his personal sound that no one would hear, the one no one would know, the beat of a war drum, beat of his heart.

When he got to the corner of Sproul Road and Elderberry he noticed something, an annoyance interrupting his internal battle rhythm like a vacuum cleaner on the other side of the house. It was the haunt of a sound coming over the dark slopes of the cemetery, somewhere deep in, an amplified acoustic guitar, atonal, real wise-ass shit above the rumble of an engine, a pickup truck maybe, higher and whinier that the semi he'd just mastered like a cowboy on a prize bull.

Kids, punks. Probably rip-cording beers, tearing up turf, and spray-painting the headstones. Meagan the Pagan liked sneaking out her window, climbing down the trellis, and tooling around in here when the weather was better, he knew. She probably liked the shitty song too.

Now gunshots.

On the recording, gunshots, oh fucking bravo, oh, fuck you Meagan, you snotty dark witch. You probably think it's politically deep and socially hip, groundbreaking and personally insightful. Let's go protest the Second Amendment! Let's go talk about firearms when we don't even know how to sharpen a kitchen knife. Let's all sit at the table and share.

He turned the corner and started walking faster. His left hand was out again, bumping along the wrought iron gateposts. He could see his driveway across the street half a block down and the external lighting that cast a dull glow across the front of the yard, rain spattering along the top of the oversized yellow mailbox on a post, painted over with birds, flowers, and peace signs.

Mother had done the "artwork" herself when Dad left, that very day. She'd cancelled a class. She'd gone to the basement and taken out two cans of old metallic enamel and semi-gloss latex, plus the paint kit Connor had used for his model car in the Pinewood Derby for Boy Scouts that fall. She'd found a stiff four-inch China bristle brush and three pencil-sized jobs for detail, and she'd painted the bathroom, covering it with birds, nests, and trees, but not artistic birds, nests, and trees, but rather, abstract versions of birds, nests, and trees that looked like watercolor shit made by preschoolers on crack. She'd taken a break outside on the grass by the porch on a blanket eating hummus and saltless organic rice crackers. Then she'd done the mailbox. She'd forced Connor to come out and stand there looking at it, holding hands with her.

Oh, yes.

They needed to have a talk.

Something caught the fleshy part of his index finger, felt like a paper cut, a steel splinter maybe, and he instinctively brought his hand to his mouth to give it a suck. Made it worse. Fuck it, let it bleed, let it swell, he just didn't care anymore.

He and Mother were going to have a talk.

Connor crossed the street and walked up the driveway. The house was part of him, but he looked at it now as if part a stranger. The lights were on in Meagan's room, not the overhead ceiling light, but the table lamp by the window. The bottom of the window was open, probably because she was smoking and blowing it through the crack. The trellis had wild ivy in it that had already taken hold of the house and worked its way around the far corner. Great yard work, Mother. The downstairs lights were off. Mother was upstairs, probably working. That would be good. He hoped the interruption was going to be startling.

He moved around to the near side of the house where Mother had planted the butterfly bushes. They were overgrown, dangling into the skinny walkway between their place and the Jazinskis' tree hedges, and Connor had to use his forearm to block the flower clusters away from his face. Didn't feel good like the graveyard trees spilling over the border railing. Felt like Mother's fingertips caressing his emotions, ever so softly. But he suddenly wanted to feel the molestation, *needed* to feel it to know it was real, again and again to feed the black fire, and he started circling the house, purposefully nudging against the bushes and shrubbery, and each time the leaves brushed his face he bit back a scream.

Like the dark meditation against the black gatepost he lost track of time, but then again, he did not, and if he'd had to count laps, it had been five or six so far, nine or ten at the most, and he was done with this now, God damn, he was ready.

He turned the corner and hopped up the back concrete steps. The rain cut off under the overhang, making it spatter dramatically around him on three sides. Sounded like applause. He opened the screen door, stuck in his hip. He got out his key, snapped over the deadbolt on the inner door, and stepped onto the tile. His sneakers squelched. He snapped on the light, making the kitchen look hard-edged and clinical. He was dripping rainwater, breathing heavily, and he looked down at himself. His pants-cuffs were blotched half up the shin from his walk through the puddles.

Dirty boy.

His clothes hung on him cold and heavy. On the counter by the toaster was the bright ceramic Tweetie Bird cup, and he dipped in his fingers, lifting out the keys to the Rav 4.

Smart, dirty boy, no running for you, Mother. It would be just like you to burst out of here crying, playing the victim, but I'm going to make you sit and take it in and listen to me. I'm going to tell you who you are, make you listen to my diagnosis.

He made his way across and through to the shadowy middle room, skirting the circular table in the middle, painted forest green with the three stools around it sporting red padded seats the way they had at the Country Squire Diner or, as Mother had said, at the Woolworth's counter where it was proven that people of privilege took the small things for granted. To the sides on the walls were the long blank stares of Mother's Greek and African masks, her pictures of tree-climbing goats, and in the corner next to the cabinet with the fancy dishes there was that trash-sculpture that looked like a robot in a Shakespearean pose.

That one really did it for Connor, remembering as if it were yesterday, yet feeling it as would the stranger, what it was like growing up with this lame-ass shit all around him, what the kids must have thought when he was young enough to still have boatloads of friends, slowly dropping off one by one because of yellow mailboxes, butterfly bushes, and Shakespearean trash sculptures.

He passed through the front room, hand on the banister, stairs underfoot. They were wood. Why no carpet? In the whole house, no carpet, all wood, as if Mother had figured hard floors and less comfort made her family seem "real" and down to earth and more charitable.

Well, Mother, it's time for a talk.

Time for you to listen for once, hear the truth about your damned self.

At the upper landing he looked back toward the front of the house. Meagan's door was closed. Good. Stay put, Sis. I've got some things to say to you as well . . . not so important as the matters I plan to discuss with Mother, but some housekeeping, some clean-up. Stay in lockdown. This might be awhile.

He looked the other way. Down the long hall, his door to the left was closed and Mother's door across the way was open, spilling light onto the floor. Straight ahead at the rear, the bathroom door was closed. There was a strip of light under the bottom and faint threads of steam. One of her marvelous marathon showers. One of her shitty contradictions. Buy bulk, no name brands. No frozen pizza, no chips, no Hershey's syrup, no Reese's Pieces. No meat, especially the good stuff like lamb, because they kept the poor things in cages too small, no processed anything, all tasteless. Boycott lettuce picked by abused immigrants, boycott Ben & Jerry's because the products were grown with pesticides, boycott anything to do with animal testing, animal fats, anything red, and while meals turned into a torture of picking at shit, moving it around the plate, and the constant bargaining, Mother the good Samaritan took showers lasting up to forty-five minutes, saying water was the purest thing on earth, straight from nature itself, and she was going to enjoy every last bit of it the way flowers did; flowers and trees and conifers and grasslands, naturally and beautifully, *"no matter how much your father complains about paying the water bill."*

Don't worry, Dad. I got this.

There were two candles burning on the floor in front of the bathroom door. Two slim pillar candles with see-through cylinder vases. For ambiance.

Oh, I got this.

He walked past her room, fists bunched at his sides, neck cords up, jaw hard, and he took a short glance in passing from habit. Her computer was on, strange. She never did that. She was so hype about her precious dissertation, so frightened of losing it or otherwise fucking up the file, that she always saved and shut down. Always.

He veered into her bedroom. Messy and *"strewn,"* that's the way things looked in here. First, there were all the silly stuffed toys, the hand puppets and figurines scattered all over the place, the stepchildren, her token allegiances to Jonathan Swift's fascination with circus freaks, and where there was a sideshow there was a dumpster explosion, and there were clothes on the bed and more bursting out of the closet onto the hardwood floor. They had crawled out of the drawers hanging there, and they were falling over the backs of chairs and her hamper and her footstool and the nesting tables like dead hombres in a bad western. With a small grin, he thought,

*If I were your father . . .*

He looked at the desktop computer. On the screen there was a document that didn't have the block paragraphing of a "research paper." It looked like a story and was titled:

*The Sculptor*
*Manifesto of a Murderer*
*My Partial Confession*

Connor Mullin was no longer smiling. He walked slowly across the room.
He sat down in his mother's writing chair.
And started to speed-read.

# CHAPTER 15
# SORDID CONCLUSIONS

Connor Mullin hadn't moved except to click the mouse. There was a small puddle that had gathered under the chair, he'd seen it out of the corner of his eye spreading right, but it hadn't fully registered. His clothes had stiffened on him—creased, cold dead-weight—but the inner side of his left leg felt warm. In a vague way he knew he'd urinated on himself and from a great distance, it seemed, there was the question of whether any of the piss had made it down to the rainwater on the hardwood, but it was difficult to connect these trivial things.

The world had become this manifesto, this confession . . . this piece of misdirection that was meant to have the police and the Feds spending endless man-hours chasing down a manufactured "criminal" while Professor Becky Mullin sat back in her messy room, in her weirdo house, laughing up her sleeve. It made a sick sort of sense. She had direct, personal access to any number of college coeds through her classes of course, but more importantly, her assigned conferences that started out as teaching functions, all subject/predicate bullshit, but soon turned into her favorite thing, a therapy session in disguise, as these fragile, naïve girls opened up and drew out in detail how they patterned their lives.

*God,* how many times had she rehashed the sob stories, describing the way so many of these freshman girls came to her office early September, gliding in with their short-shorts, tight blouses, perfect hair, and French manicures, all initially presenting themselves with an air of maturity and confidence, yet usually breaking down before the second paragraph of their first compare/contrast essays, spilling about their impossible class schedules, their haphazard study habits, their crazy social calendars, and the hours typically spent in the cafeteria versus the library, the lounge versus the Learning Commons . . . the specific slots they saved for "me-time" and where specifically they crept off to spend it . . . the dorm-visitor restrictions, the way the laundry machines didn't work sometimes and where you had to go to get a load done, and how much they missed their dads and their mommies, and the apple tree out the back window, and their pet cat and their best friend Kristen, or Addy, or Brittany or Elena (pronounced Ellen-ahh), and the way some asshole above them kept dribbling a basketball on the floor at all hours of the night, and that some of the boys were like high school all over again but bolder and drunker and a few of them handsomer, and a crowd of them on floor three had a fight club, and that most other girls could be hysterically funny and then vicious and critical, and we all make brands for ourselves on Instagram, some of them slutty, but what's a girl to do . . . and this is when we tend to sleep in, and this is when we always sneak out, and this is how you trick front-door security, and this is when we go to the bar, and walk the campus alone, and attend frat parties with a rape-buddy we always try to lose after knocking back one or two, and this is my life . . . my crazy, disorganized hissy-fit.

Open books, all of them. And even though Professor Becky Mullin offered what seemed genuine interest, she was merely skimming the chapters, focusing most on those "boring" back pages, the indexes, the blueprints illustrating habits and tendencies.

Most importantly, their timetables.

Simple psychology. Mother was divorced, in some ways bitterly, and she was surrounded at the college by hot young chicks wearing provocative clothing, at least in early fall and starting mid-spring. She carefully determined which she would murder, disfigure, and put up on poles, and just as every fiend had to have a release-valve, she talked often about the various choices at the dinner table, of course out of context, focusing on the idea that it was some sort of grand family lesson that even the pretty girls needed comforting . . . a wonderful consolation prize for her own homely kids in that these gorgeous vixens came to her office and often had a good cry. Her favorite detail about teaching was that she kept a box of Kleenex in her office on her desk and three spares in the drawer.

Scarecrows.

Dolls.

Her tribute to "Swiftian" freakery, all capped off with this false manifesto, ironically filled with far more truths than one would expect, and that is what made it so hideous. She'd used pieces of Meagan in this, the gratuitous and violently "poetic" images that made for good shock-metal videos. Connor himself was represented in terms of the way someone in a position of law enforcement (or security) would think, and also by the mechanical know-how, the trucks, and the technical jargon. There was even some "Dad," in there between the lines with his dry sense of analysis, and so Mother wasn't just a rapist after all. Nor just a thief or even a killer. She was a heinous slaughterer who grafted . . . suturing in her family to make herself into Frankenstein's monster by choice.

She was a jealous fiend in a position of unlikely authority.

She was an author (of sorts) and an editor by trade, using her questionable academic talents in a format that matched up better with her strange creativity. She'd been put on earth to punish these girls, and now she'd created a "murderer" so far from her own profile that law enforcement would literally waste years chasing down empty leads and mistargeted suspects. She'd finally come into her own.

Two questions left.

How did she do the killings, as in, what were the specific mechanics?

And how was she strong enough to actually haul the bodies around, especially after impaling them? She was five foot five and skinny as a straw.

Time to read between the lines. Time to give it a second go-around. This ugly piece of writing was an absolute masterpiece, not Mother's, but Connor's. It was the proof he'd need to bring her in, bring her down. He'd be known for this, renowned even, famous.

He leaned in to the screen.

And felt the hard barrel of a gun pressed to the back of his head.

# CHAPTER 16
# HELLO, IT'S ME

"What have you been writing, Officer Mullin?"

Connor knew the voice, but it was out of place here, couldn't nail it.

"You're awfully wet," she continued. "Where have you been, Officer? No, screw that, let's cut right to the chase. What were you doing out in the graveyard? Story research? Nice manifesto you've been working on. Got some new info to add?"

Connor closed his eyes and then opened them slowly.

"Erika Shoemaker," he said.

"Bingo. You've been a busy little beaver. Who's the guy you're working with? Which one of you rigged the captain's tires to blow when we got just past the high school? Cute trick making us walk across Sproul Road in the rain."

"What guy?"

"Why's the shower running?"

"My mother's in there. This is her computer."

"A bad boy with mommy issues. Fits with the fiction your accomplice is throwing around, but there's always some truth wrapped up in the bullshit, now isn't there?"

"You've got it wrong, Erika."

"You call me Ms. Shoemaker, you rank piece of shit. In fact, call me mister."

"You sound like—"

"Shut up. What's with the candles? You and Mommy have rituals?"

"That's disgusting."

"Snug fit. Wear the shoe."

Connor tried his very best not to sound condescending.

"The danger," he said, "is in the shower. It is clear and it is present and it is my mother that has the explaining to do."

"Oh, that's rich," Erika spat. "You want me to go knock on the door? I'm not leaving your royal presence for a moment. I've got my revolver cocked and ready and I'm not moving. I'm not going to make you stand up or put your hands over your head, no maneuvers, no dancing. In fact, I don't think there's anyone in the bathroom at all. When I first followed you in, the rain let up a minute and I heard the shower. I thought it was you, and I tried to wait you out. I waited and waited and that water's been going for a while now, hasn't it? Looks like you enjoy the sound of it. You put the candles out there, did you? Maybe she's out on a date and you're wishing it was you. Sitting here writing manifestos on her computer. You digging through her underwear drawer too?"

"How would I know which is which? You taken a look around here?"

"I'm not here to look, Officer Mullin. There are experts for that."

"Then what are you here for?"

"To listen."

"To what?"

"You. Read to me, Officer. Read your confession. As I said, I'm not moving this gun from the back of your head and I'm not moving my sightline. We're stuck here and we will be for a while. I'm bored. Read me your manifesto, your big false lead. I want to hear it in your voice."

"I won't."

"Then I'll kill you. If you think I won't you're mistaken. After what I've seen today it wouldn't even be a stretch."

"You're clearly bluffing."

Something slapped onto his forehead. It was her non-shooting hand. Something dark hooked into his vision, and she stuck her fingernail into the bottom of his eye, underneath it, right at the lid-line.

"All right!" he barked. He had brought up his hands to cup over the soft spot, and they were suspended in the air, shaking. She took it out, but not fast enough. He was bleeding or tearing, he couldn't tell which.

"Read," she said.

"Okay, Jeez."

"Talk like a man, Officer Mullin. Own up. This isn't a boy's crime."

"But I didn't—"

"Read."

"But—"

"Read. You dirty, toxic son of a bitch."

Connor cleared his throat.

"Okay," he said weakly. "Here goes."

# CHAPTER 17
# A LOVELY READ

*The Sculptor*
*Manifesto of a Murderer*
*My Partial Confession*

There's mist on the football field.

To the right is the small construction site they fenced off between the Annex and the Writing Center, and there is a mound of brown dirt next to a stationary wet saw and a work station under a canopy.

There's a squirrel skittering along the low branch of a maple with drooping leaves.

Below that, two female professors are having a conversation by the steps that lead to the library. The stocky one is smiling. She has square wire frames, a big nose, a nondescript dress, and thick ankles. She nods in agreement a lot. Her expressions are animated, and it is obvious she has made a name for herself with her verbal ability.

There's an eyelash under my fingernail, and I figure it came from number twelve, because she was a blonde.

I walk over to the guard shack at the far corner of the ROTC dormitory, hit the keypad, and enter. I write on the log that I am on shift, and I take the small radio out of the charger plugged in by the microwave.

"2579842 present," I say.

"Check," comes back through the tinny speaker. I slide the sunglasses off the top of my cap, bring them carefully to my face, and hide my blank expression behind them. A pair of freshmen with a dented steel bucket walk by and purposely look away, as if I don't know that they plan to upkeep the tradition of egg-bombing the nude statue that stands in the fountain between the cafeteria and the Quad. Clever boys, but they've got it all backward. It is not their identities that are important, but rather the fact that part-time security guards wearing aviator sunglasses and blank expressions stay faceless.

I watch.

And no one watches me doing it.

*

If I fall in love with you, I might want to make you immortal.

It's easy to fall in love with a girl, each a storybook graced with God-given introductory pages that are written upon, edited, and rearranged into later chapters of beauty. Their journey is a splendid blur of mascara, lipstick, liner, bows, bands, ringlets, and flips . . . locks tucked thoughtfully behind an ear or hanging loose to the shoulder, freckles, coy grins, sharp cheeks that redden when you cross the line just a bit, and eyes that do that brief sparkling dance if you tell her she's pretty at just the right moment.

And so many flavors!

There are strawberry blondes, and ash blondes, and flaxen, ginger, and honey blondes, there are chestnut brunettes who come off soft, warm, and girly, and those sharp copper redheads who use a lot of rust and green around the eyes for seductive distance and brazen coquettishness. There are jet-black bangs and sable braids, teased up auburn and wet tawny on the beach, there is the willowy girl working the library reference desk that you can't help but envision on the bed in her underwear on a Sunday morning, knees drawn up to her chin and painting her toenails, and the haughty ex-cheerleader you ache to turn into a "good girl" who folds her hands, arches her back, and nods earnestly when you tell her things. There's the long-haired girl with the button nose and big charcoal eyes, and the platinum blonde with the white-rimmed sunglasses and cappuccino tan who was just born to be captured on Fanavision at the ball park.

Delicious.

And let us not let go unmentioned the serious artillery: the pleated skirts, the jean shorts, the low-cut blouses with silky folds and buttons unfastened, the black thong-straps positioned above the low waistlines of tight hip-huggers, and the long sleeves tight to the arm and extended to the middle of the palm. And, of course, there are the legs, the long legs with that vertical line accenting the thigh, the muscular legs that make you believe you could fuck like some spectacular athlete, the smooth legs you are dying to run your fingers across like exotic glass, and those legs the lightest blondes let go unshaven, making you swell inside because it's just so darned personal somehow.

Still, this is all window-dressing. No matter how the given female has prettied up the package or grown into her curves and lines, it is her innocence that finally draws us. She can be knowing and closed and clever and calloused, but in the end she wants to let her eyes soften and melt into yours. It is unavoidable. Women are the warmth of the world.

And I am their sculptor.

*

There's a steady rain drumming along the roof of the truck.

I own my own side business called *Pressure Washing and Steam Cleaner's Inc.* It is a bland name, an industrial, faceless label, and my truck is an old mid-sized moving truck I bought at auction, sandblasted, and repainted this old battleship gray. I have a twelve-foot ladder lashed down to the roof with bungee cords, but the ladder is for show. So is the truck. While there is indeed a pressure washer back there in the trailer, and an Emglo compressor to power it, there are no steamers, no wet/dry vacuums, no spare hoses, no replacement filters, no detergents, no pickle barrels filled with rags, old leather tool belts and power drills, no miscellaneous fasteners, no brooms, and no squeegees and mops for the run-off.

Just one cold box eight feet long by thirty-six inches high held down by yellow polyester ratchet straps, one power washer tied down in the back-right corner next to the compressor, and a fifty-foot length of heavy gauge extension cord. I don't need anything else, because I only have one customer. The local supermarket. Every two weeks or so I power-wash the wall on either side of the pharmacy dumpster, and of course I do it for free. What else would they expect from a faithful part-time employee who moonlights as a college security guard on his off-days? Gosh. Someday regional might even grant me overtime, or even holiday hours in return for the favor!

I park, adjust my name tag, exit the truck, and turn up my collar. The door squawks when I slam it shut, and for the millionth time I wish I could operate out of a van. But vans and mid-sized Penske movers and U-Haul units are designed for homeowners who don't like using high ramps. I need fifty-two inches from wheel's bottom to deck, just like a sixteen-wheeler.

That way I can access the loading dock.

My title at the supermarket is officially a "Closer," a part-time, intermediary evening manager, who comes in at 8:00 P.M. to break down the product stacked and shrink-wrapped in the back-room storage area across from the three trailer bays. Then I wheel the grocery and non-food items on U-frames out onto the floor and into the appropriate aisles. At midnight, when the store officially closes to the public, I am alone, doubling as the stand-in Night Time Crew Chief, since my boss is out on disability. Lots of packing-out for one guy, and some would complain about being the lead player in this one-man circus.

Not I.

When the clock strikes twelve, I can finally go to receiving, cut the red plastic tie, and yank the chain hand over hand to crank up the ribbed steel garage door. There is a sheet on a clipboard hanging on a hook, and I will jot down the date and time that I broke the seal, writing in the "Reason" space, *Freezer maintenance.* Not that it really matters. I could write *Check,* or *Police dock area,* or *Verify timed lighting*, and no one would ever read it or care. The clipboard sheets are fail-safes to match up with the seal numbers in case anything is stolen.

But I'm not taking anything out of the supermarket tonight.

I'm bringing something in.

*

Cold box.

A flat-top freezer on rollers, eight feet long, three feet high, sometimes adorned with two sliding glass doors as cover panels, other times left bare and open-port. There are three freezer tubs outside on the dock apron that have gone down. They have required a tune-up for a week or so now, and I am always the first line of defense upper management "puts right on it," before they call in Redco with a real work order.

I bought my own freezer last year from an Acme that went out of business in a suburban location seventy miles west of here, and my new used cold box looks exactly like the cold boxes out on the dock apron and the seventeen others positioned all through the store. There are twenty-three surveillance cameras on premises, yet there is only one camera that covers the loading dock area, set outside above the bay door and facing the woods behind the property. The apron yawns thirty-two feet off to the right, like a big lip hugging the wall. The dock is accessible to trucks at its far-right edge, so the camera records what goes in and out of receiving, but cut from view are the trucks themselves, let alone the three or four odd freezer units lined up at the far edge waiting for a tune-up.

When I go out, get my truck, back it in, and finally roll my personal freezer unit from the back bed and out across the apron, it will look as if I am bringing in one originally from the dock area. I have covered the top with a black cloth, since the grainy recording from the surveillance camera will simply make it look as if the shadows are playing across an empty cavity.

Not empty.

I move out to make my way to the employee parking area. Moments later, I am thankful that the security camera doesn't have sound, because the dock plate I left outside makes a sharp clanging when I drop it down between the dock bumpers and the rear side of the truck that I just backed in. It's dark inside my rig, and I undo the straps, feel my way to the back of her, and give a push, walking her out of the truck and back across the dock lip.

Once I am in, I pull down the bay door, shut the padlock, and tie on a new red seal to it. I bend back down and push my cold box past the receiving shack, and through the red swinging doors of the meat room. It's cold, and that's good. It feels like work, like good work, like solid work, the type that grounds you. I put on a smock. I put on my goggles.

It's time to make a new doll.

*

Stainless steel work tables and cutting boards five inches thick. Sharpeners and scales and the auto feed mixer/grinder, and the poultry cutter and the patty former and the packaging unit that's always running out of plastic.

And of course, there's the industrial meat saw. I love the hulking, off-silver thing. Looks like something that came from a collector's basement, and I am attracted to the *nostalgia* of it, the way that every time I see it, that song in every grandmother's favorite musical comes to mind: *"Let's start at the very beginning. A very fine place to start."*

Industrial meat saw.

To the eye of the amateur it could go in any metal shop and stand in as a stationary band saw. And while I certainly do appreciate the throwback look, the ripping blade scrolled onto it and the song in my head, I am just as thankful for the floor beneath it, all smooth red brick with a drain twenty feet long down center, rectangular grates, and seven-inch cork inlay surrounding it. After the work is done tonight, after I wipe my brow with a sterile cloth and soak the trade materials in my triple sink arrangement (clean, rinse, sanitize), after I fill the gun reservoir with concentrated industrial acid cleanser so strong it dissolves hair build-up in zoo animal cages, and after I blast the machines and blitz that smooth floor-brick with the wall mounted, gooseneck pressure sprayer, and finally squeegee the waste to the floor drains, I will have long removed any traces of DNA that might have been hanging around. Board of Health wouldn't have it any other way.

Meat saw.

I adjust the upper guard to accept stock up to nine inches. Overkill, I admit. Her throat is barely six inches in diameter, poor skinny thing, but I wouldn't want her to catch and snag. It is a real pain in the ass to have her by the waist and the hair, and get stuck in this preliminary, crude pass. Once it bucked the blade and caught up on her cheek. Yes. Number three, my only miscarriage.

I lean down and peel off the dark cloth.

Her name is Melissa. Lucky number thirteen. I haul her out, and she almost slips through my arms because I had her oiled and surrounded by forty-five Igloo Maxcold ice cooler bars. I adjust and walk her over to the saw, King Lear carrying Cordelia.

After I remove her head, I am going to eat her eyes. It is ritual. I don't particularly enjoy it, but certain obligations must be fulfilled; windows to the soul preserved. Feels right, like a hard lesson. Like morals. For the removal of these precious orbs I am going to try using the three-and-a-quarter-inch boning blade tonight, even though it will be like surgery under a rock. The serrated spoon doesn't really cut worth a damn, and it's annoying to get the remains of the extra ocular muscles caught between your teeth with no chance to floss right away.

Yes, there's a pop and burst, like a cherry tomato. No, it doesn't taste like chicken. Yes, I am careful when I do this because it's really gross if it flies out of your mouth and you have to eat it off the floor.

*

Now, with the preliminaries done, it is time for creation. It was a clean cut, no danglers, and the headpiece is up on the table. I have arranged my cutting tools biggest to smallest, and in three groups—Breaking and Skinning, Lance and Fillet, and Carving and Slicing—and I bring her head before me to move the damp hair off her lovely face. I tie it back in a ponytail for her, this long, loose, curly redwood perm with gold sunset highlights. The cavities where her eyes were seated stare out in pure, childlike wonder. She has straight teeth, sharp cheekbones, and featherings of wine-blush to accent them. Beautiful.

I reach for my first instruments and hold them over her for a moment, poised, ready, teetering on the brink of it. In my right hand I have the ten-inch breaking knife curved up like the weapon of some oily thief in a third-world desert marketplace, and in my left I hold the five-inch skinning blade, angled slightly, picking up gleam. A conductor about to start his symphony. The painter standing ready with two brushes instead of just one.

I lean in and set to work.

And the colors are spectacular.

*

I attended art school back in the day and studied Pointillism: small distinct dots applied in patterns that form images best seen from varied distances. Georges Seurat developed the technique in 1886, a branch-off of Impressionism, and it was quite popular until computer animation made it all rather obsolete. I suppose the most practical example of the thing nowadays is newspaper print, the dinosaur that can't be killed, but what has been lost in modern artistic relevance has been revived through metaphor.

We are too close up to our world nowadays to really "see" anything. Existence has become so ultimately accessible through virtual search engines that we have become a generation addicted to freeze-frames and short climaxes. We are egotistical self-hunters, obsessed with admiring the heads on the wall, our lives no more than the blur we ignore between texts and Facebook postings and shock-clips on YouTube. We have become background to our own theatrical presentations. Lifetime scrapbookers.

Time for some distance. Some breadth. Some perspective. Some awareness throughout the routine between poses.

Some wow down in the trenches.

*

There are gulls in a V formation, flying toward the promise of morning sun still hiding behind the horizon, the mountain tunnel, and the power station.

If I was pulled over and the trailer was searched right now, the given officer would find a very dead girl named Melissa Baumgardner lying rigidly in my used cold box, her face rearranged in what would seem random cuts, gouges, and ribbons, head clearly removed then sewn crudely back on, a thick wooden dowel lovingly inserted so far up her rectum that our good officer would be able to see the business end of it in the back of her throat if he or she took the time to force open her jaws.

Actually, the dowel is one of those antiquated window poles that janitors at my local elementary school found in the basement and threw out last month. And the cuts, gouges, and ribbons, the lacerations and the gradations I could only get right by wheeling in a deli meat slicer and making five passes, the second set of eye craters, the back-up nose hole and twin mouth-orifice I dug out of her left temple, cheek, and jawbone, all that would seem the grisly work of a madman.

But I am not interested in the view of the officer, nor in the report of some criminal psychologist. I know very well what I am.

I am an educated man who holds menial jobs like the rest of us caught up in this thinly disguised middle-class recession . . . a creator, a messenger aiming his craft at your transitions, the times between movie shorts, the dead minutes that are the real moments of your lives: the trips to the bathroom, the times you make breakfast and fill out the Post-It Notes to stick on the fridge, the moments at work when you look at the clock, those stretches in the car when you drive between "meaningful" destinations.

I have mastered Pointillism, an art that can only be properly registered from a distance, and the cuts and gouges on Melissa's face are anything but random.

Today I am going to use this abandoned jobsite that has a dozer, a gargantuan pile of gray crushed stone, a walk-behind saw, and a crane. I am going to park my rig as if I belong here, walk around the truck wearing my hard hat and safety vest like a veteran, haul out my masterpiece, and mount the end of the smooth stake I impaled her with into the unmarked flagpole base I stole from the ROTC storage garage back at school. It's a *Wizard of Oz* moment, yet a haunted one, because Melissa isn't a scarecrow (as the public would call her) with hay sticking out of her neck and a goofy smile cut through the burlap, but she is rather a blurry, bloody form under plastic.

I untie the bottom. I look both ways and see that the highway is momentarily clear. I reach up and unveil her.

I don't hesitate even for that last hungry, parting glance reserved for maestros and lovers. I put my head down, get back in my truck, and haul my ass out of there. The sun is about to break over the horizon.

According to the traffic patterns I studied, most vehicles frequent this stretch of road between 5:28 and 7:40 A.M. Early risers. Go-getters. My work will have left its mark long before this. I drive off at 4:55 A.M., and just as I round the curve that changes the sightline three hundred yards up, I look in my rearview and see headlights.

I smile.

My first customer!

According to what I have heard on the news, there will be an average of two hundred witnesses before rush hour, and around a hundred and fifty more before the police can make it out to the crime scene and take her down. The latter observers will just see a horribly scarred victim hanging limp on a pole, yet they are not my concern. It is the former, the virgins, the ones who speed by before traffic comes to a standstill, the early birds listening to their favorite radio stations, caught in the soundtracks of their lives, not thinking, not living, not really looking at the road before them because it has been memorized and placed into some fuzzy, collective background as they zone into the comfortable fabric of their respective transitions.

At a pass of fifty-five miles per hour, Melissa will offer a coy smile and mouth the words "love you" . . . her image in the rearview—a scarlet seductress fluttering off a series of winks, puckers, and kisses. At sixty-three miles per hour, she will crease her forehead, and then air-whisper the phrase "To arms!" to the receding image in the side-mirror—a crimson Native American princess, striped with war paint, shouting after you in a wide-mouthed cry of betrayal. And at anything over seventy-two, she becomes the red mask of terror, face rippling with G-forces, head slowly turning with you as you fly by, black eyes going from half-lidded semi-slumber to widened awareness, lips forming the words "mine forever," the image dwindling in the glass—a petrified witch-queen, lips raised up and curdling.

Rest assured that each time I have left a doll, I have hit the next exit, circled back, and tried to film her on my cell phone in passing. No go. Thankfully, there is something about the craft that makes it camera shy. Even the steadiest hand yields nothing but muddy blurs of gore. Know that my art is pure, and that on some level religion is probably involved.

My girls are fashioned for bald observation, to form ghosts in the mind, phantoms guaranteed to wander through your dreams and appear sporadically in the fabric of your everyday routine as empirical memory. The real stuff. No instant replay, no secondary sources. Transitions become important again, and there is something to talk about. The scrapbooking, at least for a moment, takes second fiddle to a reality played out in real time.

Fear.

Live.

It is really a simple equation.

*

A cluster of pigeons flap into the air and then settle back down around the green monument modeled after some Age of Enlightenment guy with a powdered wig, stern eyes, flaring nostrils, and a long furling coat.

There is a brook and a walking bridge. There is a war memorial surrounded by decorator spruces and a garden with a fountain. Across the park due north, a larger cobblestone avenue stretches uphill to the law library, the amphitheater, and the bell tower. To the right, the park is bordered by 5th Avenue, which features a number of red brick buildings making up the University Health Center and a line of light poles, each bearing the school flag. This is a huge urban university, population more than thirty thousand, and their football team actually played a bowl game on ESPN last year.

It is my day off, and I am sitting on a park bench at the edge of the walkway. A male jogger goes by, and three janitors cross from the other direction, one of them pushing a gray cart with a bunch of spray bottles and an eighteen-inch floor broom sticking up out of the deep corner well. I see a security guard drive by on a ten-speed, and I note that like all the officers on foot I have observed, he wears a gray button-down jersey made by the same company that manufactures the three hanging in my closet at home. Of course, the circular shoulder patch is different, but I can buy a duplicate in their university bookstore's sports and decal section, then simply sew SECURITY in silver stitching along the bottom curve below the icon. The bike rider is the thirty-first security guard I've noticed on campus, and I walked it for a mere twenty minutes before sitting on this bench and watching the pigeons. Clearly the philosophy here is to flood the territory, create a uniformed presence, and it is likely that most don't know each other, especially the ones working the different eight-hour shifts. Finding the seam in those shifts and walking the shadows as "one of them" will be child's play, striding cap-brim down with "casual fatigue" beside my ten-speed, unmounted, as if my shift just recently ended. No questions, no worries.

And beneath the brim of my cap I'll be watching.

This is a perfect hunting ground: lots of trees and alleys and side streets and lots, construction areas with dark walkways bordered with tarps and scaffolding, and subway tunnels connected by poorly lit entrance stairways. This is a teeming labyrinth of lecture halls and cafeterias and auditoriums and apartments, all with easy access if you're smart enough to know where to find the service entrances. It is as easy as walking your ten-speed, identifying the blind spots between cameras, choosing your mark, and learning her come-and-go.

It is the top of the hour, and the park fills up with students. There is an Asian girl walking next to a tall nerdy guy with wild curly hair, a long neck, and spooned-out monkey ears. He is a disaster and she appears not to notice, nodding in quiet support of his exaggerated exclamations, and yielding shy smiles when he clearly jokes poorly. She has straight black hair tied back with a thin green ribbon that matches her eye shadow, and she wears a black skirt. Slim hips. No backpack; she hugs her books in front of her chest. She has on black tights, and her legs are thin, toned, and strong. She walks like a dancer. They are five feet from me now, and he hits a home run: blurts something relatively clever, and she leans in toward him, turns up her face, surrenders a genuine smile that reaches her eyes, then the sun, the whole world.

I die a little inside and fall head over heels in love with the girl. I want to know her, comfort her, and find out her dreams and how she feels about her father. I want to caress her cheek with the back of my knuckle and hold her in front of a hearth fire.

I want to make her immortal.

*

Often when I am in the Target looking for cheap sweaters, or on the third floor of Macy's checking out coffee makers, or at Staples trying to find the right printer cartridge, people stop me and ask if I work there. I smile and gently admit I do not. Then they forget me. I am someone and I am everyone. I am the clerk at the service desk, the guy in the blue jumpsuit checking under the hood, the one who cuts your spare key at the hardware store, the man stocking shelves at Home Depot. You give me access to the pipes down in the basement and always let me in to read the water meter. I run your credit card at the rental place, check your coat in the lobby, and bring up room service.

And you never bother to notice me.

# CHAPTER 18
## DOOR #1

Connor Mullin fell as silent as the grave. The manifesto was worse in his voice, far worse, and he was sure that Erika Shoemaker was going to shoot him right there in cold blood. He wondered if he'd retain consciousness just long enough to see the blood burst onto the computer screen. There would be meat in it. Red runners. It would make for a fine coda, nice gift wrapping.

"Erika," someone said.

She hitched—thank God she didn't pull the damned trigger.

"Captain!" Connor said.

"Don't listen to him," Erika said.

"I'm innocent."

"He's not."

"Quiet, the both of you," Canfield said from the doorway. "Erika, keep your revolver right where it is. Don't take your eye off him. Who's in the shower?"

"No one," Erika said.

"My mother," Connor said. "Captain, please let me explain. Tell Ms. Shoemaker to let me turn at least halfway around so we can have eye to eye, you'll see it in my face, I swear."

"Quiet, son. Erika, why did you not check the bathroom?"

"Working on keeping my revolver right where it is and keeping my eye trained. Talk about quiet—"

"Sorry, stocking feet just like you. Officer Mullin, where is your firearm?"

"Captain, I assure you—"

"You are not in a position to assure me of anything. Where is your firearm?"

"Bed across the hall. Slung over the bottom post, right side, in a Cheyenne holster with a long leather belly band."

"Why am I not surprised?" Erika muttered. Canfield moved his heavy frame out of the room and returned quickly.

"Holster's empty," he said.

"Interesting," Erika said. "But you're going to be more interested in what our boy has been writing on the computer."

"Maybe and maybe not," Canfield said. "Where's your gun, Officer Mullin?"

"I don't know."

"You dump it somewhere in the graveyard?"

"No."

"You're soaking wet."

"I was caught out on the highway."

"There are soil marks on your pants cuffs."

"There was erosion on the roadside, 476."

"Your hand is bleeding."

"I was bumping it along the iron posts, got a splinter."

"Graveyard iron, putting you at the scene. I thought you were out on 476."

"I was. I got thrown out of an Uber by Finch and Cabrera."

"They'll corroborate that?"

Connor paused.

"Probably not," he admitted. "But there's a trucker. His rig is in the parking lot by the chapel. He's the one who picked me up, just go ask him."

"Yes, convenient," Canfield said. "I saw it on my way in just as you saw it on your way out. Probably gone by now."

"Captain," Connor said, "my mother is the Scarecrow Killer. She calls herself 'The Sculptor,' and the proof is right here on the screen. I can explain every nuance, every fabrication, every angle she took to create this red herring. I've got the inside line. I know how she thinks."

"Good," Canfield said. Connor sensed him approaching and felt Erika move right, making room. Canfield's big hand was on his shoulder. "Get up, son. Hands to the thighs, push, and stand still as a stone for me. Then I'll guide you around. Let's go out into the hall, just the three of us. Nice and easy. Then, like a good boy, you'll knock on that bathroom door for us."

"She's probably listening on the other side at this point, Captain."

"Really."

"She's not stupid. Who do you think has my service revolver?"

"I'll take that chance. You'll make a good human shield. Up."

Connor pushed up as he'd been told. Now there were two gun barrels pressed to his head, Erika's more centered and Canfield's smaller one dug in under his left earlobe. Connor winced. Canfield moved him, and it was an awkward dog and pony show, the three of them moving out into the hall.

It was colder out here, almost drafty. The candles made the shadows jump up the walls. Perfect context, due left, the trim around the linen closet was riddled with cracked paint as was that of the bathroom straight on, and there was steam misting through the slit at the bottom of the door like tendrils of vine, snaking, disappearing.

They moved it forward.

Up close, the shower sounded like the roar of a waterfall.

"Open it," Canfield said. "Slow and steady, please."

Connor reached for the knob. Of course, the second Mother saw it move, locked or not, she'd know her adversary was positioned directly on the other side of this cheap bathroom door, hollow core, wood façade, nothing but thin slats on two sides with perforated cardboard or plastic between. Connor's pistol would put a smoking hole through both panels as easily as it would his stomach, intestines, and spine. And BTW, human shield, hell, both Canfield and Shoemaker had conveniently moved to the sides a crucial couple of inches.

He was alone here, hung out to dry.

He could picture Mother on the other side of that door in her off-white terry velour bathrobe, sweat beaded along her narrow forehead, gun centered, hard smile carved up the side of her face. She'd left that manifesto for Connor to find . . . to make him either a partner or a patsy, maybe even a silent, inactive co-conspirator who could use his position on the force to help her tie up loose ends.

So why the candles?

To remind Connor of his own weakness and femininity.

Why not just ask for his help outright?

Because it was more effective to measure his loyalty this way, better than a "therapy session," where he'd have been aware of how effortlessly she could twist him. This was pure. And for her, better sport. If he knocked softly on the door, she'd have known he was in the fold. If he tried to break it down, she'd have been waiting.

Now it was an even easier determination for her. He had guests.

Connor turned his hand, the knob turned, the door was not locked. Connor pushed.

And everything inside went red, raining blood.

# CHAPTER 19
# NOW YOU SEE ME

Captain Canfield stared into the bathtub over Connor's shoulder and recognized a number of things simultaneously. First, glaring before them with the curtain drawn back was a replica, or better, some sort of footage of the dead body he'd found in the open grave back at Saint Mary's, down a short slope and fifteen feet right of Cindy Chen's desecrated resting place. He had lowered himself into the deep cavity. He had briefly searched the victim, no identification, but he'd guessed she lived here at the Elderberry Street address that they'd decided Erika would cover initially.

Here, the representation of the dead body was tinged red, making the image look like the projection was doused in blood. The shower was superimposed as the rainfall in a deluge of crimson droplets that cauliflowered and disintegrated across her proportions. When he'd discovered her folded over like this in the wet graveyard cavity, he hadn't noticed any cameras, too dark, and it wasn't going to be any easier finding the projection device in here, at least not primarily. Similar to the image the killer had put in Canfield's broken window back home, this felt like looking straight into a laser.

He squeezed shut his eyes instinctively, the neon-red afterimage searing and stinging, and something shoved between himself and Erika, all shoulders and elbows.

"Hold!" he shouted. It was both an order to Erika not to shoot blind, and to his junior officer not to make a run for it. Erika obeyed. Connor did not. No surprise; Canfield would have probably done the same thing if accused of killing a woman, dumping her in a hole, and literally wearing the trace evidence indicating that he ditched the weapon somewhere in the cluttered cemetery ground-soil.

The surprise was the kid's exclamation.

The woman in the grave and projected here in red-negative was Connor's mother; Canfield would have bet his life on it. When he'd found her there, he'd noted that she was middle-aged, and the yellow rain slicker with the flower patterns on it had looked like something only a Boomer would wear.

But on his way shoving past, the kid hadn't said "Mom."

On his way pushing past, he'd said . . .

# CHAPTER 20
# NOW YOU DON'T

"Sis."

All three of them had been temporarily blinded, but Canfield was fairly certain "Sis's" room was the one straight back down the hall opposite the bathroom. On the way in he had noted the window out front with the lamp on behind the curtain. The window had been cracked open at the bottom, and beneath was a trellis covered with ivy. The killer had told them a teen was involved, and so . . . enter "Sis." Was she still in her room? Maybe. Teens were reclusive. Maybe she hadn't heard them all this time. Maybe she had heard them and had climbed down the trellis. Maybe she'd climbed down the trellis far earlier in the evening and knew something about the body in the grave.

Connor's feet pounded down the stairs with the confidence of someone who not only knew the layout of his own house with his eyes closed, but who had guessed that "Sis" was somewhere out in the storm. That, or it was a straight escape having nothing to do with her, it didn't matter. Instinctively, Canfield reached out for the wall to get his bearings, and from above there was a creak and a snap, like a foot coming through a floorboard or more like a trapdoor opening.

Something fell on them, multiple things, a downpour of what felt like beanbags with edging, brittle and spinous. He put his hands up over his head and heard Erika scream. There was a stench difficult to identify—moth-dust, petrified paper product, some kind of dry rot—and whatever it was, it fell around them like a dust storm, covering their feet, rising up to the shin.

Canfield took a step and felt another dichotomous sensation, things squelching and simultaneously piercing.

Bones. Quills and shafts.

They were dead birds.

Erika was moving off and screaming in pain, disgust, fear, did it matter? Canfield switched gun hands and reached out for her. Luckily, he got fabric. He pulled, it stretched, she lashed out, he felt her hand breeze by his face.

The front door opened downstairs, and the sound of rain swelled in through the foyer.

"Erika," Canfield said, eyes still squeezed shut. He got his other arm around her. "Stop, Erika. No."

"We've got to chase that fucker down!" she rasped.

"No," he said, pulling her close. "Let him go."

"What?"

"It's enough," Canfield said. "Enough of the games, enough taking the bait."

He felt her breathe.

"Enough," he said softly. "Just hold. We've been reacting predictably, first going by the book, then buying into the con, the ultimatums, falling for the threats and the sound effects. No more. Just. Hold."

He held her. She breathed hard into the hollow of his shoulder and steadied.

"This is what we are *not* going to do," he continued. "We are not running out into the rain as the killer has predicted we will. We're going to wait until this red glare works off our eyes. We're going to wade through the offal at our feet and inspect the room down the hall there to see if Connor's sister is hiding under her bed or inside her closet. Then we're going to search the whole premises to make sure there isn't a terrified teenage girl trying to crawl into the darkest corner."

"What if she was the one who took the gun from her brother's holster?"

"There are a million possible avenues, Erika, but we need to stop leaping."

She pulled away to arm's length, but they both still kept their arms around each other. He let his eyes open, then closed them, opening again and letting them flutter. The red afterimage was passing, more dull traces now. Erika was doing the same. She had a couple of feathers in her hair. There was a scratch on her forehead, and she looked very pale.

"Only one of the 'guaranteed three' are dead that we know of," she said, "if that red thing in the tub is the first casualty. We haven't even been introduced to all four players at this point, and we can never assume the alleged fatalities might not have been prevented if we followed Connor Mullin into the night. Not to mention the one in that group who wasn't necessarily 'doomed' if our intervention was, in fact, successful. We go off script, we'll never know."

"Then we'll never know. You've got to release yourself from that liability."

She stared up into his eyes a long moment. Easier said than done, he knew. He glanced past her at the carrion on the floor.

"Careful skating through here," he said, though he didn't really have to. Now that they could see, it was obvious. The dead fowl around their feet were mostly what appeared to be black birds and barn swallows, and they had been primed to injure them when they ran after Connor. Not only were they dead, but they'd all been wrenched like dishrags, making the fragile bone-work poke through. Canfield didn't know if he was more enraged at the cruelty or amazed at the depth of planning going all the way back to the taps on his front door that left them shoeless from the get-go. Even the candles had multiple meanings and purposes. Both were buried to the rim, both standing, one burning, one not. Canfield smiled thinly. If either of the canisters had kicked over causing a fire, his first instinct would have been to stamp out the flames.

Down the shadowed hall, the dead birds looked like small-scale heaps of landfill, the bones, wings, and tailfeathers protruding like fractured Chinese architecture. Sado-art at its finest. He hoped Erika wasn't looking at this with such depth, noting the killer's meticulous and multi-leveled superiority, but he knew she probably was anyway.

"Game's over," he said evenly. "We're staying put even if there's a new ultimatum. We are going to take apart the mousetrap, right here, nice and slow."

He released Erika and started to move carefully through the birds.

"Where are you going?" she said.

"First things first . . ."

He got back to Becky Mullin's bedroom, pushed in, and immediately went for the Panasonic cordless phone sitting in the charger by the printer. He lifted it out, hit "Talk," and got nothing. Expected. He put it back in its cradle.

"The closer neighbor is on the other side of the hedge to our left," he said, pawing around the clutter on the desk for a cell phone, hoping to get lucky. "Together, you and I are going to walk over there and ask to use their phone so I can get everyone on the force reeled back in from the goose chase. I'll call the Broomall station and request a team to help us in here and out at the gravesite. Their territory. Our people will assist, and I'll send a crew of ours to my place for immediate processing. Eventually I'd like to know how that 'Robinson' character delivered an unstamped letter to your in-bin in a restricted area, especially if it turns out that Connor Mullin wasn't involved, but I'll take what I can get when I can get it. For now, we bring in the cavalry."

"But Captain," she said, "if it isn't Mullin, the accomplice could be part of that very same cavalry."

"Noted," he said, "but an assigned team makes everyone the other's watchdog, at least for the operations tonight. I'm stopping this now, putting it all in plain sight."

"You call the station, Captain, and everybody dies."

Canfield turned. Erika looked frail in the archway. She shivered. If he'd had the time, he would have taught her the SUL safety muzzle positioning, but at least she was pointing her weapon at the floor. She shrugged rather helplessly.

"He said he'd wipe out the whole force, Captain. Blood on the windshields and body parts in the storm drains."

"Yes," Canfield said, "I heard him loud and clear, Erika, but he's an unreliable source. He admittedly lies about lying . . . and what real evidence have we seen of his ability or willingness to do real violence? There is a woman who may have been killed by her own son, he who may be involved with this, maybe not, and there has been nothing else to go on except laser-pictures, fake torture, falling birds, and false history. Seems we have a domestic tragedy on our hands and nothing else but a whole lot of theater."

"That torture video looked pretty real."

"Looked, yes."

"Those bombs set under the squad cars outside my apartment were legitimate."

"And un-detonated."

"There are a lot of people on the force, Captain. If you go this route, there's astronomical potential for catastrophic 'liability,' to use your own word."

"Yes," he said. "And it's all a bluff. A damned good one, too."

He approached the computer area.

"So no more games, no more horror stories."

He went down to his knees and crawled under the desk. Modem, wires, power strip, dust. He reached in and snapped off the switch, making everything around him go dim for all but the pale glow of the overhead.

He stayed there on all fours, waiting.

Nothing. No television flipping on, no amplified voiceovers. Maybe he'd one-upped this son of a bitch. Maybe not, but he had to stick to the plan now.

If the phone came back on and rang, he wouldn't answer. He would not let himself be compelled. He had command now, a position, something with a definitive perimeter. In effect, he had put the lights on in the funhouse, and all the jack-in-the-box puppets were sprung and bobbing loose on their springs.

He backed out from under the desk.

And Erika was no longer standing there in the doorway.

# CHAPTER 21
# WILLFUL PARASITE

Meagan felt the car come to a halt, and when the engine cut off she willed herself to keep breathing regularly. She'd planned this. If she held it and he unwittingly outlasted her, maybe checking his phone or looking for something in the glove box, her pent-up breath could burst out too hard. Soft and even, girl. Easy-breezy, rainbows and ice cream.

He talked to himself while he drove. He farted too, twice actually, and the second one had been a lingerer. Given that her head was positioned a mere inch behind his seat cushion, she'd almost retched, but it was the mumbling that really creeped her to the core. It was her name. In his mouth. Muttered over and over in that gravelly voice, calling her a *"dumb bitch"* and a *"poor kid,"* a *"hypnotized weasel"* and *"stinking dead meat."*

She had no doubt that he'd meant to rape her, and the quick glimpse she'd gotten of him loping across the parking lot had filled her with such disgust she thought she might vomit. He was this forty-something fatso-walrus in a drenched yellow T-shirt and oversized jeans too short up the ankle. He was the type that wore a polyester vest and pushed a broom at the mall, leering at you while you window-shopped . . . the greasy cook who pushed out through the red swinging doors to watch you head past toward the bathroom . . . the old-timer at the CVS eyeballing you over his half-rimmed granny specs when you reached up for the top shelf in the vitamin section.

Of course, any girl in her right mind would have run home and run home fast when he followed the truck to the other side of the graveyard. He'd done it to make her think he was her shining knight who'd chased off the bad man, coming back soon to gallantly help her out of the grave. It was a textbook kidnap-rape-and-dismember scheme . . . an absolute no-brainer.

But he'd made her kill her own mother. And he was going to pay.

When she'd pulled the trigger in the pitch-dark grave minutes before, there was a short report and a millisecond of muzzle-flash. The person coming at her had looked hawklike and hooded, similar in a way to the skull icon erected for her in pixels coming from her cell phone. She'd shot her mystery man, she was sure. He thudded dully against the far dirt wall, and for a moment Meagan had stood there shuddering in the dark. Then, her mother's voice:

"Sunflower . . ."

A trick. No fucking way.

"Mother?"

"Please, dear . . ."

Meagan dropped the revolver. It was a dream, a pitch-dark dream, and a whine was building up in her nose, and she waved her hands in front of herself, hard as if she had eaten something too hot.

"Move the plywood," Mother said wretchedly. "I want to look at your beautiful face."

Meagan started to cry.

"Don't," Mother said. "No time."

Meagan sucked in her lip, but it popped back out again, quivering. She was moaning, wringing her hands. She turned toward the near wall of dirt, shuddering. She breathed, summoned her courage, tilted up her face, and reached above her head as her mother had told her to do. She went up on her toes and slapped up at the barrier. It jumped and moved a few inches. She stretched more carefully and scraped it over the best that she could. The moon poured in with the rain. The plywood was halfway off. She turned back, and sticking out just past the shadow-mark she saw her mother's Ugg boots, her muddy calves, and the edge of her raincoat.

In a rush, Meagan fell to her knees and reached into the shadows, pulling her mother to her, putting her face inside the slicker-hood so they could be cheek to cheek.

"Why?" she said. "Why did you follow me, Mother?"

"I've done it before," she gasped, "so many times. I know about the trellis and the hole under the gate and your special place. I was worried about you. I had a feeling you'd fallen into a relationship with an older man, and I wanted to protect you. I didn't want you to know that I knew, so I put on the shower and put candles in front of the door so you'd think I was occupied if you got home first. Then I came here and saw the gifts on the hill. I was terrified, mystified that I'd arrived before you, so I found this grave and I hid in it, listening in. I'm so very sorry."

"No, I—"

"No nothing, Sunflower. I don't blame you, don't ever think that."

"But—"

"No time!"

Meagan bit her tongue. It hit her, really hit her, that these could be her mother's last words. This wasn't happening. It couldn't be.

"My darling," her mother continued. "On my computer . . ." She gasped for breath and swallowed heartily. "On my computer there is a document. I never hit 'Send.' You must go back and hit that button."

"What, Mother? Why?"

"It's what I went to your room initially to tell you. I wrote something, for a publisher, for money, and I never wrote so quickly and effectively. I finished an entire chapter, final draft, in record time because I was born for it. I wanted to show you before sending it off. I wanted to share it with you, maybe work on the future chapters together, talk about it, connect, really connect. Don't you see, Sunflower? It was a horror chapter, like your music, your imagination, your artistic sort of worldview come alive in a burst of dark beauty . . . what you've been trying to translate to me for years. It was to be our binding tie. Read it. Send it. There won't be a book now, but I want the publisher to see it."

"Why?"

"Maybe they'll release it on its own."

"What's the difference to me, if you're gone?"

"You'll see it in print, real print, not just a Word file . . . not just something your mother wrote for a handful of academics, but something real, something relatable, something for us, for everyone, for the soul, for the world."

"Mother, please."

"You'll see it, Sunflower . . . you'll see that something I wrote made a difference."

Meagan looked upward for a moment and let the dark rain bounce off her face.

"Yes, Mother," she managed.

"Good. Then there are three things you need to do, please."

"Yes, Mother?"

"Get your cell phone and—"

"I left it on my night stand."

"Then go right home and call the police. Tell them of the man who caused all this. Next, go to my room and hit 'Send.' Third, but really first, let me be the root for you to grow in the hollow."

"Wait Mother, please," Meagan said. "What does that mean specifically?"

"Can't you let me be poetic if even for a moment?"

"No! Christ, Mother!"

"But it's vulgar."

"Mother!"

"All right! I'm the root, you're the flower. You're not tall enough to get out of this pit, so use my body as a stepping stool."

"Yes, Mother," Meagan whispered.

It was the last thing they said to each other. Becky Mullin went slack in her arms. Meagan expended a bit of time weeping, and then she started carrying out her mother's last wishes.

*Use my body as a stepping stool.*

After tossing the service revolver up and out onto the grass, Meagan had dragged over her mother's body, folded it across itself, and climbed it to get out of the hole. She'd heard it gasp under her boots, releasing pent-up gasses or something, and it made her climb faster, moaning gibberish. Out in the cold open air, she crawled on her knees a few feet, trying not to puke, taking in deep wet breaths. Far right, there was the whine of the pickup, the drone of the music, the inarticulate shouting, and Meagan reached for the gun, grabbed it, pocketed it, and slowly pushed to her feet.

*Go right home and call the police.*

Yes, Mother.

Meagan told herself to turn, to go back toward the gate-fencing to see if the hole was still there so she could crawl through fast as she could to get help.

*Go.*

She started to lumber, to jog and to run, but not back toward home. Before she even realized exactly what she was doing or specifically why, she found herself making for the hill of keepsakes, climbing it, feeling her legs burn, feeling everything around her turning redder and redder.

Her mother was dead.

She fought up that hill, crested the peak, and halted, bent over with her hands on her thighs. She spit in the grass. Breath heaving, she lifted her head, eyes blazing, rain making rivulets down her face. She straightened. She tilted her chin defiantly and proceeded to make her way through the field of flat ledger stones, lurching, picking up speed with the green statue-lady watching ominously from behind.

*Mother said it wasn't my fault.*

She reached the edge of the field and crashed through bushes shaped like the hats of archbishops. Scratched her face, didn't care.

*That man killed my mother.*

Breathless, fighting for that second wind, she turned north and started jogging through the maze of headstones, then trotting, then running all out, and by the time she got to the edge of the grave-lot she was pitching forward, zigzagging with fatigue. She made for the signpost that said SECTION 2 / ST. LUKES DRIVE, and she reached out and grabbed hold, swinging halfway around it. She was smiling brightly, shoulders heaving. Across the chapel parking lot, the rain moved across in dark sheets, and there were two vehicles, two choices. Deeper in by the chapel garden there was the dark form of a big truck with lumber on the back-trailer part. It reminded her of Connor and the dumb-ass shit he found fascinating, and common sense screamed that the guy fake-chasing the pickup hadn't shown up in a big rig. His car was the shitty black Ford whatever parked like a drunk by the marquee board between two spaces, straddling the line with its tires up on the grass, fucking perv!

And he killed her mother . . . a woman so sweet and starry-eyed that she thought she and Meagan would write stories together . . . the ultimate oddball-weirdo living in fantasy land. Always had been. She was a pain in the nuts, a child, a beautiful damaged child, and this man stomped into this graveyard and took her.

No worries. Meagan was going to avenge her mother's death.

She was going to stalk him, haunt him, and kill him. Like a horror story.

*Oh, Chapter 2 is going to be a real motherfucker, believe it.*

His car was open, and in the back he had one of those sunshade protectors you put across the windshield so the steering wheel didn't burn your tender fingers in the summer, fucking lame-ass, and she got in under it, feet first across the back seat, reaching back out into the rain to pull shut the door.

It smelled in here like McDonald's food, old man sweat, and Armor All. The floor on the driver's side was cluttered with Wawa coffee cups, a few old newspapers, and what looked like crushed packs of Newport cigarettes. It all would make noise if she even gave off a twitch.

He was coming.

His voice was carrying, calling her name, so it was time to pull a submarine, now. But she had to have just one quick look at him. Taking the edge of the cardboard as if she was gripping the brim of a cap in a breeze, she pushed up to see over the bottom rim of the window. Could he see in here as she could see out? Too late now to go worrying about it.

He came loping out from the scatter of headstones, a big fat walrus with a fat walrus moustache, eyes like black charcoal, his face a white smear. Biting back a short scream, Meagan immediately buried herself on the floor between the seats, pulling the cardboard over her as best she could. She was on her side and the hump was right against her hip, too hard, gears with no grease. The driver's door opened.

He shoved himself in, and it made the whole car bow down. Her head hit something and she squealed, but the howl of rain from the outside saved her. If she could have put cloth in her mouth to bite down on, she would have. If she could have changed her mind and opted for the hole in the fence back on what seemed the other side of the world at that point, she might have. He started the car with a roar, and pulled out as if his hair was on fire.

It was a rough ride. There was a screeching turn and two short stops that had rolled Meagan up against his seat, mashing her face against the base of it. There were a couple of sharp uphills, and though Meagan had a hand free to push back against the seat base, when they banged over a pothole ten minutes in she literally had to clench herself silent. Her bones hurt. Her muscles felt raw, and when the engine finally went off she tried her best to keep breathing regularly.

They were here.

Wherever that was.

The door squawked open and he grunted lustily, pushing himself off the seat and out into the rain. The car rose on its shocks, and he slammed the door so hard it left a ringing sound like aftertaste.

Meagan kept her breath steady, in and out, girlfriend, rainbows and ice cream. She started counting to sixty. Then she'd do it again, then once more. Then . . .

Then, she'd "write" Chapter 2.

For you, Mother.

I'm going to show you how to make a damned difference.

# CHAPTER 22
# PICKING THROUGH THE PENTHOUSE

Canfield moved cautiously out into the hallway. The red effect from the bathroom had gone out and there was only light from the one candle, playing off the heaps of birds in flickers and starts. He could see downstairs. Rain spattered into the foyer through the opened front door as Canfield made his way down the hall to the sister's room. He had five shots left. Erika's sudden disappearance made little sense, and there was something here, something behind the bedroom door, something flapping.

More scary bird metaphors? Canfield's recurring nightmares as a child were always those of fighting wild birds that were gouging out his eyes and pecking his face to shreds.

He'd always woken up at that point, bolting up in bed, swiping at the air.

Captain Canfield clenched his teeth and turned the knob to open the sister's bedroom door. The flapping noise had kicked up memories, yet more disturbing than the distraction was the idea that this miscreant, whoever he was, had known about a dream Canfield had been plagued with as a child in the first place. Or maybe it was the mother being "themed." Or one or both of her children. There had been birds painted on the mailbox, and in the bathroom; he could have sworn he saw rough winged outlines scrawled on the walls. Or themes be damned, maybe the killer was simply smart enough to find universal motifs that scared people enough to think that the references were tailored. It was the same principle fortune-tellers used to work their cheap con . . . a parody, almost laughable, but you never accounted for how effective it could be when it was your palm turned up under the lamplight.

He pushed into the room.

The shadows were long, falling across the unmade bed, scatters of clothing, books and folders, knickknacks and DVD's, and retreating to the back edges of the tabletops, desktops, and bureau were the forgotten kiddie projects—misshapen ceramics, watercolor art on stiff marbled paper, animal figurines made of popsicle sticks. Canfield did a slow 360. At the upper periphery, as if watching darkly, were all the posters of demons and black rose gardens and Gothic iron crosses and multiples of some pale blonde female guitarist Canfield didn't recognize, as well as a few featuring that laughing skeleton with the long gray hair that everyone and their mother knew from the old Iron Maiden albums. Right above Meagan's bed was a large poster with four guys standing on the filler stones between and around a set of train tracks. Along the top border, it said *April 21st – Courage is Born From Fear.*

The "flapping" was the shade pushing back and forth against the window each time the wind changed.

Canfield moved to the closet and opened the door. Crammed. Clothes stuffed together on the hanger-bar, and below" were layers—a shelf loaded with old board games, and beneath it, abandoned stuffed animals, canvas pouches and discarded boots and sneakers, sandals and travel bags. As noted, most of the girl's current apparel was tossed about, on the floor, coming out of the drawers, like mother like daughter.

He bent and looked under the bed. Shadows, stationary forms, a wicker basket, a couple of old binders, an instrument case—clarinet or flute maybe—some kind of folded-up exercise machine or maybe a futon frame or something like it. No one hiding. The girl had gone out the window and climbed down the trellis; he would have bet his pension on it.

And so, where was Erika Shoemaker? The flapping shade had been a coincidental distraction, and the more Canfield thought about it the more nonsensical this whole thing appeared. No one had kidnapped his administrative assistant . . . he would have heard it. He'd been under that computer table no more than a moment or two, fifteen seconds at the outside when he'd held still, listening for more booby-traps popping off of their catch-springs. And that was the point: he'd been *listening.* He'd heard absolutely nothing, and she wouldn't have just wandered off, at least it didn't seem so.

He tried to picture himself calling out to her down the stairs, and seeing her come into view with a bottle of Tropicana, shrugging and saying, *"What? I got thirsty."*

Didn't fit.

He pictured himself going into Connor's room and finding her sitting on the ottoman with her hands tied behind her back and her lips sewn together with fishing line.

Didn't play. There hadn't been time to set up the horror show. She'd simply vanished, for no reason, and instead of shouting and running around, Canfield did what he always did when he hadn't a clue as to how to proceed. He played it close to the vest, quietly and methodically.

He moved back down the hall to check Connor's room, and the second look, this one measured, reaffirmed his initial impression. The kid was riding a horse in his own strange rodeo, his room the haunts of a childish child, yet everything arranged with a military neatness, as if he was his own father, threatening to throw away the whole kit and kaboodle if even one accessory was left out of place. The gun belt on the bedpost that looked like something out of a spaghetti western hung above a collection of toy trucks in a blue plastic treasure chest, the Hess Christmas trucks, nine years' worth, in front of that in a tidy row. The bureau and desktops were filled with miniatures from Dungeons and Dragons tabletop games, and the shelves were laden with neat mini-book racks filled with what appeared to be alphabetically ordered comic books, graphic novels, motorhead stuff, and weaponry-fetish, from *Arkham Asylum* and *The Sandman: Preludes & Nocturnes* to *Car and Driver, Motor Trend, Firearms News,* and *American Handgunner.*

More generally, the place simply assaulted your eyes with fast-food restaurant colors, bright reds and yellows and oranges and such. Much seemed to be part of a cheap ad for cartoons and gaming paraphernalia: controllers and discs, a Mario figural calendar, a lamp that looked like a bowling ball with teeth, marked "Chain Chomp," a Minecraft lava lamp, a Zelda Triforce cookie container, lots of Pokémon stuff, Yugioh posters, Teen Titans water bottles, and a Dragonball Z hand soap dispenser.

Canfield no more thought this boy was a killer than he was excited about his wearing a badge and a firearm. More contradictions. Lots to rethink. And still, no Erika Shoemaker.

The bathroom was empty as well, the laser image long nixed. Canfield peered in briefly but didn't take all that much time doing it. He'd get a better look at the projection device up by the showerhead later; they all would. He checked the linen closet: nothing but towels and sheets and blankets and pillow cases, and there was no way Erika could have climbed up through the trap door to the attic. She was shorter than Canfield, and he would have needed a stepladder himself.

Once more he ducked into the mother's bedroom. Vacant. He looked in the closet, under the bed, nothing. He ventured back into the hallway, moved down a few feet, and then he froze where he was.

At the bottom of the stairs in the living room, Erika was standing there, facing the opened front door. She was motionless. Rain was coming in, spattering the floor before her bare feet, and she turned slowly, staring up at him.

"Captain," she said. "Bill . . ."

She looked different. Her wet hair was combed back, tied into a ponytail, and she was wearing makeup now, lavishly applied, rich green eyeshadow and heavy mascara curved up in thick cat's-eye wing lines. The shadows made her face long and strange, the overall effect cold and masklike.

"I had to go to the bathroom," she said dully. "There's a half-bath by the kitchen. I looked in the mirror. Scratch on my forehead, felt ugly. Found a Girl Boss Goodies Mini Cosmetics kit in a basket, and a Procter and Gamble powder palette. He got away. Killer-boy out in the rain. Murder-Mister killing college girls with his Murder-Master."

"Erika," Canfield said, "you're in shock." He moved to the landing.

A shadow suddenly filled the front doorway, a massive shadow with a red cap, white hair, monster hands, and a cheap windbreaker. He ducked in under the archway and grabbed hold of Erika, lifting her, pinning her to his chest as she kicked and screeched, blocking the shot.

The giant grinned up at Canfield, showing his horse teeth.

He yanked Erika backward, out into the rain.

# CHAPTER 23
# BEHIND THE CURTAIN

Connor Mullin shattered the passenger-side window with a paver he pried up from the walkway that ran through the chapel garden. He'd been more than polite; he'd knocked first. His big dumb friend had pulled an Elvis, and Connor was pretty sure he could hotwire this big ole hog without too much of a problem. It was probably as simple as wedging off the ignition bezel, dropping down the lower cover for the column, and twisting it over with a short wrench.

Hoisting himself up and crawling through the dark portal, he thought of little else in his future besides starting the rig, turning it around, and getting his ass out onto the highway. His eyes still smarted, showing everything with that red laser tinge at the edges. As far as the projection in the bathtub was concerned, he had wondered about who manufactured it about as much as he'd presently planned out his immediate future, not much, priorities.

This was survival.

His oddball, pseudo-perceptive mother . . . actually a cunning, cold-blooded Jekyll and Hyde . . . was now dead, lying somewhere out in the rain with Connor being tied to her death in terms of metal splinters and residual soil. The Captain had said the markings on Connor's pants cuffs had put him, quote, *"at the scene,"* after accusing him of ditching his gun in the cemetery, and so it was clear that the red-tinged image in the tub had been filmed in a grave out here. And whether or not it was actually graveyard dirt, highway dirt, or a combination of both on his pants . . . and regardless of the bad weather and unstable setting most probably preventing the Crime Scene Search Unit from retaining any sort of conclusive corroborating evidence either way in terms of footprints, hair and/or fiber at the given kill-site, and their knowing this, Connor was pretty damned sure that a slug from his own Glock had ended his mother. And the killer was his kid sister Meagan, talk about a lose-lose.

Had she seen the manifesto on the computer and confronted the evil professor?

Was Meagan the accomplice?

Why the candles? Why the graveyard? Why now, what the fuck?

Again, Connor Mullin had priorities, and there was no more time to go tooling around out there trying to unhitch the cab from its trailer than there had been to go putting puzzles together. Back at the house he'd burst down the stairs blindly, struggling to get the car keys out of his pocket with his pants drenched and sticking to him like a second skin. Outside, when he was just starting to get his eyes again, his first painful glimpse had been of the Rav 4 in the driveway, down on its rims with four flattened tires. Another factoid for the grab-bag filled with unanswered mysteries, and he'd taken off back the way he had come toward the chapel parking area, expecting Canfield to be close behind him and sirens cutting into the night.

But there had been neither of those things. More mysteries, and now that he was sitting in the driver's seat of a sixteen-wheeler he was about to steal, he couldn't help but briefly wonder why the Captain had said he was in stocking feet as was Erika. Why were they together in the first place, and why had she said their tires had blown? That made for a lot of bad Firestones, I mean, shit, could Mother have engineered all this even with an accomplice? What was she thinking, fucking up her own getaway car?

Priorities. No time for fluff. Stick with the program.

Connor reached down for the ignition and the keys were in it, another weird-ass co-inkee-dink. Now, why would that big old boy lock his keys in here like this? It was as if he'd gone off to take a piss with a spare in his pocket, keeping the truck prepped for his own fast getaway.

*What would you be running from, big boy?*

He turned the key. The truck roared to life, and there were new shapes that came up in the light of the instrument panel, additions to his left set at his elbow just below the rim of the window, and to his right snaking up out of the console.

Both were covered with fancy black dust-covers of the sort that magicians used to hide rabbits in hats. Connor reached across himself to the form on the left and slid off the fabric, unveiling a strange sort of tablet or iPad with three small-screen monitors fastened together by swivel hinges like a trifold vanity mirror. Connected by parallel offset bars was the keyboard, split in half at the 7, U, H, and N buttons, the pair of devices placed at eight and four o'clock just beneath the steering wheel. Each had a small palm rest and a foam touch-tab where the index finger would be positioned.

"This sure as hell ain't Hewlett Packard or Dell," Connor muttered. He looked to the right and let his hand rise slowly, finally pinching the gauze of "item #2" between his thumb and index finger and sliding it off as if he were some snotty proprietor uncovering a royal jewelry display. Okay. On a gooseneck mount, it was a rectangular video monitor screen. The apparatus was paper-thin, like a tablet turned short side down, but it didn't look like a tablet. It looked more like a jumbo-sized cell phone with strange icons at the bottom, all of them with slight imperfections as if they were carefully designed rough drafts stamped onto the plastic before marketing removed the ticks and proportion lines. One was a tooth. One a dead palm tree. The third was a pair of binoculars.

To his left, the trifold computer screens lit up suddenly; his hands had migrated to the keyboard palm-rests under the steering wheel without his really thinking about it, and he'd inadvertently brushed his finger on one of the touch-tabs. He glanced over and gasped.

The left screen had his mother's "Sculptor" manifesto on it, page 1, he remembered it well. The center screen had what appeared to be an earlier version of said manifesto, with a shitload of red markings. Someone had gone on "Track Changes" and edited the document for her. And the computer screen to the right had a list in micro-print, hundreds of email addresses, those seemingly belonging to newspapers, magazines, television stations, and entertainment blogs.

Connor leaned forward. Hundreds hell, this was *thousands*. It was alphabetical, starting with aaa.contact-us@html.com, and by the bottom of the screen it had only gotten to abbotsvilledailytimes@oped.com. Connor looked back to the center-monitor with the editing marks. It was the page from his mother's work that was talking about leaving Melissa Baumgardner's corpse at the jobsite. One of the paragraphs had originally read simply:

"The dowel is one of those antiquated window poles that janitors at my local elementary school threw out last month. And the cuts and gouges would all seem the grisly work of a madman."

With the additions in red, it said:

"Actually, the dowel is one of those antiquated window poles that janitors at my local elementary school found in the basement and threw out last month. And the cuts, gouges, and ribbons, the lacerations and the gradations I could only get right by wheeling in a deli meat slicer and making five passes, the second set of eye craters, the back-up nose hole and twin mouth-orifice I dug out of her left temple, cheek, and jawbone, all that would seem the grisly work of a madman."

Connor used the touch tab and rolled the document back a few pages, then forward, then back all the way to the introduction. There were sections basically untouched and others with such heavy editing it was almost completely rewritten. As for the former, the supermarket portions were almost utterly void of the red markings, as were the introductory pages describing the campus, while in terms of the latter, there was an abundance of straight redactions in what Connor would have referred to as the "Hot Chick" section, starting with the "strawberry blondes, and ash blondes, and flaxen, ginger, and honey blondes" stuff, and ending with the commentary on the legs the lightest blondes let go unshaven. Deleted were about three more pages of description his mother had written . . . all tits and ass and midriffs and "gams" . . . detail after detail going more and more micro, all the way down to a rather clinical argument that the square behind the knee was the sexiest creation on God's green earth, preceding a strange paragraph through which she demonstrated through "classification and division" the value of pores, birthmarks, and melanin.

Concurrently, most of the additions came in the parts where she had tried to go techno, like the paragraph that eventually had become:

"I have a twelve-foot ladder lashed down to the roof with bungee cords, but the ladder is for show. So is the truck. While there is indeed a pressure washer back there in the trailer, and an Emglo compressor to power it, there are no steamers, no wet/dry vacuums, no spare hoses, no replacement filters, no detergents, no pickle barrels filled with rags, old leather tool belts and power drills, no miscellaneous fasteners, no brooms, and no squeegees and mops for the run-off."

Originally, his mother had simply written:

"I have a ladder tied down to the roof, but it is for show. While there is indeed a sprayer and a motor to run it, there are no buckets or mops."

The balance of the edits followed suit in reference to content, along with some sentence-to-sentence stylistic stuff. Connor was no English major, but it seemed his mother liked to drone on and on about things, and while the editor had kept the credibility of her "swag," as it were, there were distinct corrections that made the thing flow better without going too far off the rails.

And all done by the giant simpleton? Really?

By instinct Connor double-tapped, and the marked-up document winked out in what looked like a backtrack to some sort of home page. Like the icons on the monitor on the gooseneck, the graphics looked unfinished, professional, but seemingly what would have been left on the drafting table before going to marketing and production. There was a symbol in the top left corner, a light blue cube up on its vertex point and a title—*Track Ranges.* Below that was a short explanation: *Editing and Enhancing App: neural style transfer using encoder/decoder architecture to splice editor's narratorial tendencies to subject's text, according to the former's documented writing patterns found on social media and other published platforms.* Next were some very basic instructions and guidelines—stuff about loading the editor's history via the "gamma" port (whatever that was), keyboard instructions for merging the work of the subject and the overlay of the editor, and something next called "Instantaneous Publishing."

Again, all this from the simpleton? All this stuff had a homemade feel to it, and besides tossing around the seemingly ludicrous idea that this big stupid man was inventing super-tech in a basement somewhere, Connor again asked himself:

*Fucking why?*

He used the left touch-tab to try and scroll through the finished document on the far left. Nothing. No cursor. He tried touching the screen. Nothing.

*Ha. You got screen-freeze, champ.*

The blood ran out of his face; he suddenly got it.

His mother and the big boy had been partners. She identified the targets and he did the heavy lifting, but they'd been having issues, both thinking the other was planning some kind of betrayal. She used her bizarre creativity to initiate this false manifesto as they'd agreed, and all along the big boy had planned for Connor to be the surprise ignition-switch, possibly the fall guy, finding his mother reading and re-reading her "masterpiece" after sending it along, glued to the screen, supercharged with the revisions sent back to her as if they'd turned her into some kind of dark Shakespeare. Riled up as he was, Connor was meant to confront her, expecting the response of a timid, manipulative professor and instead getting the wrath of a serial killer newly exposed. Things would have escalated, emotions heightened, and instead of a family squabble, a "talk" or "hard intervention" as Connor had planned, one was meant to actually take out the other, with Captain Bill Canfield waltzing in ready to finger the victor as the Sculptor Killer.

But she'd had second thoughts late in the process, figuring Big Boy would pull a double-cross by sending the document from her computer leaving it traceable to forensics, instead of from his newfangled system as they had initially agreed. She panicked, she paused, she never hit "Send," and so Big Boy had had to go to plan B, drawing her out of the house while Connor was leaning his forehead against the cemetery gateposts half blacked-out with cold rage. Next, Big Boy killed Mother himself somewhere deep in the graveyard, yes, in a hail of gunshots while Connor was letting his hand bump along the iron posts thinking the gunfire came from a heavy metal song; and to avoid leaving physical trace evidence in the house, Big Boy had figured he'd had just enough time before Connor got home to come back here to his command center and hack into her computer now that she wouldn't be able to literally see him doing it before her very eyes, sending the document back to himself, running it through *Track Ranges,* and then beaming the edited version back onto her computer for Connor to find. Hot damn, if he hadn't circled the house multiple times like an animal, Big Boy wouldn't have had the time to pull this all off.

But Connor *had* circled the house, and it had worked out perfectly for the big bastard.

So why wasn't the email transaction completed? Why wasn't the mailing list connected with the new document and sent to the masses?

The old unexpected wild card.

In accordance with this newly erected "Plan B," Connor—drenched with rainwater and covered with soil marks—had found the document and had gotten caught reading it by Captain Canfield, whom the killer had baited in with some kind of anonymous tip, but miracle of miracles, LOL, instead of chasing Connor into the night, Captain Canfield went and threw the one wrench into the gears that would fuck up any tech-wizard's shit, even the high-end space-age systems with super-apps, trifold screens, and split keyboard pads tailored with hand-molds.

LMAO, Canfield must have turned off Mother's computer before Big Boy could connect the email addresses, cut and paste them, upload them one at a time, whatever: Connor wasn't a tech-nerd that way and he had no idea how involved was that last crucial step for the big guy. What he did know was that the rig had been left here unattended. Trace evidence be damned now, the better half of "The Sculptor" was going to the house to plug back in Mother's desktop.

And all too soon he'd be back, unless Captain Canfield took him down.

*No offense, Chief, but my money goes on Big Daddy.*

Connor laughed hollowly. He couldn't believe that he had actually thought the trucker he'd "randomly" met was a mentally challenged man-child filling in horse outlines with crayon in coloring books, and the depth of this conspiracy was mind-boggling. Were Finch and Cabrera in on this? Others at the station? And what about Meagan if she wasn't actually her mother's killer? Was the red image in the bathtub for her? Where was she? What was her supposed role in this horror show?

Connor's jaw dropped.

He'd been looking at the monitor on the gooseneck without really looking at it, eyes resting there while he'd been thinking about his kid sister. Now he was looking for real again: at the icons stamped at the bottom in seeming rough draft with the tick and proportion lines. It was the one in the middle.

It wasn't a palm tree.

It was a sunflower.

# CHAPTER 24
# BEAUTY IN THE EYE OF THE RIPPER'S BEHOLDER

Captain Canfield ran into the storm. Cold stingers to the face, the front lawn was muddy, his clothing lay on him like lead. It was dark, the wind shaping the rain in what looked like the billowing cloak of some massive dark horseman, with intermittent moonlight coming through the road foliage and cemetery border trees.

Canfield took a position in the grass, gun leveled. He didn't have a clear shot, not as a sniper would have had with a rifle with a scope.

Across the street on the sidewalk was the huge figure. He was smiling. His feet were spread, his left arm clamped around Erika's waist, his right palm pressed to her mouth. She was straining hard, arms pinned to her sides, feet kicking insane bicycle pedals against his thick legs. Her T-shirt had ridden up; you could see the shape of her waist. Her ponytail had come loose, and wet strands were plastered to her forehead and jawline like skull-fissures.

The big man spoke. His hat pushed a shadow across his forehead, but below that his skin looked bad—spoiled and cracked like a leper's. It was the caked-on makeup. The moisture out here had begun to erode it.

"Captain," he called. "Advantage perp. You can't risk discharging your firearm. And your prerogative is clear. As the first officer on the scene, you are to look after the safety of the victim before securing the arrest. And if the citizen endures physical harm at the crime scene, you are obligated to care for the injured before arresting the offender." His grin became monstrous.

"Officer," he said, "I'd like to report an injury."

He took the hand covering her mouth and groped it up the side of her face. She squirmed, kicking harder, and he pawed at her, fingering. She jerked her head, and he smeared the cat's-eye makeup in a hash-mark up her left temple. He pulled back across, and she let loose a gargled scream, kicking like a frenzied horsefly held by the wings. He mashed his hand-heel into the other side of her face, slipping down along the bone like wet marble, and this time he streaked thick mascara onto her cheek, hooking down like an athlete's smeared eye-black. He made an adjustment, and with the base of his thumb, his ring finger, and pinkie he cupped her chin, holding her still. He had to work it like the old Spock Vulcan "live-long-and-prosper" sign, but he spread his middle and index fingers back across the bridge of her nose, then started spider-crawling them up toward her right eye.

Canfield screamed "No!"

The monster's two fingers were poised like a claw, uneven tongs.

He pushed in, over the eyeball, deep into the socket. Blood squirted up over his middle knuckles. She screamed herself raw, her kicking went nuclear. He let go of her mouth so he could work in the thumb, forming a pincer-grip. For a bare moment it cleared the horrific sightline; he dug in his fingers, and Canfield could see Erika's eyeball slip from one side of the socket to the other as the monster worked in deep, trying to get to the back of it. Blood wept down his wrist, but the rain washed it away, making the effect seem ghostlike and illusory. He yanked, her head jerked forward, give, but no climax. He couldn't pull it home, stubborn muscles and nerve fibers proving their elasticity, and he re-angled his elbow, bunched, set, and ripped that eye straight out of its socket.

She stopped kicking.

Thick blood welled in the dark crater and poured down her cheek. The rain doused and diluted it, ebbing down her face with the beat of her heart, tendrils and threads gyrating there on her cheekbone like algae floating off coral in a current. She was twitching, hanging there in his arms. He slapped her cheek and she jolted awake, shrieking incoherently, body in spasm, the broken doll, the lunatic stage-puppet.

He set her on her feet in front of him, bending his knees so she was still mostly blocking the line of fire. Both big hands moved to her hips to steady her, and he walked her back to an oak tree.

He whispered something in her ear. It took a moment. Then he smacked her hard on the ass and barked:

"Go!"

He ducked behind the wide tree and she ran, faster than one would have ever expected, moaning and crying, lumbering desperately away toward Sproul Road.

Canfield pounded after her, grass to driveway. Cutting across the corner of the neighbor's lawn, he noticed quite academically that they had been gardening, planting shrubs. Passing through the line of them at the perimeter, he stepped on a trowel. It hurt, fucked his rhythm, and his ankles banged together; he went down. He hit the street, skinned an elbow, quick-rolled, and somehow managed to cradle the gun without having it blow a hole in his stomach. He didn't allow himself time to recover. He sprang up and broke into a straight sprint, thinking, *Knees high, push hard, strong kick, arms in sync,* and by the time he caught up she was almost to the street lamp. She stumbled and collapsed, trying to grab hold on her way down, and he caught her from behind just in time to save her from falling onto her face. He went to the ground with her, held her, turned her so he could look at her.

She'd been truly violated, disfigured, it was real, no illusions. She had two faces now, the left profile all sleek cuts and angles, the makeup bird-winged up off her left eye giving her a futuristic look like a runway model, yet turned to the right, her profile was that of a ghost-witch, her long skull and jawline accented by the rough crater peering at you with blank recognition. She looked very much like the kind of thing you bought in an island hut, stuck on a voodoo stick with beads hanging off the fist-guard. She was sobbing, still convulsing.

Canfield wanted to comfort her, but he didn't know the words. He wanted to give her some kind of gentlemanly reassurance, but he didn't know that song either. What came out was mechanical, almost programmed.

"What did he say to you?" he said softly, flatly. He felt terrible about it, but he was who he was.

"What?" she said. "What? When, Bill, what?"

"Easy," he said. "What did he say to you in your ear? Just now. I'll catch him, but I need all the data."

She started weeping again and buried her face in Bill Canfield's chest, shoulders shaking.

"He told me," she said, voice muffled, "that I had to run hard, I had to run like the wind, toward Sproul Road. He said that I had to run straight into traffic. He said he was going to flush my right eye down a toilet, and if I didn't run as fast as I could he'd hunt me down, find me at the hospital, at work, in the parking lot, the grocery store, my apartment."

She pulled back and looked up at Canfield with her left eye.

"He promised he would give me round two," she said. "He promised he'd rip out the other one."

# CHAPTER 25
## FINE PRINT

Connor reached for the monitor on the gooseneck. He wanted to hit the middle icon, the one modeled after the nickname his dead mother had given to his weird sister, but he was doing this methodically, left to right, like reading. He hit the tooth icon, and the screen lit up, blue tint, black writing, unexpressive font.

It looked like an instruction book, dry and technical, but by the time he got to the sixth line or so he felt differently.

This was not a page from some tech manual. It was what looked like something you found in a lockbox in a secret compartment under a floorboard in one of those strange horror movies where the images left stains in your mind like spatters of blood and black ink.

It was the big boy's diary. An inventor's journal.

Connor backtracked and reread the text.

"Megapixel camera design modeled after capsule endoscopy technology, utilizing evolution of tablet data recorder in the form of microchips integrated with enamel of molar offered by donor. When first contacted by saliva of the host, the tooth will burst to a form that can be swallowed, releasing micro-nanobots designed to migrate to the retinal field in order to transmit the electrical pulses, and therefore the host's visual field, to the observer's computer screen."

Connor rested his palm on top of his head. Yes, on second read it made about as much sense as the first go-around, but here again was where it got mega-strange. It said:

"Tooth donor, Bridget Ballentine, taken and nullified outside Handschumacher Dining Center, 3210 Chestnut Street by food service entrance, behind dumpster hidden from street-view, where target would typically purge after gorge. Blunt-force trauma to base of skull, wrapped in plastic, transported to lab. Molar extracted, #19. Body retained for Hollywood crucifixion."

"What the f—" Connor muttered. He speed-read the rest of it, a list of this "Bridget Ballentine's" particulars: her height and weight, how many "Dragon Dollars" she had in her account, how much in checking at Citizens Bank, her medical condition (Bulimia Nervosa and chemical depression), the position she played for the Drexel University basketball team and all her statistics, the dates of her last three monthly cycles, her team practice schedule, her game schedule, the last four times she'd done laundry, the last three times she went shopping, her class roster, her appointments with her advisor, her therapist, home visits . . .

*"Her come and go,"* Connor finished in a hoarse whisper. He touch-tabbed the icon shaped like a sunflower. He expected his sister's name in the title, but instead it said, "Host."

Underneath was what looked like the criminological sample profiles Connor had had to read at the academy. They'd usually made his eyes cross. He had preferred learning through muscle memory or modules more spatially oriented, like choke defenses, arrests of persons, restraint and use of force, and patrol operations. This, however, was the good stuff, real fly-on-the-wall shit, like sneaking into the principal's office and happening upon an open folder on the desk, written about you by the school psychiatrist, a registered social worker, and a lawyer from the state.

"Meagan Mullin is a peculiar species defined by superlative homicidal circuitry, tending toward ritualistic, brutal fantasy-schema. This potential killer filters life-phenomena symbolically, within a matrix of impulsivity, savagery, and reanimated sexuality as translated through dark music. Still, what others might use as a channeling device, she utilizes as an instrument of simultaneous and dichotomous glorification and dissociation, and considering her low self-esteem and distorted self-image of personal inconsequentiality, her behaviors reflect self-perceived invisibility where others with similar pathology might veer toward narcissism. Hypothesis: Meagan Mullin under certain circumstances would exhibit extreme and proficient homicidal action as well as the more technical and specific aspects of the modus operandi and the signature that would define this kind of offender. In victimological overview, it has been suggested that even seasoned professionals in law enforcement would fall prey to her cunning. It has also been proposed that she would choose violence over reason, even if her actions would implicate her in the very crimes she would try to avenge."

Connor's mouth was hanging open, and he shut it, making his jaw clack.

*He put nanobots in your eyes so he could watch you kill someone, Sis. Fucking why?*

He hit the rough icon shaped like binoculars.

# CHAPTER 26
# THE APPAREL OFT PROCLAIMS THE MAN

Detective Bronson burst through his front door. He had desperately wanted to pull over at a Wawa or greasy spoon to borrow a phone, or better, he'd wanted to drive right to the station to kick off a search for the kid, a "Megan Alert," not fucking funny. But there was the issue of the DNA of hers that he quite possibly could have ingested. There was also the map on his wall, the smut on his hard drive, and let's not forget the dead body tied to the pipes in his basement. He'd half expected to find detectives from his own division waiting for him in his living room. If they didn't immediately brand him as the killer, he would most likely be considered an accomplice or a copycat, and it wasn't clear how to wipe this thing clean. What bothered him more was the idea that he yielded even higher value to the killer if silenced . . . same stomach contents, same wall map, same hard drive, same cellar dweller . . . all minus his statement and eventual testimony. Bad binary. Either way he was positioned to wind up in a box tonight, jail cell or morgue drawer.

So why the goose-chase to begin with? Seemed to be overkill, pardon the pun.

He tossed his keys on the desk, removed his firearm from his waistband, and looked over at the basement door, partly ajar. Check, stick to priorities, keep measuring options. A more relevant and pressing issue at the moment was whether or not the body downstairs was a body at all. He'd only gotten a glimpse of her. For all he knew, she was stagecraft.

Wishful thinking.

He peeled off his shirt. Shoes and pants too, socks and then undies. What a sight, he was shivering, that graveyard had been cold as a witch's tit, and he folded his arms across his chest, figuring that if he was going to open himself to the mechanism he'd been serving and enforcing for twenty-odd years, he was going to do so in his Sunday best. Fuck it, even though the act in itself could be interpreted as one of obstruction, he wasn't going to be body-shamed, possibly doing a televised perp-walk in obesity-jeans and a drenched yellow T-shirt with bacon-neck, no sir. He was going to take a quick shower, get into his good suit, pin his badge to his lapel, and after briefly checking the corpse in the basement for verification purposes, he'd call this thing in, done deal, full transparency. If the landline was down as the killer had claimed in what seemed like years ago, Bronson would drive to the station.

The better side of the binary.

He reached for the flannel-lined rugby bathrobe he'd thrown over the back of his computer chair and pushed his arms through, tied it tight. Of course, he could always do it the other way. His house had been burgled . . . by the Scarecrow Killer no less, hell with him, the son of a bitch was no sculptor . . . and Bronson could process the scene for its physical evidence right here and now on the sly with the slim hope that it would be deemed admissible. Behind him on either side of the empty hearth jutting into the living space, there were his storage chests packed with the many containers and satchels and cases and small plastic tub-units that made up his multifaceted field investigation kit.

He kept those heavy chests padlocked like owning a safe, and he didn't care that they made one side of his spacious living room look like a contractor's trailer. First of all, who the fuck was looking? But more, when it came to the tools of his craft, he revered the parts and parcels the same way a gun collector kept his most favored weapons tucked away in oak and leather cases with alligator binding and shape-molds on the inside covered with felt. His general evidence collection kit was a true thing of beauty, chock full of so many more specialty implements than the standard scissors, wire cutters, tweezers, pliers, and knives, that the captain had suggested he open his own hardware/medical supply chain. His latent fingerprint collection kit, his casts-molds-impressions and marks kit, and his post-mortem fingerprint and cadaver taking kit all had been mentioned as "excellent and exemplary" in a statewide multi-precinct memo circulated by the governor last year, and his massive photographic kit had paraphernalia that rivaled the equipment currently used by big magazines, he knew, because he had investigated a robbery during a shoot *Vanity Fair* was doing in Suburban Square last year, and their head camera-operator had told him so personally.

It was tempting to break out the toys for a sweep. No one knew the place like Bronson, and he could cover it stem to stern. It would also open him up to the suspicion that he could have quite effectively tainted the scene or destroyed evidence, and he wasn't going to risk anything past a clothes-change and shower . . . nothing more that would kill the slim chance he might walk away from this clean, call him a dreamer.

He picked up his Sig Saur and made for the stairs. He wanted a drink, something to knock back that was hard, but he knew there'd be no booze tonight, no fucking relief. The good died young, the unappreciated wasted their Sundays kneeling and praying for the wicked, and fall guys trying not to be fall guys pulled tedious, frustrating, sober all-nighters.

He walked the stairs and toward the top the air started to feel strange, the shadows menacing, as if they'd affixed themselves to the creases up here, gaining substance like moss. It was all in his head, he knew this, but all the same the killer had been in this house. Bronson was a professional, but he was still human.

The bathroom vanity lights spilled a faint glow onto the hall carpeting, and Bronson half expected a shadow to cross suddenly through it. He shivered again. This was horror movie stuff in a cruel twist of gender reversal, starring Detective Bronson as the scream-queen, alone at night and naked under a bathrobe, about to slip out of it and step into the shower. Not only was the room going to seem claustrophobic, but it had mirrors that misted like London fog, a curtain that masked the sightline, a targeted water-spray that affected sound retention, and white porcelain enamel that would showcase the blood in the starkest of contrasts. It was also about to get hot and steamy and supple and dewy, and a shapely woman basking in it just to get stabbed repeatedly was somehow burned into our view of glorious Americana like waving wheat, barbecues, and homecoming parades.

Bronson took a deep breath through the nose. He was the sad parody, Mr. Fat-Neck, Man-Tits, Hairy-Back, Belly-Flab, about to get wet and vulnerable.

Worth the risk, though. Like garden-hostas and wild ivy his suit "covered," and when he'd just washed his hair and pushed a comb through it he always looked like the job, it was all he could ask.

He walked into the bathroom and saw it the way the killer might have seen it earlier today, poking around, profiling him. It looked like what you'd see exposed from under the suit, the room given up on, the small magazine rack by the toilet on the floor with one of its chrome feet bent, and next to it an empty jug of Gallo merlot with dark red sediment hardened at the bottom. There were floor-tiles that were chipped by the sink. The tub needed re-grouting, the curtain had a thin line of black mold at the bottom, and there were calcium deposits caked on the shower head. Clearly, it was the last room he thought about and the first a woman would notice. He'd long let things go behind the scenes where it mattered, only maintaining the shell, the game face, the suit, easy target.

Bronson put his gun on the back of the toilet tank where he'd be able to reach it in a pinch and shook himself out of his robe. He paused there, and then he bent to pick it up off the floor. There was a hook on the back of the door and he hung it there, looking at it. A meaningless gesture at this point, maybe, but he had to start somewhere, didn't he?

He turned on the shower, extra hot, and when he stepped over the lip and under the jets, he felt like a country pig about to get wacked through the jugular. Vulnerable, hell. He felt exposed to the damned world, ball-sack swinging in the breeze like a party piñata. He jerked the curtain closed, the metal hooks making that tinny scraping sound along the bar, and for a second he just stood there looking at the highline stripe pattern on the vinyl. Then he leaned forward to pull the front side back cautiously. He reached out. Turned the lock on the door, and when he pulled back in he gave himself a silent "1-2-3" and went for it all at once, ducking his head under, curling in his thick fingers, rubbing vigorously. When he soaped down he did it hard, dropping the bar twice, but getting everywhere possible almost to spite anyone who thought they could frighten him out of doing a good, thorough job, even propping each foot on the far rim back by the shampoo and doing his shins and between his toes, bottom of his heels, under the nails, places he usually never bothered with. By the time he turned off the water everything was tingling, and when he ripped the curtain aside and grabbed out for a towel, he saw his skin was bright pink.

He patted his face dry and then stood there for a second, both hands holding the towel under his chin in a way that felt strangely feminine. He looked at the locked door. Usually he kept it open to let out the steam; he was a perspirer and he hated breaking a new sweat before putting on a fresh set of clothes.

He stared at the door. So easily could someone have crept up the stairs just now to wait patiently for him to finish. The fiend could very well be lurking there on the other side right here and now, wearing a grinning rubber clown mask—crazed, rolling eyes in the peep-holes—standing ready, holding a shotgun, a butcher knife, a crowbar, an axe. Bronson leaned over and got his gun off the toilet tank. He flipped the towel over his shoulder and reached for the door. Slowly, he turned the lock. Swung it open.

Nothing. Just empty hallway and a brush of cool air. He let out the breath he'd been holding and stuck the gun up onto the sink. No problem, business as usual.

But drying off, right after doing the yank and pull three times across the back, he thought he heard something.

Something foreign.

Something specific.

Something downstairs, east or west undetermined.

He dropped the towel in the tub and grabbed for his robe on the back side of the door, heart kicking. It was an old house. Often there were settling creaks, once in a while a good "pop," but that's not what just happened.

Knocking in the pipes?

Not that either.

This hadn't been a perimeter noise, nor something in the foundation. It was more intimate than that. Personal somehow. Closer, a clicking sound.

And Bronson was the pink-skinned scream-queen with no time to put on decent clothes to be stalked in. He pulled the belt of his bathrobe hard into a square knot.

He got his gun off the sink and moved out into the hallway.

# CHAPTER 27
# DO YOU SEE WHAT I SEE?

For the life of him, Connor hadn't been able to make sense of what was on the monitor at first. There was movement, dark streaks, blurred shapes, and perimeter ghost-lines, but nothing cohesive, not quite. He thought he'd possibly registered different sides of a residence from the exterior, but it could very well have been an old warehouse or factory. He'd also seen weird shapes, always opaque and fleeting, a pitchfork stuck in the ground, a steel tine rake next to a set of concrete stairs, a spade shovel at the bottom of a wall, a set of hedge shears, blades-down in a bucket, a long-handled ice chopper propped up on a rock, and it was all streak and smear, as if he'd stumbled on a display of bizarre farm-art in film negative shown under a blacklight.

A flash. Everything went bright and over-exposed, and then it all snapped into focus. It was a spotted skeleton with green hair lying on a tangle of Christmas lights in a wheelbarrow. Shadows jumped in and out of the skull sockets as if someone was holding a torch, and suddenly the sightline "blipped," like one of those subliminal things where you filmed a blank card for a frame, not quite altering the continuity, but putting a tiny nick in the flow to make it disquieting. A hand came into the shot from the right. It was his sister's hand; he would have recognized that chipped black nail polish anywhere, the edge of her sleeve too. She was wearing that gaudy motorcycle jacket with all the zippers, and she was holding one of those multipurpose wand-lighters you used for the gas grill.

Connor marveled at this "nanobot" thing. He was seeing what his sister was seeing as she was seeing it. Weird shit. Odd context, like looking through a Michael Meyers killing mask.

The flame went out, everything blackened. She cursed. He felt it come out of the monitor like percussion, though he hadn't actually heard anything. It was like being inside her head with the sound turned off, because Big Boy hadn't figured a way to hook up the audio, and when the wand flicked back on there was another of those blips. Of course, it was Meagan blinking . . . the human video camera via the weird chips set loose by the exploding tooth she'd ingested, go figure, sure man, happened all the time.

The skeleton lying before her was a rubber Halloween-decoration, and clearly she was in somebody's tool shed.

*First place I'd go if I was in a residential survival scenario, hunter or hunted.*

He thought of the red laser image of his dead mother, her manifesto, his missing gun, the strange command center he was currently sitting in, and the stranger big stupid boy-man who obviously wasn't so stupid.

*What are you mixed up in here, Sis? And where the fuck are you now, give me a smoke signal, anything . . .*

Her left hand came into the shot suddenly, and she had what looked like a jumbo turkey baster with blood droplets in the tube section. Taken from her coat pocket maybe? WTF! She tossed it and seemed to go for her coat pocket again, this time drawing out a roll of duct tape. She inspected it for a second in the wavering light, a quarter-roll left, and it disappeared out of the shot, most likely back into her jacket somewhere before she held the flame high and moved it across, shadows licking into the corners of the space.

There was an aluminum extension ladder leaning back there with dust webs floating between the rungs. There was perimeter shelving stuffed with cartons and jugs, and cluttered in front—a pile of leaf bags, a bike without a front tire, old screens, and an edge trimmer leaning against a piece of weather-faded wooden slat fencing. There were recycling cans, trash barrels, some old wicker, a broken bedframe, a lawn umbrella, and a gas mower with a busted starter handle.

To the right, however, was the cool shit hanging on hooks set in wooden rack mounts fastened to the walls.

Tools.

There was a Porter Cable reciprocating saw, a Bosch jigsaw, a Ryobi drain auger, and a cordless power drill. There was a blower, a heat gun, an electric planer, and an array of handsaws, all with the blades facing away on diagonal.

Propped below them, there was a cluster of lawn tiki torches. Meagan reached and lit the wick on the nearest one, re-leaning it so the flame wasn't poised under anything flammable. It immediately started leaving a black scorch mark on the corrugated wall steel.

Meagan turned, and both her hands came into view again, grabbing at a coil of orange extension cord that was sitting on top of a grime-spotted mini-fridge, and suddenly her hands went in and out of the frame almost rhythmically, as if she were doing the "Floss," backpack-kid dance in slow motion. She was going through her pant loops, making a belt.

"To hang shit off of," Connor whispered, entranced.

By the time she was done fastening things to herself he was awed. And mystified.

First, she had turned around a patio chair, using its cushion as a work table, and onto it she had dumped out a plastic CVS bag she'd probably brought from outside. It had been half-filled with acorns. Really? For whom, kid, for what? Then she stepped in and between things, going for the back-shelving unit, and there she snagged two glass jars filled with washers, wingnuts, and an assortment of screws, both coarse thread and sheet metal. She mixed it all together on the cushion with the acorns and, handful by handful, re-loaded the bag. She propped up her foot and took a box-cutter knife from her sock, which had blood-traces on the retracted blade she thumbed out, as had the turkey baster, and she spent a few moments nipping off lengths of the Christmas light wires. Some were already cut into pieces, as she'd been at them earlier, it would seem. She affixed the CVS bag to her makeshift belt. Then she tied on a wood-handled splitting hatchet, a hacksaw, a wood saw with a ripping blade, and the heat gun. The box-cutter went back in her sock. There was a fixture mount for landscaping shaped like a spike with an arrowhead, and that went into her other sock.

Oh, and one more thing.

Oh, Sis.

Oh, yes.

She hauled down the Milwaukee 2727-21HD; Connor knew the model number well, he'd YouTubed this sucker. Pint-sized and bad-ass, only 10 × 10 width and height. So beautifully crafted and so very deadly.

It was an 18-volt compact, battery-operated chainsaw.

Meagan walked out of the tool shed, and the moon must have moved from behind a cloud, because Connor could see now. The rain had tapered off, and she was in a backyard moving toward a big house, which was darkened and antiquated—looked like some kind of Colonial—two ramshackle stories with gambrel roofing and curved eaves, dormer windows staring out dully.

A man lived here, Connor sensed it, a man who tried things and abandoned them . . . the sense of tired helplessness here in the sprawling backyard blatantly obvious as Meagan moved across it. There was a campfire pit that had mudded over, blackened cooking grate there in the middle caved down on one end. There was a picnic table lying on its side, two sawhorses with a sagging piece of plywood between them, pickle barrels filled with wood scrap, a rusted steel drum, and a back deck connected to the house with weeds and cattails clustered underneath it. Off to the side, about fifteen feet to the left, the grass was worn down to a rough patch of dirt shaped like a rectangle. He'd worked on a car there and had never bothered re-seeding or laying down sod.

*You don't tie up your loose ends, Hoss. You don't like doing dishes.*

Meagan raised her glance to the skyline and did a slow pan, turning back the way she had come. The backyard property line was surrounded by thick foliage, the tool shed like a dark mausoleum at the back edge, the rising backdrop of dense woodland only interrupted by a line of trees with an L-cut to let wires through. Whoever this sad sack was, his place was utterly isolated.

*No one to hear you scream, Hoss.*

The sightline shifted, blurred, and refocused. Meagan was doing an inspection, looking downward, checking the equipment she'd tied to herself with Christmas lights and an extension cord, and Connor was reminded of something. It was a story that he'd had to read in twelfth grade by Ernest Hemingway, called "Big Two-Hearted River." Connor had hated it at first, boring shit about a dude going fishing, but there had been a moment where the guy had loaded himself up with a bottle of grasshoppers around his neck, a landing net hanging off his belt, and a long flour sack slung over his shoulder, flapping against the backs of his legs. Hemingway had said the dude felt "professionally happy," and Connor, being a gadget-geek, had related.

He couldn't see his kid sister's face.

But he would have bet dollars to donuts that she was professionally happy.

She turned and looked in front of her at the wooden steps leading up to the deck with the gas grill, a beach chair, and the door that most likely led to the kitchen. But she didn't go up the steps. She went to the right.

Far right, to the corner where the electric meter was bolted to the wall. Her gaze slowly went north. There were age stains shadowed up the brick and crumbling mortar in the joints all the way to the first overhang.

Connor smiled; he knew where she was going.

Meagan wasn't seeing mortar joints, edging, and overhangs. She was looking at hand-slots and footholds. Girlfriend was going climbing.

Just as she'd been doing for years via trellis.

# CHAPTER 28
# LONELY HITCHERS

To spite himself, Captain Canfield was not surprised at how many people passed you right by on the street if the woman who had been weeping blood into your shirt shadowed you now, one hand gripped to your shoulder, the other covering her empty eye socket ever so modestly. It was what they would call a "Catch-22," the conservative choice of walking back a block to knock on a door seeming better and better every moment they wasted "saving the time" trying to expedite a quick ride out here. Three drivers had stiffed them. The fourth was coming on fast, a low riding jet-black Mustang GT kicking up road-rain behind in a plume. Canfield stepped to the left lane in front of it.

The car swerved around him so deep it almost banged up on the curb.

"I'm a cop!" Canfield yelled.

"Fuckin' retard!" the driver roared back in passing. Canfield watched him speed off and turned, looking back up the road. He drew his firearm, and while he didn't like showing his hardware to innocent pedestrians when he was out of uniform, this was ridiculous. He only hoped the next driver he saw wasn't some hot-shot or nervous Nelly keeping a .38 in the glove compartment.

Headlights.

Smaller car.

Off-white Mini Cooper advancing timidly, bad muffler, probably had engine condensation dripping out the tailpipe, and as it got closer Canfield could see the driver pulling herself up to the steering wheel and staring over it in dawning alarm. Though the rain had stopped, the wipers were still going, and she looked like an old schoolteacher or college librarian with graying hair cut page-boy style and thick black Prada glasses. She slowed to a stop, and Canfield moved to the driver's side. She'd let down the window enough so you could see her bangs and her frightened eyes over the rim, and Canfield bent in, trying his very best soft-sell.

"Ma'am, if you please, I'm Chief of Police Bill Canfield, Lower Merion Township. I need for you to drive us to the hospital, now. Bryn Mawr is the closest, up Haverford Avenue. This is Erika, my administrative assistant. She has been injured and needs immediate medical attention."

"Oh, my word," the woman said. "Would you like me to move over and let you drive, Officer?"

"No can do, ma'am. No wallet, no ID."

She stared up at him for a moment, eyes big.

"Then how do I know you're a police officer?"

"You don't. I have a firearm. I'd rather not point it at you, ma'am, but I will. Still, I'd appreciate you saving me the paperwork. Uh, now hold on a second here, you're not looking at me, ma'am, look at me, please. You're about to drive away."

"No, she isn't," Erika said. She had moved in front of the vehicle. One hand was resting on the hood. The other came slowly off her eye.

"Oh. My. Word," the woman said.

Erika had the wind behind her, blowing the wet strands of her hair around. The area below the ravaged socket had swollen and bruised, and beneath that the blood and makeup had forked down her face like reptilian vein-work.

The woman said nothing, but there was the soft clacking sound of oiled metal on metal.

She'd brought the locks up, and Canfield reached for the door handle. To get her out of the vehicle. Looked as if he was going to break the law after all. She was no longer in any condition to drive.

*

She wasn't in much of a condition for anything else either, and Canfield knew he'd have to have her looked at as well. They'd frightened her almost to a state of paralysis. He'd put her in the back seat and had asked her to place a call to the hospital for him so they could have people ready. First, she couldn't find her phone in her purse. Then there wasn't enough light, and she needed her other glasses, and then, as Erika's breathing became more and more labored and Canfield drove faster and faster, she claimed the two of them were making her *"exponentially nervous,"* and it was a new cell phone her son Reggie had gotten her for safekeeping when she went out, and she didn't like it to begin with because the key tabs or "whatever in God's name they called them" were too small to work with. Worse, it had a lock on it that required you to make patterns between the dots on the screen, and she couldn't remember the shape. It was like a home plate in baseball, her Reggie had told her, with an added part where you had to make an X, but she couldn't recall where it was in the sequence.

She started to cry, and then she couldn't find a tissue, and then she smudged her glasses, and then in a quaking, blubbery rush she asked Canfield if he was the Scarecrow Killer.

"We're here," he said. "Just up ahead."

The Emergency Room entrance was at the far end of a U-shaped lot area and positioned under an overhang through a brick archway. Canfield screeched around and in, stopping short in front of the glass doors. He and Erika got out simultaneously, but when he came around to pull the passenger seat forward Erika sagged, barely holding on to the door. Canfield got her by the waist, and the woman in the back refused to move, too petrified. There was someone behind them now, and Erika was hyperventilating.

"Ma'am," Canfield said, "I'll send someone for you, but please, if you could manage to park over there it would help."

He didn't wait to see if she could comply. Erika's legs caved, and he almost had to drag her in through the revolving doors.

The waiting area to the left had some takers, maybe seven or eight people, and Canfield moved Erika toward the reception desk. The unit clerk was typing something and talking casually to a doctor in green scrubs standing behind her, yet when she noticed the grand approach, she trailed-off mid-sentence. Canfield suddenly wondered just how much of a problem it was that he didn't have his badge to flash, and when he got to the counter he wished it had been positioned lower so he'd have towered over it.

"I'm Chief of Police," he commanded. "Captain William Timothy Canfield of the Lower Merion Precinct. This is Erika Shoemaker. I know it's your show, but I'd appreciate it if we could work out the insurance and emergency contacts later."

The clerk was a thick woman, short-haired and earthy, and before she had a chance to respond the doctor came out from behind the counter and called for a wheelchair. It came quickly, and another nurse joined them with a mobile blood-pressure monitor stand on wheels. She wrapped a cuff around Erika's upper arm and put a pulse oximeter clip on her finger. The doctor was a thin man, graying, soft lazy eyes, but his voice was firm and reassuring.

"Okay," he said, squatting down to Erika's level, taking her hand. "Take a nice deep breath in through your nose and out through pursed lips. Smell the roses, blow out the candle, that's it, well done." He took a moment to do it with her and called back to his clerk, "Regina, call X-ray and Phlebotomy. Call MRI and get a hold of the surgeon on call. And hunt down Joe Lincoln, no . . . sorry, better for this would be Jahnui Acharya, Ophthalmology."

He looked up at the nurse with the bleached-blonde hair and high forehead. "What's her SAT?"

"Eighty-one percent, Doctor."

"Regina," he called, "she needs a nebulizer. Contact Respiratory and have them bring a vent." To the nurse he said, "Find a non-rebreather mask. Let's get her into a room and pack that eye." He got behind the wheelchair to push it, and on his way out with the small group he told Canfield to wait out here, he'd report what he knew when he knew it.

Canfield nodded. When the doctor had first started giving orders Regina had gotten right on her satellite phone, talking softly into it and intermittently writing down the doctor's most current directives on a legal pad as fast as they were thrown at her. Multitasking. Canfield was impressed, almost relieved, yet suddenly the clerk looked at the device in her hand as if it had grown legs and antennas.

"Lost contact," she muttered. She picked up a spare sitting on the desk and hit a button, next shaking her head, nothing. There was a muffled ringtone, and she reached into her shirt pocket for her cell phone. She held it in two hands, stared at it, then hit the off-on button with her thumb.

"Ma'am," Canfield said, "what's wrong, if I may?"

"No cell phone either," she said reflectively. "First a weird text, then nothing."

Over Canfield's shoulder something was going on, he could feel it, and the clerk stood up, looking past him. Canfield turned.

On the other side of the glass was a man in a trenchcoat sleeping open-mouthed with his head back and a woman with a bandaged thumb looking at a magazine. But all the others were standing now, looking at their cell phones, tapping them, making gestures to each other. Canfield spun back around.

"Ms. Regina, ma'am, what did the text say?"

"Um . . ."

"Ma'am, please."

"I think it was for you," she said.

"For me?"

"That's right."

Canfield gripped the counter with both hands.

"Word for word," he said. "Now."

Her neck reddened.

"Word for word, sir," she continued, "it said, *'You were right, Billy C., my good jolly friend. It's much more effective to just fuck with the Wi-Fi.'*"

# CHAPTER 29
# TRIFLES

Bronson came off the stairs cautiously, two hands on the Sig Saur, trying to discern what that noise was exactly. Tough call. It had been a ticky-tack sound difficult to place.

He turned right into the darkened hoarding room, thinking for the millionth time without really thinking that he had to clean up this particular shithole. He held his breath, felt along the wall, and flicked on the light. Before him there were piles of cardboard boxes—some with the flaps torn off, short tables, stacks of red plastic mechanic's bins filled with hardware and batteries and solder and tape-spools next to piles of papers and accordion folder cases stuffed in packing boxes for the air conditioners, the microwave, and the vacuum cleaner, all of it looking very much like that proverbial "junk kitchen drawer" supersized. The space was so crammed, in fact, that it would be tough for a person to hide in here, and Bronson worked his way in for a few obligatory pokes behind the file cabinets he could reach and the two closed-back shelving units that weren't flush to the wall.

Nothing. He backed out, shut the light off, and walked carefully the rest of the way through the serpentine path to the kitchen. The more he thought about it, the more it had seemed like a "stove" sound maybe, similar to the ticking of the gas igniter when you turned on the burner, yet the key word was "similar," as in *not quite*. Igniter-ticking was consistent, uniform. This sound had possessed a different personality, random action, like something falling. The first thought that had come to mind was one of those ball-in-a-maze games his mother used to occupy him with back in the day, where you turned the board every which way to get the plastic ball down through the slots and dividers.

Stepping carefully into the kitchen, he looked quickly across at the double doors leading to the deck. No scary silhouettes, no blurs of movement. He reached over, snapped on the kitchen overheads and the back-deck floodlight, nothing out there. He glanced up at his cabinets. Now that it had been more than a few seconds the tonality of what he'd heard from upstairs felt more and more indiscernible, and rather than question whether he'd heard it at all, he continued in faith with this lingering suspicion that it had been a kitchen noise, a piece of elbow macaroni tumbling onto the linoleum, a coffee bean, an almond, maybe he had mice again and they were into his dry stock.

But there it was again, a clicking, clearer this time, and it came from back over his shoulder in the living room, a sound that evolved, first hollow and echoed, then up close and blunt to dead quiet.

Someone was dropping things down the chimney.

Bronson moved back through the hoarding room to the main living space, strode into it, and stood still for a moment facing the fireplace, heart pounding so hard he felt it up in his ears. The first one of these that he'd heard must not have bounced out, but the second one had. His carpeting was a dim gray, and the small object sitting on it a foot from the hearthstone looked like a turd pellet from either a huge rat or a very small dog.

Bronson moved closer.

It was an acorn.

He went down to a knee between the storage chests, trying to remain calm and rational, weighing things logically. While it was alarming as hell that someone was up on his roof, *actually out there right now,* checking to see if he had his throat damper shut or not, it was clear that the son of a bitch didn't have much common sense when it came to basic building construction. Unless there was some cockeyed plan of running a tube down here and gassing him out, or even more cartoonish, dropping down a few killer snakes, there was nothing up in there but a dead end. It reminded him of that old classic horror film *Child's Play,* where there was a puff of dust and Chucky dropped down into the fireplace like Santa's grinning, bloodthirsty stepson. It made for a good camera shot, even better when Chucky kicked away the screen, but the writers were irresponsible with their research, or worse, condescendingly arrogant in their belief that viewers were that ignorant, and this is why Bronson never went much for horror movies. Chimneys didn't work that way. If they did, rain would get in, wouldn't it?

He moved the gun to his left hand and picked up the acorn. He supposed he wouldn't have known about the structural elements of chimney design either if his hadn't been in disrepair to begin with. He'd hired a contractor last summer to renovate the crumbling thing with a new flu liner and a replacement for the missing throat damper. Not that Bronson was about to go chopping wood and taking his wine in front of the thing on a bearskin rug, but it wasted heat and energy and he'd thought of reselling someday. The contractor had shown him the plans. Above the firebox, the smoke chamber was offset, key word *offset,* with a horizontal slot connecting it to the throat as the limited space through which smoke could pass. Bronson didn't recall the exact measurements of said "slot," but it had been mere inches in width, big enough for an acorn to fall through with a good bounce, but no killers, no Chucky dolls.

The contractor had tried to fuck him on the price, so Bronson had backed out, going up on the roof himself and capping the crown with a piece of plywood and a couple of Tapcon masonry screws, all energy-conserving-purists be damned.

He shook his head, grinning with disgust.

The killer had pried up the poorly anchored piece of wood and was tossing nuts down the chute. Like a kid. Bronson's smile turned the other way. He thought about the victim in the basement, the light show, the needles.

*Well, okay, fuckhead, you've showed me your hand now. You're a mastermind coming in here with nobody home, but mano a mano you're weak . . . good in the studio, but you can't pull it off live on stage.*

Another sound came through the chimney, but it wasn't an acorn.

It was a shucking sound and a clinky thud, as if someone had taken a grocery bag stuffed with pennies and ran it down the shaft to land on the smoke shelf.

*A bomb?* Bronson thought. *But why? You have a key?* Then he thought something else, and thought about the idea that thinking that thought in itself had put him two steps behind.

*"Why not just lace my spaghetti with Meagan Mullin's powdered DNA?"* he'd asked the killer earlier. "*Why the dog and pony show?*"

*"Where would be the sport in that, Detective Bronson?"*

Another sound blared out suddenly, distinct and high-whining, far out of context, but too close for comfort. It was an engine sound. A revving lawn-mower sound, but smaller and nastier, louder now, shrieking down the chimney like an air-raid siren.

Bronson began to push up, but he was overweight. Bad knees. All those times he could have found a treadmill or an elliptical machine, or even gone for a walk, yet deciding to sit and stew at his desk. It had all made him slow, and he was a full two steps in back of the eight ball. He was an arm's-length from the fireplace, and he knew it was best to roll hard right or left but the storage containers on either side of him nixed that idea.

There was no flu liner up the chimney narrow, just bare brick walls. Just big enough to fit in his cordless chainsaw and drop it bar-down, with its trigger tied to the "on" position.

The long, thin slot by the smoke shelf could concentrate and channel out shrapnel.

Turning his hearth into the mouth of a cannon filled with canister shot.

He heard his Milwaukee chainsaw come down. He heard it land, rip the bag of "clinky stuff" angry and hard, and the next sound was mighty and terrible, like putting your ear to the garbage disposal with the guest silver caught in the blades.

He saw things sparking in the fireplace—Mexican jumping beans, metal hardware like woodscrews maybe, nuts, bolts, washers, and wingnuts it looked like, all kicking hard ricochets, and he had just enough time to put his forearm in front of his eyes before assuming what the other dark objects were that he'd seen exploding straight into his face.

*Acorns,* he'd thought. *I'm going to die of sharp, severed acorns.*

# CHAPTER 30
# TRIFLES, PART II

Bronson didn't die. He hadn't passed out either, not quite. It was like being in a half-sleep on one of those long summer days with the flag flapping lazily outside your window, smoothly transitioning you through dreams of waves lapping up on the shore, wind filling the sails of small schooners, a grand clipper ship, your parasail taking you high across oceans and valleys.

Only here, it wasn't a lapping sound. It was a high insectile whine, and it wasn't a dream state but a nightmare. He saw, in his mind, vicious bugs, killer bees, angry wasps, all trapped in his fireplace, swarming in there, darting and weaving, flying out in a savage alarm dance and landing on him, thrusting their stingers into his face, working those abdomens like pump-jacks, hard clockwork.

The whining slowly died down and stopped with a sputter and grind, and the nightmare bled into another, the sobering kind, the dawning dread of sluggish waking that reminded you that you had taken a desperate dive forward into the fray with your forearm rooked in front of your eyes, and most of the shrapnel had whizzed over your head.

A lot of it, however, had stuck you like a pincushion.

He was nose-down on the hearthstones, soot in his mouth, everything warm and stinging as if someone was pinching his face with multiple pairs of handyman's pliers. The buzz of the chainsaw was still in his head even though it had stopped, still ringing, slowly fading, and there was something else now, off to his right.

Ticking.

Not like an oven igniter, a piece of macaroni, an almond, or even an acorn falling down the chimney. This was even more random, and Bronson got an image in his head of a toddler playing bongos with his rattle on the coffee table. Then he came to altogether and pushed to his knees.

That was no toddler.

It was the Scarecrow Killer outside his window, tapping it with his ring-finger, mocking him.

Bronson was on his feet. Multiple times now this son of a bitch had made him ingest things, disgusting things, a teen's DNA, gutter water, silt, and now soot, physicalizing the metaphor that Bronson had eaten shit his whole life, taken it on the chin, played second fiddle, never firing his weapon in the field.

Bad horror movie, right?

The "good" cop, the timid lawman, the one who always played by the rules, would have approached the window with extreme caution now, careful not to shoot when there was an opportunity for negotiation, for talk, cooperation, a deal.

He brought his non-shooting hand to his face. There were projectiles stuck in his forehead, at least four, sharp pointed wood screws by the feel, one of them buried through the left eyebrow at least two threads deep. The tip of his right ear was gone. There were acorn shards peppered all over his face, embedded like Rocky Mountain wood ticks, and his nose felt broken right on the bridge where a pair of eyeglasses would sit. Freshets of warmth ran down his neck and the sides of his chin; he'd been opened in ribbons.

Clicking at the window again. It sounded like that old kiddy fanfare riff, *"Shave and a haircut . . . two bits,"* and Bronson thumped over and shot right through the closed curtains.

Twice.

Glass blew into the yard, and the wind sucked out the short drapes, snapping them into the darkness like flags. Taped to the upper sash, hanging down center and gyrating like lunatic marionettes, were three strands of green Christmas wire with duct tape wrapped down at the bottom in rough crosshatch, pocketing what were most likely small rocks, aggie-sized, perfect for getting picked up in the breeze and knocking randomly against living room windows.

Ticking again.

Now it was the window on the other side of the hearth nearer to the front door, deeper-sounding, throatier as it were, not a stone but a knuckle this time possibly, the most common soft-knock, the quickie one-through-seven count.

Bronson stepped around his kit boxes and backed in to slide along the wall, ducking under a couple of nails he'd banged in for a large Monet print his mother had bought him that he'd realized he detested after a week.

Knocking again on the window, slightly more insistent, a one-through-five as if to say in sing-song, *"Hello, I know you're in there . . ."*

Bronson would have preferred to be positioned on the other side of the window frame for the more natural pivot to a balanced shooting stance if he decided to go front-on, but there was his reading chair in the corner that he never used and the lamp next to it that he never turned on.

Three knocks now, rising impatience, separated by a half-second each.

Bronson reached up for the curtain rod, sitting in the open grooves of a pair of cheap Kwik Hangs. He reached with his gun-hand. Got the edge of the hollow rod nestled in the mouth of the barrel and shoved it off and away. The drape-set fell clumsily to the carpet, and Bronson chanced a glimpse around the edge of the jamb.

He'd expected to see one of three things: glare, darkness, or a hint of movement.

None of the above. The window was bleeding.

It looked as if some horrid beast had pawed up to the glass and coughed blood onto it, with a blast-center in a rough circle that dripped crooked runners down to the rail. Bronson impulsively leaned over another inch so he wouldn't be straining his eyes so hard sideways.

The window imploded. The punch was terrific, and the hail of glass whizzed past Bronson's nose so close he felt wind. There was something dark in it, long and bird-beaked thumping down and kicking head over heels amidst the jumping pebbles of glass. It smashed against the leg of his oak desk, spun, and snapped against the far wall, denting the paneling.

A pitchfork. Taken from the tool shed, no doubt.

Bronson had his back to the wall, knees bent almost to a sitting position, gun straight out in front of him. He was panting. His eyes felt as if they were rolling in his skull. He was sweating into his cuts, and the stinging was more than an annoyance.

Someone hammered the front door, one dull thunk, single shot, as they did in a horror movie Bronson had actually appreciated at the time, called *The Strangers*. It took everything in his willpower not to waste bullets firing into three inches of solid oak, but just in case the prick was going to whack at it again, he decided to break the pattern of predictability. With a loud grunt he hauled himself up straight out of the squat, stomped across the floor, threw the deadbolt, and pushed.

Nothing. Stuck. He looked down, and from under the bottom edge he saw a row of metal nubs poking through. It was his steel-tine garden rake, kicked under to jam it. In terms of guessing ahead, the killer was up now three to zip.

Another crash, and Bronson whipped around. That sounded like the side window in the kitchen, to the right just above the sink. He lumbered across past the stairs to the hoarding room, and snaking his way through, he saw through the archway all the glass sprayed onto the kitchen linoleum like bright savage jewels. Closer, he saw that his Bully Tools spade shovel had crash-landed and wound up tip-down somehow, D-handle propped against the dishwasher like a farmhand leaning on his plow, catching a Marlboro.

Bronson crept forward to the edge of the hoarding room's carpeting, gun raised, finger inside the trigger guard. He was greasy with sweat and with blood, some still slick, some congealing, tough to think straight, and there was something wrong with the background in there, in past the breakfast table, something different. It was the double doors to the deck. The wooden handles on the outside had his manual hedge trimmers jammed through them. To prevent his escape, or at least slow him down.

Another implosion, this one muffled, the utility room through the kitchen to the left, and suddenly he got it. This wasn't about his wasting bullets or his possibly deciding in a pinch to go grabbing the pitchfork or shovel, running through the glass in his bare feet, and smashing through the doors to the deck where the killer had a thousand places he could be waiting out there to plug him. This was about making it so Bronson couldn't cover all points of entry. If he stuck with the living room, he'd have no angle on the sink window or the utility room. If he took a position in the kitchen, he couldn't see the living room. He was being forced into making a choice.

It would have to be the main living space. Considering the grade and the adjusted back deck, the kitchen window was a foot and a half or so above eye level. The utility room window was on the same plane and the smallest of the four, so chances were that the killer would come in through one of the hearth windows. And if he did do it the hard way from out back, Bronson would see him coming through the hoarding room. He'd have a split second, maybe two, and he could take cover, kneeling behind the far side of the oak desk or one of the contractor's boxes.

But the anticipatory positioning would expose his flank to one of the hearth windows, God *damn* it, he couldn't dot his I's and cross his T's logically and methodically with his face smarting and burning and throbbing like this!

Bronson turned to make his way back to the living room, picturing a gunfight in close quarters, the smell of it, the pain of being hit, the finality. Blood dripped into his right eye, and he wiped at it with his sleeve. His face felt like a tossed salad under a heat lamp. He stepped out, and there was a girl standing in front of his desk, breathing hard as if she'd just run a marathon, staring at the serial killer tracking board glued to the wall. She was a redhead, short, maybe fifteen or sixteen, slightly chunky, drenched hair pulled back behind her ears and held in place by the weathered John Deere cap of his that she'd evidently found in the tool shed. She had on a black motorcycle jacket, dark jeans, and weird knee-high punk boots, and she'd wrapped an extension cord around her waist. Tied to it like some lunatic carpenter's tool belt, she had a hatchet, two hand saws, and Bronson's heat gun, at least he thought that's what it was; it hung on the far side of her and he could only see the edge of the perforated guard nozzle. She was holding a service pistol between her two hands, barrel down. It was standard issue, the type the precinct's patrol officers carried. Shoulders still heaving, she looked over, face covered with gore. It was war paint, self-applied. Like the hearth window, there was a "blast-center," in this case her nose, and from there the blood pinwheeled off in jagged lines as if she'd gone to her back and squirted herself with a monster syringe. Decades ago trick-or-treating, Bronson had seen a similar effect when his elderly neighbor, Mr. Jacobs, had dripped red dye on a porch pumpkin.

"Meagan Mullin," he said.

She raised her gun and pointed it. Bronson raised his. For a second they were in stalemate and the air seemed to crackle. Slowly she lowered her weapon. Bronson held his position. He was about to tell her to drop it, but she turned to a sudden blur, so quick to speed it looked like a special effect.

The tools on her waist whipped around her like blades in a blender.

She burst away to the left and clapped down the stairs to the basement.

# CHAPTER 31
# UNVEILED

Right up until he saw the wall map, Connor Mullin was having the time of his life. His kid sister was a boss, no lie. When she hefted that chainsaw over the rough lip of the chimney and dumped it down, he'd clapped his hands together like a birthday boy getting a cake with extra sugar-lace and modeling chocolate. When she shimmied quickly back down to the ground and pressed the pre-made rock puppets to the living-room window with a piece of duct tape, he'd had his hands clasped below his chin like a nineteenth-century maiden getting flowers, and when she was waiting with the pitchfork outside the window farther down, the one with the blood blasted on it, he'd nodded his head up and down as if he'd guessed right about the type of pitch Aaron Nola was throwing to strike out Freddie Freeman.

In terms of the window-blood, now the turkey baster and retractable razor knife with the streaks on the blade made more sense. He'd always suspected that Meagan was a cutter, and he figured that the "procedure" was performed in the tool shed minutes before he'd picked up this broadcast, where she found a dirty sleeve of red plastic beer cups or maybe an old rusty mop bucket to spurt into, didn't matter, the special effect was pure "fire."

More so, she had the victim in the house on the run. Everything he did, she'd anticipated, and by the time she got to the back of the house and around to the room where she'd planted the ice chopper, Connor was more than a fan, hell, more like a *fanatic* as he sat there going over the steps in her routine so far, looking for flaws, finding none. In terms of straight terror with stone knives and bearskins to work with, she was craftier than Rambo. And while one might have originally thought the circular saw and the auger would have made better projectiles, like bowling balls smashing through plate glass, Connor saw that physics-wise, the lacrosse-style whip-action she'd manufactured with the long-handled gardening tools was nothing but epic.

Meagan was a fucking Alpha male.

*God,* didn't Connor laugh hysterically at *that* one, pounding the steering wheel, making the tripod monitor shake in its mount. He was still laughing in fact, almost to tears, when on the monitor he saw Meagan pick two jagged glass pieces out of the window frame under the rock puppets, and next, shove in a paint-spotted ground cloth she'd planted there to be used as a buffer. She stepped up on a hose-reel storage container, climbing up through, and once in, Connor saw the wall map as she did. A serial killer's testament to his own grisly handiwork.

Then he saw a very bloody Detective Bronson come in from a darkened room to the left. He was in a strange bathrobe, gun in hand, and Connor saw his own service revolver rise into the shot when Meagan pointed her weapon.

He stopped laughing.

His mother was the Sculptor Killer, or a critical part of the Sculptor Killer "concept" and its initial vision, doing her part profiling the targets and creating rough drafts of spectacular misdirection. The big stupid man-child was her muscle and brainiac in terms of the tech, and now it was clear that Bronson was their stooge with access, planting the letter with the magazine cut-outs in Erika Shoemaker's in-bin and planning to "sell" that fake manifesto from the inside, keeping everyone in the precinct off-scent, pounding the pavement and questioning every supermarket manager and college security guard in the tri-state area to no fucking avail, most likely for months, even years.

All good, but Big Boy had had other ideas, an internal double-cross, where one corner of the triangle took out the other two with the help of a pair of specialty contractors as it were, Mother's children. Connor was the first pawn, meant to be hyped for a confrontation, then getting so super-juiced finding Mother with the manifesto that possibly, repeat *possibly,* he might have gone and iced her himself, and if he didn't, same difference, Big Boy would lure her outdoors to tie up that loose end. Connor was the fall guy either way. Meagan was to be fed bits and pieces of this thing strategically so that she'd take care of Bronson like a hired assassin. Then she'd most probably be eliminated. It was heinous and perfect. The false manifesto, supposedly penned by Connor himself, now showed in plain black and white his "clear guilt," which he would categorically deny, while spending the rest of his life trying to incriminate his dead mother. He would never be able to link in proper context the "simpleton" truck driver with white hair who gave him a ride, because Big Boy would go MIA, and regardless of the results of Connor Mullin's inevitable court appearance, three working, conflicting theories would have been effectively created: mother as killer, Connor as killer, or the mystery security guard/grocery store worker (or someone specifically *not* those things who falsely claimed to be) who ingeniously framed both parent and child. Big Boy would run off into the ether untouched.

Come to think of it, the son of a bitch was probably hoping to save time, figuring that Meagan and Bronson might just take care of each other. It wasn't like the movies when it came to guns, not always, with one shot making your eyes go blank and your body go ragdoll. Often when hit, you finished what you started, adrenaline and all that, and Meagan had just run down to the basement. This was trench warfare. Bang, bang, both down, both continuing to shoot their magazines empty, a real possibility. And of course, Connor's gun was the one to be smoking. Big Boy would probably find a way to remove the powder burn from his sister's cold dead fingers and plant a new set of Connor's prints on the grip and the trigger. Sure, why not? If the bastard could invent semantic psycho-phonetic editing devices and nanobot eye movies, the last part of the frame-job would be elementary.

When she'd burst down into the basement Connor had gotten a jumpy view of a thin set of stairs, the masonry wall to her left, rough with layers where the patching compound had sloughed off. At the bottom there was a rickety end table knocked over in front of some white masking cloth that had a strange shape shadowed behind it. The corner had come loose top right, the dog-eared flap revealing a piece of rope circled around the piping, affixed to something just below the sightline.

Meagan ripped down the cloth, and Connor gave out a primal holler of fear and alarm.

The figure tied to the pipes was spindly and gaunt, too long and too pale, a human spider on a massive insect-exhibit board. She had needles going down one side of her, connected to tubes trailing off right. Her eyes were blank staring whites, her mouth covered with duct tape fashioned into a heart-shaped smile. Through her parchment skin you could see the shape of her clavicle, each rib, the points of her hips.

Ladies and gentlemen, Bridget Ballentine—tooth donor, her molar to be used as the physical carrier for affixed nanobots.

Welcome to her Hollywood crucifixion.

Immediately, Connor reached for the gear shift. Detective Bronson wasn't just the stooge here. Looked as if he was the group's torturer, their executioner who prepared the kidnapped victims for the jobsite road-shows here in his chamber, the "lab" most probably stocked up with blood-spattered splash basins, chains over razors, hot brands, meat hooks, cattle prods, and curved knives . . . battle hatchets, cleavers, tasers, and bone drills.

The first round went to Meagan, no doubt about it, but she'd been stuck in the arena with one bad fucking hombre.

Well, help was coming. Connor had wheels here and big ones at that. Though he hadn't recognized the residence from the view of the backyard, he knew Bronson's address from a few weeks ago when he'd been assigned to escort the detective home after he was threatened in open court by the cousin of a defendant he'd nailed for criminal mischief and arson.

Connor looked in his driver's-side mirror. This was going to be a bitch to turn around, a bitch to get moving, a pain in the ass on the winding roads once he turned off City Line Avenue.

He didn't have a game plan.

But wheels were wheels, all the same. Especially these. Sixteen-wheelers were totally "fly," and fuck it, they made for good battering rams.

Maybe Connor didn't need a plan.

Maybe he'd just drive this bad bitch right into Bronson's living room.

# CHAPTER 32
## GOOD TALK

Bronson moved to the edge of the basement doorway and leaned up against it, gun in both hands, muzzle angled away just below the chin line. Some of the blood on his face was still oozing, he could feel it seeping down his forehead, in the crease on the right side of his nose, along his left sideburn, and under that ear. It was partly dried in some places too, hardened like eyeshadow on the left, putting the lid at half-mast. He was afraid to rub it, brittle flecks, little knives, and he could feel a big rosy cheek-apple beneath, a clown-dot pinching the skin. How fast was there infection? Who knew, but the throbbing had become more pronounced, like the beat of a great drum with rips in the head, making it so he knew the design of his cuts and sores without looking in a mirror.

Was the girl down the basement stairs actually the Scarecrow Killer? His instincts said no, but she'd fucked him up pretty good here. After he'd been tricked into swallowing the horse-pill, the instructions had been to go save Meagan Mullin, so wouldn't it be just perfect if she'd engineered the whole charade from the start? The killer had used a voice-changer app, after all, and Bronson knew that regardless of the overall improbability, he had to be ready for all possible scenarios.

Either way, this was shaping up to a no-win confrontation.

If she was the killer she was going to come after him trying to finish this, and he was going to have to put her down. If she wasn't the killer, she probably thought that he was, and he was going to have to put her down when she came after him. He wished he could call a time-out to think.

"Mister," she called up the stairs, voice quavering, lower range than he'd anticipated, almost musical with a hint of a rasp in it. "Please, I'm just a kid. I'm scared. I'm sorry I hurt you."

Bronson considered this for about half a second.

"Nice try," he said. "But considering my living room pushpin and yarn map and the body down there that I know you've discovered, I figure you think you've confirmed who I am. Don't act like you didn't come here for this. Listen to me. Readjust. Be open to logic. I assure you right here and now that I put my living-room road tracker together to *catch* the Scarecrow Killer, and I didn't put that poor young lady down there on the pipes. To be honest, I can't prove to myself that you aren't the one who did."

"Me?" she said.

Bronson laughed shortly.

"Don't play little miss innocent now. That chimney stunt was clever and malicious."

"Thank you."

"Not a compliment. I'm thinking maybe you're a child-prodigy, an evil genius, and maybe I want to question you as to why you're killing college coeds in the first place, and more, why you involved me. You tricked me into ingesting your DNA, making me your hostage so to speak, so why the big break-in here? Explain your grand vision. There are bodies impaled and left on highway construction sites, crucified basketball players, and this vicious attack on an innocent man, all of it winks and flashes, piecemeal tableaus, but not much of a big picture. Enlighten me."

Now she was the one considering for about half a second.

"Mister," she said. "You gotta stop playing games, playing like someone made you do what you already planned. You know I knew you were gonna pull some weird-ass shit with the blood and hair sample I gave you, and I'm sorry, I'm just a kid, I was curious, I was exploring. When I saw you at the graveyard I thought you were just a creep, I swear I didn't know who you were . . . that you were the highway killer-guy. I'm not pretty and I'm not college-age yet, I mean, aren't there rules or something, even for guys like you? It's not like we traded wedding rings or anything."

Bronson tensed.

"Meagan," he said. "What do you mean traded wedding rings? What did he have *you* ingest?"

"What?"

"Now it's your turn not to play. Spill."

No response. He heard something shuffling around down there, but for the life of him he couldn't make it out. Sounded as if she was pacing. Somehow he had to get a hold of that gun of hers . . .

"Mister," she said finally, "I'm really afraid. Don't hurt me, please. Put your gun at the top of the stairs where I can see it. I'll come up slowly, take it, and go out through the window I came in, I promise. You can't blame me. I'm just a kid, it's not fair."

"What did you ingest, Meagan?"

Another hesitation.

"You know very well, but you want me to act dumb, right, Mister? Like one of those pervo role-plays or something? All right then, I'll say it out loud for you. It was a tooth, the one you gave me."

"A tooth . . ."

"The one that burst in my mouth."

Bronson got so excited he almost came around the corner to pound down the stairs.

"Meagan!" he said. "The killer is trying to force one of us to take out the other, but it's a rigged game, we're both screwed. If I kill you, your DNA is inside me. I'm sorry to be grotesque, but I won't be able to prove I didn't . . . eat . . . or ingest part of you as a sick sort of trophy. Check the body on the pipes. Check the head, Meagan, the mouth. I'll bet you she's missing a tooth. This killer is high-tech, methods advanced, and he's set us up to look like partners. Don't you see? If one of us kills the other, the one left standing takes the rap for the Scarecrow Killings. This sick maniac is having fun with us, and the only way to beat him is to approach the authorities together."

There was no response, and it took so long Bronson had this crazy idea that she might have gone catatonic, curled up on the floor in a fetal position.

"Mister," she said. "I don't know what to do. I'm confused. I'll do what you say if you promise not to get me in trouble. Just—just put your gun on the top stair, right there at the lip so I can come up and get it."

Bronson shook his head.

"No can do, kid. I'm the adult, I'm the cop, I'm the one driving this train now."

"You're really a cop?"

"Detective."

"Prove it."

He blinked hard, trying to get ahead of this thing.

"Listen," he said. "Take that gun and toss it up here on the landing. I don't mean to sound as if I distrust you, but we're at a standstill here. I need your firearm. Walk up five steps, no more, and underhand it up here, just like horseshoes. Then when you've gotten back down to the bottom of the stairs, tell me so. I'll be able to sense from your voice that I have enough distance to come from around the corner and take the weapon off the floor."

"How does that prove you're a cop?"

He closed his eyes in frustration. Hurt to do so, he opened them.

"Look, kid," he said. "I'm Detective Bronson, and I work with your brother Connor, first-year officer, a bit green, too eager to show he's gung-ho, but a good young officer just the same."

"You know my brother?"

"Affirmative. Red hair like you, acne on the chin, peach fuzz goatee, nerd trying to play tough all the time."

"That's him," she said quietly.

"Meagan, please," he continued. "I also have two contractor's boxes filled with investigative equipment by the fireplace that no one but a cop would have in his or her possession. I've got a badge and handcuffs in the top right drawer of the oak desk you were standing in front of when you were upstairs. You give me that gun in good faith and I'll walk you through it all. Then we'll go to the police station together." He paused. "I wouldn't mind seeing a doctor too. You roughed me up pretty good."

"Sorry about that."

"Forgiven. Forfeit your weapon."

No response.

"Meagan."

No response.

"Meagan Mullin, answer me!"

Nothing. Bronson leaned closer, ear almost touching the door frame. There was a sound down there. Something oral, faintly guttural, she was choking on something, possibly her tongue.

"Meagan!"

Something fell softly, sounded as if she'd fainted.

Bronson gnawed on the inside of his cheek. If she was faking it, he'd be coming down the stairs at a gross disadvantage. If she wasn't faking it, he would live the rest of his life as the police officer who had done nothing to save a young teenager, terrified and alone in his basement. It would have been the first thing in this whole circus he'd actually been guilty of, God damn it.

"Meagan Mullin," he said, "I'm coming down there. The ceiling and the opening are configured so my feet and legs will be exposed for a few crucial moments. Do not shoot at me. I am a trained professional, and if you shoot and miss, I am going to approach you with deadly force. If you injure me and I manage my way down the rest of the stairs, I will approach you with deadly force. Moreover, I remind you that I know my basement, every nook and cranny, so if you're hidden somewhere, I guarantee I will find you. If I see you pointing a weapon at me, I will fire, no questions asked. Do not ambush me, do not point your weapon. If you do, I will discharge my firearm with the intent to put you down, no exceptions."

He listened. Nothing.

"I'm coming down now."

He turned the corner of the stairway. He half expected to see her standing at the bottom, her brother's service revolver in both hands, aimed up at him, one eye squinted shut, the other looking straight down the barrel.

Nothing. At the bottom of the stairway he could see a few feet of the rough gray basement carpeting, that's all. The slanted ceiling made it seem as if he was looking through a telescope, one that yielded—from down there looking up—what would be a wonderful view of his feet and legs. He took a second to count the steps, twelve altogether. Looking at the siderail and the cutout of the wall on the right, he estimated that he wouldn't have a good look into the basement's front end with the piping, nor a clear view to the side until he was four steps from the bottom or so.

That left his feet and lower half in jeopardy for eight steps. His left eye was half shut. If she jumped into front view, she'd have to take aim, and he could squeeze off two shots. If she shot from the side when he was exposed through the cutout, she'd probably hit arm, shoulder, or thigh, possibly the pine slat handrail if he got lucky, and he'd have a fighting chance pivoting hard off the last stair.

Third possibility, he could go down to the fourth stair from the bottom, squat and aim under the handrail through the cutout to the side, but that gamble left him open to a frontal attack if she was, in fact, waiting up against the pipes.

Or she could be choking down there while he worked through scenarios.

An idea came to him. It wasn't a question of protecting his feet, but more, making her *think* he'd protected his feet, if even for a second or two. He turned and reached back into the pantry area where he kept his winter coats and the cardboard recycling stacked underneath. There was a packing box there that he'd broken down, heavy duty, from the Oregon Meat Company from whom he'd bought specialty product just to give it a try. The elk steaks were bitter and gamey, but the outer cardboard packaging was perfect, lined on the inner side with bubble aluminum foil–lined insulation. It was a big box, and one of its panels would look at a glance as if it were made of steel, similar to a loading dock plate with that diamond pattern, the skid-proofing.

Last week he'd ripped the box apart at its seams, and he reached for the piece that had served as the top flap, about a foot and a half by a foot. Good enough. He turned back and bent down, putting it in front of his shins.

He could have gone down slowly, but that would defeat the purpose. The approach with the cardboard was only meant to cause a moment of doubt, just enough for him to thump down the eight steps where he'd become visible.

There was no time to think; Bronson pounded down the stairs, holding the fake shield at knee level, gun pointed over it. The arch of his right foot banged up on the bottom of the cardboard twice, almost making him trip and go ass over teakettle, but somehow he managed, feeling like an elephant in a funhouse tunnel. Four steps from the bottom, the space before him opened, and five feet back he saw a figure positioned behind the end table lying on its side, legs back, its mirrored top-surface facing the stairs reflecting his advance. It was Meagan Mullin kneeling behind her own flimsy barrier, two-fisting her brother's service revolver across the top edge. Her face was covered, as she had evidently ripped some of the pipe-cloth and made a ghost mask with eye holes.

Bronson dropped the cardboard, and coming off the bottom step he almost fired a shot.

But in a flash he realized that it wasn't Meagan Mullin. It was Bridget Ballentine, her body taken off the pipes and positioned knees-in, propped across the dehumidifier that had been moved from the corner by the French drain . . . you couldn't see it behind the mirrored tabletop, but Bronson immediately noticed the space it had been moved from on the floor back in there to the right, the thin layer of accumulated sediment and concrete dust on the carpet marked by the blank square in it where the machine had been parked for years. Ballentine's hands were clasped together as a balancing point on the top edge of the end table with Bronson's crescent wrench sticking out from between her dead fingers. She was wearing the mask Meagan had cut out for her, the fabric held in place by Bronson's John Deere hat, and the dead basketball player had on Meagan's black leather jacket, long forearms sticking far out of the sleeves.

Bronson U-turned toward the back of the basement. She'd meant to see if he'd shoot on first impression as he'd threatened he would, panicking when he saw the flash of a "gun" drawn on him before really registering what he was looking at, or worse, she wanted to make him hesitate that all-important one or two seconds so she'd have a clear shot at him, uncontested. He finished the turn back toward the rear of the basement and took a position, gun raised, feet spread apart.

But all he saw was the dehumidifier, of all things, sitting in the middle of the basement floor back there, fifteen feet deep and parallel with the water heater.

"Oh, fuck," he said, turning back toward the front of the basement. Bridget Ballentine's corpse had already started sliding off far left, both hands still gripping the wrench as if she'd fallen into the surf waterskiing and hadn't yet given up the rope.

From beneath her, Meagan had pushed up from her kneeling crouch, where she'd kept herself in a tight ball, masquerading as a dehumidifier hidden from view by the end table's mirrored surface. Bronson had only made it to being half turned around, craning his neck, head on a rusty swivel, too slow, and Meagan Mullin was already aiming. Without the John Deere hat, her hair was matted to the shape of her skull, the blood-streaks on her face making her look like a mannequin in a house of death, a creature from one of those shock-horror rock videos Bronson never understood, like Alice Cooper back in the day, or that Marilyn Manson character who had been so popular in the '90s. She was wearing a reddish short-sleeved midriff blouse, and without the motorcycle jacket her arms looked untoned and pale white, utterly nondescript for all but the silver duct tape around her left forearm where she'd opened a vein.

She fired, the gun barked, actually sparked, and Bronson felt it immediately.

In his left shin. It was as if someone had taken a pickaxe and punched it into his leg: cold fire, red shock.

He tried to hold on to his Sig Saur; he tried his damnedest, but instead of his fingers clamping down the reflex went the other way, and his hand opened like spasm.

*I have to look that up,* he thought, going down like a sack of bricks, gun dropping to the thin carpet. He tried to fall that way, and he landed on his side, the gun bouncing two feet from him. He reached, he stretched out with everything he had, and inches away a combat boot came down on the muzzle. Almost daintily, she slid it away with her toe, and after retrieving it she stepped back into his field of vision, looming over him. She had both guns pointed down at him now.

"Hospital," Bronson said.

"No."

"You look like a zombie cowgirl from Mars."

"Wait here," she said. "Don't move. If you try to crawl away, I'll shoot you in the other leg, right in the middle of the kneecap, we'll both watch it shatter like a piece of china. Then I'll cut off your balls with a steak knife."

"I won't move," he said.

She turned for the stairs.

"Where are you going?" he said.

"Not far enough for you to get creative," she said. "The living room, five or six paces in and then back again."

"For what?"

But she didn't answer. She was already a quarter of the way up the stairs.

# CHAPTER 33
# A HOP, A SKIP, AND A COUPLE OF THUMPS

Connor hadn't caught the whole scope and sequence of his kid sister's basement ploy; he'd been occupied. The rig was parked in front of the chapel, which had that bullshit decorative garden stuff surrounded by a rock border too high to risk running over, and instead of having access to the roundabout going behind the building, he was stymied by a huge skid steer loader and a tandem vibratory roller next to it for what looked like some mill and overlay they'd done, both machines branded "CAT" and parked behind caution tape ten feet in front of him. He could have tried cutting a hard left, but there were gravestones peppered through there, and while it looked as if there may have been a tricky path he could have risked, making a rough backward S-shape, it would have been more than likely he'd knock over some stones, leaving him in worse shape than running over the border rocks.

He'd had to try backing it up, but he wasn't good in reverse. He ground the gears twice, making the cab jump and jerk. It was like trying to use a small pair of scissors to trim hair around your ears and not being able to pick up the proper angle in the mirror: on first try he turned the wheel the wrong way, making the trailer come to that "jackknife" shape behind him on the wrong side and pointing him toward the headstones as opposed to the empty parking slots to his right; then he'd worked himself into too much of a corner and it was a chore readjusting. By the time he did the choke and sputter, shuddering back and forth enough to give him the room to squeeze around, Meagan was already hidden behind the end table with its mirrored top-surface facing the stairs. Connor didn't even know what she was doing. There had been blips he'd caught, but it had been a mishmash of movement and smear when he'd chanced down a glance. There was a flash of her cutting down the hideous body with her box-cutter knife, a streaky flicker of her using the same tool to cut holes in the masking cloth she'd already slashed into a hood shape, and a whole mess of shaky footage as he put the big rig through its choke and grind.

The last thing he'd noticed when he finally had the eighteen-wheeler turned around was that Meagan was running upstairs to Bronson's big desk in front of the wall map, where she opened a drawer and found handcuffs. Connor drove the access road to the cemetery exit, and once through the wrought iron gateway arch he had to wait for two cars to pass before making his right. He looked down at the monitor.

Bronson was lying on the floor at her feet, left wrist cuffed to the steel leg of the splash basin by the washing machine. He seemed to be pleading. Jumping into the shot then was the hacksaw Meagan had taken from the shed. She had her palms on either side of it, and she moved it up and down like a small kid having fun with a steering wheel. She put down the hacksaw and pulled up the wood saw with the ripping blade. Same motion, but on the left side she pinched the tip of the blade between her fingers so she wouldn't poke herself.

Connor started his turn onto Sproul Road; he got it.

She was making him choose.

Something moved, something at the edge of what Connor was focusing on, and it took a second for him to register exactly what seemed off-kilter, something to the right, something odd. He looked in the passenger sideview mirror showing the rear of the trailer, doing the jackknife shape again, this time the proper way, as he made the sharp right. There was a man back there, climbing up on the back of the flatbed. A big man with white hair and a red baseball cap.

Face grim, Connor gunned it immediately, popping those gears, making the engine roar. The whole rig jounced with it, and the man almost fell right off the back, arms doing huge windmills.

As the rig straightened, the rear-side view vanished, and Connor hit the button to lower both windows, reaching out for the driver's-side mirror.

Sprockets screaming, he had to switch gears, and for a bad moment he feared he would stall out, trying to pat his fucking head and rub his tummy, standing on one foot trying to square dance in a hurricane, but he managed to smooth into acceleration and adjust his mirror to show the very back corner of the trailer. He switched gears again, getting a good rhythm with it, and motored past Cardinal O'Hara High School on the left.

Big Boy hadn't fallen off. He was poised at the peak of the back edge of the load of pine, crouched like a California surfer. Jaw steeled, Connor bore down, working it up to forty, then fifty, then fifty-five miles an hour, rushing past the Sproul Bowling Lanes, the emotions inside him exploding every which way, crazy firecrackers. The severe desperation he'd felt thinking Meagan was caged in with a superior foe had turned on a dime moments ago when he saw her reigning supreme, making him stoked to get the hell over there to share a damned victory dance. But this new development was a different rocket-ride altogether. Christ, it was like being bipolar! Bronson wasn't the beast Connor had suspected, but the man trying to maintain his position on top of the wood back there was.

He was coming to kill Connor Mullin, right here in this cab.

*Not if I can bounce you off, motherfucker.*

Connor geared up and worked that gas pedal. Big Boy was in for a hell of a ride. And if he decided to stay put, hunker down, and hold on? Well, fine, Meagan was a fucking god, and Connor was bringing her the last sacrifice. Together they'd solve the Sculptor Killer mystery, and he'd serve her the head of the snake on a forty-ton silver platter.

Big Boy clearly made the choice to stay put and hang on, and Connor saw in the mirror the man's red hat fly off into the night-wind as they approached the place where suburban roads briefly met major arteries at the edge of a short overpass foregrounding the Springfield Shopping Center and running perpendicular to Route 1, which ran underneath it.

The turn onto the Route 1 North ramp was a tight hairpin left, and Connor screamed headlong into it working the wheel, almost tipping it, bashing sidelong into the short concrete retaining wall with the passenger side of the cab, followed hard by the trailer slamming home, scraping and screeching.

*That's gonna leave a mark,* Connor thought, grinning wildly. There was another shock and a bang as Connor over-adjusted, pinballing against the concrete on the other side, but when he straightened it out and bounced down the ramp and onto the highway, he saw the beast had held on by lying flat and hugging that wood back there for dear life.

Connor roared down the long hill, gaining momentum, passing the beer distributor and the gas stations at the bottom on either side, and bolting up toward the Pilgrim Gardens Shopping Center. Looking in the mirror again, he saw his adversary had come a bit closer, still down on his stomach, trying to shimmy up like a union worker on a phone pole, the fucker.

Connor roared through toward Junction 3 where Route 1 automatically became City Avenue, and he started jerking the wheel back and forth swerving lane to lane through and around all the slow pokes, making a van going the other way blare its horn as it passed and two cars in front of him screech over, one into a bar parking lot where it plowed down a sign advertising hot wings and special ranch dressing, and the other into the entrance to the Llanarach Hills Apartments, running over a low row of shrubs and a thick host of flowers that burst like confetti.

Connor crossed West Chester Pike on a red light: lucky for him traffic was light. Horns screamed. Someone nipped the back of the trailer, but it didn't alter Connor's trajectory. He didn't lose any of his load; it was ratcheted down tight as a drum. He didn't lose his stowaway either. The freak had advanced to the halfway point up the wood. He was still shimmying bit by bit on his stomach like a big white leach, an inch at a time, but he'd gotten close enough for Connor to see his face. The mirror was shaking, but Connor could have sworn the man was wearing a mask of pale clay, slightly misshapen, divots and dents, and Connor realized it was heavy stage makeup, now smeared as if he'd tried to rub it off and only partly succeeded.

It also looked as if he were smiling.

Connor switched gears and floored the thing, foot literally pressed to the floor.

*Smiling, are we? Okay, fucker, we'll see what you do when my kid sister goes up one side of you and then down the other.*

Connor flew past a spatter of vehicles, which all seemed to have quickly gotten with the program and hauled ass over into the right lane for him, and he shot through Haverford Avenue like a runaway train. Past that, there was a gradual downhill leading to a rise, and coming over the crest at Lancaster Avenue it seemed the tires left the ground, the truck banging down, the long trailer following suit. By the time he passed the Point Apartments at Merion and Drexel Avenues he'd gotten it up to eighty-three miles per hour, bouncing, and banging, and flying . . . oh, my. When he roared under the crosswalk at Saint Joseph's University, he was going well over ninety. Just exactly how he was going to alert his sister to this particular situation was unclear. Just where all the cops were hiding with an eighteen-wheeler plowing through a major throughway at the edge of a city was another enigma, but Connor didn't have time to get out his detailing brush. This was a broad-strokes-only zone, and getting to Bronson's place and crashing this big bad bastard right through the front door was all Connor could let himself picture.

Past Saint Joe's, the scenery got noticeably and familiarly "urbified," and Connor got ready for another tight turn, the hard left onto Conshohocken State Road, where he'd pop back into Lower Merion Township, minutes away from Sir Bronson. But drawing nearer, he saw that there was some kind of Vision Center they'd recently built on the near corner, with this pre-fab pseudo-fancy stone monument showing the logo and address flanked at the edge of the sidewalk.

He'd wanted to cut that corner.

He did it anyway, leaning hard with the wheel, tearing across the grass deep in by the parking area, just missing the row of cement tire bumpers.

The banging was fierce, real bucking bronco shit, and the trailer rocked and jockeyed behind him. In the mirror, Connor could see that the man was still holding on, a bit bigger in the mirror now, maybe twenty-five feet from the cab at this point.

Connor had lost speed, but not that much, and he vaulted down the dark street, noticing the amazing dogleg-left coming up, but driving all the faster, God damnit to hell! He clenched his teeth and curled his lips, approaching hard, and he cut a slant right through the two opposing lanes, in effect cutting *that* corner as if he were lopping off a bad piece of gristle. Luckily the street was as barren as his plans, or he would have certainly been up for vehicular homicide on top of everything else, and by the time he flew over the short bridge and wound through to where the road dumped him onto Montgomery Avenue, he'd worked up one hell of a sweat.

He turned right onto Levering Mill Road, fast as he could without capsizing. Then the quick left, the right, and the soft left at the Y that would bring him to Bronson's place. The woodland was thick in here, and the overlays of branch-work blotted out the light of the moon. The truck's headlights lanced into the darkness, making the approach seem tunnel-like, and Connor made the last turn, cutting his third corner of the evening, taking out a huge wild bush that looked like Japanese knotweed and then Bronson's mailbox, snapping it beneath the undercarriage like a piece of kindling.

It was a short way to the house, shorter than Connor remembered it, and he slammed on the brakes, literally standing on the pedal. Bobbing and starting in the headlights was Bronson's Ford Crown Victoria, parked sideways on the crushed stone and cinder he used as a rough sort of parking roundabout rather than grass out front with a walkway. Connor had remembered this as well, but he'd recalled Bronson keeping the car off to the side. Here it looked as if he'd simply swung it in front of the door for convenience. Probably because it had been raining, and his hasty park-job shortened the "landing field" considerably. It also meant that instead of bashing through a wall, Connor was simply going to bulldoze the car against the front door. It would act like a buffer, defeating the purpose.

Or would it?

Connor had no time to work out the physics in his head; he'd already committed to stopping.

There was a harsh rasp and roar as the tires kicked up sprays of road grit and cinder, and Connor broadsided Bronson's car like a matchbox. He thought he heard the Ford's tires snapping off their axles, but it could have been something else; everything was a blur. Almost comically then, everything came to a stop inches from the house, and caught in the blare of the headlights was the tip of the rake handle sticking up, the tines below—out of the sightline, jammed between the rail and the threshold of the front door.

There was a ticking sound, the stalled engine winding down, and it smelled like oil, blue smoke, and exhaust. Somewhere off in the distance an owl hooted, and it gave Connor the sudden answer of how to alert Sister-Alpha, that is if she hadn't heard the raucous approach out here. A trucker honk! And he didn't have to request it with an elbow bend, fist pump. He was in the driver's seat!

He reached for the lanyard cable hanging down from the left corner of the cab, and there was movement in the open window. A hand groping and grabbing, a big-ass hand, and Big Boy had clearly made his big advance when they'd turned down Levering Mill in the shadows of the tunnel-branches where Connor wouldn't have been able to see back there even if he had been looking.

Connor slapped at the monster-paw, but it was as if it had a mind of its own, getting a grip across the bridge of his nose, a thumb back in one ear, the middle finger burying itself in the other.

Connor gripped at the thick wrist with both his hands, but it was like trying to move iron.

*He can't kill me while he's lying on the roof, palming me backhand like this. He can't possibly kill me with one hand, he can't.*

Connor heard a voice, from the simple one who had told him about growing up down South and coloring in horses with crayon, only the tone and inflections had changed, no longer "simple," but silk-smooth and exacting.

"Remember what happened to the Prince of Dorne?" he said.

Connor remembered, of course, who wouldn't? *Game of Thrones,* season 4, episode 8, when The Mountain burst the dude's head with his bare fucking hands, duh. But he went in through the eyes, not the ears, and Connor measured miserably what a backward testament this was to a moment of directorial greatness.

He strained over a last look at the monitor. His sister was picking something up off the basement floor. It wasn't a handsaw. The hand on his head started exerting the real pressure, vice-like, and for the second time that night he wondered if he'd retain consciousness long enough after the kill-moment to see the spatter of blood on the screen.

He did.

And just before darkness, he thought:

*Yes, I'd guessed right, there's meat in the runners.*

# CHAPTER 34
# A TASTY LICK OF OMNISCIENCE

The was a big man in the cab of a big rig, and he had put the awkward baggage back in the sleeper compartment, buried under the comforter and a half hamper of laundry he'd dumped there. He'd closed the trifold computer screen and pushed it down behind the side of the seat on its spring-locks, and he was just completing the process of wiping off the monitor and collapsing the gooseneck to slide it down out of view in its slot when the girl jumped up on the stair on the passenger side. She had blood streaked on her face like a bicycle wheel with streamers twirled on the spokes, and her red hair was flattened to the shape of her head. She stuck a gun in through the open window.

"All right, Crud-Face," she said. "You're going to drive me back to my house at 503 Elderberry Street in Broomall, right now, no detours, or I'm going to take out both your knees, shove the hot muzzle up under your nose, and blow your motherfucking head off."

# CHAPTER 35
# THE WORKPLACE IS MY SANCTUARY

Captain Canfield had never been so goddamned happy to see a parking lot full of black and whites in his life. The Lower Merion Precinct Station House. Headquarters. A proper hierarchy of command, sophisticated equipment, strict order, superior numbers.

Back at the hospital, it turned out that Canfield didn't have to hijack a vehicle or borrow an ambulance. Before adopting that measure, thinking methodically, he had taken a moment to test the validity of the apparent communications shutdown right there at the emergency room sign-in counter. Though he'd semi-bluffed earlier that evening that he wasn't a "tech-nerd," he was aware that the "Wi-Fi" didn't have anything to do with satellite phones, and he pretty much knew that cell phone power came from a number of different sources simultaneously. Whatever this was, it was specific to the hospital employees and patients, most probably temporary, and so he ordered the clerk to get on the PA system and have all building occupants check satellite phones, radios, and cell phones, everyone from security all the way down to the janitorial crew.

Within the first two minutes, the woman who worked register number four in the cafeteria, name of Adeline Jones, came rushing around the corner (limping actually, she walked with a cane), face flushed, calling out to Canfield that she'd picked up service on her cell phone. The whole Wi-Fi thing was just another big hoax, and by the time everything else came humming back up to function, Canfield had already begun dismantling the ugly charade in its entirety from the ground up, first ringing the station to demand that dispatch call back all units responding to the false terroristic scenarios, and then ordering the ranking officer on night crew, Captain Phil Hammond, to gather the troops to meet at the station, all hands on deck, including those on day shift and overlap, as many as he could get a hold of currently off-duty from Patrol, Traffic, and Detectives. He also requested that Rochester and Franklin call in their three primary teams from Vice as well as Rotterdam and her ten most experienced officers from Juvi, all the rock stars and crucial supporting players to report to Command Central for a powwow, right away, yesterday.

Adeline never got back her phone.

Canfield hadn't waited around for a squad car to pick him up either. The woman in the waiting room with the bandage on her thumb, Roxanne Ryan, had a brother on the force over in Radnor, and she decided her injury wasn't so bad after all. She had a Prius and didn't mind going through red lights.

She drove him to his necessary pit stop, resulting from his second phone call. When he rang the neighboring Broomall station, Lieutenant Swan, a new transfer from Pittsburgh, insisted Canfield swing by, show his face. Canfield had expected this, and he appreciated Swan's caution and insight. This whole crazy affair had been based on clever impersonations and false reports, many of which had been called in to the Broomall facility itself as the killer had indicated earlier, and before deploying officers anywhere else Swan wanted to make damned sure Canfield was who he said he was. There was a photo on the federal database as well as Bill's fingerprints; he'd be out of there in no time.

Canfield would have done the same thing.

And it wasn't too far out of the way.

"We're here," said Officer Webster. The "meet and greet" at the Broomall station had taken twenty minutes, forty-three if you counted the driving time, and after sending Roxanne home and thanking her for her service Captain Swan had quickly done the identity verification and put Canfield into a Broomall patrol car like royalty: sirens, flashers, the works. And now that they were half a block from the Lower Merion station house, Canfield felt real relief for the first time that evening. The familiar lot was packed, cars backed up actually waiting in line to get in where all the spots were taken, and they were parking in the access lanes and up on the median grass. They were good men and women, soldiers, real-life heroes coming in on their off-time to help right the ship and go get the son of a bitch who'd thrown their operation into a tailspin.

"I'll get out here," Canfield said. "That parking lot's a damned jungle."

"Yes, Captain."

He nodded.

"My thanks for the lift, Officer Webster."

"Pleasure."

Canfield reached for the door handle.

The car radio barked.

"Officer Webster, emergency message just called in to us—Lower Merion dispatch to Broomall dispatch. Captain William Timothy Canfield is to stay put. Explosives were just found in his station house basement similar to those wired to the squad cars earlier at the Shoemaker residence. High possibility that there are more hidden in the building, and it is believed that Canfield is the inadvertent trigger."

The captain clenched his teeth and put his palm up to the door glass. It was still crowded outside the facility, but the movement of the pattern had changed. They were evacuating. Too slowly.

And the parking lot exits were gridlocked.

# CHAPTER 36
# A TESTAMENT TO MY DEAR MOTHER

Expressionless, Meagan Mullin stood in her mother's room in front of the desktop computer. On the screen was an email with an attachment, and it was addressed to Helen Juniper of HarperCollins Publishers. The attachment was a long short story titled "The Sculptor," and it was her mother's last wish that it be sent to its final destination.

Meagan had no idea if Helen Juniper really existed. She had no idea if the Scarecrow Killer, whom she'd just left behind in the basement of his ugly-ass house, had manipulated her mother into writing this the same way he'd managed to make pixels come out of cell phones.

Didn't care.

It was her dead mother's last wish.

Meagan Mullin heard the distant drone of approaching police sirens, and she didn't care about that either. She reached for the mouse, moved the cursor, and clicked "Send." And when the big hand fell on her shoulder, she quickly reasoned that he couldn't have come in the front door, she'd locked it. He hadn't broken a window downstairs either, she'd have heard it.

He held her still and palmed a rag hard into her face with his other big paw. Smelled like furniture polish or some kind of heavy industrial cleaning fluid. She swooned, and the last thought she had before losing consciousness danced through her mind in the spirit of one of those childish tongue-twisters where all the consonants sounded alike.

Wasn't "Peter-Piper."

It was,

*Crud-Face climbs trellises quickly and quietly.*

# CHAPTER 37
# HEART TO HEART / EYE TO EYE

Meagan Mullin jerked awake. She was sitting, tied to a steel chair, not too tightly, but enough it seemed to have kept her from slumping over onto the floor while she'd been unconscious. In front of her was a set of lab tables with those gas jets like the ones they had in high school that were never connected to anything. There were test-tube racks, beakers, laptops, and a bunch of blinking shit Meagan couldn't identify for the life of her, all of it punctuated with switches and connectors and twists of wire spliced and pigtailed into thick, complicated weaves that snaked back to a power source hidden behind a set of large canisters that looked like basement water heaters and a few large spools of cable of the sort the utility guys used when thunderstorms knocked out the electric.

Far left, there were computers stacked like a wall of amplifiers at the Wachovia Center, and next to those, farther in and catty-cornered, were ten or eleven huge gas ranges with chef pots, stew pots, stock pots, casserole pots, pressure cookers, turkey fryer pots, and a bunch of pharmaceutical glassware on burn-stands, all in use—heating various liquids, some of them bubbling over, twisting up vapors. Smelled vinegary, industrial, like the rag that had been pushed into her face. There were other tables in front and to the near right cluttered with more of the scientific paraphernalia, like microscopes, magnifying glasses, goggles, rulers, scales, measuring devices with glowing meters,

X-Acto blades, a drafting board on a tabletop podium, tweezers of different lengths, snips, tubular constructions that made sharp pitches and angles, soldering stuff, welding stuff, power tools, and gas canisters with curly-cue tubing and gauge-clusters.

It felt like a warehouse; she gazed upward. Above her the ceiling was at least thirty feet high, made of what appeared to be concrete with exposed girders, studded crossbeams, and nests of wide elbow piping.

She looked over to the right—hospital feel over here, definitely. There were steel operating tables along the wall, and a bunch of stuff Meagan did recognize from her anatomy/nursing elective: knives and power drills, scalpels and splitter forceps, orthopedic surgery saws, electric osteotomy saws, a reamer, a joint saw, and an invasive oscillating saw, all propped on individual stands and affixed to wall-mounted brackets. There were cabinets on wheels and those bolted to the concrete, sinks with sprayer units to the far side, an industrial floor drain, and a cloak area with various aprons, smocks, and polyethylene bibs.

Suddenly startled, Meagan jerked her head down farther right. There, just back of her shoulder, was a woman lying on a gurney, asleep, not dead, her chest was moving ever so slightly, black bands strapped across her hips securing her there. There was an IV in her arm, and her face was packed on one side with thick white gauze material fastened with surgical tape angled over her forehead and under her chin. She was the most beautiful woman Meagan had ever seen, besides Liz Buckingham of Electric Wizard, of course. Nordic features. Looked as if the wound was to her right eye.

"Meagan Mullin, it's time that we had a chat."

The voice came from behind her, soft but grotesque, like stepping on a slug with bare feet. Meagan snapped her glance frontward, she wouldn't look first, no fucking way.

She suspected she'd be tortured.

He'd probably been in it with the Fat Walrus all along, maybe as partners, and she made herself go blank inside. Like a piece of paper with no writing on it, like wood. He could very well torture her, but she didn't have to tell him jack-squat.

A shadow fell across her on the left side, angling past across the concrete floor and pitching up along the facing of the closest lab table the way things looked double-jointed when you stuck them in water.

Right beside her now. His presence was thick, she could feel it.

The form passed in front, turning, taking his position ten feet before her.

Black cleated PVC knee boots, size nineteen at least, maybe twenties. Gator-green coveralls, pant-legs spattered with faded chemical stains in what almost looked like purposeful "random" patterning like one of those old-fashioned maps of the continents. Huge hands, long hanging arms. She looked up at his face.

He had on a scarecrow mask. It was homemade seemingly, weathered burlap, loose shank of rope tied around his neck to gather the rough fabric in accordion folds, leaving the excess of flap-work draped along his wide shoulders and sweeping down across the top of his chest like a demented sort of lion's mane. On either side of the mouth-hole he had a coarse stitched grin going up both cheekbones, higher on the left, stitching between the two sides of the nose-orifice making it skull-like. Bald crown with worn leather patches sewn into it, his blue eyes glinted at her through the peepholes.

He leaned to grab a steel folding chair, and it looked small in his hand, like dollhouse furniture. He spun it, set it backward, and sat, folding his forearms across the backrest. Meagan swore she could feel his animal heat even from here, and she tilted her chin up at him.

"What's with the mask?" she said. "My mother's story was titled 'The Sculptor.'"

"Yes, there's no mask for a sculptor, yet I can surely be both."

"You killed my brother."

"How do you know that, Meagan?"

"He was behind us in the truck. He smells gross just like you or your partner said right before showing me pixels of sunflowers and dandelions. I didn't put it together at first because it was faint and out of place and mixed with all the other truck smells, but now it makes all kinds of sense."

"My partner, you say?"

"The Fat Walrus."

The giant didn't respond for a second.

"Meagan," he said finally. "Meagan Mullin, my child. I want you to know before we move forward that killing Connor was a challenge, more so than your father, who whined like a tween and broke like a twig. Now that we have that formality covered, I imagine in fairness that you have a lot of questions. For my part, I will answer them with absolute candor and accuracy. You must do the same, however. No lying. No hedging. No making things rosy."

"My father's dead?" Meagan said flatly.

"Yes. Do you have something you want to say about it?"

"No."

"Don't want to talk about how you feel?"

"Never, your turn, tell me the whole story."

He cocked his head ever so slightly.

"You won't know the whole story, Meagan, at least not this evening if I decide to let you live through it. The sum-total would be impossible to tell and rather impractical to try and lay out in its proper chronology. I promise, however, to provide you with highlights. Honest ones, with all the detail you care to handle."

"Fine, where's my leg?"

"You mean Detective Bronson's leg?"

"Yes. I want it."

"Of course. It is on ice. It will be returned to you when we are done here."

"Good. You may have been partners, but he's the one who killed my mother."

The man's eyes seemed to be smiling.

"No, Meagan. I killed your mother, through you, of course. And Detective Bronson wasn't the Scarecrow Killer, nor the Sculptor Killer or a copycat, nor the stalker you assumed him to be."

He stared at her for emphasis and then reached down into his side pocket, drawing out a small device that looked like a television controller with a pointer. He held it up, hit a button, and traced in the air a large rectangle shape, leaving green pixels behind like soft glowing stars. The rectangle then filled itself in, becoming a piece of dot-animation that looked like one of those 1970s reel-to-reel tape set-ups, spinning. Next, from speakers positioned somewhere off to the sides a recording came up of the killer's voice enhanced through the robotic mixer-app along with that of Detective Bronson. It was dialogue about smut on his hard drive; Bronson was being blackmailed. The giant reached up to the floating animation and spun the reels, fast-forwarding to a later conversation involving Meagan herself. Detective Bronson had been given a choice. It was to save Meagan or the girl on the pipes.

The killer hit one of the controller buttons to shut off the tape. Then he made a wiping motion across the presentation and the image vanished.

"You see?" he said. "He was just a good cop, trying his best to rescue you from the likes of me."

"He wasn't a good cop," Meagan said. "He was weak and he was stupid, and how do I know that recording is real? What do you mean you killed my mother, fucking why?"

The man studied her.

"One thing at a time in due time," he said. "About the recording, I agree, you have no way of verifying its authenticity. That's part of it, so deal with it. Moreover, you know damned well that it *is* real, so let's stop playing silly mind games that are well beneath both of us. I'll get to your mother in a moment, with great respect I might add, but first things first, I'm not done quite yet with what went on with Bronson. Explain what you did after handcuffing him to the splash basin."

"Why?"

"I want to hear it in your own words. While I recently watched the replay on my visual monitoring system, your explanation would provide context and perspective left incomplete by the lack of audio."

"What do you mean by 'visual monitoring system'?"

"Baby steps. What did you do to Detective Bronson and to what purpose? Be clear."

"Fine," she said. "I thought he was the Scarecrow Killer and I told him I wanted my bullet back. I told him to cut the leg off just below the knee, and I gave him a choice. The hacksaw would be smoother, but slower. The ripping saw would be quicker, but it would probably hurt more. He refused to do it, so I cuffed his other wrist to the other leg of the sink, and I used the hatchet to chop off part of a finger. I told him I'd go down a knuckle each time he refused. When I got to his ring finger he caved, begging me to uncuff his cutting hand. He went with the ripper."

"And looking back, how do you judge his performance?"

"Weak and ineffective. He tried to shove it through deep on the first push and the blade didn't catch, it just scraped down the shin-bone curling up skin. He cried out like a girl. He tried to get smart then, tried drawing it backward just below the knee to carve out a starting groove. By the time he had it ready, he was shaking, and this time when he tried pushing a good rip, he punked out going too soft, getting stuck halfway through the pass. He had to see-saw the blade out, and it was wet with blood, his hands greasy with it, and he was drooling and crying. By the time he finally got the damned leg sawed off, I couldn't understand a word he was saying. Wasn't listening anyway. I told him he needed to cauterize the wound. I gave him the heat gun, and I told him that if he didn't use it he was going to bleed out. As an alternative, I told him he could be quick about it and use the landscaping spike to end himself. I told him he could ram it straight through his own throat if he liked, right in that puckered hollow under the Adam's apple, but he hadn't the courage. Couldn't do the heat gun either. He bled out. I was glad."

"He was innocent of what you suspected. Are you still glad?"

"Yes and no."

"Why both?"

"Yes, because he came for me in the graveyard like a lame-o perv and his overall weakness made me feel ill. No, because I killed an innocent man. *If* I killed an innocent man, that is. I don't know if I believe anything you say, whether or not you say I'm playing games when I tell you. This question-answer bullshit is a game in itself, and at least I can admit that I'm doing it. So now it's your turn. You want to tell secrets, then spill 'em. Why me? Why here and why now? And why the fuck haven't you snapped me in two like a twig at this point, just like you say you did to my dad?"

Silence. He was just . . . *staring,* and when he finally spoke it was so soft it made Meagan want to scream and thrash as if she'd been covered with larva.

"I haven't broken every single bone in your body, dear Meagan," he said, "because you've left me in a predicament myself, similar in a way to your current internal struggle with the idea that you now know—and you *do,* in fact, know—that you effectively tortured and murdered an innocent man you thought was a monster. For me, I have been forced into a paradoxical choice, something I always so effectively architect for my lab rats, ironically. You have me angered and awed, undecided for the moment, and regardless of what happens following our discussion tonight, this is something of which you can be proud. I have never been undecided."

"Until now."

"Precisely."

"Why are you angered?"

"You robbed me of my ending."

"And why are you awed?"

"Because of *the way* you screwed up my ending," he said. "My research on you indicated that you could be devious, but I never could have predicted the kind of offensive you unleashed on Bronson. And while you are still young and developing like a green tree limb, you are not who you think you are, nor who I thought that I thought you were." He folded his hands on the backrest. "You are like me," he said.

"I'm not."

"You are. Keep this clear, measured facts, nothing rosy, don't make me remind you again. You can't lie to me, Meagan, I'll know it."

"Yeah, you have research on me. How long were you watching me, learning me?"

"Years. All of you."

"All of us . . ."

"Yes, the perfect roster of players that made for the perfect tangled web. And it should have unfolded with flawless precision, even with the improvised storylines I originally left room for."

"Improvised?"

"Of course. It enriches the game. I worked out pathways and one or two counter-paths for most scenarios, but mathematically it would have been impossible to cover every potential response. Some I left up to chance, providing the spark and letting it fly off toward the paper and silk, so to speak." He put up his "hold-on" finger. "Of course," he continued, "this left me open both ways, first for spectacular aesthetic brilliance, yet also catastrophic failures. A perfect example of the spectacular was, and is, your mother's manifesto. It was of ultimate importance that this be created, at least in rough draft, solely by her. Far, far scarier and effective that way. And trust me, Meagan, it was . . . spectacular."

"And I am your failure."

"Partly, yes. The part of the unexpected I couldn't reconcile."

"What else was unexpected?"

He studied his fingernails briefly, then dropped his hand back on the back of the chair.

"Nothing I couldn't handle," he said. "The original plan was that your mother would hit 'Send,' thinking she was going to publish a new kind of dark fan fiction. She'd go to your room to share the experience with you, find the room vacant, and follow you to the graveyard, where I had manipulated the gate posts to allow for her to crawl through, something I wouldn't have originally thought she would do, but remained sure that she would from past observations of this behavior, even in the snowy months, getting soaked, getting dirty. That was how deeply she loved you."

"You fucker."

"No time for names, dear. The keystroke she didn't make changed the game. Two towns over, Captain Canfield's home computer was already successfully infected with the malware that would collect the three thousand emails I'd pre-loaded to blogs, newspapers, television stations, and radio outlets, forging the headers, and writing everything on to his hard drive. It would also have set off the explosives I'd had planted in the Lower Merion police station basement, behind the cardboard storage boxes in the far right corner of the old records room, under the heating unit, and tucked just inside the lip of a floor drain they'd used for a shower area before the renovations to the east wing and the additions of the lot trailers back in 1973."

"So everyone would think Captain Canfield was the Scarecrow Killer."

"So *many* would have thought Captain Canfield was the Scarecrow Killer. Discovered in the station rubble would have been the replanted spine of the thesaurus he regularly used, now to be believed to have been utilized to help him make notes at work that he took home in order to write the false manifesto on his PC. Detective Bronson would have been named as both his co-conspirator and intended patsy, and forensics and the techies would have claimed they could prove that the high-density explosives were detonated by a signal sent from Canfield's cell phone, which I had pre-rigged with a triggering device he wouldn't be able to explain away even though he'd left the phone at home on his bureau throughout the entire fiasco."

"But you only wanted 'many' to believe this. Why not everyone?"

"Legends aren't made of neatly tailored, tied-up loose ends. Improvisation, remember? More frightening than a nightmare are multiple versions of a fatal truth, and I intended to leave the public the implements they needed to become master-authors of their own collective horror story. Canfield would have felt responsible for the multitudes of officers killed in the explosion. All brothers and sisters in blue. All men and women under his command erased in a blast he'd have felt he could have prevented if he'd only been able to decipher my phone impersonations . . . if he'd insisted upon a safe house for Erika Shoemaker, his administrative assistant lying there next to you, instead of taking her to his residence . . . if he'd driven back to the station instead of the Saint Mary's Cemetery on a killer's goose-chase . . . all parts of this, Meagan, of which you weren't involved, but you can trust the fact that all my psychological data on Captain Canfield would indicate that he would have taken his own life once in jail. I even figured for some sort of media appearance before he was incarcerated, or even during the process, where he would have said on live television, *'We submit,'* or something of the sort, anything to save more lives in his mind, yet it would have been inevitably viewed by the public as a way to deflect blame. He'd have been absolutely crucified in the court of public opinion. The idea of Bronson as the mastermind, and Canfield the patsy, would have stopped gaining legs the first day, though about a third of the majority would have believed Canfield had not acted as a lone wolf and was in fact involved in a conspiracy with Bronson in some way, shape, or form along with others in the department. Faith in the police would have sunk to an all-time low, a beautiful thing, but that was only the beginning."

"Of the legend."

"Of the virus . . . the way we spread rumors and glorify conspiracy theories. According to my calculations, ten percent of the public would have thought your mother was the killer, double-crossed by Connor, Canfield, and Bronson. Eleven percent would have believed an assortment of different familial combinations of lies and betrayal, such as the absentee father killing everyone and paying off the police . . . you and your mother as partners with your inadvertent participation . . . mother and son as partners . . . your mother and Canfield as lovers . . . Bronson as the perverted ringleader excluding yourself . . . Connor as the ringleader excluding your mother . . . Connor and Bronson fighting for control with your mother interfering, and so on and so on. Point is, there would have been a deluge of rumors, spreading, metastasizing."

He paused for effect.

"And the most glorious part, Meagan, would have been the statistical contradiction, the overlay that would have defied all the numbers. I figured that seventy-three percent of the public, including many of those who were to believe one of the above-mentioned scenarios, would have harbored a strong *simultaneous* belief that everything other than the manifesto was the actual misdirection, and supermarket profits would have plummeted considerably. Colleges, especially in Pennsylvania and Delaware, would have reported major enrollment issues with students dropping upcoming Summer One courses. People would have been spooked, terrified, immobilized. Most of them would have believed, from a perspective of logic and tangible evidence, that 'The Sculptor Killer' had been stopped, but they also would have believed on a gut level that the killer was still out there. It would have been stunningly contradictory, yet eerily present, an undeniable fact, lingering in the air like poisonous gas. Then, for the sake of horrific climax, I would have killed one more coed. It would have left the tri-state area reeling."

"But my mother didn't hit 'Send.'"

"Correct," he said. "Of course, I could have just taken over the computer and done it for her, but it was critical for me to know why she delayed, primarily from an analytical perspective so I could account for the possibility in future scenarios. I had to let the story-game change in real time, and seventeen minutes later when you entered the grave with her as predicted and she made it her last dying wish for you to hit the 'Send' button for her, it became even more important for me to see if you lived through your confrontation with Bronson so you could expedite her will."

"That was the improv?"

"That was the beginning of the necessary adjustments. It was then that the Captain entered your home, and going against all my psychological data on him, he pulled the plug on the computer. It broke with protocol, something I hadn't accounted for, and now I couldn't detonate or send any emails if you wound up being stopped somehow before, during, or after your encounter with Bronson." He paused. "Yes, Meagan, while I am tech-superior, I am not a magician, and I was forced to unveil a series of alternative plot-lines. Originally, mind you, instead of unplugging anything, Canfield was supposed to chase your brother into the night after finding him there in the house reading your mother's masterpiece. Erika was to get to Connor first and kill him in the graveyard or out on the perimeter sidewalk if he didn't crawl through the gate-hole. I had temporarily exited my rolling command center and was waiting out there at point-central by the green statue for backup just in case Erika did not succeed, and I had originally planned to catch up to you at the Bronson residence to take care of you after you took care of Bronson. The original plan was that you were to become a haunting cold case, the Sculptor's doll never found. If you had not survived your confrontation with Bronson, I would have eliminated him quickly and painlessly."

Meagan wanted to spit right in the man's mask. She didn't think it would reach.

"How do you know the Erika-lady on the gurney here would have killed my brother?" she said. "Seems kind of extreme for an administrative assistant."

"I know she would have killed him, because we'd planned it, Meagan."

"She was in on it?"

"Of course. No one had easier access to her in-bin where my original letter was planted this morning, nor the station's basement where she positioned the explosives."

"How did she get maimed?"

"I ripped out her eye."

"She's in this with you, and you did that to her?"

"It was part of the alternate story-line defense. If the captain ever went off script, as he did, changing the play, she had an emergency spaghetti-syringe in her hair filled with Lidocaine and a vasoconstrictor, sodium hydroxide, and sodium chloride to numb the eye area to make it so all she'd feel is pressure, like getting a tooth pulled. She was lucky the syringe didn't fall out in the rain. Lucky also that she had a chance to haul off somewhere to make the injections and cover any hasty needle marks with the cat's-eye makeup."

"You yanked out her eye."

"Yes."

"She let you yank out her motherfucking eye . . ."

"Yes. And I almost pulled the wrong one, too, she was fake-kicking so hard. And I wish I could have left her there at the hospital for the intricate surgery they'd been arranging for her, but I had to get her out before the cavalry arrived. It was fortunate that Canfield's night crew was stretched so thin from my prior false terroristic threats that recalling everyone and restoring department order delayed the deployment of a proper security detail for Erika until they'd evacuated the station forty-five minutes later and the captain had settled back in with a fortified command. After I put the rag over your face and rushed over to Bryn Mawr, I was glad to find that all I had to deal with was hospital security. I had planned to dial the operator and report smelling smoke in the NICU, but it wound up that there was no need for the alarms and the drama. After they sterilized Erika's wound, packed it, and taped her up in Triage, they left her there to get her another blanket, two packs of Saltines, and a plastic cup of juice. The nurses had additional responsibilities to attend to before returning, the surgeon was delayed, and it was all the time I needed. I had used a food service bay for the entry, and I walked her out through the ambulance depot. I was wearing scrubs with a surgical mask over my face. Covered her with a sheet like a cadaver. No one ever questioned it."

"Why wouldn't you just let her stay, playing the role? Wouldn't her testimony against Canfield have fucked him up royally?"

"Her potential testimony had been made irrelevant. By the time I brought you back home to execute your mother's last wish, my window to effectively take care of Canfield had shrunk considerably. As I stood there behind you, I estimated that the explosives had been detected by then and the police station already evacuated, or at least nearly so. A shame, really. Canfield had ordered in much of the day staff, and if I had been able to get you to your mother's computer ten minutes earlier, just ten short minutes, I could have taken out almost two hundred officers. It would have been magnificent; blood on the windshields and body parts in the storm drains, like the omen I promised our dear Captain Canfield. His public flogging and following suicide would have been *guaranteed,* as I had worked extra incriminating evidence into this alternate plot-line. There was a woman in a Mini-Cooper, Henrietta Schmidt, who would have sworn that Canfield was the one who actually disfigured Erika. There is a hospital desk clerk, Regina Montague, who got a cell message from the apparent co-conspirator calling Canfield a "good, jolly friend," and finally, Officer Webster, who would have testified that it was Canfield's order to park far enough away from the station to maintain a safe distance from the explosion."

He sighed.

"Unfortunately, those points became moot. I had built in a minute's delay for the detonation, and I utilized it after you hit the button. I aborted. No reason to blow up a building with no one in it. That, however, left Canfield with no sense of guilt, no reason for suicide, and it also afforded him all the tools available to finally see who left that note in Erika's in-bin. He would have figured it out, and quickly too. I had to remove her from the hospital and make her disappear."

Meagan smiled thinly. "So all your stories won't work now, ha."

"On the contrary. Rumors can grow from multiple gardens, and even without Captain Canfield as killer, there's enough fertilizer out there to sprout all kinds of weeds."

"You lost the game, though."

"I'm still here."

"What are nanobots, anyway?"

The man froze. Softly, he said: "Where would you know of that word, Meagan?"

"In the truck," she replied. "In the console between the seats under one of the panels. There was a small white Dixie cup like they have at the dentist, and it was filled with what looked like a thousand tiny splinters. On the outside of the cup it said 'NANOBOTS' written with a Sharpie or something. What the fuck are nanobots?"

"When did you have a chance to look in my clutter-catcher?"

"When you were trying to back out of Bronson's driveway. By the second try, when you scraped over the hump and bumped into the tree, I had your rhythm down . . . the same timing every time you looked back in your sideview. What are nanobots?"

His eyes in the holes had gone sharp like knives.

"Nanobots, Meagan," he said evenly, "are tiny robots. They are .01 to 10 micrometers, and can be injected into the blood. Scientists hope to use them in medicines to kill cancer cells or deliver drugs to target tissues in the near future, but as I already told you, I am a few years ahead of all that. Mine are more advanced in many ways, including the fact that they go mobile at point of first contact with the esophagus, each unit minifying itself for the route of travel through the muscle wall, no need for needles."

He leaned forward, hugging the backrest to his chest.

"Remember when I told you, Meagan, that I had your episode with Detective Bronson monitored? Remember the tooth you stuck in your mouth because your coat was flapping around and the gun was in the way in the pocket on your dominant side? Well, affixed to the exploding tooth were nanobots. A form of artificial intelligence. They migrated to your retinal field so I could watch what you did as you did it."

"Migrated? Like being alive?"

"Close enough. And my nanobots are aggressive, like hornets, like parasites."

"They're alive, in my eyes, like right now?"

"In a word, yes."

"That's disgusting. How many?"

"Only one each. I told you, they are aggressive, but you wouldn't feel just one of them gently penetrating your retina and working its way through the optic nerve to lie dormant and settled. These mechanical creatures remain docile when isolated. They would only be theoretically unstable if agitated, competing for positioning. You don't feel them presently, do you?"

"No. So you can see what I see as I see it?"

He leaned back and folded his arms across his wide chest.

"Yes, I can watch on my monitor, but you should know that I have developed other types of these units as well. Remember, my interests cross a broad and populated spectrum. Psychology is just as important as scientific observation and technological innovation, and I have developed other types of nanobots that affect behavior, feelings, and logic, more specifically in terms of manipulations in the hypothalamus, the temporal lobe, and parts of the cerebral cortex."

"Mind-control."

"No. Mind-enhancement. Erika was my first subject for those particular prototypes, my only subject so far actually, and it has proven to be a major success. She has experienced the privilege of imposed suggestion and free will, the perfect new hybrid."

"Did she volunteer at first to be infected with your psycho-type nanobot bugs?"

"No."

"Then it wasn't free will."

He stood. Stepped forward.

"And this isn't philosophy class, Meagan. I've made my decision. You are like me. Too much like me, and therefore you cannot not be trusted. And so, with your premature intrusion into that which you were not invited, Dixie cup and all, you have written your own special ending. You will be liberated by my behavioral technology as has Erika Shoemaker, with two new nanobots, and then I will deal with you accordingly. First, however, I must ask you to give me the blood I am owed."

"What blood?"

"The blood you put in the pill bottle and placed on Cindy Chen's grave with strands of your hair. There wasn't much to work with altogether, and what was available was wasted on Bronson in pill form. He was graced with the privilege of ingesting you for the good of the game, but he was grossly undeserving, as you have so eloquently illustrated. You will bleed for me, Meagan, right now. You'll bleed heavily, and I will absorb you."

He raised the controller and pressed something. The ropes fell away, not standard hemp, but something with snap-catches. Turning away then, he searched the lab table for a cup or a beaker. Meagan quickly dug into the right front pocket of her slim fitting jeans.

For the Dixie cup filled with what looked like a thousand insignificant splinters, the small Dixie cup that she'd taken from the clutter-catcher when the Scarecrow as Crud-Face had been occupied maneuvering the semi . . . the Dixie cup she'd pressed over like a small crumpled envelope and stuffed away in her pants like a klepto. She hadn't known whether or not it would come in handy; it was instinct. Maybe this monster was right about her after all . . .

She opened her mouth, leaned back her head, and dumped it all out under her tongue. Felt like a thousand tiny needle-points.

She'd just crammed the collapsed cup back into her jeans, when he turned around and approached her, graduated glass cylinder with a hex base in one hand, Bronson's box-cutter in the other. Meagan hoped he wouldn't ask her a question and force her to answer.

"Do not try to cut me," he warned. "I am aware that the thought will cross your mind, but please know for certain you would not be successful. From your seated position, the best opportunity would be the frontal thigh area, but what are these coveralls made of exactly, and how much would their slack affect your quality of penetration?" He was gigantic, close over her now, like the shelf of a mountain. "And know, my dear Dandelion, that if you do attempt something nefarious here, I will have no problem ripping out the contents of your throat, burying my face in the void, and wolfing down the leftovers like a street urchin with a bowl of hot gruel." He went for a quick change of tone. "This is ritual," he said, slowly handing over the tool. "My dear, you can take as long as you want and be as meticulous as is appropriate . . ."

He trailed off when she grabbed the box-cutter straight out of his hand, pushed out the blade, and opened her mouth. Quickly, she turned the tool in her fist like an ice pick and pierced it down through the center of her tongue.

With two hands now and a muffled scream, she worked it forward and away, splitting the soft pink organ in two. The pain was exquisite. Blood jetted upward and outward, back of her teeth, a spray in the shape of her breath spattering hot on her knuckles. She made herself avoid swallowing, and she dropped the knife at his feet. He didn't back off. He passed her the cylinder, muttering something about how he admired her for making the transformation into something beautiful and snakelike, forked tongue of Satan, and she took the glass, pressed her lips hard to the opening, and spat hot blood down into the tube . . . blood that was peppered with as many as a thousand aggressive nano-bots, ready to migrate to the retinal field like angry black hornets the second they hit an esophagus.

It filled fast to about the three-quarter mark, he was eager, couldn't wait, he grabbed the glass cylinder. She hoped he wasn't going to take his time going for atmosphere.

He raised it up to his mouth-hole. Meagan was bleeding profusely. Down her chin. Down her chest. In her mouth, up the back of her nose, she was trying not to choke, making sure not to swallow.

He put the glass to his lips inside the mask and tipped it back, drinking hard, drinking deep.

Suddenly he stopped right there where he stood. Slowly he lowered the graduated cylinder, staring at it. She had spit into it about 70 milliliters. It was down to the 20 mark; he'd gulped it down like a hungry little baby with a bottle, and Meagan could tell that he'd just registered the teeny-tiny splinters in his mouth, down his throat, hell, maybe all the way to his stomach by now.

He dropped the glass and ran back for the basins.

Meagan spit hot blood to the concrete. She'd hit an artery, her mouth was a geyser, she forced herself again not to swallow. Back by the sinks, the huge man had turned on one of the curved overhanging spray units, hot, you could see the steam rising out of the deep industrial sink like a smoke machine. He leaned over the lip and turned the faucet head up at himself, straight into his face, and right up the mouth-hole.

He screamed into the hot spray.

Meagan turned and broke past the lab tables, stumbling back for the ovens. There was no time to think, no time to gloat. How many of these nasty little things had she herself inadvertently let go down her own throat? How long was it before one bled to death when the tongue was cut in half down the middle? How many seconds did aggressive nanobots take to minimize and migrate from a serial killer's esophagus to the flip-side of his eyeballs? She spit again, gasping for breath, her tongue pounding, dull pain on the edges, white hot on the inseams.

She swallowed. Couldn't help it, her time would be shortened now, and the pieces of her tongue felt like mud-flaps, making her think suddenly of her brother and his insane and silly obsession with trucks. An overwhelming sadness took hold of her, and she turned to see how things were progressing behind her.

Not good for him, that was for sure. He was stumbling around, hands up at his face, fingers clawing at his eyes through the burlap. Before, she hadn't gotten a good look at the back-room scenery, and now she saw that behind the beast was the rear of the warehouse space—crammed with what looked like camera equipment, mirroring devices, stands and weird lighting umbrellas, scopes, reflectors, and what might have been lasers.

Back in the farthest corner was his bed. It was a mattress on the concrete, and this was somehow sadder than Connor and his mud-flaps.

It was hot back at the gas ranges, and Meagan turned to shut them all down quick as she could. It seemed to take years. She knew it really took seconds. One at a time then, trying not to shake, Meagan methodically turned each burner back on to the position just before kicking off the igniter-ticker that would spark up a flame. The smell of gas wasn't sheepish.

The monster was coming. He'd made his way across the space mostly by feel, partly blinded, and Meagan knew it wasn't like getting shampoo in your eyes. She tried to imagine what it felt like to be stung on the inner side of your eyeballs by hundreds and hundreds of yellowjackets. He'd advanced to the lab tables now, and he banged head-on into a mobile steel assembly work station on wheels, tipping it over, sending glass and detailing tools to the floor. He stopped where he was and took his hands from his eyes, trying to see her, to mark her, to memorize a pathway.

They shared a brief glance.

Through the mask-holes his eyeballs were reddened like cherry peppers, and Meagan could have sworn she saw things wriggling in them.

Suddenly his eyes ruptured hard. The discharge was fibrous.

*Silly String,* Meagan thought crazily.

He screamed, grabbed his face, and came crashing forward.

He tried to make his way back to the ovens, but he kept bumping into stuff, sweeping at things, knocking shit over, sending shit flying. Meagan ducked off to the side and made her way across to the groupings of the gas canisters that looked like the things used by scuba divers. She didn't have the slightest idea how to read a gauge or how to open a valve, but she turned every knob she could get her damned hands on. She looked back a few feet. Unlike science class, the lab tables with the gas jets might very well have been hooked up in here, and she made her way flipping the levers.

She wondered if he'd stockpiled some of the same explosives here that he'd planted at the police station. She wondered if she could set them off without knowing exactly how they were designed to be detonated. She wondered if she'd released enough gas at this point, even if he managed to get to the burner knobs. Was the space too big, the ceiling too high?

Back by the ovens, the giant was stymied. He'd somehow blocked his own way with upended lab equipment knocked about helter-skelter, and it appeared he was trying to text something into a cell phone by feel. Meagan had no idea what it meant, but she knew one thing. If he was trying to blow the place up, he was welcome to it, first come first serve, here's your hat, what's your hurry.

Meagan glanced back at the woman on the gurney. The lady's eye was open. She was trying to say something.

Meagan approached and sat next to Erika Shoemaker.

"I don't want to burn," the woman begged.

"We were both going to burn anyway," Meagan said, her breath a red mist. It sounded like a mishmash, but from the look in Erika's eye it seemed she'd gotten the general idea. Meagan felt a distinct sort of stinging coming up behind her eyes, disquieting, gaining volume. She leaned back and fingered into her left pocket to get out her lighter, the hot pink one with the black hearts and skull designs. She'd had it for three years, and it was the one she took to the graveyard to smoke weed, to the parking lot behind the Panera Bread in Lawrence Park when she'd had that occasional urge for a Marlboro Light, to every concert she'd ever been to, holding it up in the electrified darkness to salute to the music she loved so damned much.

She thought of Herbert and April 21st, Electric Wizard, Iron Maiden, Black Sabbath.

Thought of her family.

Thought of those girls stuck on poles on the highway.

With her free hand she took hold of Erika's, squeezed it softly, and then she flicked up a flame.

# CHAPTER 38
# THUNDER AND BRIGHTENING

Deep in North Philly, in a cluttered section of cross-streets, there was an unofficial dumping area for old bricks and concrete rubble, a tire farm, a spattering of condemned houses, some weed-filled lots, and a massive train yard that hadn't seen a locomotive since 1992. There was an old ball-bearing factory with huge exhaust fans, smokestacks, and grime-caked draft hoods on the roof blocking out most of the night sky on one side of Dauphin Street. Like a bookend three blocks away south, there was the dark hulking shape of the abandoned forge once rented out by Mount Airy Steel.

Benny Beckerman was picking through a trash bin by the guard shack at the entrance of the tire dump. The bin was blue. Was it the yellow or the blue ones that held toxic waste? Hell if he could remember. It wasn't being used for that anymore anyway. There were sneakers in here, beer empties, a dented hub cap that had that shiny inner part that was supposed to spin, and a McDonald's bag, bingo.

Beckerman picked at it, feeling for something besides empty cardboard with ketchup, special sauce, or creamy ranch slathered on the inner flap, though he knew how good it was to suck down one of those Sweet and Sours even without the meat and potatoes.

Suddenly something felt wrong, something in the air making your ears want to pop.

Part of the old forge exploded. The sound was thick at first, as if God had taken his massive hands and given a hard, flat clap, turning the night a bright, blinding white. Beckerman looked up into it with his eyes squeezed half-shut and his teeth bared. This was followed by a percussive "boom" that sent a fireball into the sky that was bright orange tinged blue, then bellied out to a fourteen-carat yellow laced black with smoke.

Beckerman dove to the street, banging his knee, skinning his chin, arms crossed up over his head.

It rained brick, rock, and pieces of steel; there was smoke in the air, you could taste it in the back of your throat. Beckerman was about to try to get up, and there was a secondary explosion, the sky going bright again. The delayed percussion shook the ground and vibrated straight through him. Beckerman had been tazed once, caught hawking stale soft pretzels he'd found in a dumpster outside the Link after a late-season loss to the Cowboys. This was worse. This one he'd felt in his balls and his tailbone like rape.

A siren. Two of them now.

Beckerman scrambled to his feet, slinking down the nearest dark cross-street. He didn't need the questions, didn't need to be anyone's witness.

Vibrations were one thing.

Jail cells were another, and whether or not he'd been unfairly pegged for a shit-ton of bad luck in his life, he wasn't about to go sucking blame, not tonight, not for bumming around, walking the shadows, and jonesing for a scrap of someone's Big Mac.

# CHAPTER 39
# SOMEONE TO SEE YOU

Canfield had stolen a twenty-minute nap in holding cell number three, and when he woke up seeing bars, for a second, he'd panicked. He bit it back, he knew where he was, who he was, how he got here. He pushed up and swung his feet around over the edge of the cot, elbow-points to the knees, and he rubbed his eyes hard with the pads of his thumb and index finger. Reality. Master it. Order.

He'd pulled an all-nighter here at the station. Considering the multiple precincts involved, the immediate intervention of the FBI, the warrants being sought for, the searches being executed, the evidence being collected, and the long line of potential witnesses, it was ironically clear that when they finally folded down the tents of this particular circus there wasn't going to be anyone to arrest.

Michael Robinson, the Scarecrow and Sculptor Killer, had died in the old forge up by Dauphin Street in North Philadelphia last night. It was believed that he took Erika Shoemaker and Meagan Mullin with him. There was DNA evidence he'd left back at Canfield's place, but all three body identifications were going to be difficult. Initial reports indicated that the explosion wasn't limited in cause to the gas lines Robinson had working as a result of hacking the PGW computer system and masking the usage, and the running hypothesis was that there had been a significant stockpile of specialty devices that had been inadvertently ignited. According to the reports, the officers in the Search Unit first on site had attempted to widen the crime scene to a three-block radius, because within the property borders, there was nothing left but rock dust in a crater. Of course, every inch traveled off the given blast site meant the deterioration of a mile's worth of integrity, and Canfield didn't think they were going to be able to make much out of debris that wound up in the gutters.

The press was having a field day, and Sergeant Kennedy had done a pretty good job with her team positioned in the parking lot and all entry and exit points in the building, keeping all the reporters off premises. Still, everyone in the station house had cell phones and laptops, and there were televisions in the break room and the patrol supervisor's office. They'd all heard pieces of the manifesto that had been sent to three thousand news outlets and blogs. Some of the broadcasters were reading the whole thing over and over again on air with no breaks, similar to the stunt that the Albuquerque, New Mexico, radio station pulled in the early '90s, playing "Stairway to Heaven" back to back for twenty-four hours in order to hype up a change in format from New Age to Classic Rock.

"The Sculptor," the story, was becoming a hit, and as a result people would start wanting to believe he was still out there, if it bleeds, it leads, and this left everyone open for mayhem . . . copycats and wannabes . . . unjust accusations of college security guards and supermarket store managers . . . wild theories . . . ghost stories, especially since all the evidence had been vaporized. He's dead? Where's the body? Canfield could see the headlines already. It would make everyone's job harder, maybe even lessen public confidence in the police in general, but they would stand firm and stick to procedure. They'd take the long way, the professional route, methodically going about their investigations, doing much and saying little publicly. They'd do what they did best. They'd put it all through the system. It was a dinosaur, but it would prevail. The institution would hold like it always did.

He reached for his shoes and slid them on, and then he stood and reached for the backup uniform jersey he'd put on last night when he'd re-established command. He buttoned up thoughtfully. For his part in this, he thought he'd be okay in terms of liability. Every decision he'd made he could defend, and while he didn't get the killer himself, never realizing until recently that Erika Shoemaker might have been playing stooge for this miscreant, he didn't think Michael Robinson would be able to frame him posthumously. One of the first things Canfield had done when he'd gotten back inside the building last night, before even changing his shirt, was send a team to his private residence. He had them check his phone. Yep. There was an app put on there that looked like a detonator. And considering Robinson's technical obsession with computers, Canfield had anticipated that there would be some kind of monkey business that had been done to his PC. Sure enough, Detective Dagostino found the malware. He reported that it was an attempt to do that "spoofing" jazz the brainiacs in the Computer Crimes Division were always talking about, and when the manifesto got bounced there, the detective was actually sitting at Canfield's desk, watching it happen, chewing on a toothpick. That nixed the credibility of the fake detonator app on the phone if there had been any doubt in the first place, and so with the detective's report for verification, no one would believe Canfield wrote that manifesto in the end. The creepy news? It was sent to his computer within ten seconds (or so as estimated) of the factory explosion. It was Robinson's last action on earth.

It didn't make Canfield feel too damned special, even though the phone Robinson had used for these final acts had, in fact, been furnished with a tracker app, confirming that he had indeed been right in the middle of the blast site at the time of the explosion. He wasn't so brilliant after all, was he . . . ?

"Captain," Officer Princeton said. He was standing in the doorway of the open cell.

"Yes?"

"A man here to see you. In your office. Kennedy let him through. Says he has something you absolutely must see. Evidence of some kind. Won't say what it is."

"I'll be right there."

He tucked in his jersey and took his cap off the edge of the sink. Put it on and straightened the brim. He looked in the small mirror. What he saw looking back was a cop. Sticking with the game plan.

A sudden emotional wave tried to take him down under the froth. Erika Shoemaker was dead. An entire family had been taken out, including a young field officer whose biggest flaw was that he wanted too much to impress his superiors. And Detective Bronson—one of the few people Canfield had thought of as a real friend—had been tortured by this maniac and left to bleed out on his own basement floor.

Canfield buried it. He thought of the image in the mirror, the one people depended on to keep order, to keep them safe, to keep the machinery running. He didn't have room for these kinds of emotions. They weakened his effectiveness, and besides, he had done every last thing that he could. Every decision had been the right one in the context of the moment, and he hadn't missed a damned trick. He wore that stoic face because he had earned it. Over a lifetime. He was saddened, often lonely, but that was what went with the rank.

He walked out past the evidence room, down the hall to his office.

Waiting for him there was a man. He was short, five foot six or so, wearing a black golf shirt and khakis. He had wire-framed glasses, short gray hair, and was of Asian descent. He had a manila folder in his hands. Officer Kennedy stood beside him.

"Captain," she said, "this is Zhang Wei Chen. He doesn't speak English fluently, though he can evidently read and write it fairly well. To save time, I'll tell you what he's spent the last fifteen minutes or so trying to explain to me."

The captain sat in his chair. He didn't offer his hand because he was pretty sure it wasn't going to be measured as an appropriate gesture.

"Zhang Wei Chen," he said. "Cindy Chen's father, I presume."

"Yes," the man said. Canfield gave a short nod.

"The detectives in charge of your case back in '86 briefed us on you from your interviews with them, but I'd forgotten the pronunciation of your first name, apologies."

"Yes," the man said.

Officer Kennedy went on for him.

"Last night, Captain, at 11:58 P.M., Mr. Chen received a text from Michael Robinson."

Canfield leaned back, put his elbows on the armrests, and folded his hands across his stomach. Evidently, the pirating of his PC wasn't Robinson's last Hail-Mary after all. The bastard had probably alerted Mr. Chen to the location of his daughter's body in the wooded grove behind the train depot at Merion Station on Idris and Hazelhurst Roads. Of course. Canfield hadn't had time to send a team there yet to exhume the body. There were many things that needed to be done, and if Robinson wanted to get in a final dig here through Mr. Chen, criticizing the department's apparent sluggishness, well . . . there was nothing more that Canfield could do.

"Mr. Chen," he said evenly, "whatever Robinson texted to you must be taken as evidence, and I assure you, it will be considered in a timely manner. I appreciate everything you have gone through, but there are things we need to do here that—"

"Captain," Kennedy interrupted, "Robinson didn't just send Mr. Chen a message. Robinson sent directions. To the house he grew up in, occupied now by a single parent named Stephanie Boyd. The message said that there was a confession hidden there. From his father, Mr. Hank Robinson, written in narrative thirty-three years ago. Robinson texted that Mr. Chen would find it by looking behind a loose panel in the broom closet on the first floor by the kitchen. Mr. Chen went there this morning. He brought you the confession. He wanted to hand it to you personally."

The small man stepped forward. He was thin, and you could see the shape of his skull, especially up at the temples where he'd balded back to the ears. He took the manila envelope, put it on the captain's desk, and planted his index finger on it.

"You should have known," he said. "You. Should. Have. Known."

He turned and walked out.

Canfield opened the folder. Inside it was a sheaf of papers that had faded yellowed marks at the curled edges. It was not computer paper, but the older, thicker typewriter paper they used in the mid-'80s, when Canfield was a young field officer and had fallen for a seven-year-old's masterful work of deception. It began:

*"Daddy."*

*"Hmm?"*

*"There's a dead girl in the flower bed."*

# CHAPTER 40
## CHORES

Most of the students had gone home for the summer, and to be honest, Courtney was glad. Freshman year had been rough and she hadn't made many friends. She had pale skin and a fairly large cheek mole she'd never quite come to terms with. She had oversized breasts, a thick middle. Over second semester, from nowhere it seemed, she'd developed this goofy, nervous laugh that people around here tended to measure with distaste, and to top it all off, she kept the stuffed panda she adored in the closet because someone had scribbled "Dork" on its tummy with black magic marker.

First semester, her roommate, Erin DeCecco, had spread the rumor through the dorms that Courtney had left a fish smell in the bathroom. For a month people had talked about her with smirks and called her "Salmon-girl" in savage little stage whispers. Throughout the year most girls had treated her coldly, and the boys were just rude for the most part, loud as hell, smoking and drinking and kicking soccer balls in the halls, playing cards in the lounge, the usual.

They'd all packed up and gone home, most of them taking their last finals yesterday. Courtney had signed on for a Saturday class, so she wasn't required to vacate until tomorrow evening. Floor five of Radcliffe Hall was an abandoned mess—overflowing plastic industrial trash barrels by the elevators, some old clothes strewn about, a couple of busted microwaves, and lots of sticky floor stains, mostly spilled beer and soda. The bathrooms looked like disaster zones. The only other person left on the floor was the RA, Dusty Caruthers, and when asked, she'd said maintenance didn't come through until everyone was gone. She'd said they typically mopped the block walls just as they mopped the vinyl composition floor tiles, and Courtney found this both funny and depressing.

She'd just finished half a Greek vanilla yogurt, and she decided to do a last load of laundry. More pathetic than nasty block walls were dirty clothes in a suitcase, and she dumped out half a hamper and walked the basket downstairs to the laundromat on the first floor.

The long, windowless room smelled moldy, and Courtney saw that there was a guy doing maintenance back to the left of the snack machine, patching a hole someone punched in the drywall. She had three washes left on her Banner card, and she got it out, started the load, and took out her phone to give a quick check to her social media. She headed back up the stairs, still looking at the screen.

The repair-guy listened to her fading footsteps. He'd dropped out of community after a semester and had been pumped for this job doing maintenance, especially on a campus with so many hotties. In fact, when he'd been listening to Ozzy's Boneyard on Sirius Radio yesterday, and the DJ had read that weird manifesto in between Cannibal Corpse and a song by Rob Zombie, there were parts of it he'd secretly related to. Like the stuff about college chicks, and their clothes and ribbons and lipstick and liner. He loved that horny, pretty shit, even though the guy who wrote it was clearly a fucktard.

They said he was blown up in a factory or something.

Fucking deserved it too, sticking girls up on poles.

But he did kind of have a point, about college kids compared to people who worked for a living, real work, like cutting grooves in the highway with a walk-behind saw, or doing roofing in the heat stirring tar in a kettle. Like patching up drywall in laundromats.

Some people acted like they breathed different air, like they walked around on another planet right the fuck in front of your face. Take that girl just now, for instance, the one with the cheek mole. She was cute. He'd stopped what he was doing to check her out, too. I mean, hell, he'd put down his trowel!

He was angered suddenly, more so than usual.

He'd put down his trowel . . .

*And you never bothered to notice me.*

## THE LAST ACTION OF MEAGAN MULLIN BEFORE THE TRAGIC EVENTS ON THE NIGHT OF HER DEATH

She bought an album from Eclipse Records for her best friend with the note: "Hey Fitz. Courage is born from fear, and the band April 21st will be your guiding light."

http://eclp.se/eifqd

# ACKNOWLEDGMENTS

Roxanne Ryan and Jeremy Sawruk:
For helping me invent nifty futuristic technology.

Brad Winslow:
For making damned sure that my scenes involving law enforcement had at least a shred of credibility.

Professor Vito Gulla:
For offering critical writing advice I could use.

Mary Clarke:
For reading the early drafts and identifying the dark hero before I even knew.

Susan Aronovitz:
For making clear the details needed for the hospital scene.

S. T. Joshi:
For your wisdom, kindness, and guidance.

# ABOUT THE AUTHOR

**Michael Aronovitz** is a horror author, college professor, and rock critic. He has published four novels and three collections. He lives in Wynnewood, Pennsylvania, with his wife and son.